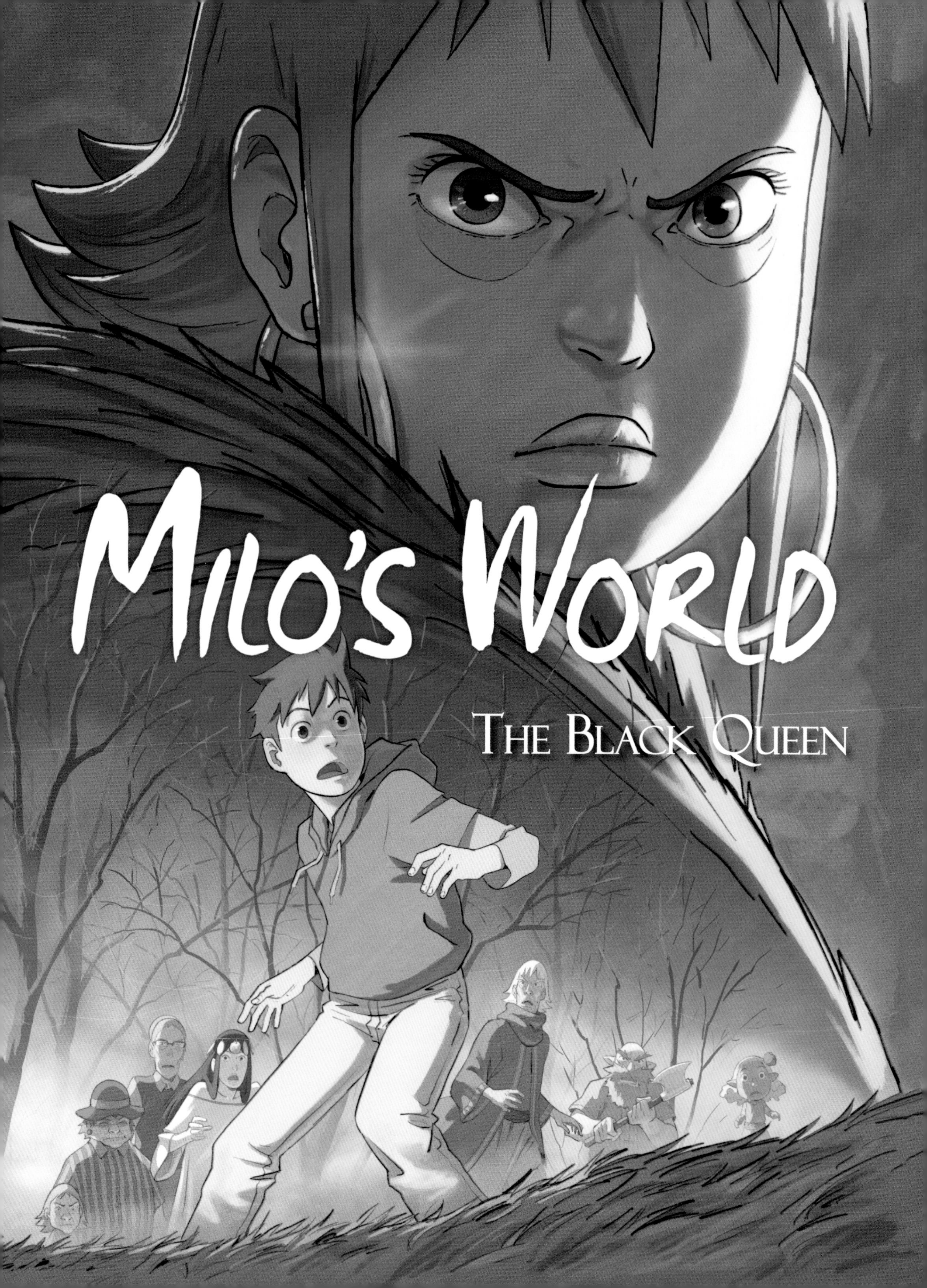
MILO'S WORLD
THE BLACK QUEEN

BOOK TWO:
THE BLACK QUEEN

WRITER
RICHARD MARAZANO

ARTIST and COLORIST
CHRISTOPHE FERREIRA

Translation by Montana Kane
Localization, Layout, and Editing by Mike Kennedy

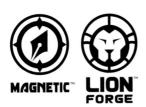

ISBN: 978-1-5493-0671-6
Library of Congress Control Number: 2019909387

Milo's World Book Two, The Black Queen, published 2019 by The Lion Forge, LLC.
Originally published in French under the title *Le Monde de Milo - tome 3* © DARGAUD 2013, by Marazano, Ferreira and *Le Monde de Milo - tome 4* © DARGAUD 2013, by Marazano, Ferreira. www.dargaud.com

10 9 8 7 6 5 4 3 2 1

For Kyoko, Minoru, and Akira.
Christophe.

To Christophe, my partner in crime...
To Alex, without whom Milo wouldn't exist...
To Rachel, Pénélope, Samuel, and Minoru, who will grow up with our stories...
To Thomas Ragon and the whole team at Dargaud...
Richard.

CHAPTER ONE

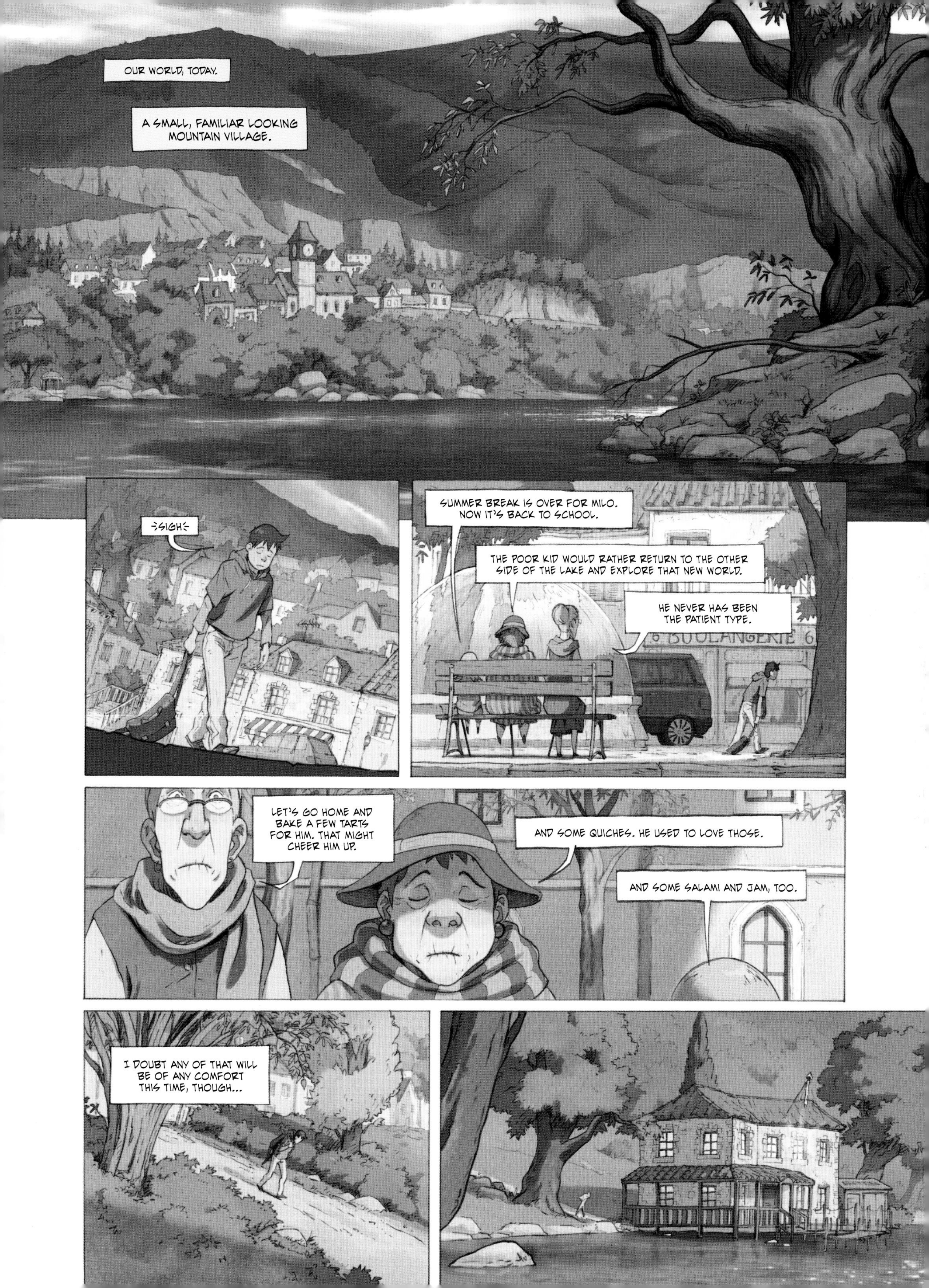
OUR WORLD, TODAY.
A SMALL, FAMILIAR LOOKING MOUNTAIN VILLAGE.
-SIGH-
SUMMER BREAK IS OVER FOR MILO. NOW IT'S BACK TO SCHOOL.
THE POOR KID WOULD RATHER RETURN TO THE OTHER SIDE OF THE LAKE AND EXPLORE THAT NEW WORLD.
HE NEVER HAS BEEN THE PATIENT TYPE.
6 BOULANGERIE 6
LET'S GO HOME AND BAKE A FEW TARTS FOR HIM. THAT MIGHT CHEER HIM UP.
AND SOME QUICHES. HE USED TO LOVE THOSE.
AND SOME SALAMI AND JAM, TOO.
I DOUBT ANY OF THAT WILL BE OF ANY COMFORT THIS TIME, THOUGH...

=SIGH=

I CAN'T BELIEVE I HAVE TO WAIT UNTIL MY NEXT BREAK TO GO BACK TO THE OTHER SIDE...

IT WOULDN'T BE SO BAD IF I COULD AT LEAST POP BY FOR A QUICK VISIT AFTER SCHOOL...

YOU KNOW YOU CAN'T TAKE THAT MANY TRIPS TO THE OTHER SIDE IN SUCH A SHORT AMOUNT OF TIME, MILO...

IT COULD BE DANGEROUS...

JUST WAIT FOR THE NEXT SCHOOL BREAK.

PFFF... YEAH, I GET ALL THAT.

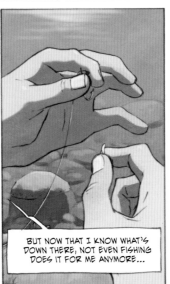

BUT NOW THAT I KNOW WHAT'S DOWN THERE, NOT EVEN FISHING DOES IT FOR ME ANYMORE...

...IT'S LIKE IT'S TOTALLY RUINED MY FUN.

PLOC!

=SIGH=

HUH?

BLOOP!

THAT WAS FAST!

WHOA! FEELS LIKE A BIG ONE!

YOU'RE NOT GETTING AWAY FROM ME, BIG GUY!

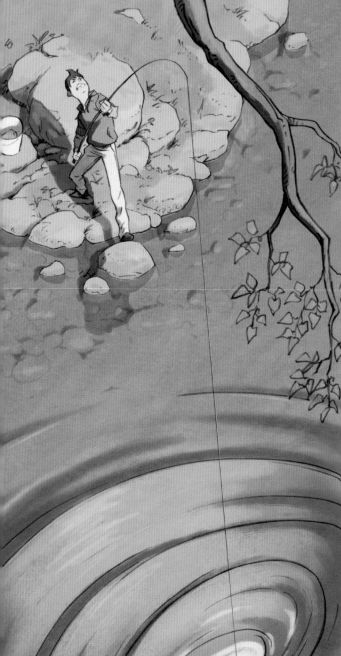

WHOA! WHAT THE--?

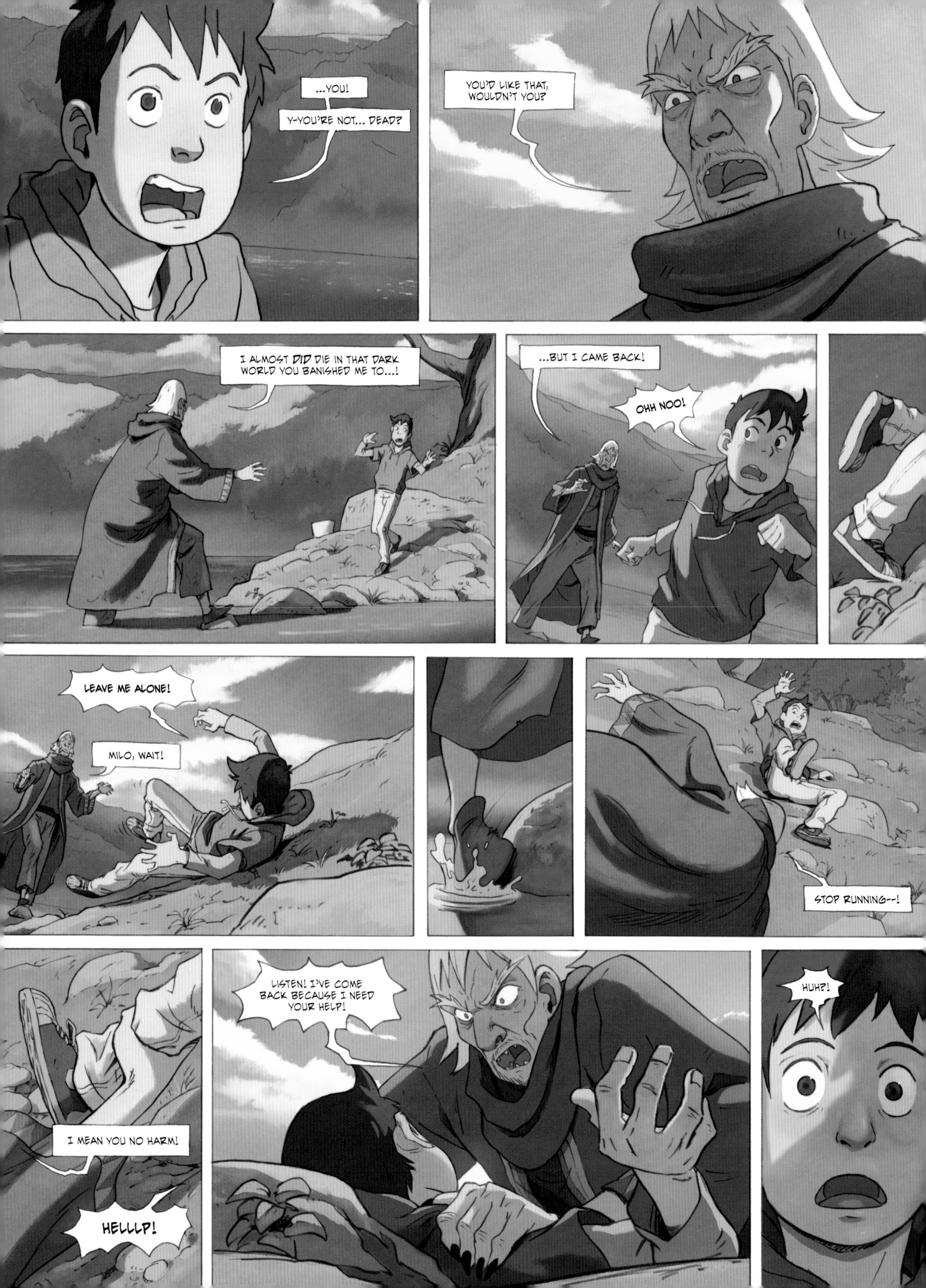
...YOU!
Y-YOU'RE NOT... DEAD?
YOU'D LIKE THAT, WOULDN'T YOU?
I ALMOST DID DIE IN THAT DARK WORLD YOU BANISHED ME TO...!
...BUT I CAME BACK!
OHH NOO!
LEAVE ME ALONE!
MILO, WAIT!
STOP RUNNING--!
I MEAN YOU NO HARM!
HELLLP!
LISTEN! I'VE COME BACK BECAUSE I NEED YOUR HELP!
HUH?!

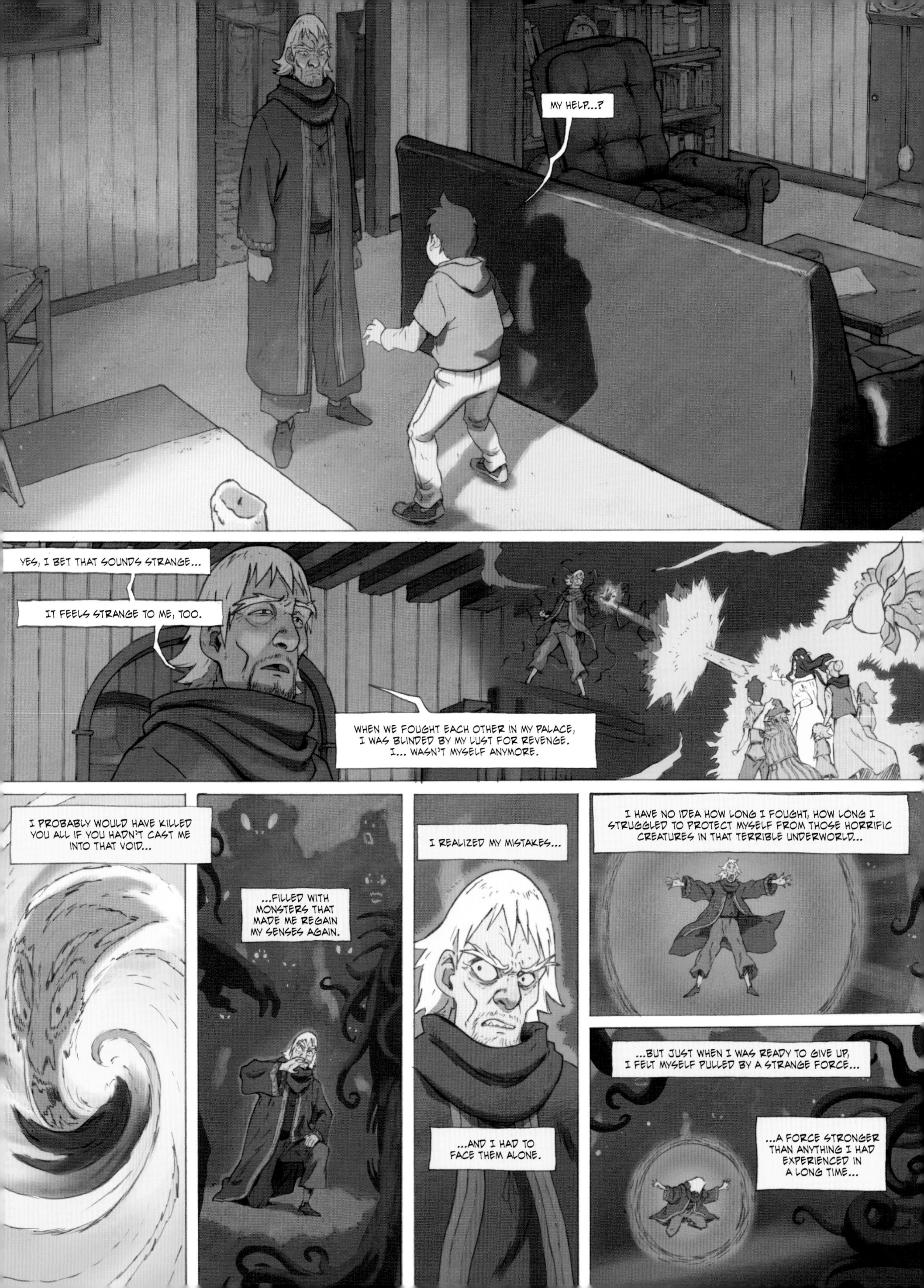
MY HELP...?
YES, I BET THAT SOUNDS STRANGE...
IT FEELS STRANGE TO ME, TOO.
WHEN WE FOUGHT EACH OTHER IN MY PALACE, I WAS BLINDED BY MY LUST FOR REVENGE. I... WASN'T MYSELF ANYMORE.
I PROBABLY WOULD HAVE KILLED YOU ALL IF YOU HADN'T CAST ME INTO THAT VOID...
...FILLED WITH MONSTERS THAT MADE ME REGAIN MY SENSES AGAIN.
I REALIZED MY MISTAKES...
...AND I HAD TO FACE THEM ALONE.
I HAVE NO IDEA HOW LONG I FOUGHT, HOW LONG I STRUGGLED TO PROTECT MYSELF FROM THOSE HORRIFIC CREATURES IN THAT TERRIBLE UNDERWORLD...
...BUT JUST WHEN I WAS READY TO GIVE UP, I FELT MYSELF PULLED BY A STRANGE FORCE...
...A FORCE STRONGER THAN ANYTHING I HAD EXPERIENCED IN A LONG TIME...

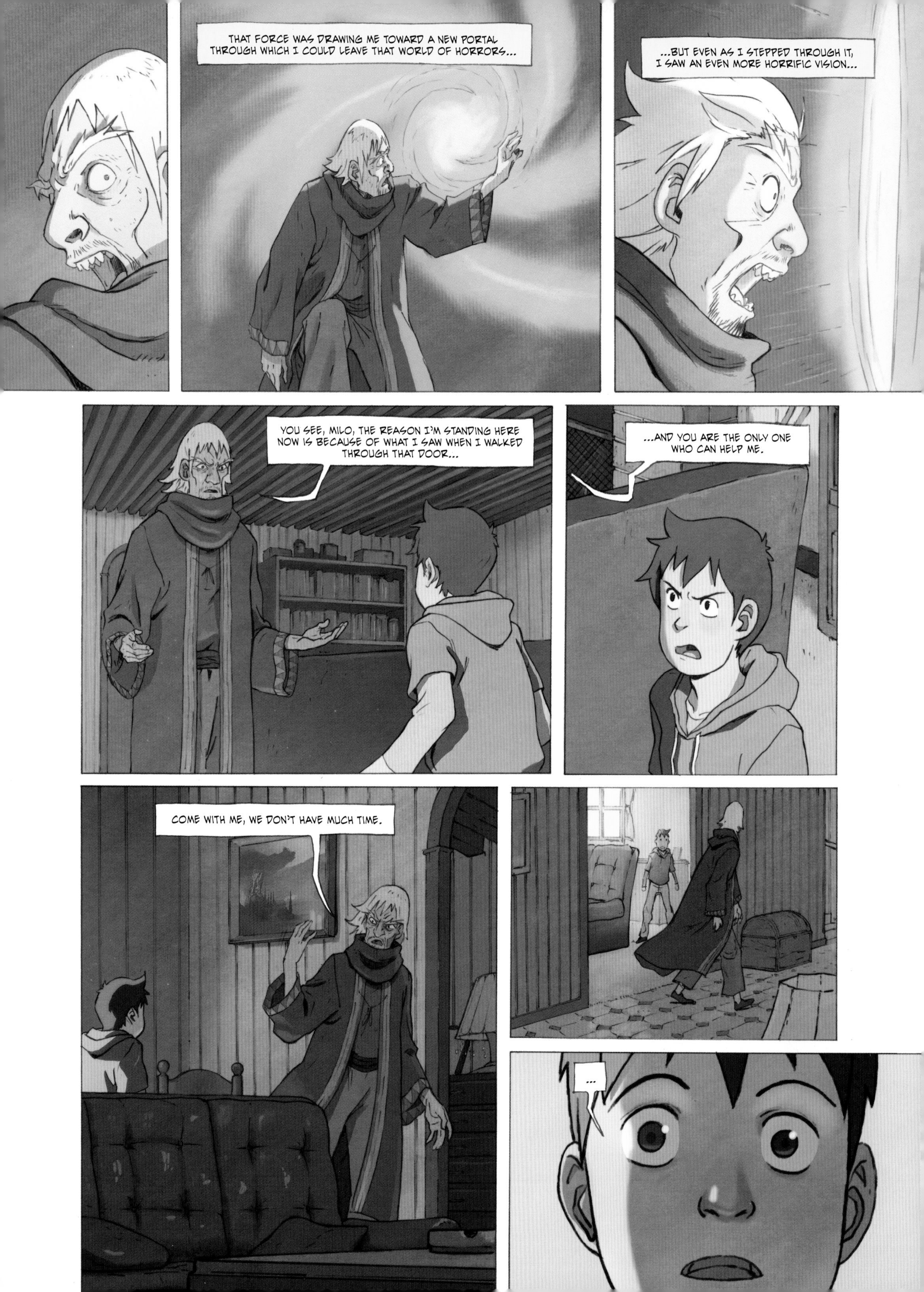
THAT FORCE WAS DRAWING ME TOWARD A NEW PORTAL THROUGH WHICH I COULD LEAVE THAT WORLD OF HORRORS...
...BUT EVEN AS I STEPPED THROUGH IT, I SAW AN EVEN MORE HORRIFIC VISION...
YOU SEE, MILO, THE REASON I'M STANDING HERE NOW IS BECAUSE OF WHAT I SAW WHEN I WALKED THROUGH THAT DOOR...
...AND YOU ARE THE ONLY ONE WHO CAN HELP ME.
COME WITH ME, WE DON'T HAVE MUCH TIME.
...

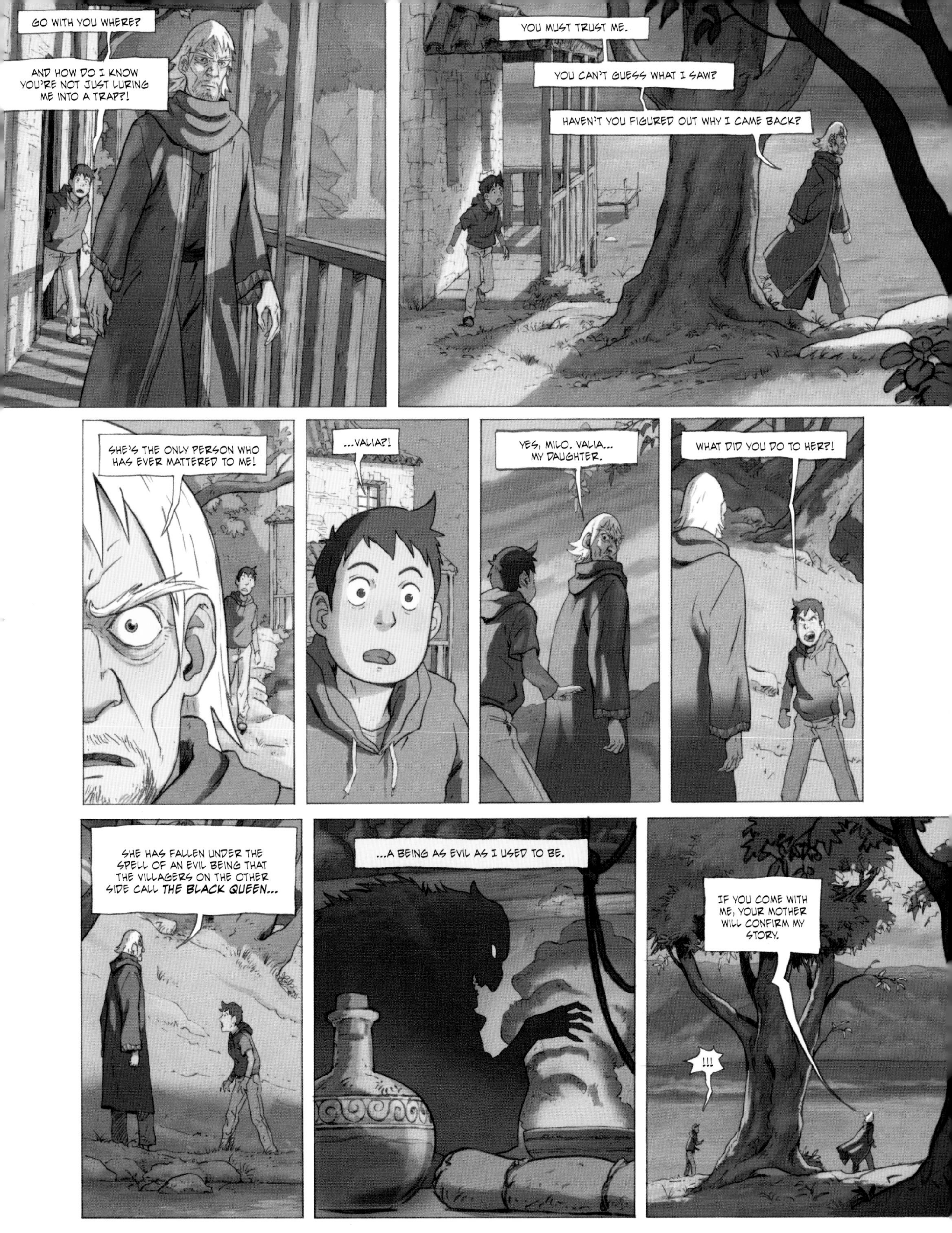
GO WITH YOU WHERE?
AND HOW DO I KNOW YOU'RE NOT JUST LURING ME INTO A TRAP?!
YOU MUST TRUST ME.
YOU CAN'T GUESS WHAT I SAW?
HAVEN'T YOU FIGURED OUT WHY I CAME BACK?
SHE'S THE ONLY PERSON WHO HAS EVER MATTERED TO ME!
...VALIA?!
YES, MILO. VALIA... MY DAUGHTER.
WHAT DID YOU DO TO HER?!
SHE HAS FALLEN UNDER THE SPELL OF AN EVIL BEING THAT THE VILLAGERS ON THE OTHER SIDE CALL THE BLACK QUEEN...
...A BEING AS EVIL AS I USED TO BE.
IF YOU COME WITH ME, YOUR MOTHER WILL CONFIRM MY STORY.
!!!

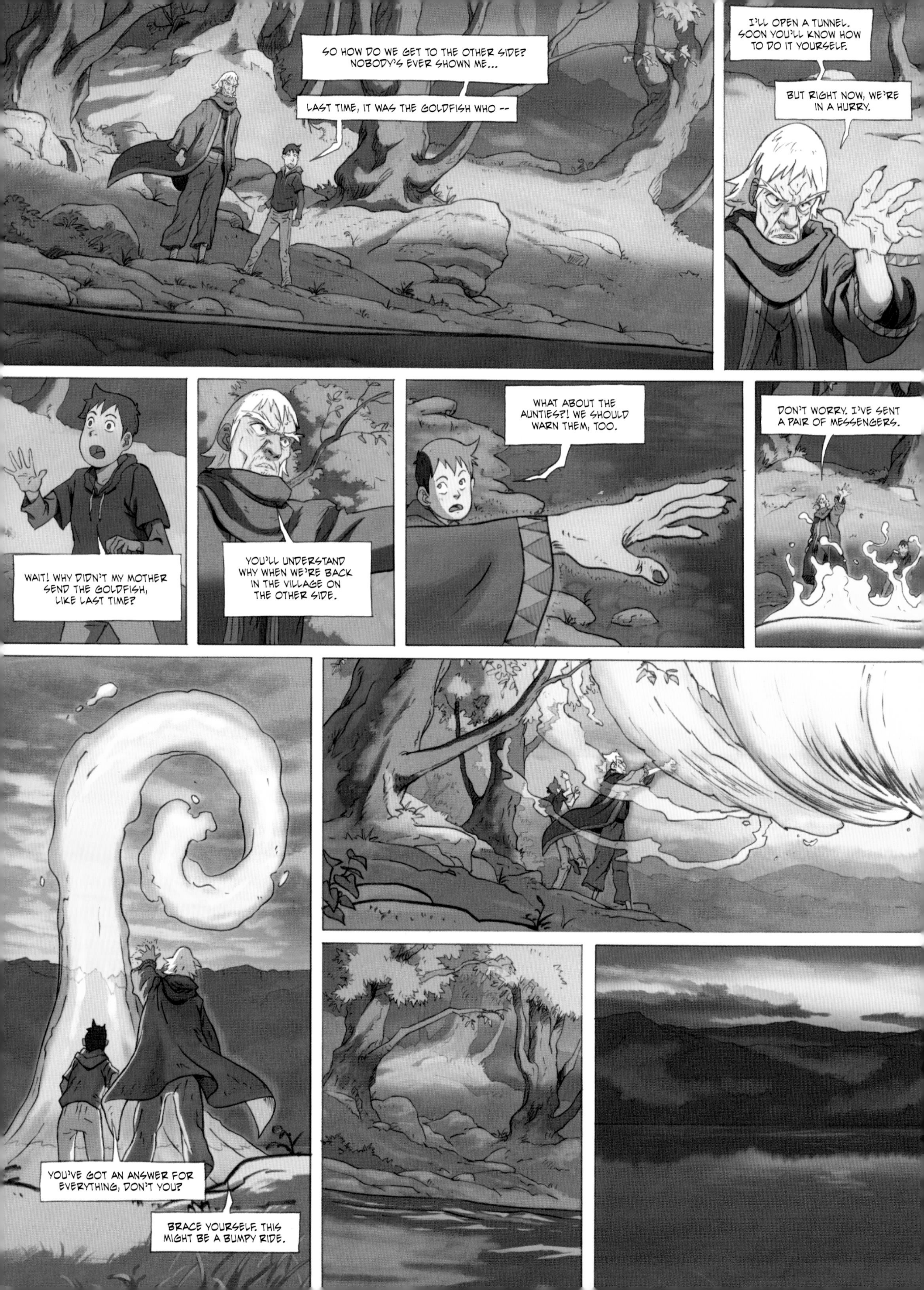
SO HOW DO WE GET TO THE OTHER SIDE? NOBODY'S EVER SHOWN ME...
LAST TIME, IT WAS THE GOLDFISH WHO --
I'LL OPEN A TUNNEL. SOON YOU'LL KNOW HOW TO DO IT YOURSELF.
BUT RIGHT NOW, WE'RE IN A HURRY.
WAIT! WHY DIDN'T MY MOTHER SEND THE GOLDFISH, LIKE LAST TIME?
YOU'LL UNDERSTAND WHY WHEN WE'RE BACK IN THE VILLAGE ON THE OTHER SIDE.
WHAT ABOUT THE AUNTIES?! WE SHOULD WARN THEM, TOO.
DON'T WORRY. I'VE SENT A PAIR OF MESSENGERS.
YOU'VE GOT AN ANSWER FOR EVERYTHING, DON'T YOU?
BRACE YOURSELF. THIS MIGHT BE A BUMPY RIDE.

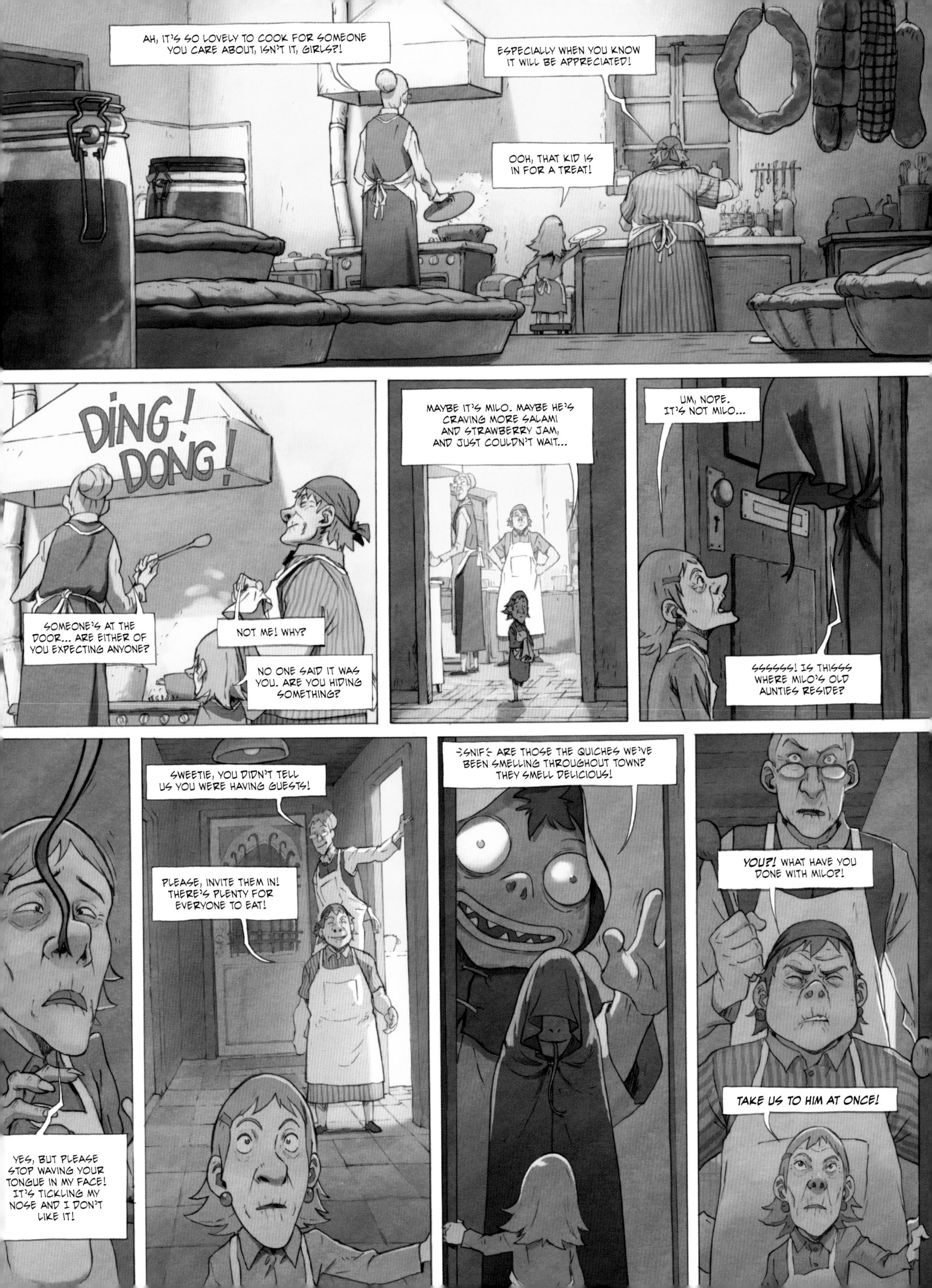
AH, IT'S SO LOVELY TO COOK FOR SOMEONE YOU CARE ABOUT, ISN'T IT, GIRLS?!
ESPECIALLY WHEN YOU KNOW IT WILL BE APPRECIATED!
OOH, THAT KID IS IN FOR A TREAT!
DING! DONG!
SOMEONE'S AT THE DOOR... ARE EITHER OF YOU EXPECTING ANYONE?
NOT ME! WHY?
NO ONE SAID IT WAS YOU. ARE YOU HIDING SOMETHING?
MAYBE IT'S MILO. MAYBE HE'S CRAVING MORE SALAMI AND STRAWBERRY JAM, AND JUST COULDN'T WAIT...
UM, NOPE. IT'S NOT MILO...
SSSSSS! IS THISSS WHERE MILO'S OLD AUNTIES RESIDE?
YES, BUT PLEASE STOP WAVING YOUR TONGUE IN MY FACE! IT'S TICKLING MY NOSE AND I DON'T LIKE IT!
SWEETIE, YOU DIDN'T TELL US YOU WERE HAVING GUESTS!
PLEASE, INVITE THEM IN! THERE'S PLENTY FOR EVERYONE TO EAT!
-SNIF- ARE THOSE THE QUICHES WE'VE BEEN SMELLING THROUGHOUT TOWN? THEY SMELL DELICIOUS!
YOU?! WHAT HAVE YOU DONE WITH MILO?!
TAKE US TO HIM AT ONCE!

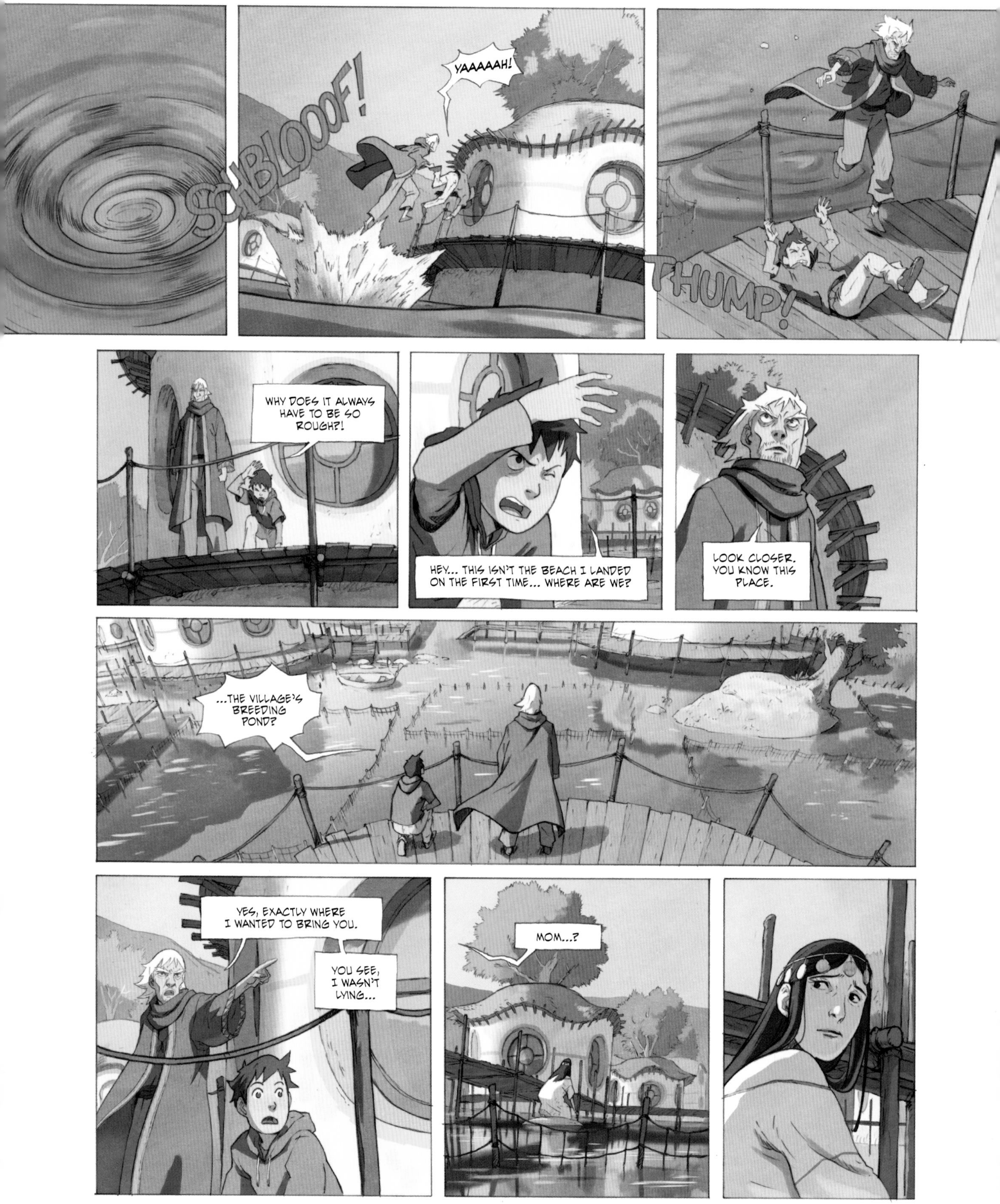
SCHBLOOOF!
YAAAAAH!
THUMP!
WHY DOES IT ALWAYS HAVE TO BE SO ROUGH?!
HEY... THIS ISN'T THE BEACH I LANDED ON THE FIRST TIME... WHERE ARE WE?
LOOK CLOSER. YOU KNOW THIS PLACE.
...THE VILLAGE'S BREEDING POND?
YES, EXACTLY WHERE I WANTED TO BRING YOU.
YOU SEE, I WASN'T LYING...
MOM...?

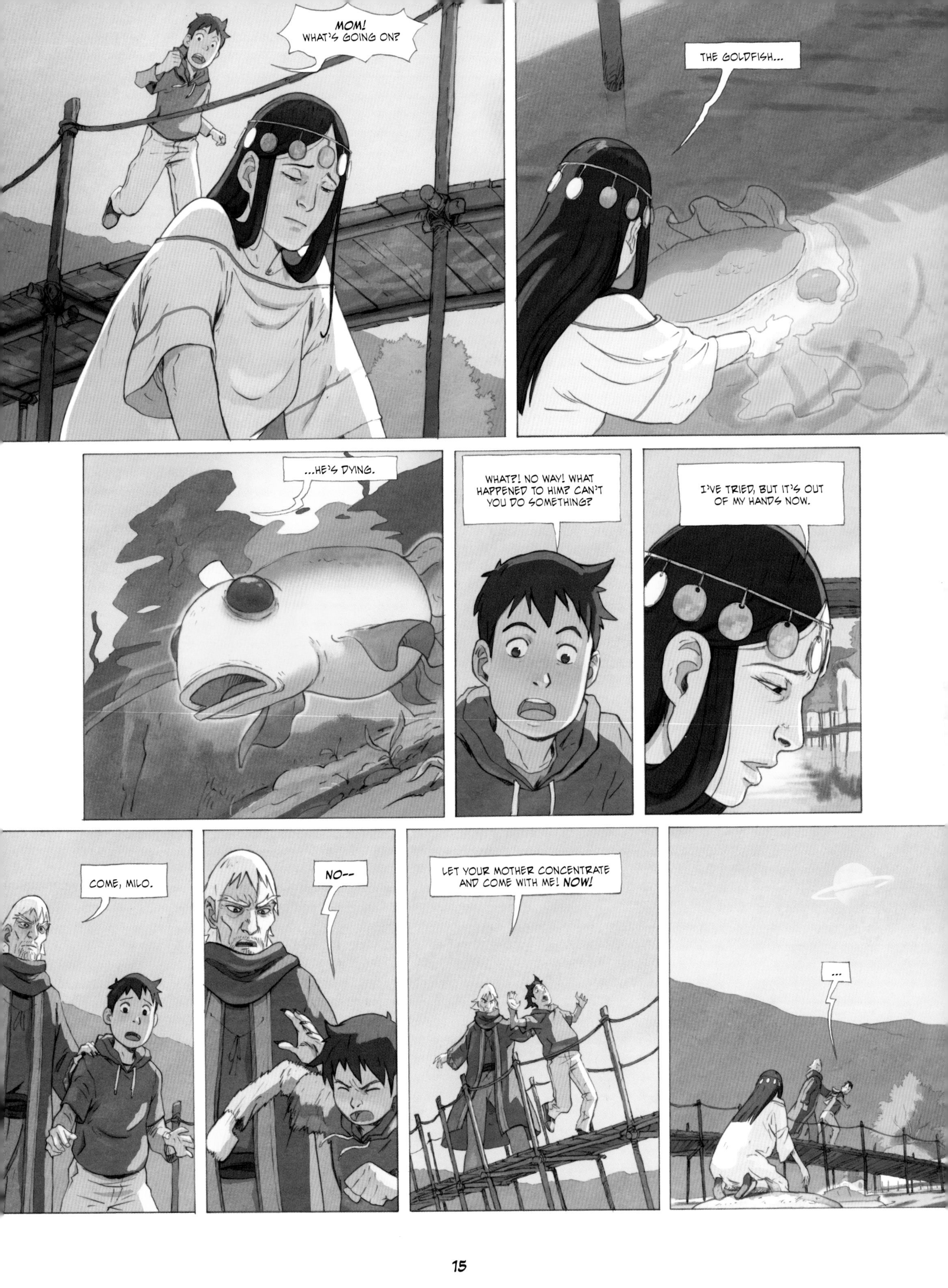
MOM!
WHAT'S GOING ON?
THE GOLDFISH...
...HE'S DYING.
WHAT?! NO WAY! WHAT HAPPENED TO HIM? CAN'T YOU DO SOMETHING?
I'VE TRIED, BUT IT'S OUT OF MY HANDS NOW.
COME, MILO.
NO--
LET YOUR MOTHER CONCENTRATE AND COME WITH ME! NOW!
...

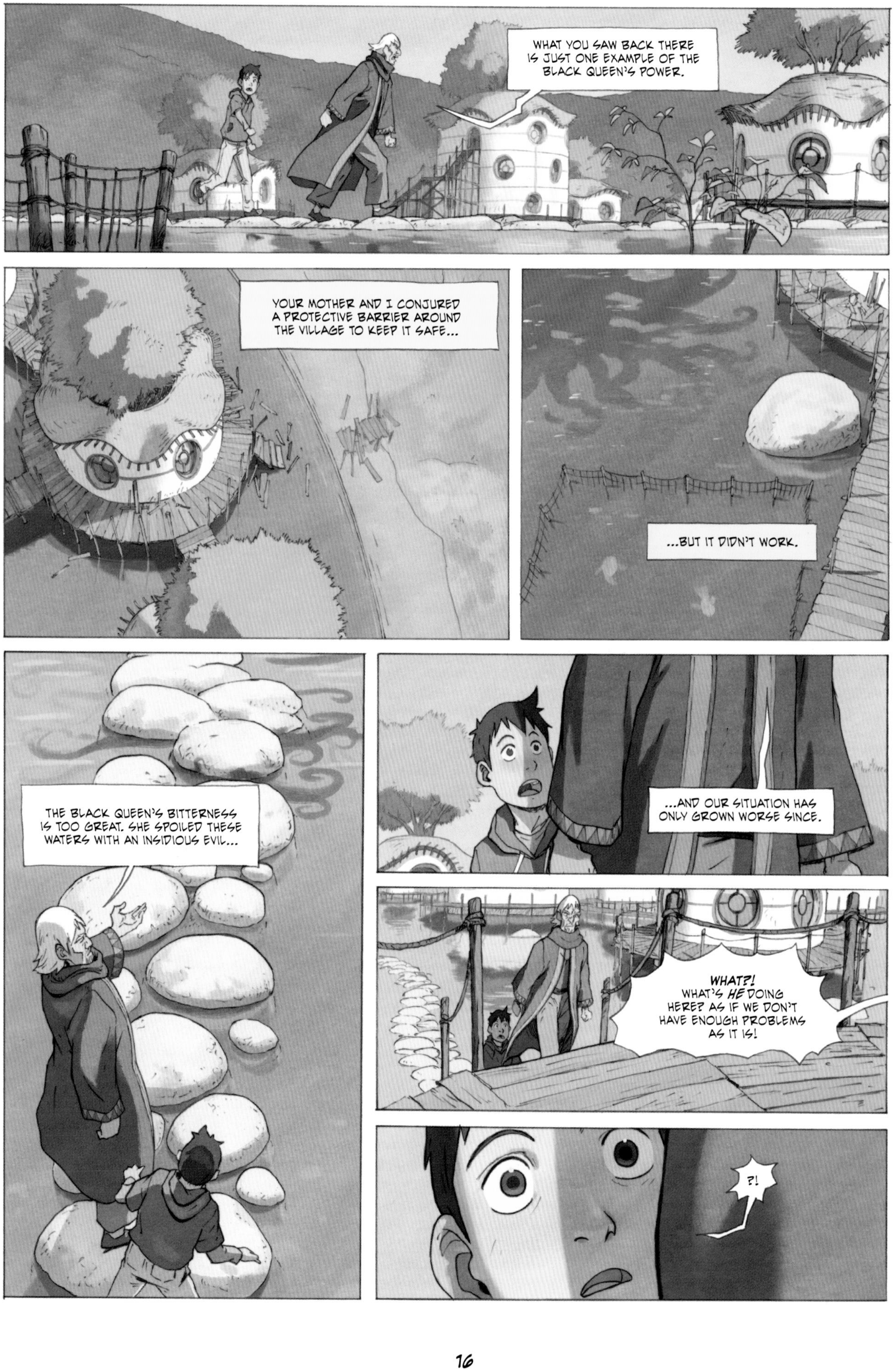
WHAT YOU SAW BACK THERE IS JUST ONE EXAMPLE OF THE BLACK QUEEN'S POWER.
YOUR MOTHER AND I CONJURED A PROTECTIVE BARRIER AROUND THE VILLAGE TO KEEP IT SAFE...
...BUT IT DIDN'T WORK.
THE BLACK QUEEN'S BITTERNESS IS TOO GREAT. SHE SPOILED THESE WATERS WITH AN INSIDIOUS EVIL...
...AND OUR SITUATION HAS ONLY GROWN WORSE SINCE.
WHAT?! WHAT'S HE DOING HERE? AS IF WE DON'T HAVE ENOUGH PROBLEMS AS IT IS!
?!

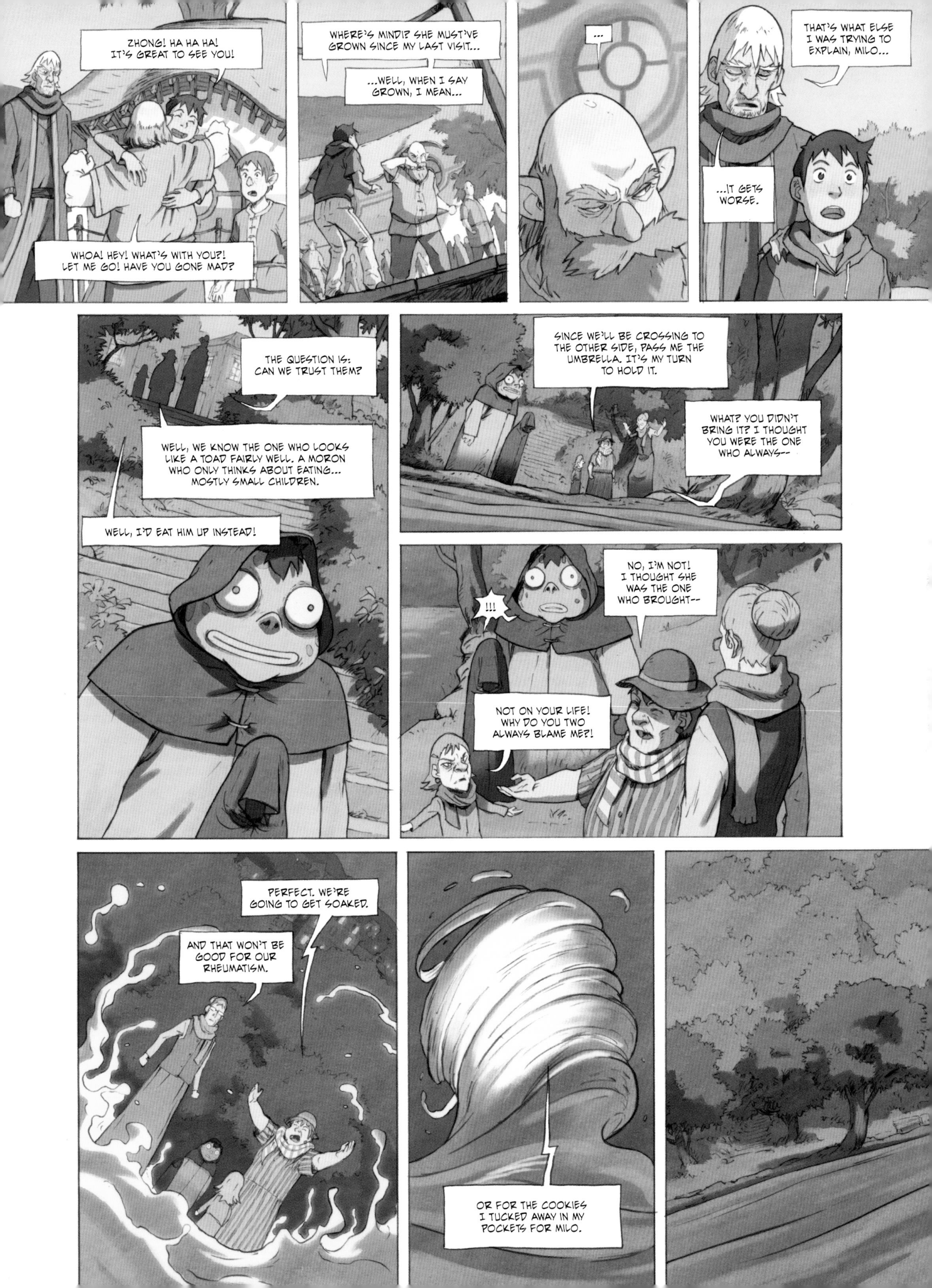
ZHONG! HA HA HA! IT'S GREAT TO SEE YOU!
WHOA! HEY! WHAT'S WITH YOU?! LET ME GO! HAVE YOU GONE MAD?
WHERE'S MINDI? SHE MUST'VE GROWN SINCE MY LAST VISIT...
...WELL, WHEN I SAY GROWN, I MEAN...
...
THAT'S WHAT ELSE I WAS TRYING TO EXPLAIN, MILO...
...IT GETS WORSE.
THE QUESTION IS: CAN WE TRUST THEM?
WELL, WE KNOW THE ONE WHO LOOKS LIKE A TOAD FAIRLY WELL. A MORON WHO ONLY THINKS ABOUT EATING... MOSTLY SMALL CHILDREN.
WELL, I'D EAT HIM UP INSTEAD!
SINCE WE'LL BE CROSSING TO THE OTHER SIDE, PASS ME THE UMBRELLA. IT'S MY TURN TO HOLD IT.
WHAT? YOU DIDN'T BRING IT? I THOUGHT YOU WERE THE ONE WHO ALWAYS--
!!!
NO, I'M NOT! I THOUGHT SHE WAS THE ONE WHO BROUGHT--
NOT ON YOUR LIFE! WHY DO YOU TWO ALWAYS BLAME ME?!
PERFECT. WE'RE GOING TO GET SOAKED.
AND THAT WON'T BE GOOD FOR OUR RHEUMATISM.
OR FOR THE COOKIES I TUCKED AWAY IN MY POCKETS FOR MILO.

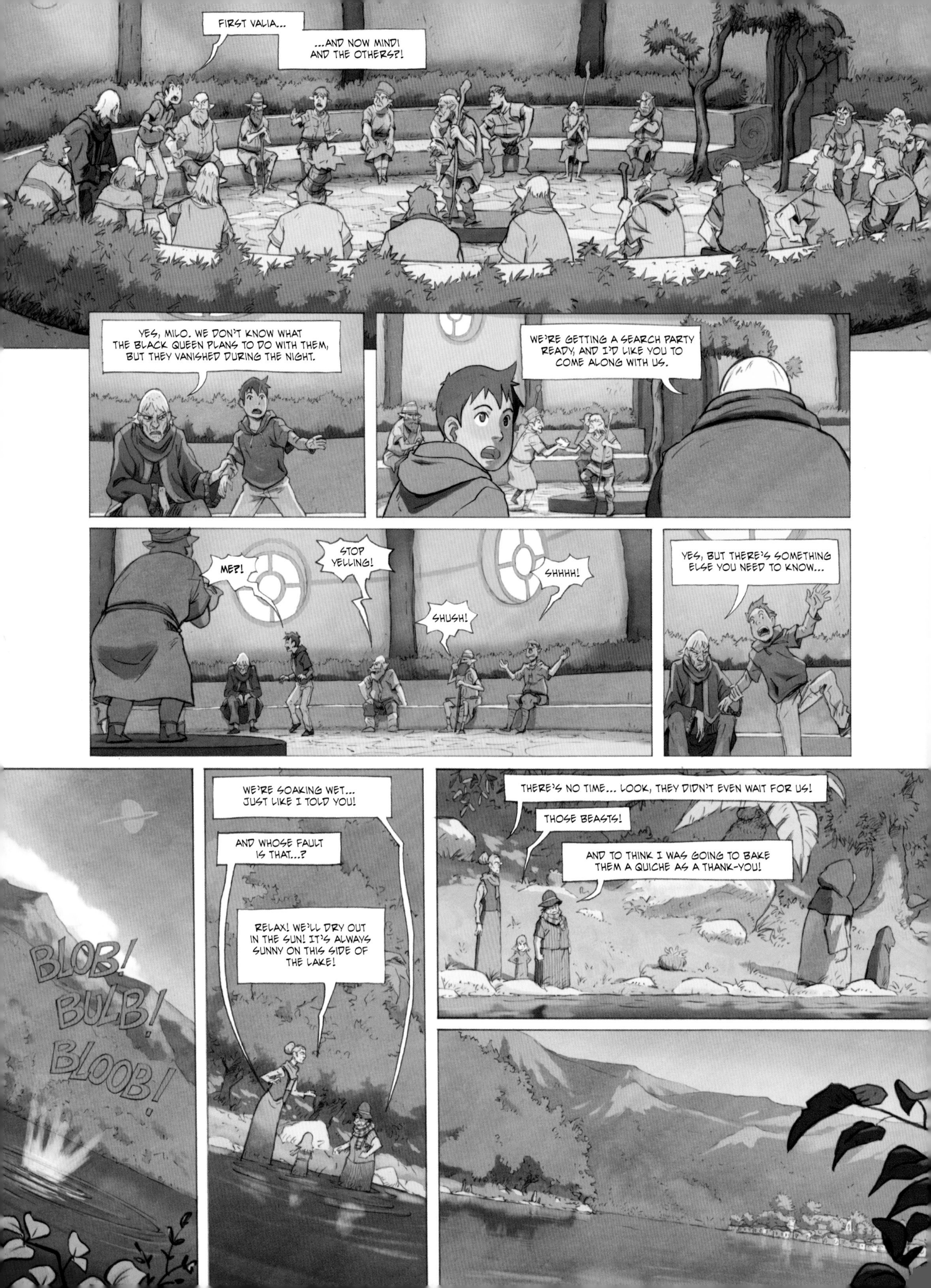
FIRST VALIA...
...AND NOW MINDI AND THE OTHERS?!
YES, MILO. WE DON'T KNOW WHAT THE BLACK QUEEN PLANS TO DO WITH THEM, BUT THEY VANISHED DURING THE NIGHT.
WE'RE GETTING A SEARCH PARTY READY, AND I'D LIKE YOU TO COME ALONG WITH US.
ME?!
STOP YELLING!
SHHHH!
SHUSH!
YES, BUT THERE'S SOMETHING ELSE YOU NEED TO KNOW...
BLOB! BULB! BLOOB!
WE'RE SOAKING WET... JUST LIKE I TOLD YOU!
AND WHOSE FAULT IS THAT...?
RELAX! WE'LL DRY OUT IN THE SUN! IT'S ALWAYS SUNNY ON THIS SIDE OF THE LAKE!
THERE'S NO TIME... LOOK, THEY DIDN'T EVEN WAIT FOR US!
THOSE BEASTS!
AND TO THINK I WAS GOING TO BAKE THEM A QUICHE AS A THANK-YOU!

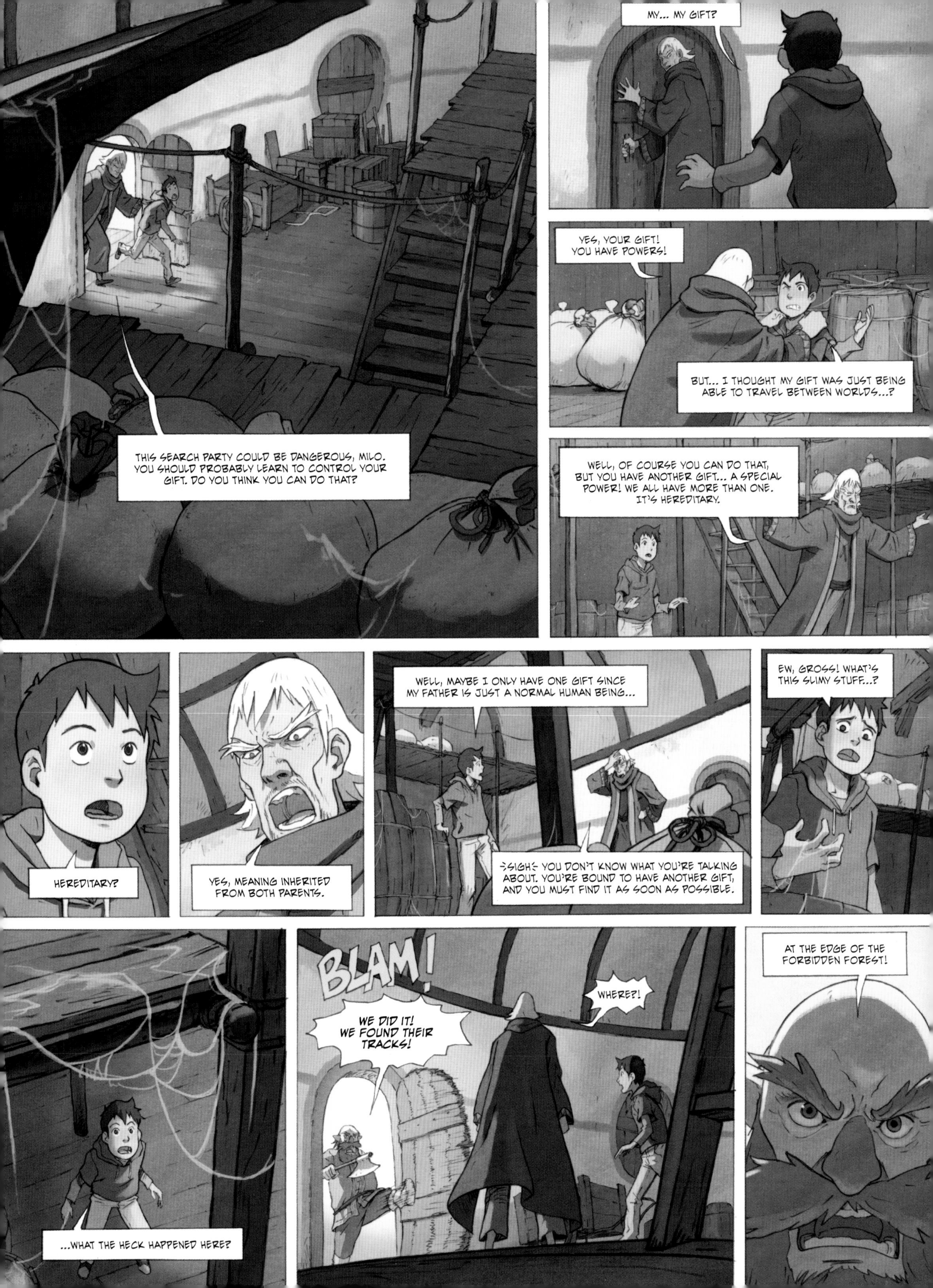
THIS SEARCH PARTY COULD BE DANGEROUS, MILO. YOU SHOULD PROBABLY LEARN TO CONTROL YOUR GIFT. DO YOU THINK YOU CAN DO THAT?
MY... MY GIFT?
YES, YOUR GIFT! YOU HAVE POWERS!
BUT... I THOUGHT MY GIFT WAS JUST BEING ABLE TO TRAVEL BETWEEN WORLDS...?
WELL, OF COURSE YOU CAN DO THAT, BUT YOU HAVE ANOTHER GIFT... A SPECIAL POWER! WE ALL HAVE MORE THAN ONE. IT'S HEREDITARY.
HEREDITARY?
YES, MEANING INHERITED FROM BOTH PARENTS.
WELL, MAYBE I ONLY HAVE ONE GIFT SINCE MY FATHER IS JUST A NORMAL HUMAN BEING...
-SIGH- YOU DON'T KNOW WHAT YOU'RE TALKING ABOUT. YOU'RE BOUND TO HAVE ANOTHER GIFT, AND YOU MUST FIND IT AS SOON AS POSSIBLE.
EW, GROSS! WHAT'S THIS SLIMY STUFF...?
...WHAT THE HECK HAPPENED HERE?
BLAM!
WE DID IT! WE FOUND THEIR TRACKS!
WHERE?!
AT THE EDGE OF THE FORBIDDEN FOREST!

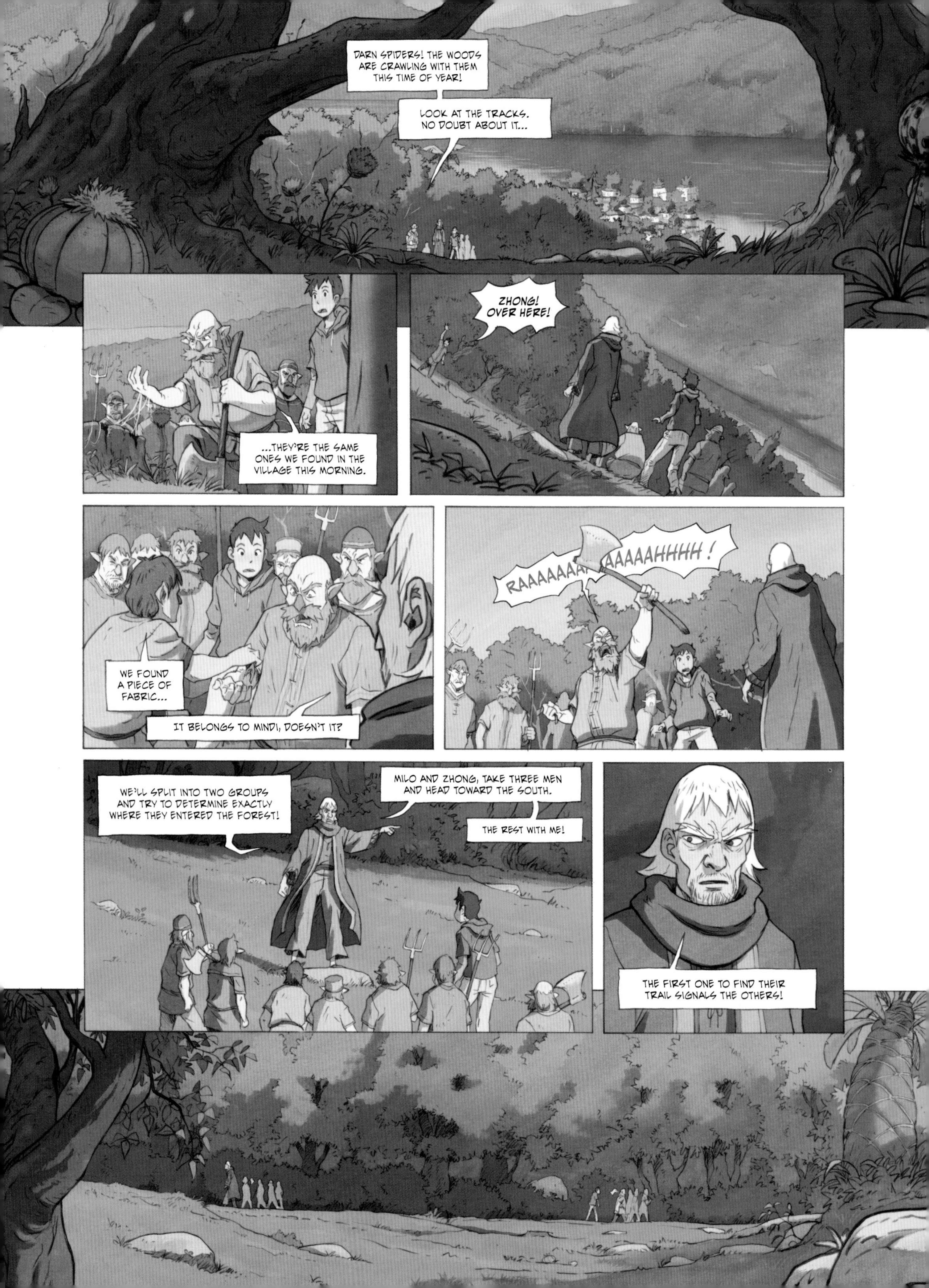
DARN SPIDERS! THE WOODS ARE CRAWLING WITH THEM THIS TIME OF YEAR!
LOOK AT THE TRACKS. NO DOUBT ABOUT IT...
...THEY'RE THE SAME ONES WE FOUND IN THE VILLAGE THIS MORNING.
ZHONG! OVER HERE!
WE FOUND A PIECE OF FABRIC...
IT BELONGS TO MINDI, DOESN'T IT?
RAAAAAAAAAAAAAHHHH!
WE'LL SPLIT INTO TWO GROUPS AND TRY TO DETERMINE EXACTLY WHERE THEY ENTERED THE FOREST!
MILO AND ZHONG, TAKE THREE MEN AND HEAD TOWARD THE SOUTH.
THE REST WITH ME!
THE FIRST ONE TO FIND THEIR TRAIL SIGNALS THE OTHERS!

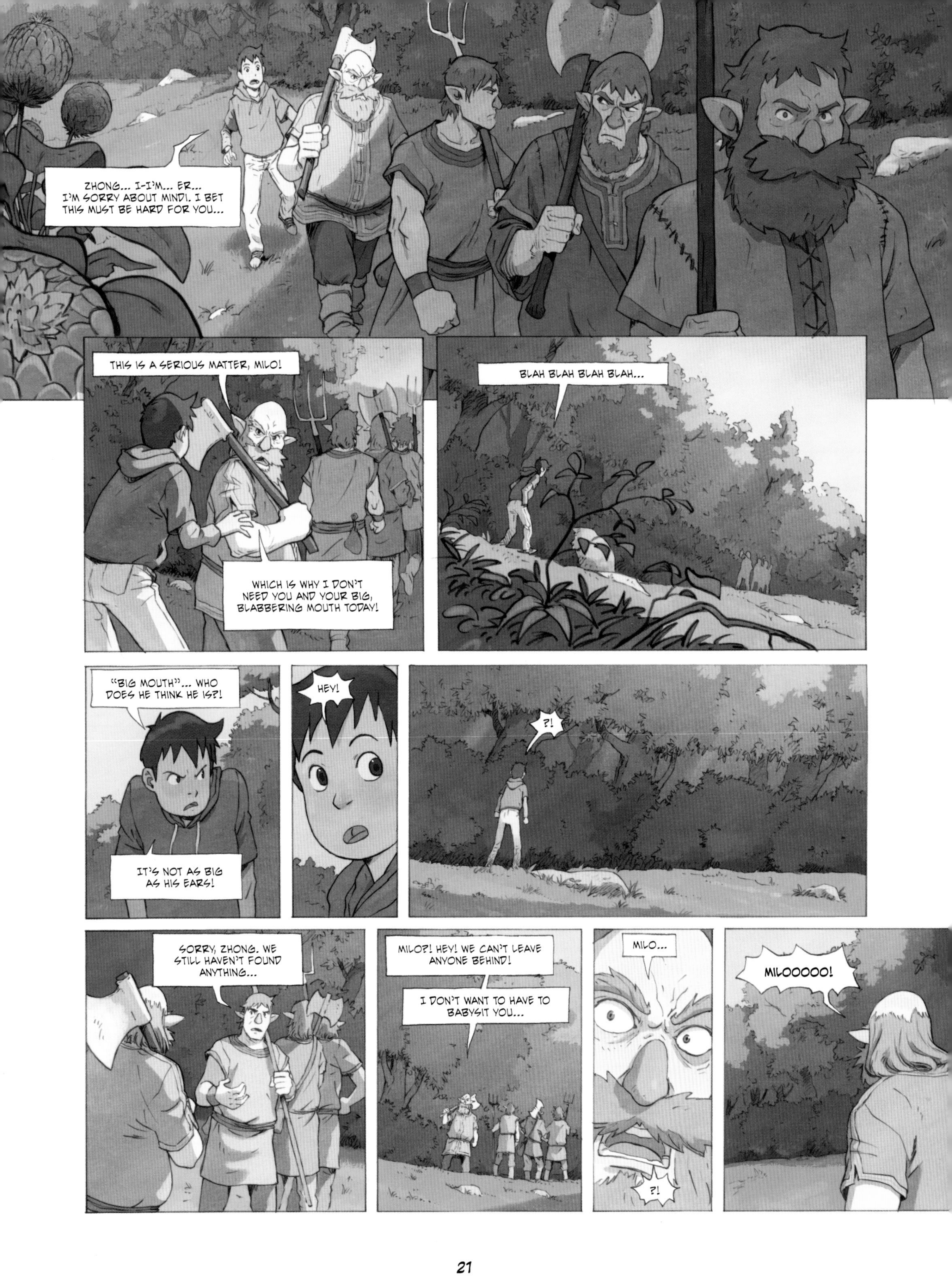

ZHONG... I-I'M... ER... I'M SORRY ABOUT MINDI. I BET THIS MUST BE HARD FOR YOU...
THIS IS A SERIOUS MATTER, MILO!
WHICH IS WHY I DON'T NEED YOU AND YOUR BIG, BLABBERING MOUTH TODAY!
BLAH BLAH BLAH BLAH...
"BIG MOUTH"... WHO DOES HE THINK HE IS?!
IT'S NOT AS BIG AS HIS EARS!
HEY!
?!
SORRY, ZHONG. WE STILL HAVEN'T FOUND ANYTHING...
MILO?! HEY! WE CAN'T LEAVE ANYONE BEHIND!
I DON'T WANT TO HAVE TO BABYSIT YOU...
MILO...
?!
MILOOOOO!

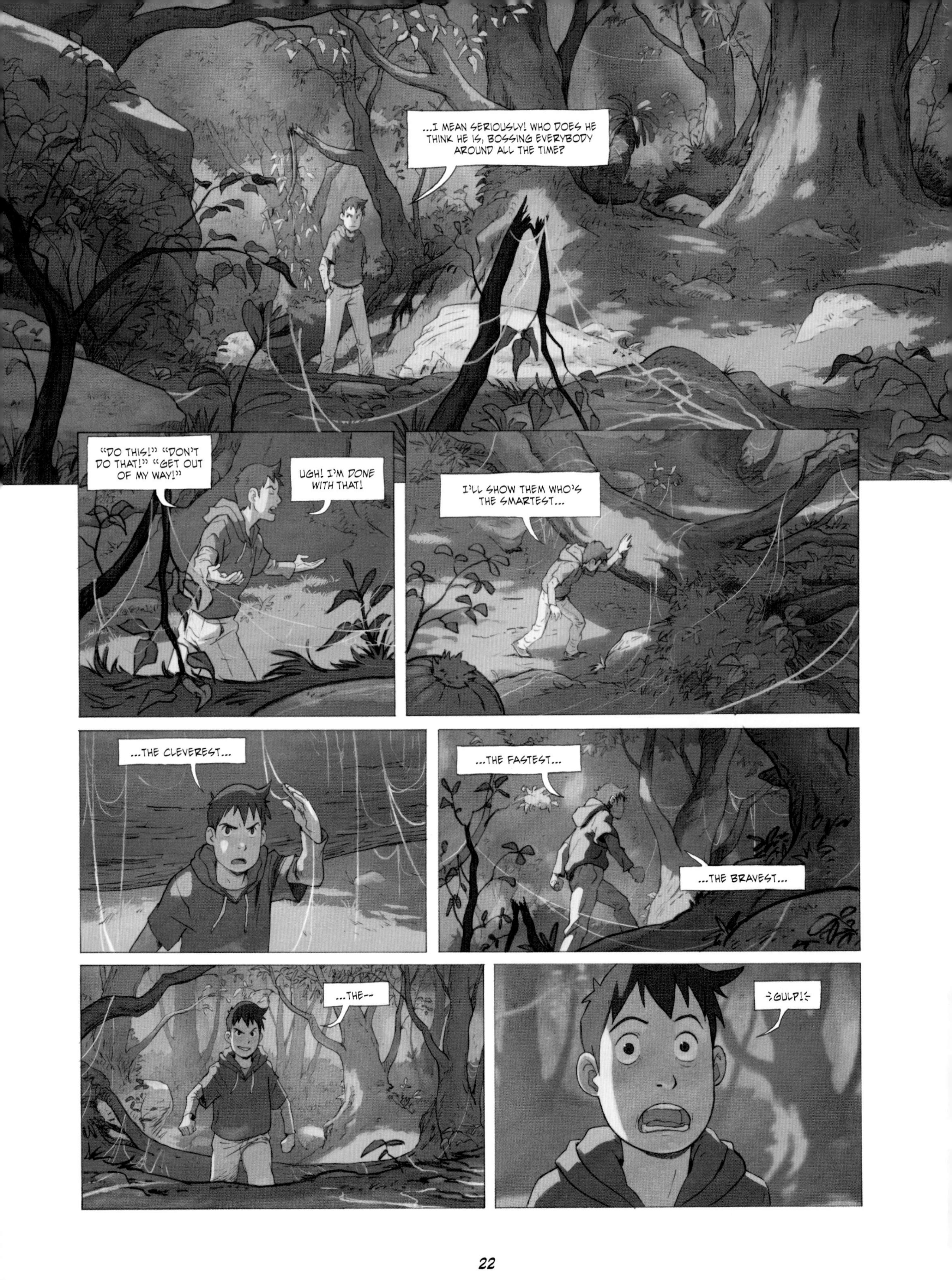
...I MEAN SERIOUSLY! WHO DOES HE THINK HE IS, BOSSING EVERYBODY AROUND ALL THE TIME?
"DO THIS!" "DON'T DO THAT!" "GET OUT OF MY WAY!"
UGH! I'M DONE WITH THAT!
I'LL SHOW THEM WHO'S THE SMARTEST...
...THE CLEVEREST...
...THE FASTEST...
...THE BRAVEST...
...THE--
GULP!

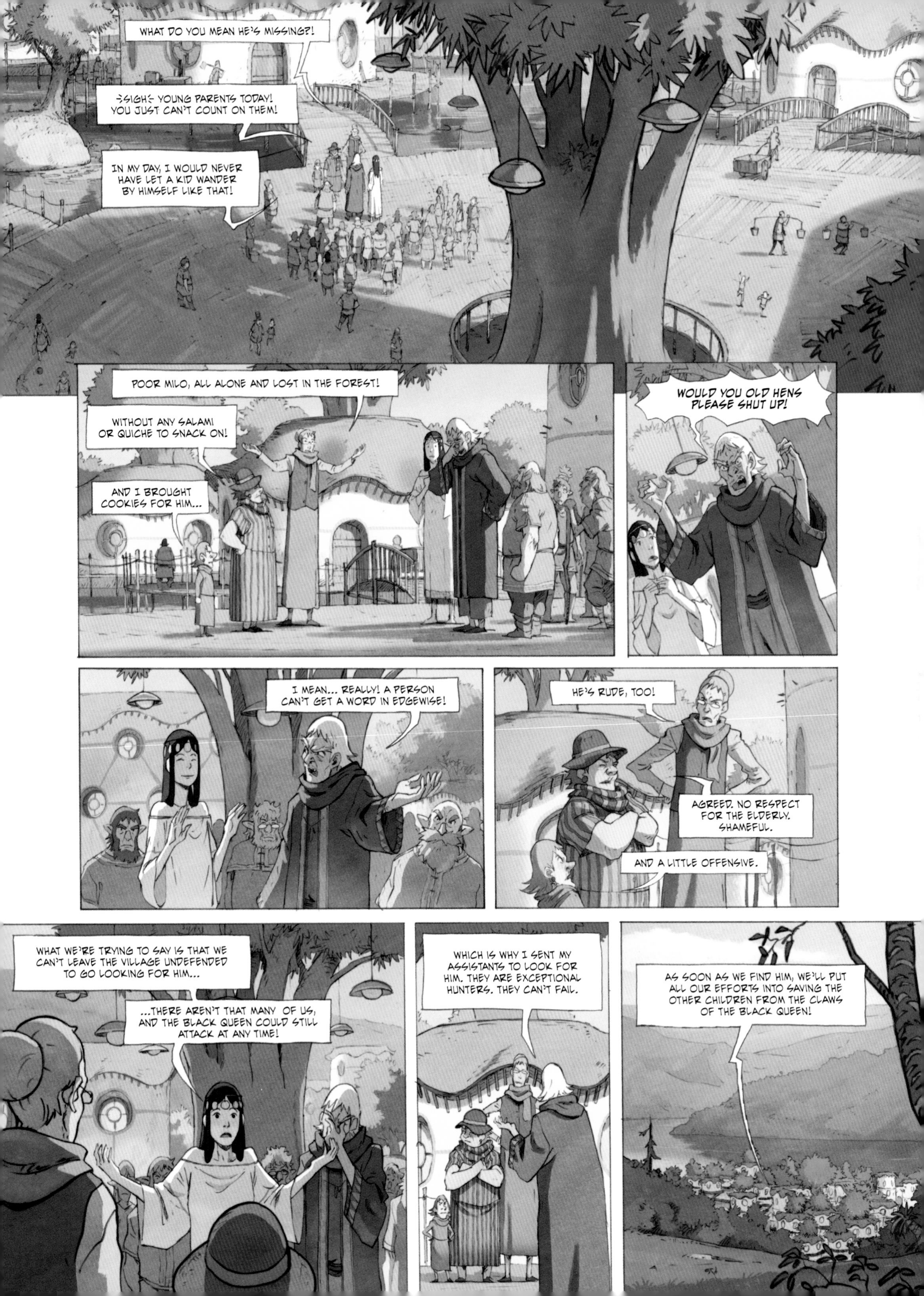
WHAT DO YOU MEAN HE'S MISSING?!
-SIGH- YOUNG PARENTS TODAY! YOU JUST CAN'T COUNT ON THEM!
IN MY DAY, I WOULD NEVER HAVE LET A KID WANDER BY HIMSELF LIKE THAT!
POOR MILO, ALL ALONE AND LOST IN THE FOREST!
WITHOUT ANY SALAMI OR QUICHE TO SNACK ON!
AND I BROUGHT COOKIES FOR HIM...
WOULD YOU OLD HENS PLEASE SHUT UP!
I MEAN... REALLY! A PERSON CAN'T GET A WORD IN EDGEWISE!
HE'S RUDE, TOO!
AGREED. NO RESPECT FOR THE ELDERLY. SHAMEFUL.
AND A LITTLE OFFENSIVE.
WHAT WE'RE TRYING TO SAY IS THAT WE CAN'T LEAVE THE VILLAGE UNDEFENDED TO GO LOOKING FOR HIM...
...THERE AREN'T THAT MANY OF US, AND THE BLACK QUEEN COULD STILL ATTACK AT ANY TIME!
WHICH IS WHY I SENT MY ASSISTANTS TO LOOK FOR HIM. THEY ARE EXCEPTIONAL HUNTERS. THEY CAN'T FAIL.
AS SOON AS WE FIND HIM, WE'LL PUT ALL OUR EFFORTS INTO SAVING THE OTHER CHILDREN FROM THE CLAWS OF THE BLACK QUEEN!

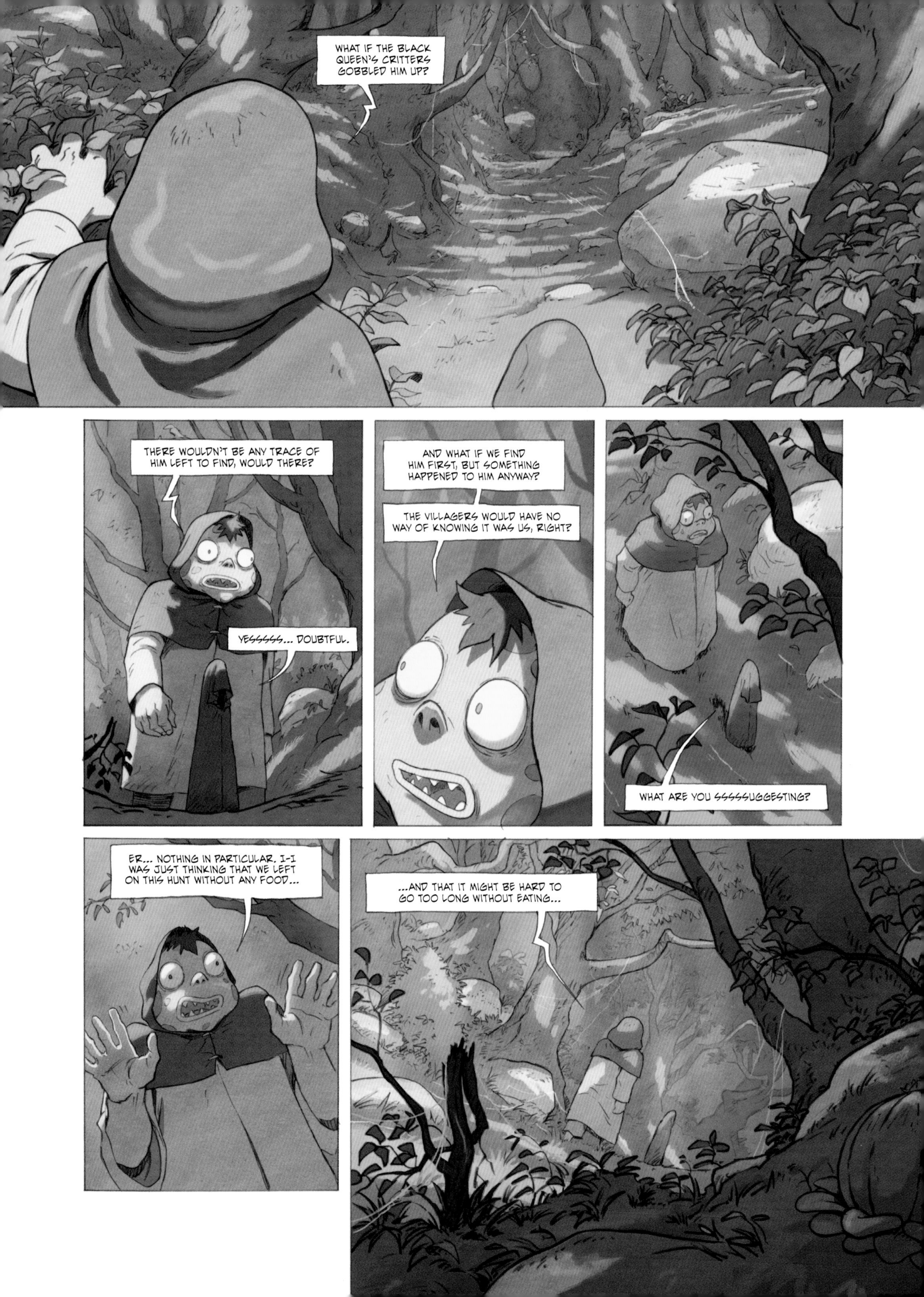
WHAT IF THE BLACK QUEEN'S CRITTERS GOBBLED HIM UP?
THERE WOULDN'T BE ANY TRACE OF HIM LEFT TO FIND, WOULD THERE?
YESSSSS... DOUBTFUL.
AND WHAT IF WE FIND HIM FIRST, BUT SOMETHING HAPPENED TO HIM ANYWAY?
THE VILLAGERS WOULD HAVE NO WAY OF KNOWING IT WAS US, RIGHT?
WHAT ARE YOU SSSSSUGGESTING?
ER... NOTHING IN PARTICULAR. I-I WAS JUST THINKING THAT WE LEFT ON THIS HUNT WITHOUT ANY FOOD...
...AND THAT IT MIGHT BE HARD TO GO TOO LONG WITHOUT EATING...

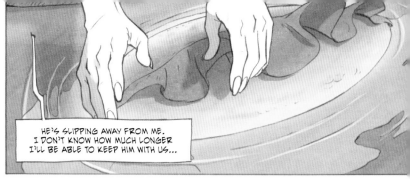

HE'S SLIPPING AWAY FROM ME. I DON'T KNOW HOW MUCH LONGER I'LL BE ABLE TO KEEP HIM WITH US...

YOU'RE DOING EVERYTHING YOU CAN.

I CAN IMAGINE HOW YOU MUST FEEL. IF THE SAME THING HAD HAPPENED TO MILO, I --

THIS NEVER WOULD HAVE HAPPENED TO MILO. EVEN FROM FAR AWAY, YOU'VE ALWAYS WATCHED OVER HIM DUTIFULLY.

WHAT HAPPENED TO VALIA IS ALL MY FAULT.

TO THIS DAY, I AM STILL PAYING THE PRICE FOR MY ANGER AND BITTERNESS.

AND NOW, I'VE FORCED YOU TO CARRY THE BURDEN FOR MY FAILURE...

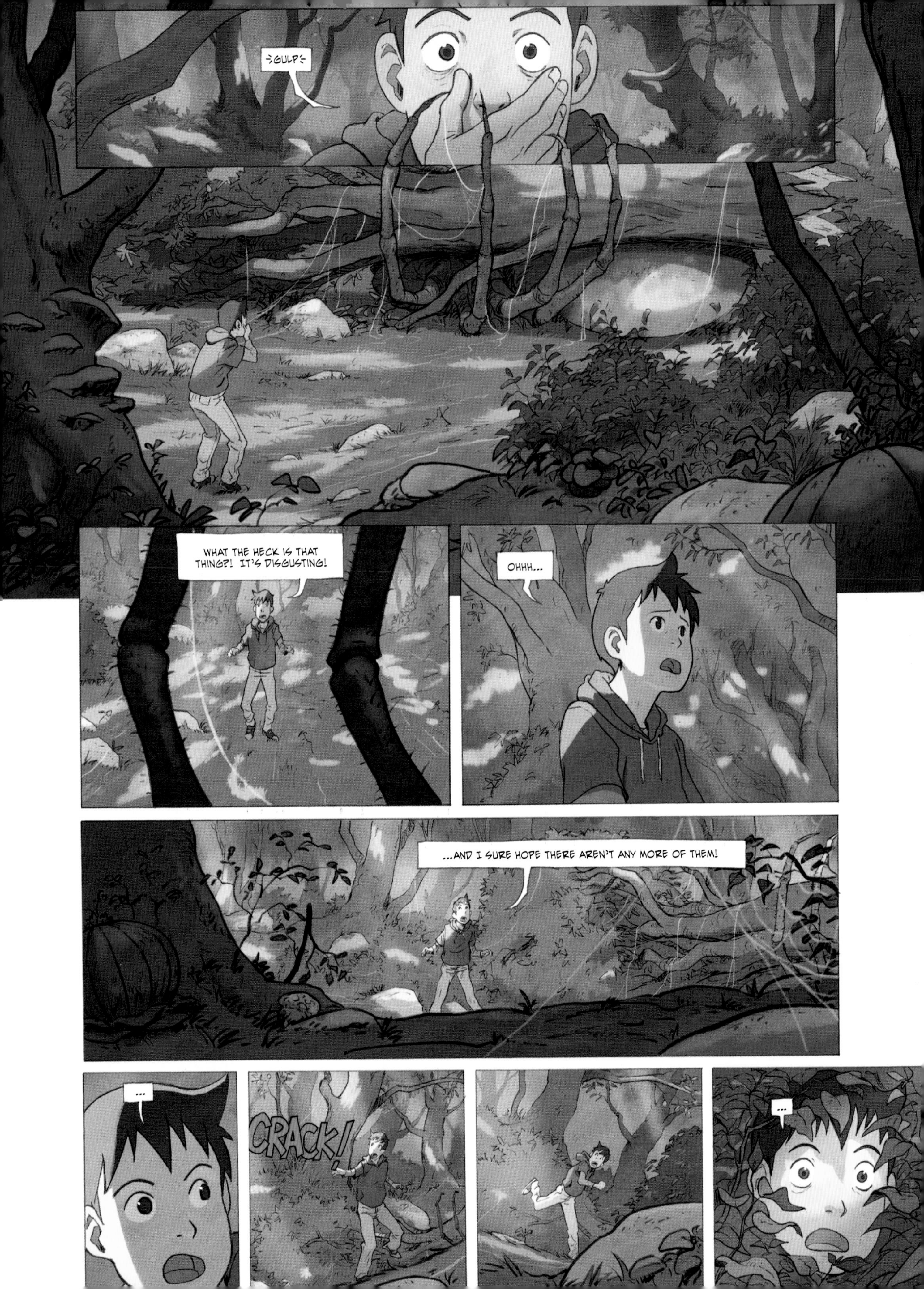

=GULP=
WHAT THE HECK IS THAT THING?! IT'S DISGUSTING!
OHHH...
...AND I SURE HOPE THERE AREN'T ANY MORE OF THEM!
...
CRACK!
...

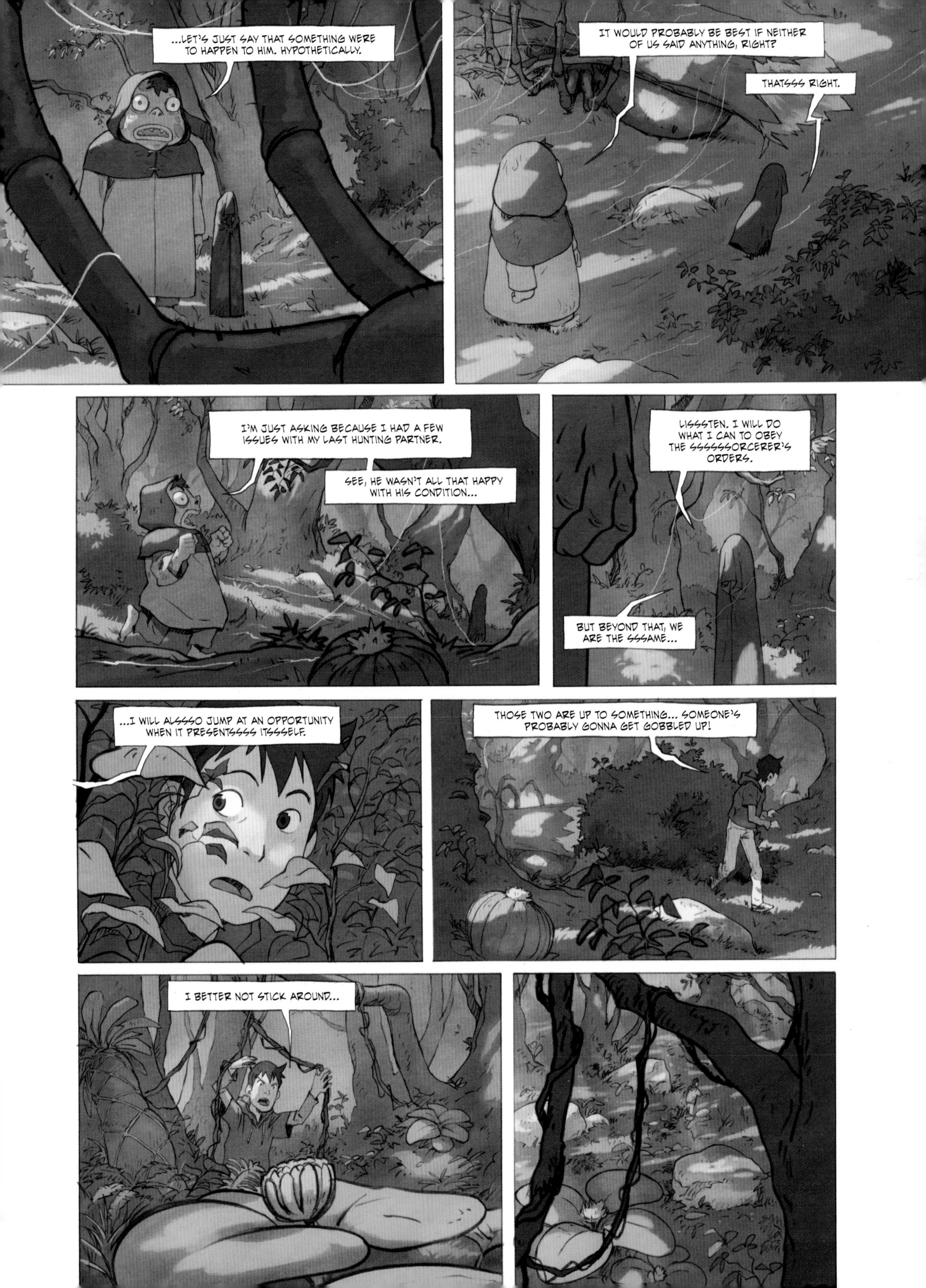
...LET'S JUST SAY THAT SOMETHING WERE TO HAPPEN TO HIM. HYPOTHETICALLY.
IT WOULD PROBABLY BE BEST IF NEITHER OF US SAID ANYTHING, RIGHT?
THATSSS RIGHT.
I'M JUST ASKING BECAUSE I HAD A FEW ISSUES WITH MY LAST HUNTING PARTNER.
SEE, HE WASN'T ALL THAT HAPPY WITH HIS CONDITION...
LISSSTEN. I WILL DO WHAT I CAN TO OBEY THE SSSSSSORCERER'S ORDERS.
BUT BEYOND THAT, WE ARE THE SSSAME...
...I WILL ALSSSO JUMP AT AN OPPORTUNITY WHEN IT PRESENTSSSS ITSSSELF.
THOSE TWO ARE UP TO SOMETHING... SOMEONE'S PROBABLY GONNA GET GOBBLED UP!
I BETTER NOT STICK AROUND...

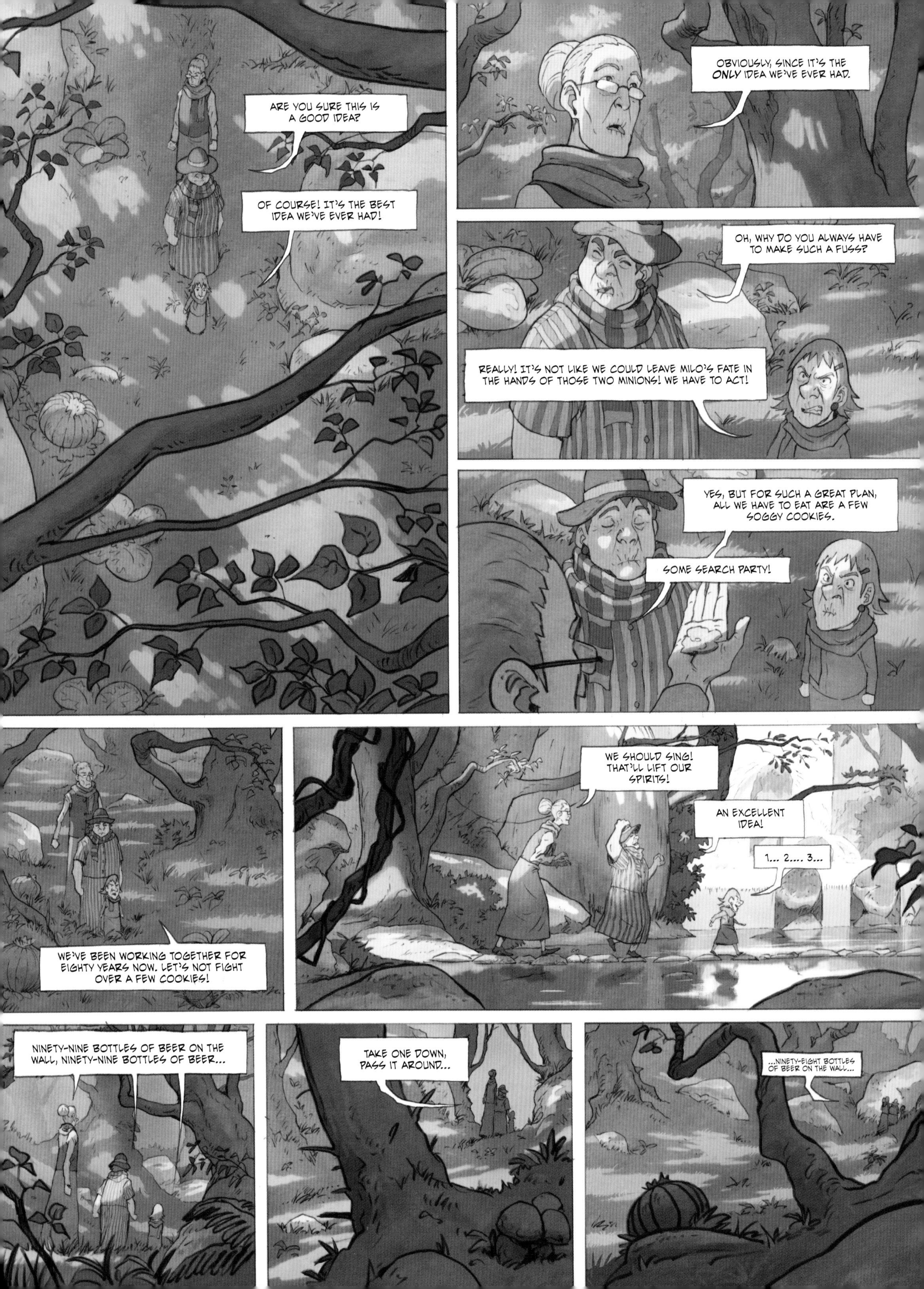
ARE YOU SURE THIS IS A GOOD IDEA?
OF COURSE! IT'S THE BEST IDEA WE'VE EVER HAD!
OBVIOUSLY, SINCE IT'S THE ONLY IDEA WE'VE EVER HAD.
OH, WHY DO YOU ALWAYS HAVE TO MAKE SUCH A FUSS?
REALLY! IT'S NOT LIKE WE COULD LEAVE MILO'S FATE IN THE HANDS OF THOSE TWO MINIONS! WE HAVE TO ACT!
YES, BUT FOR SUCH A GREAT PLAN, ALL WE HAVE TO EAT ARE A FEW SOGGY COOKIES.
SOME SEARCH PARTY!
WE'VE BEEN WORKING TOGETHER FOR EIGHTY YEARS NOW. LET'S NOT FIGHT OVER A FEW COOKIES!
WE SHOULD SING! THAT'LL LIFT OUR SPIRITS!
AN EXCELLENT IDEA!
1... 2.... 3...
NINETY-NINE BOTTLES OF BEER ON THE WALL, NINETY-NINE BOTTLES OF BEER...
TAKE ONE DOWN, PASS IT AROUND...
...NINETY-EIGHT BOTTLES OF BEER ON THE WALL...

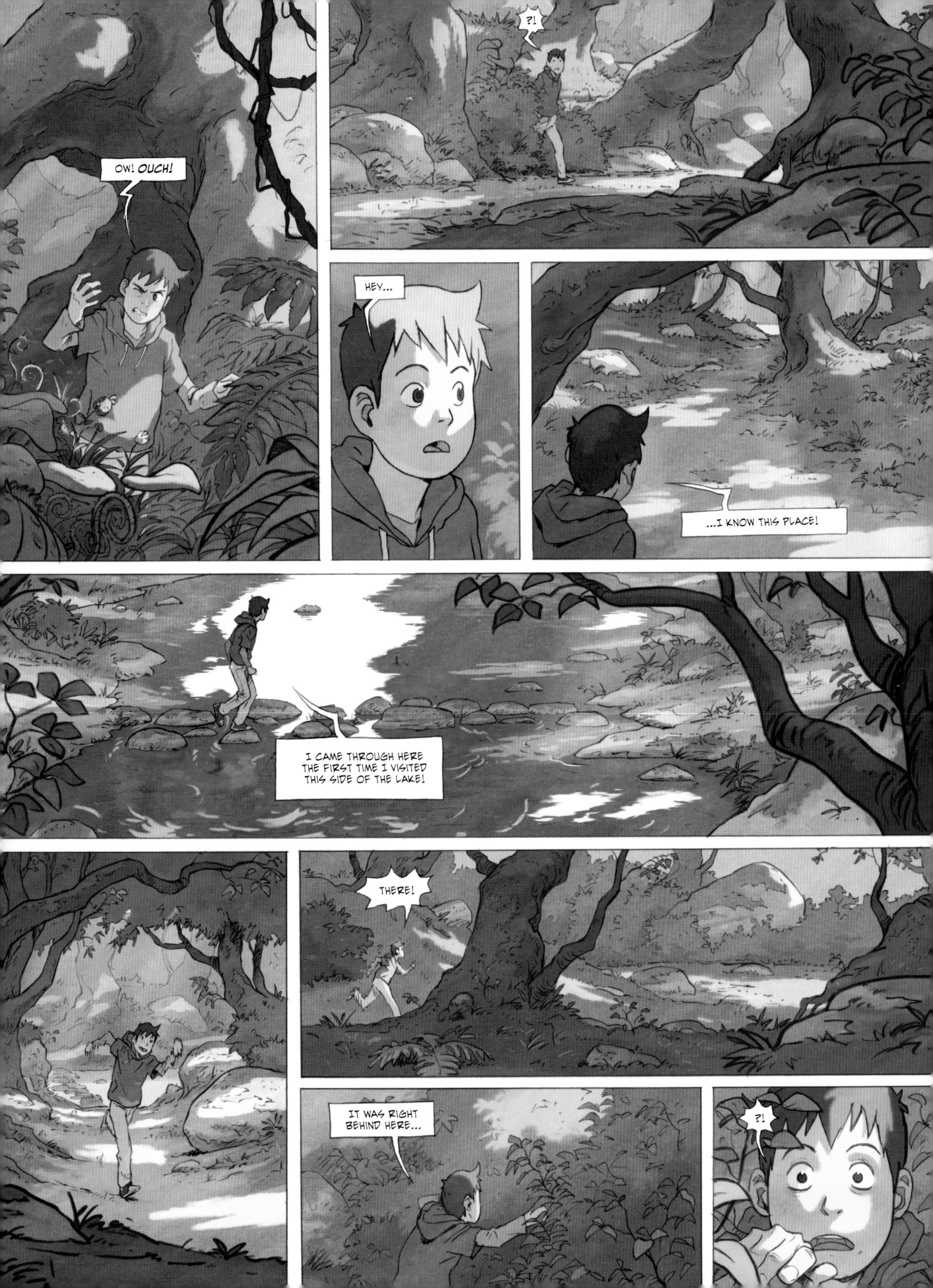
OW! OUCH!
?!
HEY...
...I KNOW THIS PLACE!
I CAME THROUGH HERE THE FIRST TIME I VISITED THIS SIDE OF THE LAKE!
THERE!
IT WAS RIGHT BEHIND HERE...
?!

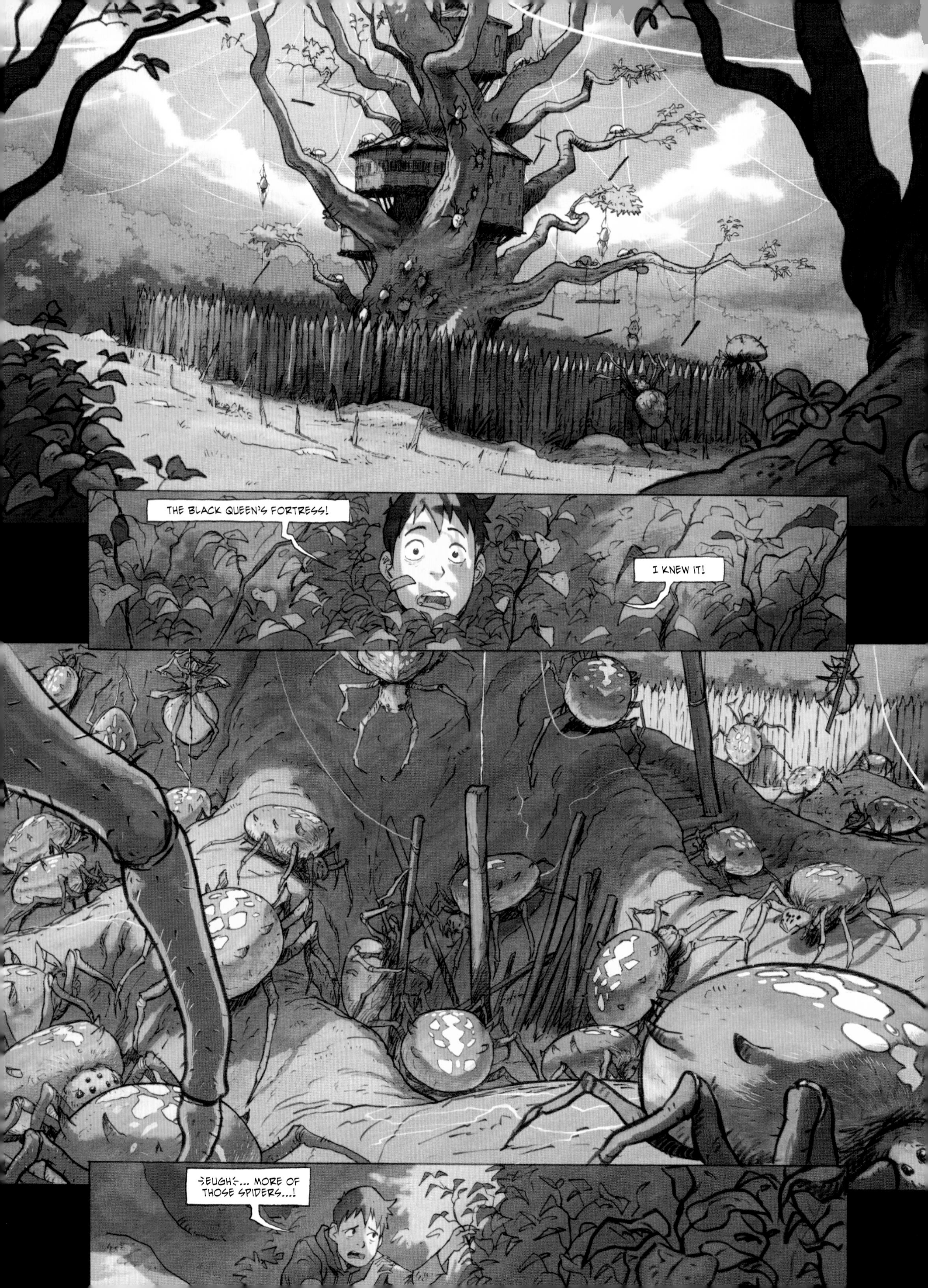
THE BLACK QUEEN'S FORTRESS!
I KNEW IT!
EUGH... MORE OF THOSE SPIDERS...!

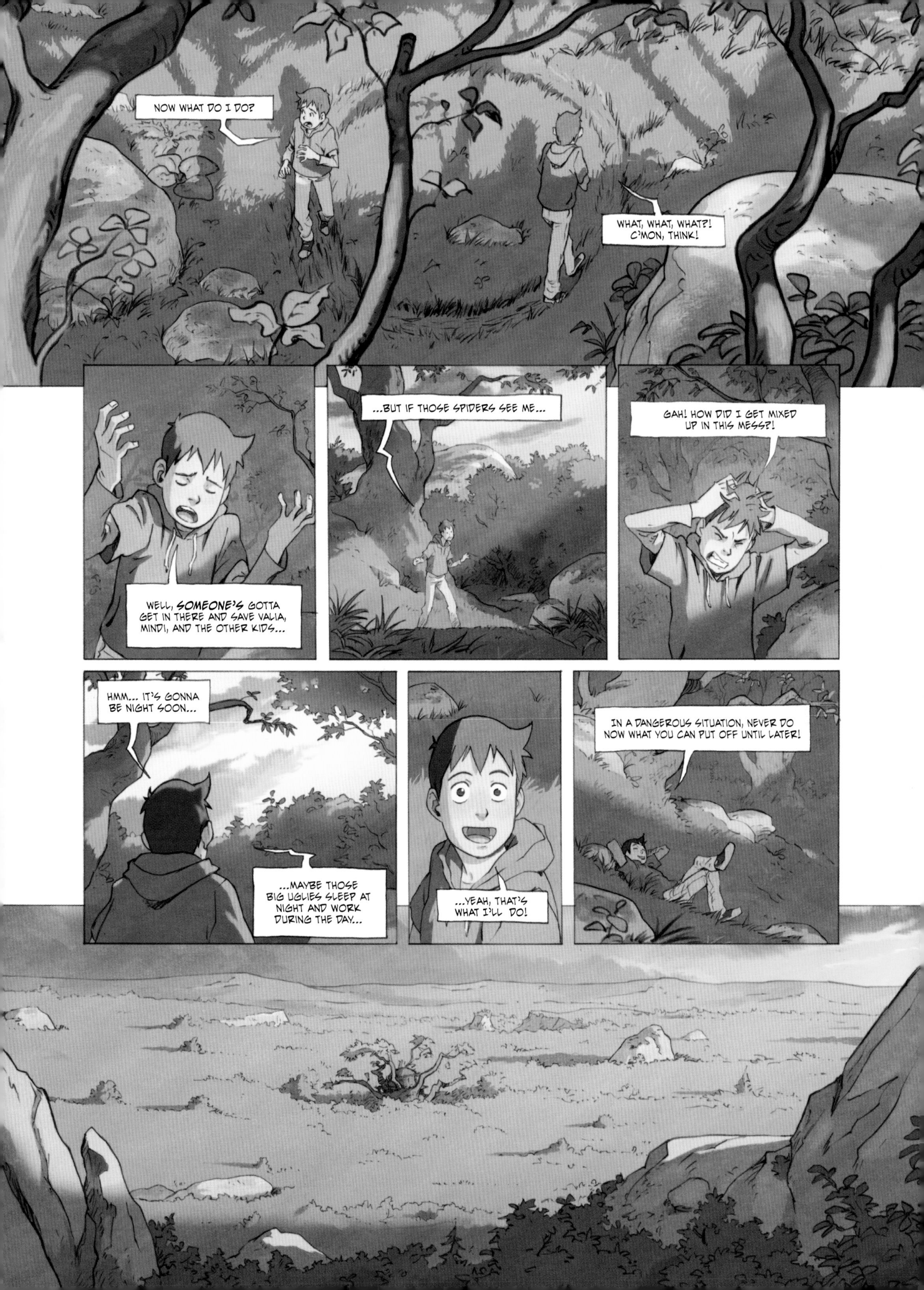
NOW WHAT DO I DO?
WHAT, WHAT, WHAT?! C'MON, THINK!
WELL, SOMEONE'S GOTTA GET IN THERE AND SAVE VALIA, MINDI, AND THE OTHER KIDS...
...BUT IF THOSE SPIDERS SEE ME...
GAH! HOW DID I GET MIXED UP IN THIS MESS?!
HMM... IT'S GONNA BE NIGHT SOON...
...MAYBE THOSE BIG UGLIES SLEEP AT NIGHT AND WORK DURING THE DAY...
...YEAH, THAT'S WHAT I'LL DO!
IN A DANGEROUS SITUATION, NEVER DO NOW WHAT YOU CAN PUT OFF UNTIL LATER!

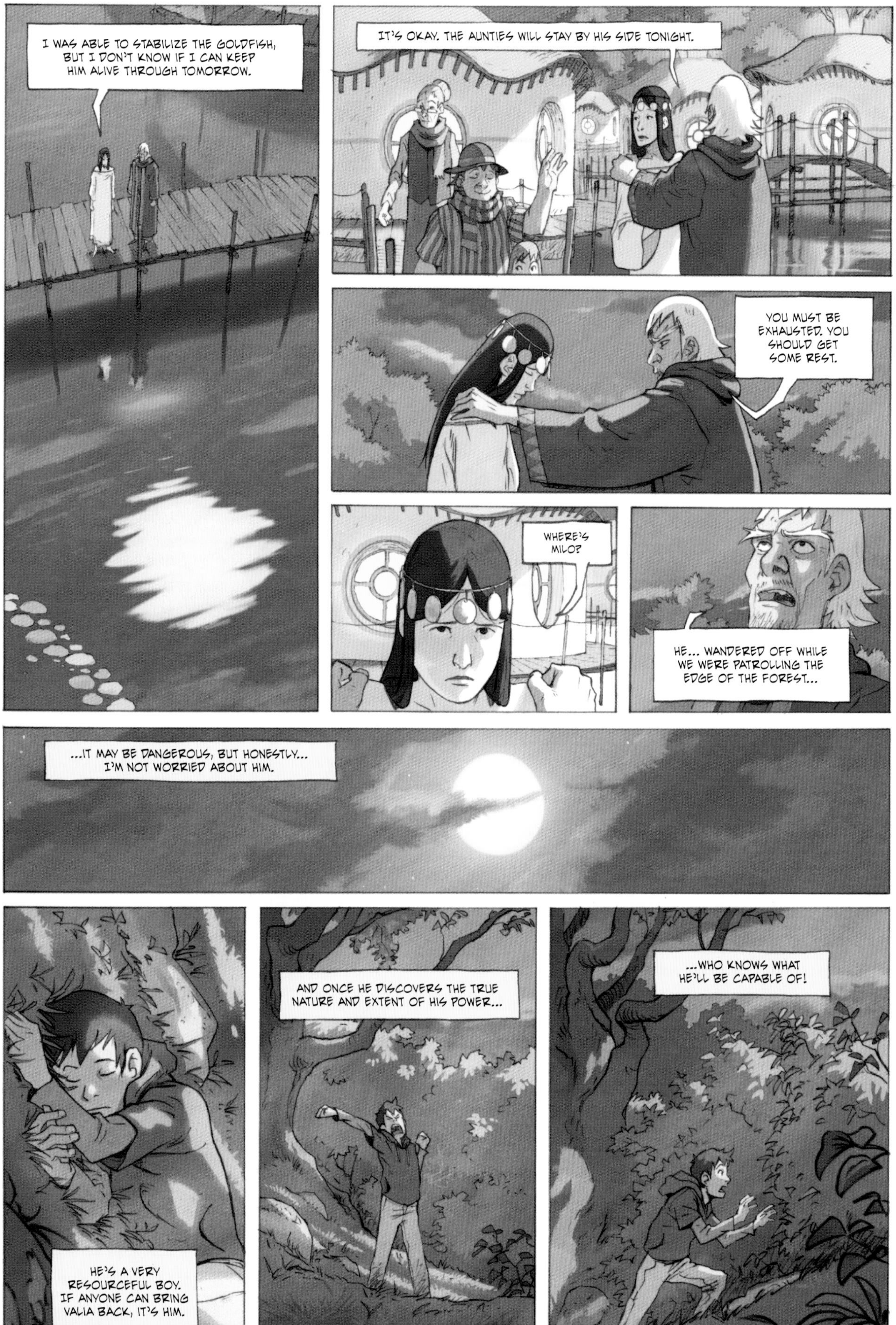
I WAS ABLE TO STABILIZE THE GOLDFISH, BUT I DON'T KNOW IF I CAN KEEP HIM ALIVE THROUGH TOMORROW.
IT'S OKAY. THE AUNTIES WILL STAY BY HIS SIDE TONIGHT.
YOU MUST BE EXHAUSTED. YOU SHOULD GET SOME REST.
WHERE'S MILO?
HE... WANDERED OFF WHILE WE WERE PATROLLING THE EDGE OF THE FOREST...
...IT MAY BE DANGEROUS, BUT HONESTLY... I'M NOT WORRIED ABOUT HIM.
HE'S A VERY RESOURCEFUL BOY. IF ANYONE CAN BRING VALIA BACK, IT'S HIM.
AND ONCE HE DISCOVERS THE TRUE NATURE AND EXTENT OF HIS POWER...
...WHO KNOWS WHAT HE'LL BE CAPABLE OF!

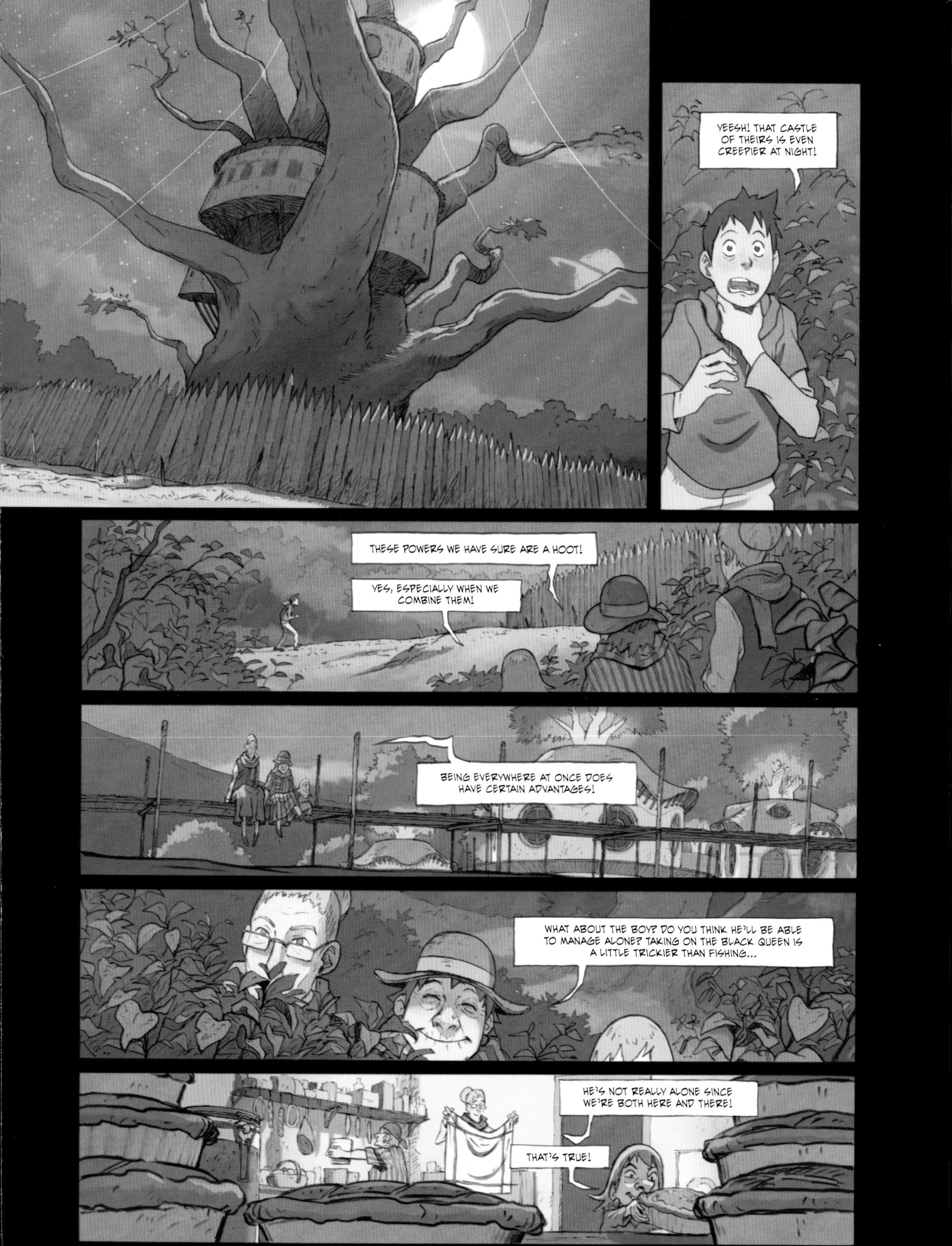
YEESH! THAT CASTLE OF THEIRS IS EVEN CREEPIER AT NIGHT!
THESE POWERS WE HAVE SURE ARE A HOOT!
YES, ESPECIALLY WHEN WE COMBINE THEM!
BEING EVERYWHERE AT ONCE DOES HAVE CERTAIN ADVANTAGES!
WHAT ABOUT THE BOY? DO YOU THINK HE'LL BE ABLE TO MANAGE ALONE? TAKING ON THE BLACK QUEEN IS A LITTLE TRICKIER THAN FISHING...
HE'S NOT REALLY ALONE SINCE WE'RE BOTH HERE AND THERE!
THAT'S TRUE!

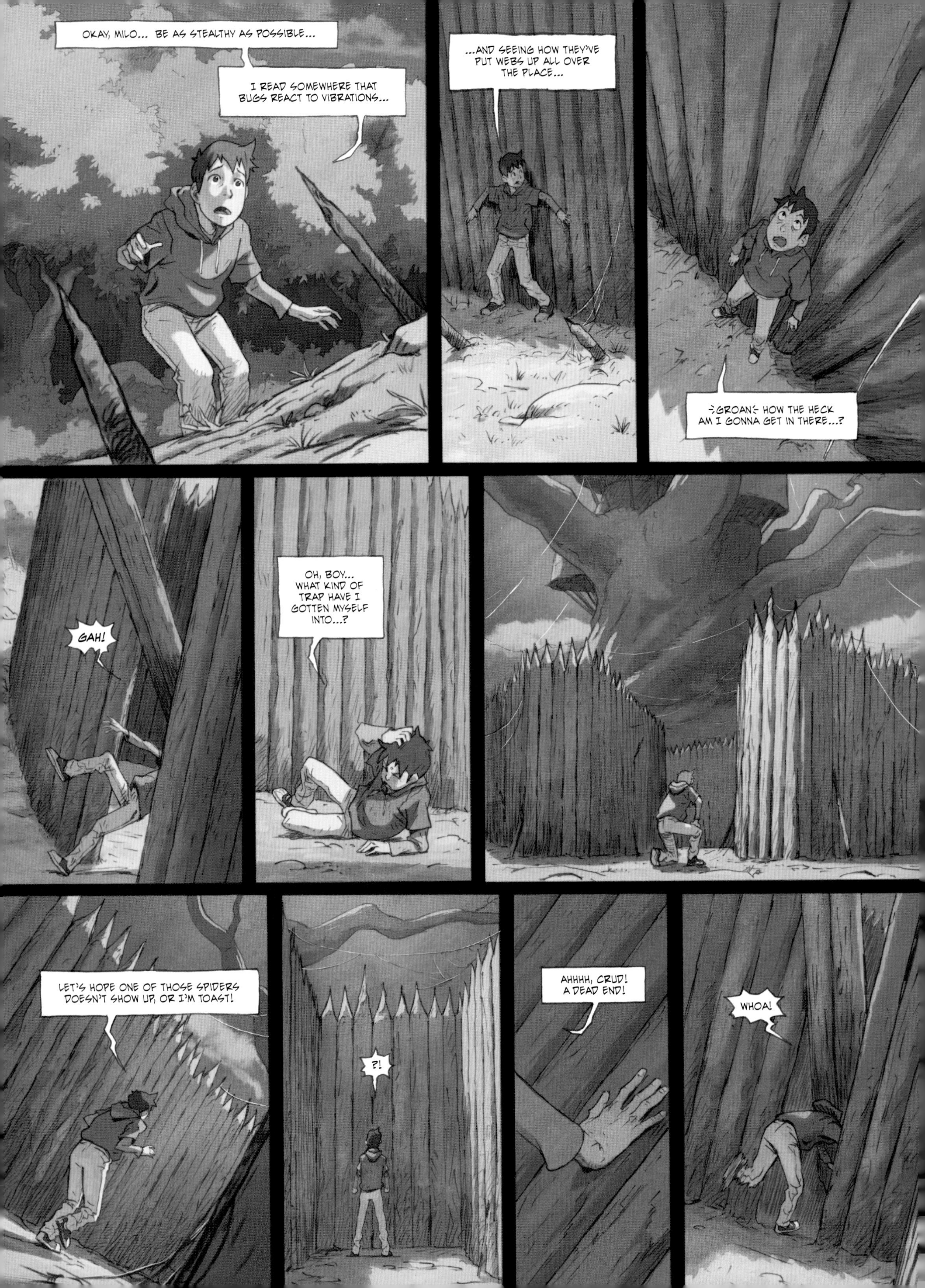
OKAY, MILO... BE AS STEALTHY AS POSSIBLE...
I READ SOMEWHERE THAT BUGS REACT TO VIBRATIONS...
...AND SEEING HOW THEY'VE PUT WEBS UP ALL OVER THE PLACE...
-GROAN- HOW THE HECK AM I GONNA GET IN THERE...?
GAH!
OH, BOY... WHAT KIND OF TRAP HAVE I GOTTEN MYSELF INTO...?
LET'S HOPE ONE OF THOSE SPIDERS DOESN'T SHOW UP, OR I'M TOAST!
?!
AHHHH, CRUD! A DEAD END!
WHOA!

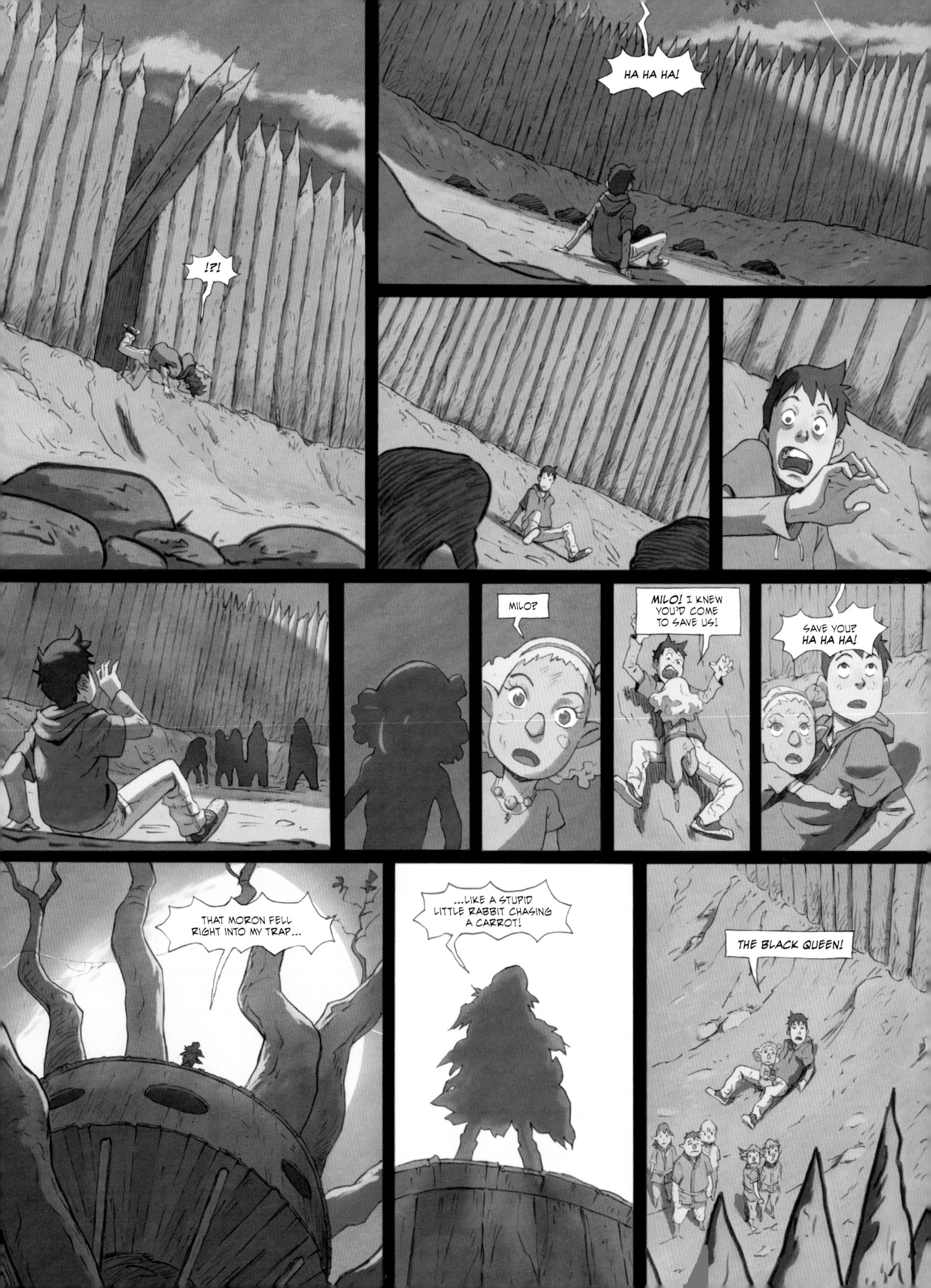
!?!
HA HA HA!
MILO?
MILO! I KNEW YOU'D COME TO SAVE US!
SAVE YOU? HA HA HA!
THAT MORON FELL RIGHT INTO MY TRAP...
...LIKE A STUPID LITTLE RABBIT CHASING A CARROT!
THE BLACK QUEEN!

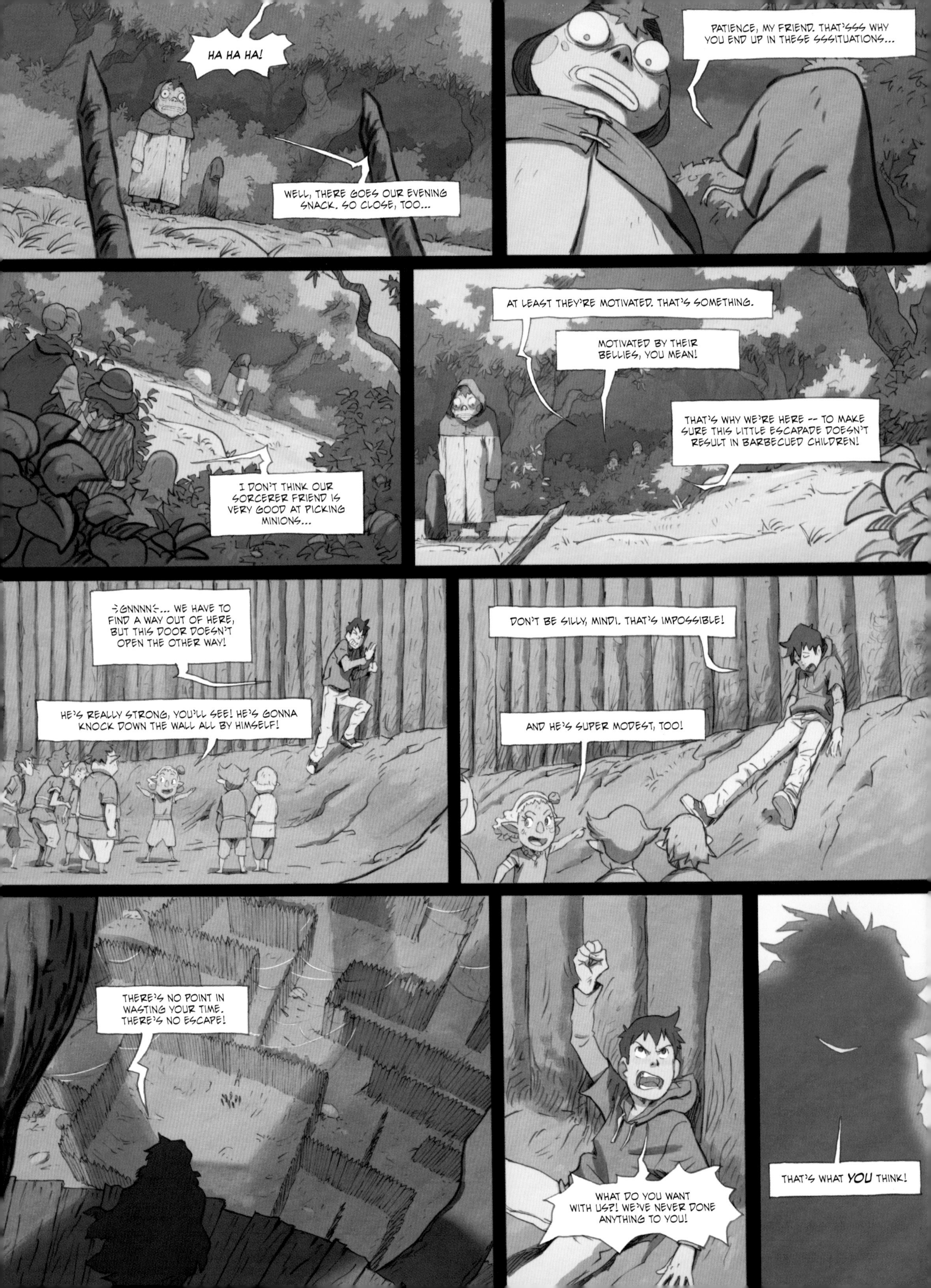
HA HA HA!
WELL, THERE GOES OUR EVENING SNACK. SO CLOSE, TOO...
PATIENCE, MY FRIEND. THAT'SSS WHY YOU END UP IN THESE SSSITUATIONS...
I DON'T THINK OUR SORCERER FRIEND IS VERY GOOD AT PICKING MINIONS...
AT LEAST THEY'RE MOTIVATED. THAT'S SOMETHING.
MOTIVATED BY THEIR BELLIES, YOU MEAN!
THAT'S WHY WE'RE HERE -- TO MAKE SURE THIS LITTLE ESCAPADE DOESN'T RESULT IN BARBECUED CHILDREN!
>GNNNN<... WE HAVE TO FIND A WAY OUT OF HERE, BUT THIS DOOR DOESN'T OPEN THE OTHER WAY!
HE'S REALLY STRONG, YOU'LL SEE! HE'S GONNA KNOCK DOWN THE WALL ALL BY HIMSELF!
DON'T BE SILLY, MINDI. THAT'S IMPOSSIBLE!
AND HE'S SUPER MODEST, TOO!
THERE'S NO POINT IN WASTING YOUR TIME. THERE'S NO ESCAPE!
WHAT DO YOU WANT WITH US?! WE'VE NEVER DONE ANYTHING TO YOU!
THAT'S WHAT YOU THINK!

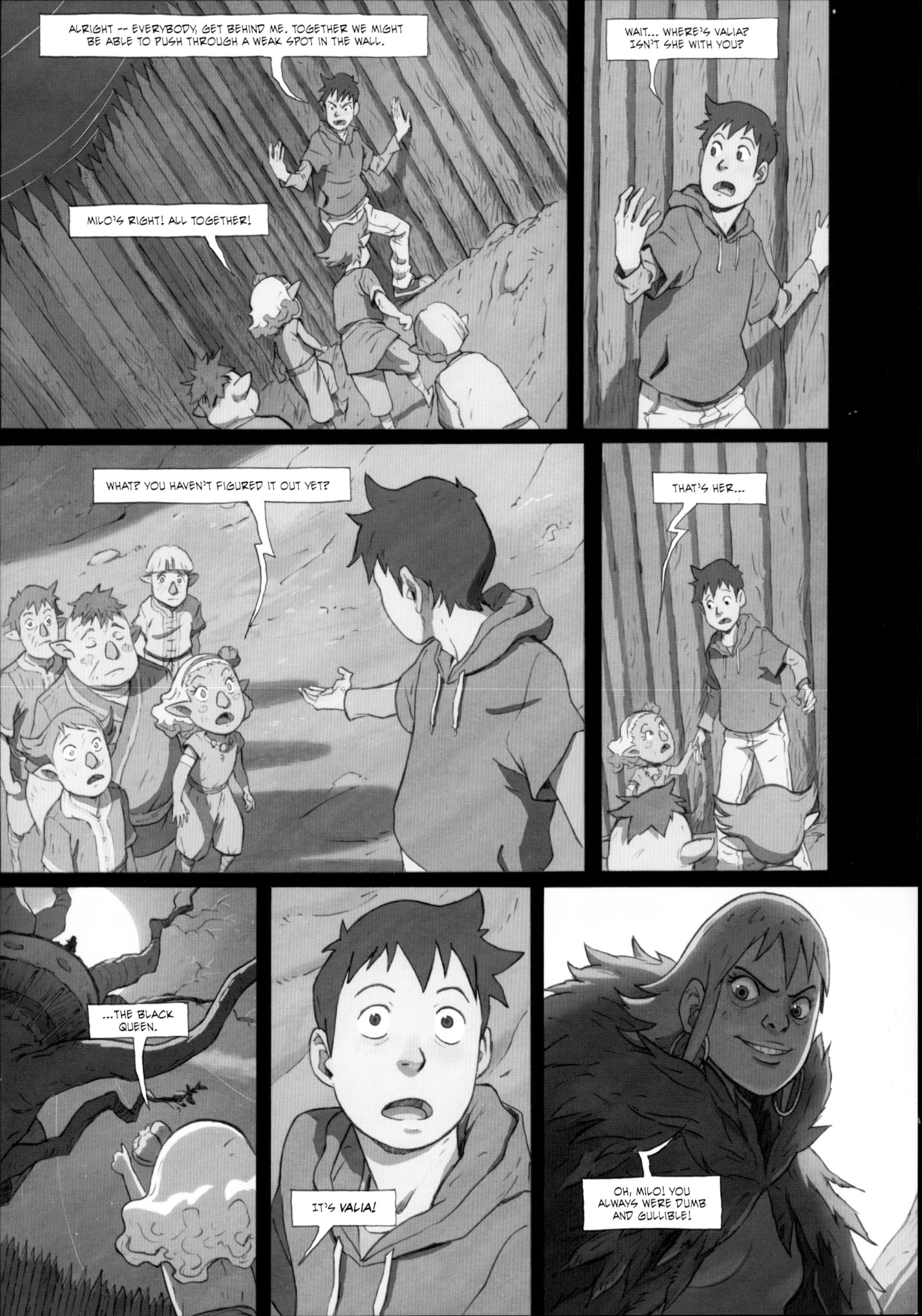
ALRIGHT -- EVERYBODY, GET BEHIND ME. TOGETHER WE MIGHT BE ABLE TO PUSH THROUGH A WEAK SPOT IN THE WALL.
MILO'S RIGHT! ALL TOGETHER!
WAIT... WHERE'S VALIA? ISN'T SHE WITH YOU?
WHAT? YOU HAVEN'T FIGURED IT OUT YET?
THAT'S HER...
...THE BLACK QUEEN.
IT'S VALIA!
OH, MILO! YOU ALWAYS WERE DUMB AND GULLIBLE!

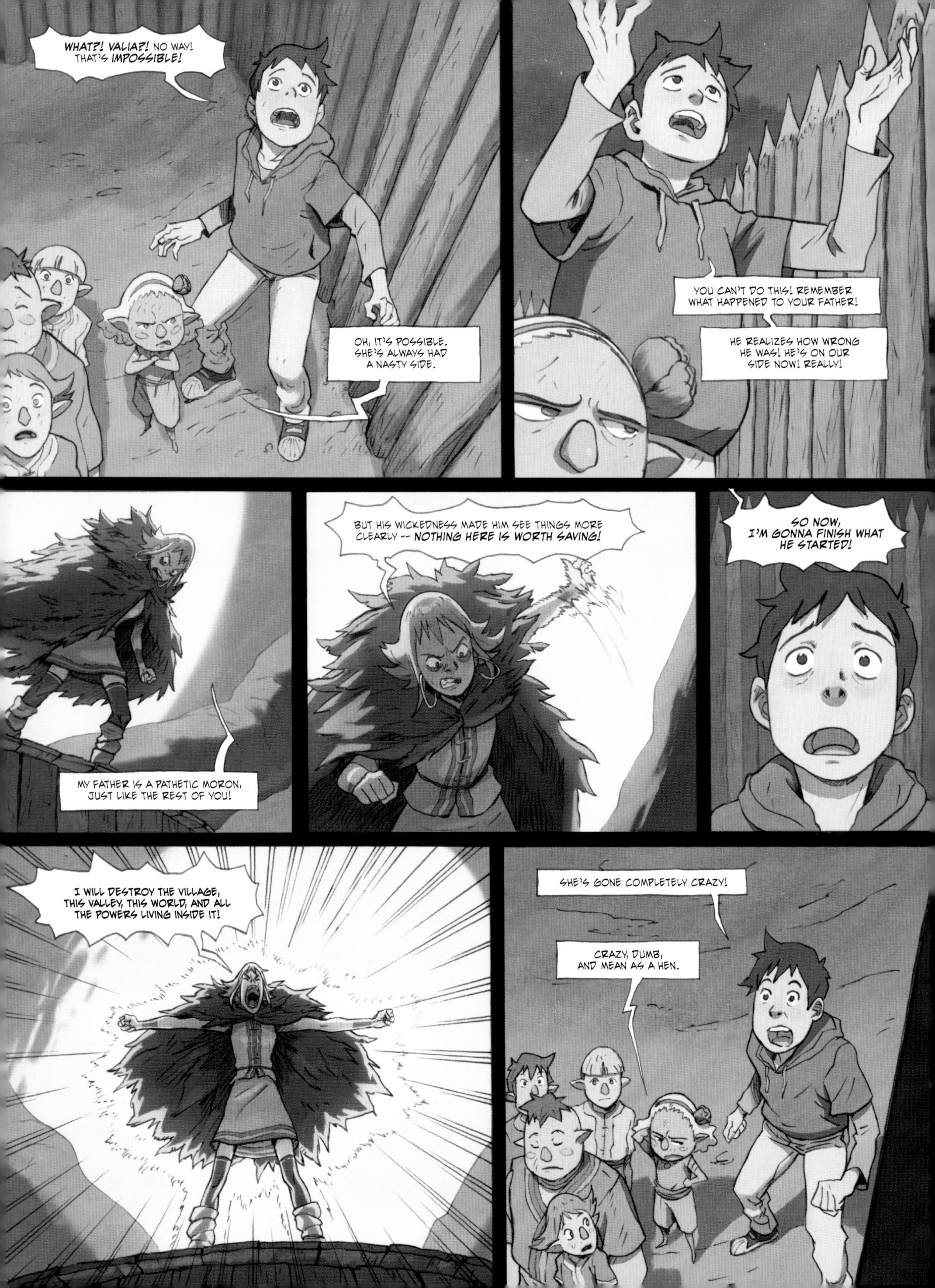
WHAT?! VALIA?! NO WAY! THAT'S IMPOSSIBLE!
OH, IT'S POSSIBLE. SHE'S ALWAYS HAD A NASTY SIDE.
YOU CAN'T DO THIS! REMEMBER WHAT HAPPENED TO YOUR FATHER!
HE REALIZES HOW WRONG HE WAS! HE'S ON OUR SIDE NOW! REALLY!
MY FATHER IS A PATHETIC MORON, JUST LIKE THE REST OF YOU!
BUT HIS WICKEDNESS MADE HIM SEE THINGS MORE CLEARLY -- NOTHING HERE IS WORTH SAVING!
SO NOW, I'M GONNA FINISH WHAT HE STARTED!
I WILL DESTROY THE VILLAGE, THIS VALLEY, THIS WORLD, AND ALL THE POWERS LIVING INSIDE IT!
SHE'S GONE COMPLETELY CRAZY!
CRAZY, DUMB, AND MEAN AS A HEN.

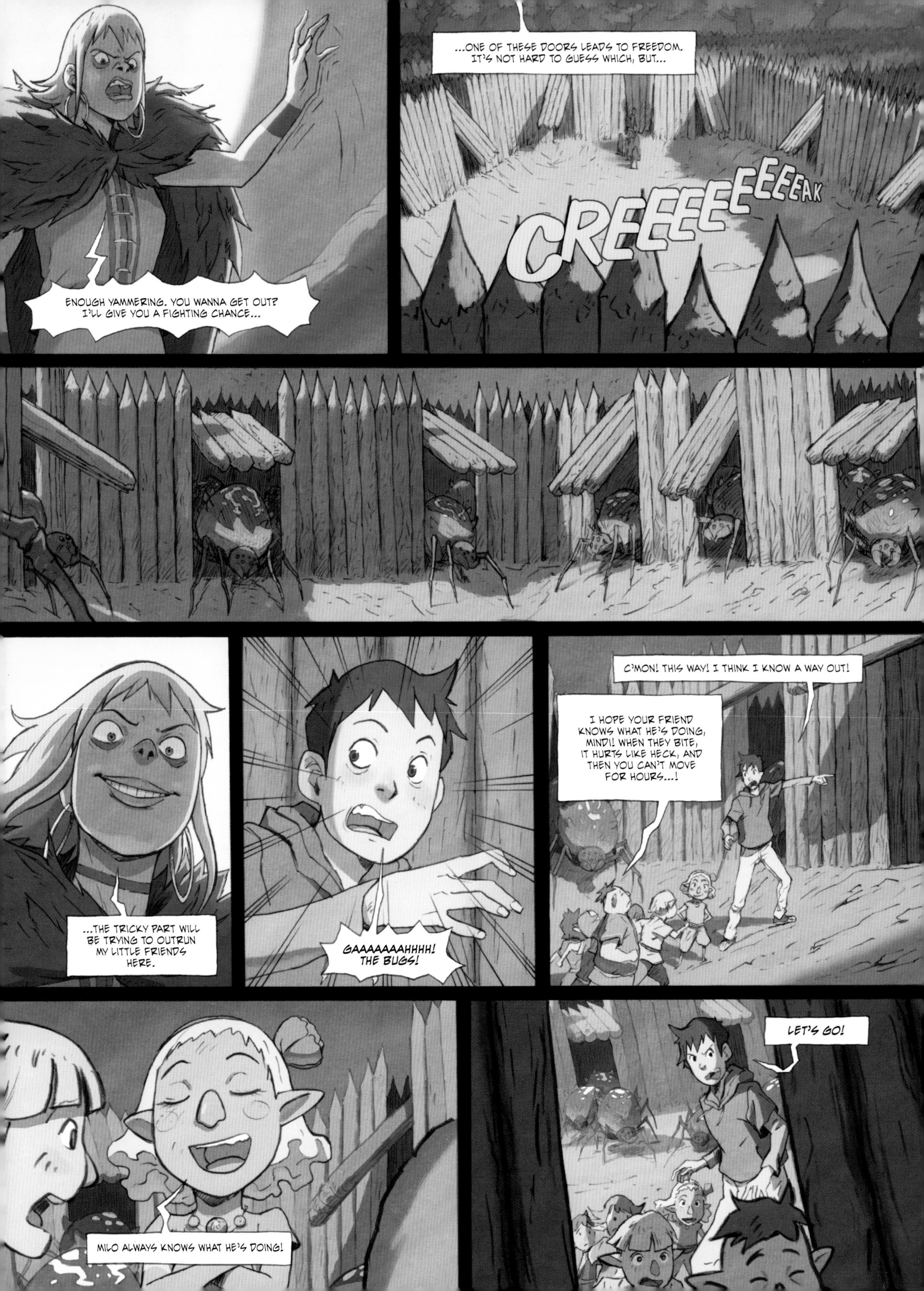
ENOUGH YAMMERING. YOU WANNA GET OUT? I'LL GIVE YOU A FIGHTING CHANCE...
...ONE OF THESE DOORS LEADS TO FREEDOM. IT'S NOT HARD TO GUESS WHICH, BUT...
CREEEEEEEEEAK
...THE TRICKY PART WILL BE TRYING TO OUTRUN MY LITTLE FRIENDS HERE.
GAAAAAAAHHHH! THE BUGS!
C'MON! THIS WAY! I THINK I KNOW A WAY OUT!
I HOPE YOUR FRIEND KNOWS WHAT HE'S DOING, MINDI! WHEN THEY BITE, IT HURTS LIKE HECK, AND THEN YOU CAN'T MOVE FOR HOURS...!
MILO ALWAYS KNOWS WHAT HE'S DOING!
LET'S GO!

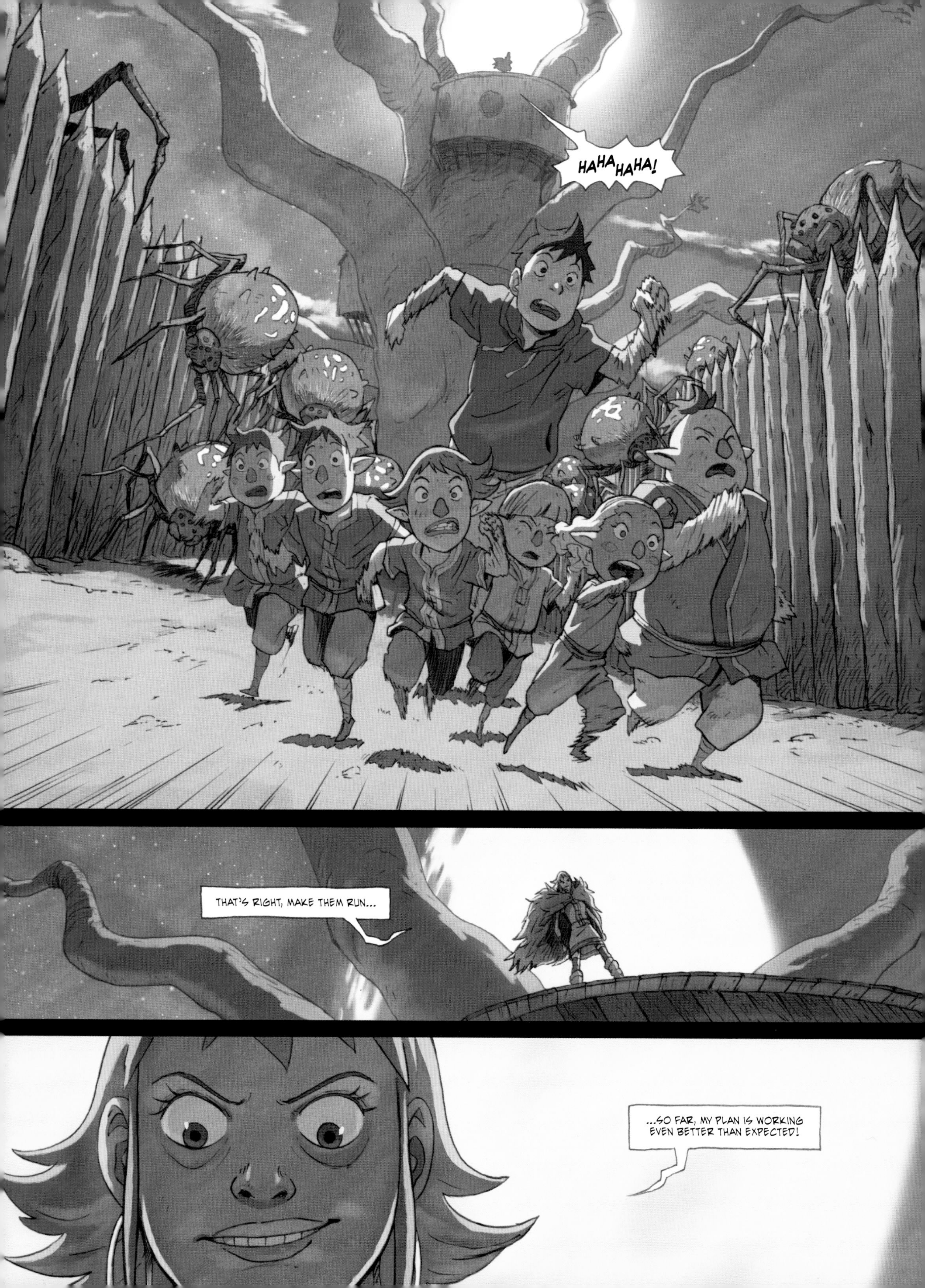
HAHAHAHA!
THAT'S RIGHT, MAKE THEM RUN...
...SO FAR, MY PLAN IS WORKING EVEN BETTER THAN EXPECTED!

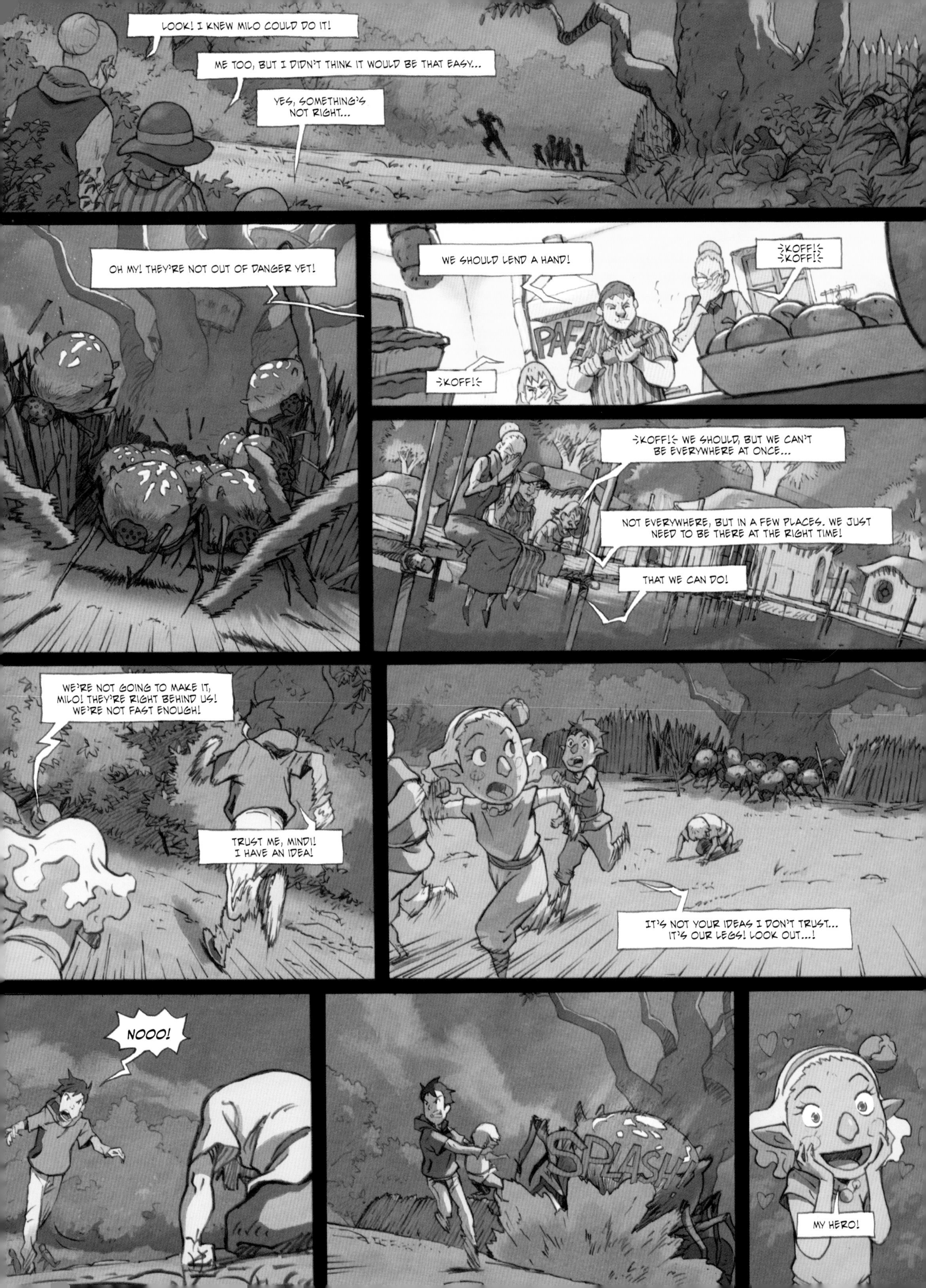
LOOK! I KNEW MILO COULD DO IT!
ME TOO, BUT I DIDN'T THINK IT WOULD BE THAT EASY...
YES, SOMETHING'S NOT RIGHT...
OH MY! THEY'RE NOT OUT OF DANGER YET!
WE SHOULD LEND A HAND!
KOFF! KOFF!
PAF!
KOFF!
KOFF! WE SHOULD, BUT WE CAN'T BE EVERYWHERE AT ONCE...
NOT EVERYWHERE, BUT IN A FEW PLACES. WE JUST NEED TO BE THERE AT THE RIGHT TIME!
THAT WE CAN DO!
WE'RE NOT GOING TO MAKE IT, MILO! THEY'RE RIGHT BEHIND US! WE'RE NOT FAST ENOUGH!
TRUST ME, MINDI! I HAVE AN IDEA!
IT'S NOT YOUR IDEAS I DON'T TRUST... IT'S OUR LEGS! LOOK OUT...!
NOOO!
SPLASH!
MY HERO!

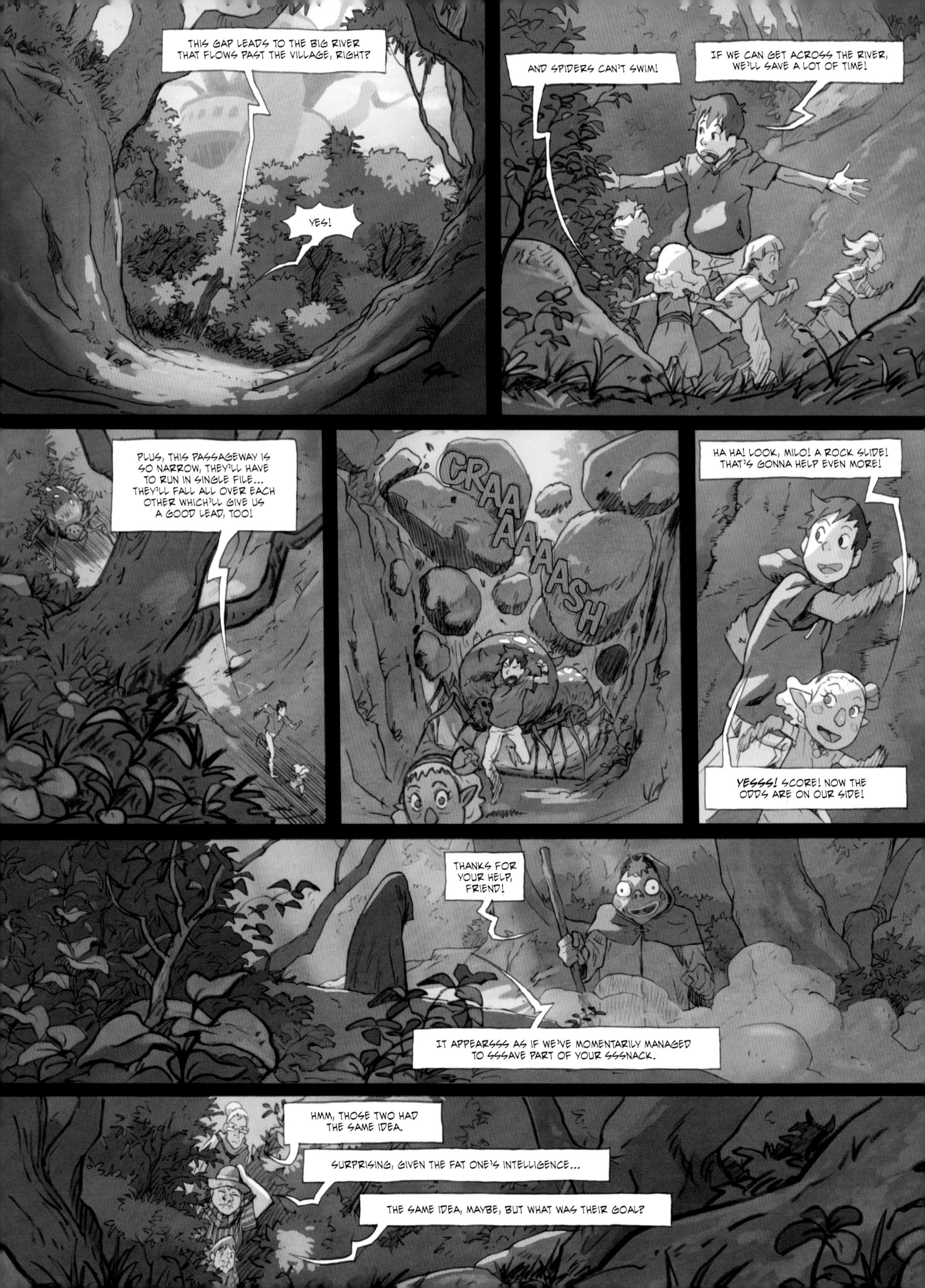
THIS GAP LEADS TO THE BIG RIVER THAT FLOWS PAST THE VILLAGE, RIGHT?
YES!
AND SPIDERS CAN'T SWIM!
IF WE CAN GET ACROSS THE RIVER, WE'LL SAVE A LOT OF TIME!
PLUS, THIS PASSAGEWAY IS SO NARROW, THEY'LL HAVE TO RUN IN SINGLE FILE... THEY'LL FALL ALL OVER EACH OTHER WHICH'LL GIVE US A GOOD LEAD, TOO!
CRAAAAAAASH
HA HA! LOOK, MILO! A ROCK SLIDE! THAT'S GONNA HELP EVEN MORE!
YESSS! SCORE! NOW THE ODDS ARE ON OUR SIDE!
THANKS FOR YOUR HELP, FRIEND!
IT APPEARSSS AS IF WE'VE MOMENTARILY MANAGED TO SSSAVE PART OF YOUR SSSNACK.
HMM, THOSE TWO HAD THE SAME IDEA.
SURPRISING, GIVEN THE FAT ONE'S INTELLIGENCE...
THE SAME IDEA, MAYBE, BUT WHAT WAS THEIR GOAL?

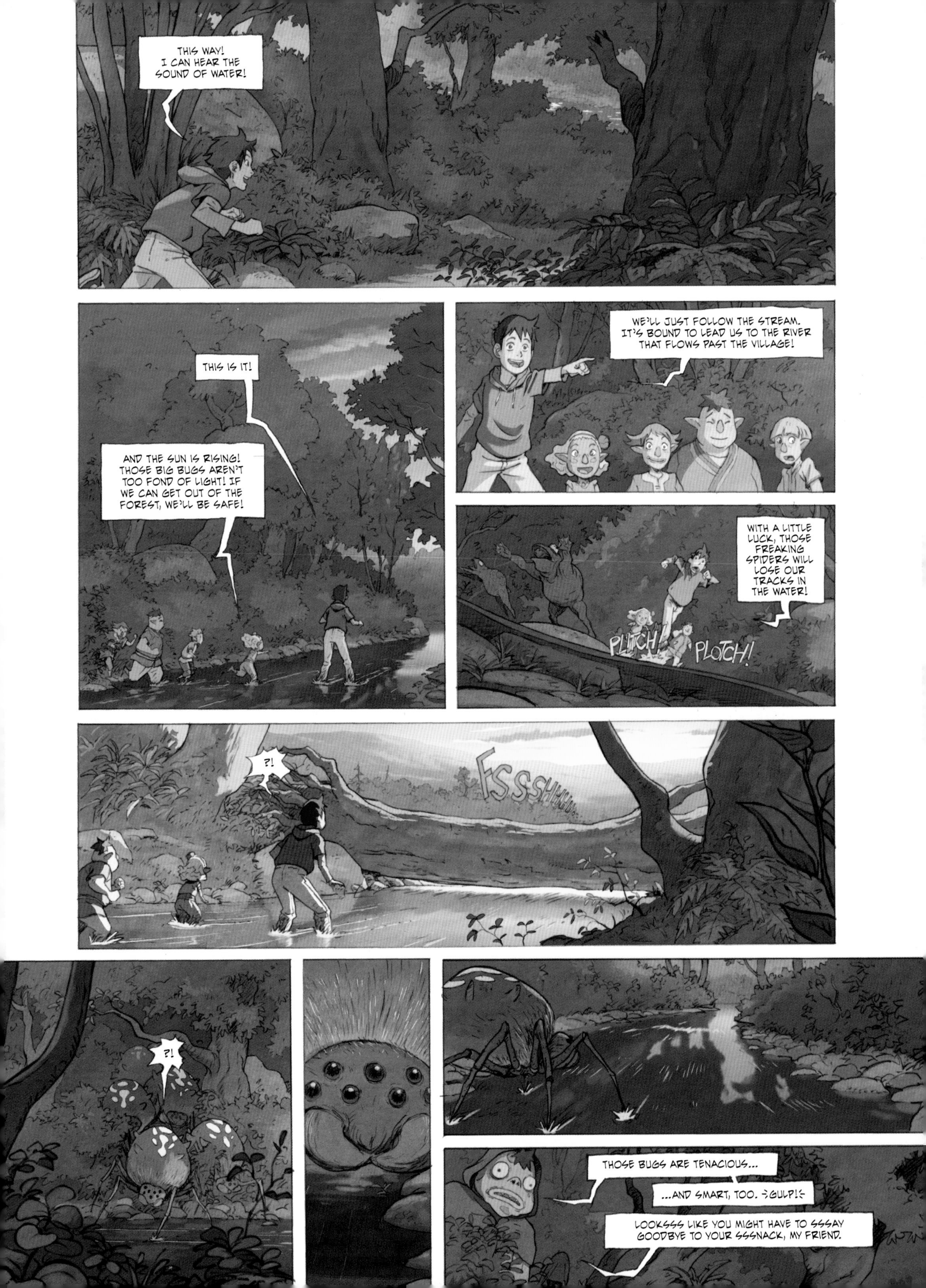

THIS WAY! I CAN HEAR THE SOUND OF WATER!
THIS IS IT!
AND THE SUN IS RISING! THOSE BIG BUGS AREN'T TOO FOND OF LIGHT! IF WE CAN GET OUT OF THE FOREST, WE'LL BE SAFE!
WE'LL JUST FOLLOW THE STREAM. IT'S BOUND TO LEAD US TO THE RIVER THAT FLOWS PAST THE VILLAGE!
WITH A LITTLE LUCK, THOSE FREAKING SPIDERS WILL LOSE OUR TRACKS IN THE WATER!
PLITCH!
PLOTCH!
?!
FSSSHHHH
?!
THOSE BUGS ARE TENACIOUS...
...AND SMART, TOO. GULP!
LOOKSSS LIKE YOU MIGHT HAVE TO SSSAY GOODBYE TO YOUR SSSNACK, MY FRIEND.

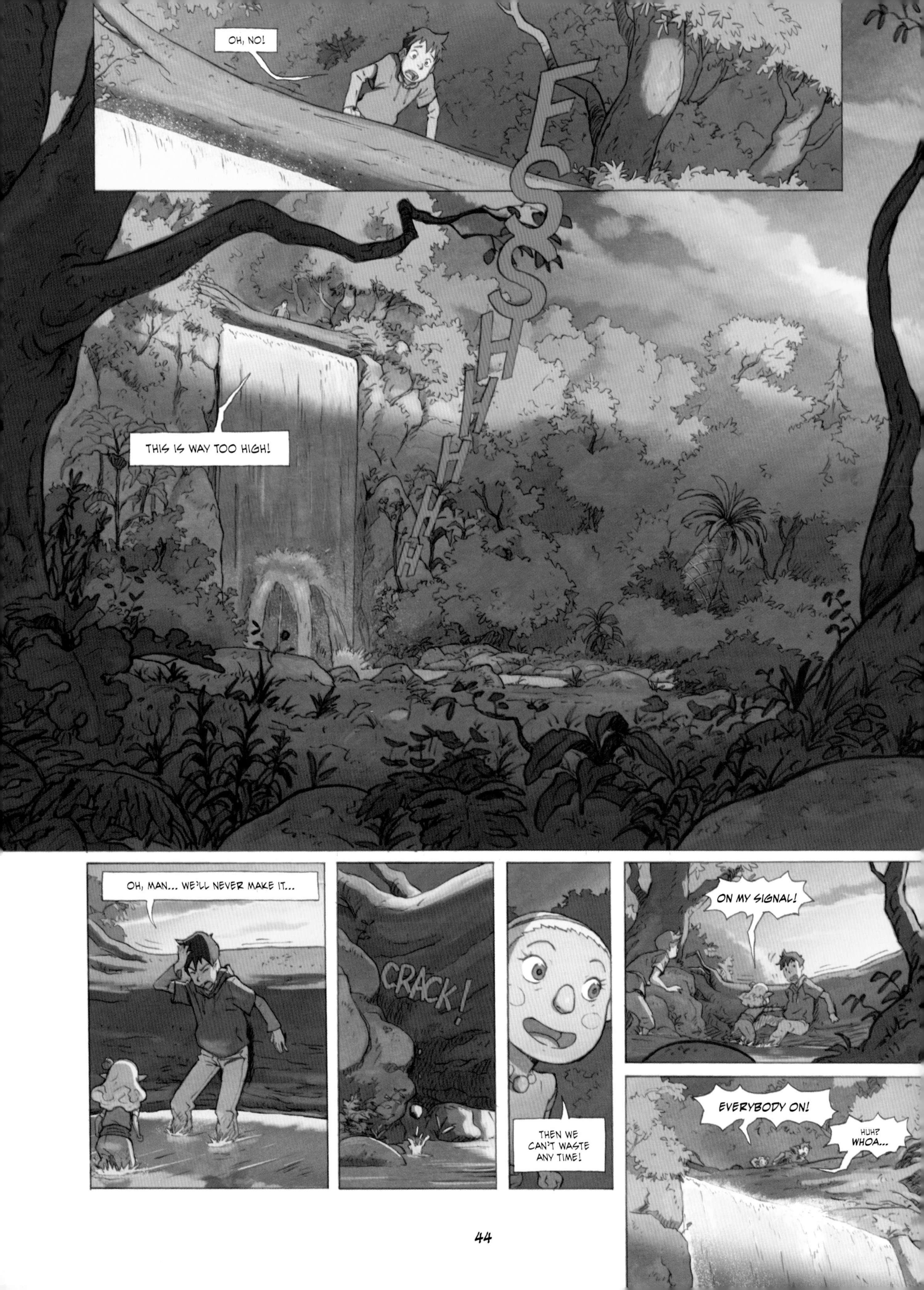
OH, NO!
FSSHHHHHHH
THIS IS WAY TOO HIGH!
OH, MAN... WE'LL NEVER MAKE IT...
CRACK!
THEN WE CAN'T WASTE ANY TIME!
ON MY SIGNAL!
EVERYBODY ON!
HUH? WHOA...

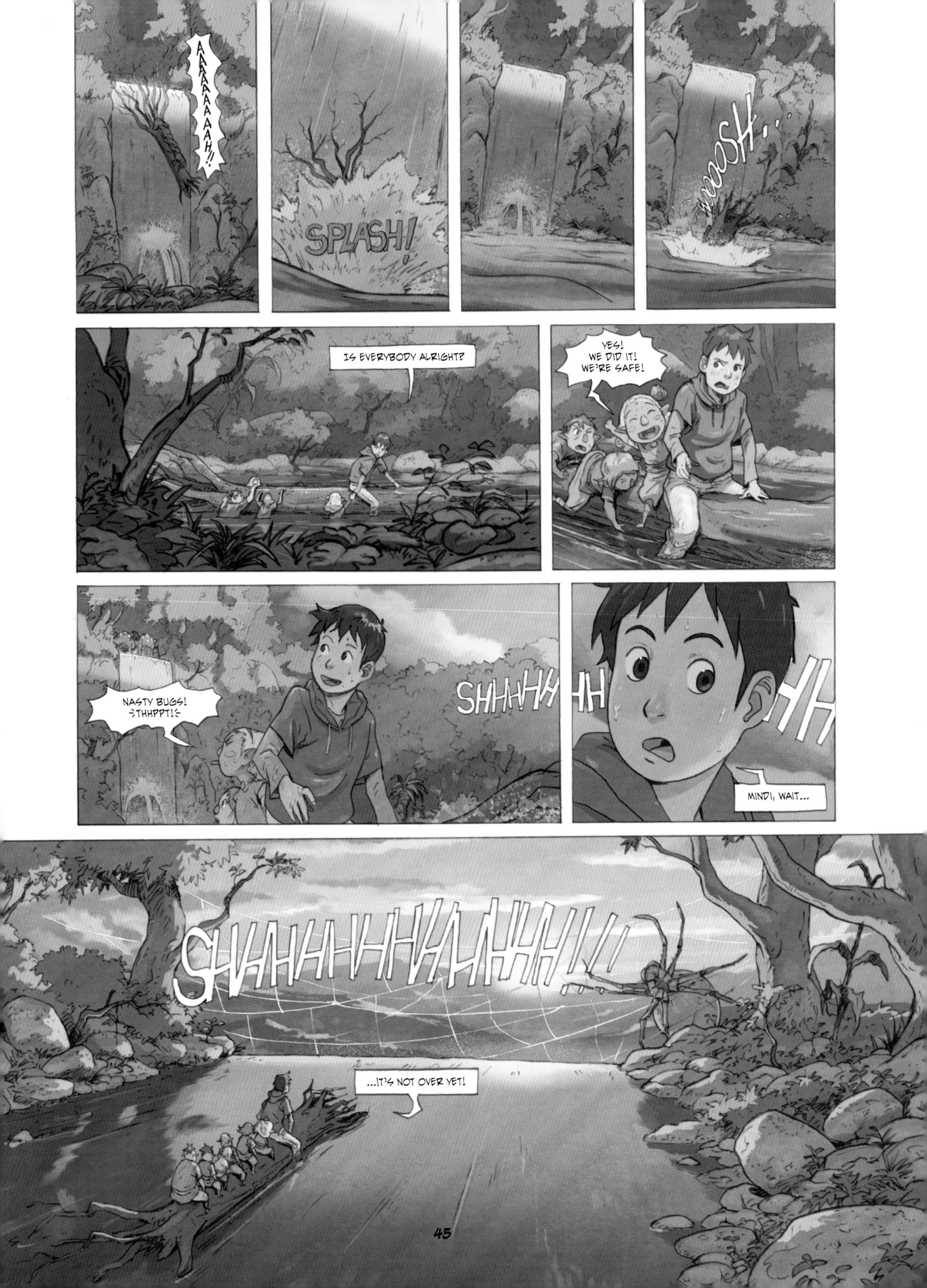
AAAAAAAAAAAH!!
SPLASH!
WOOOOSH...
IS EVERYBODY ALRIGHT?
YES! WE DID IT! WE'RE SAFE!
NASTY BUGS! THHPPT!
SHHHHHHHHHH
MINDI, WAIT...
SHHHHHHHHHHHHH!!!
...IT'S NOT OVER YET!

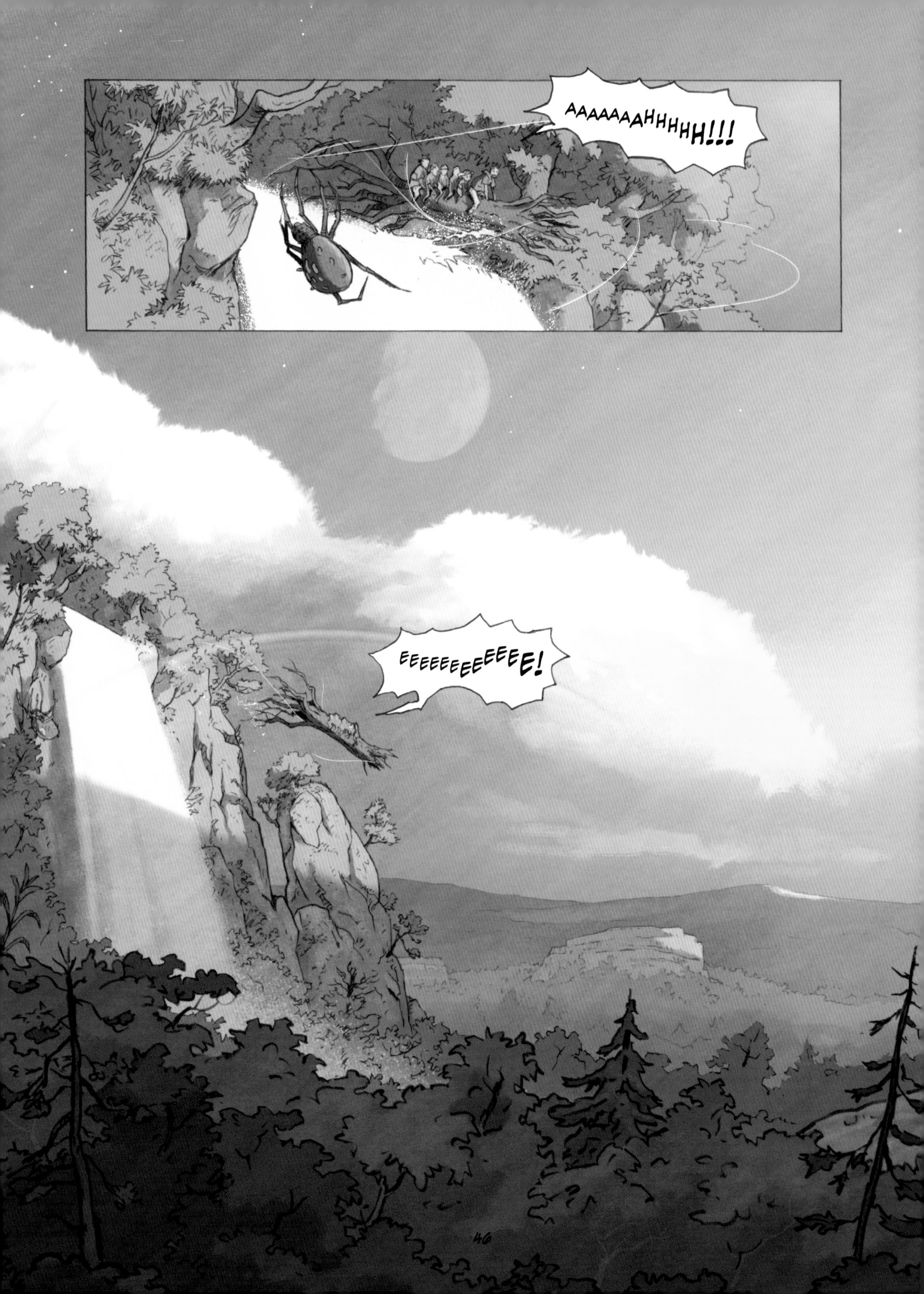
AAAAAAAHHHHH!!!
EEEEEEEEEEEE!

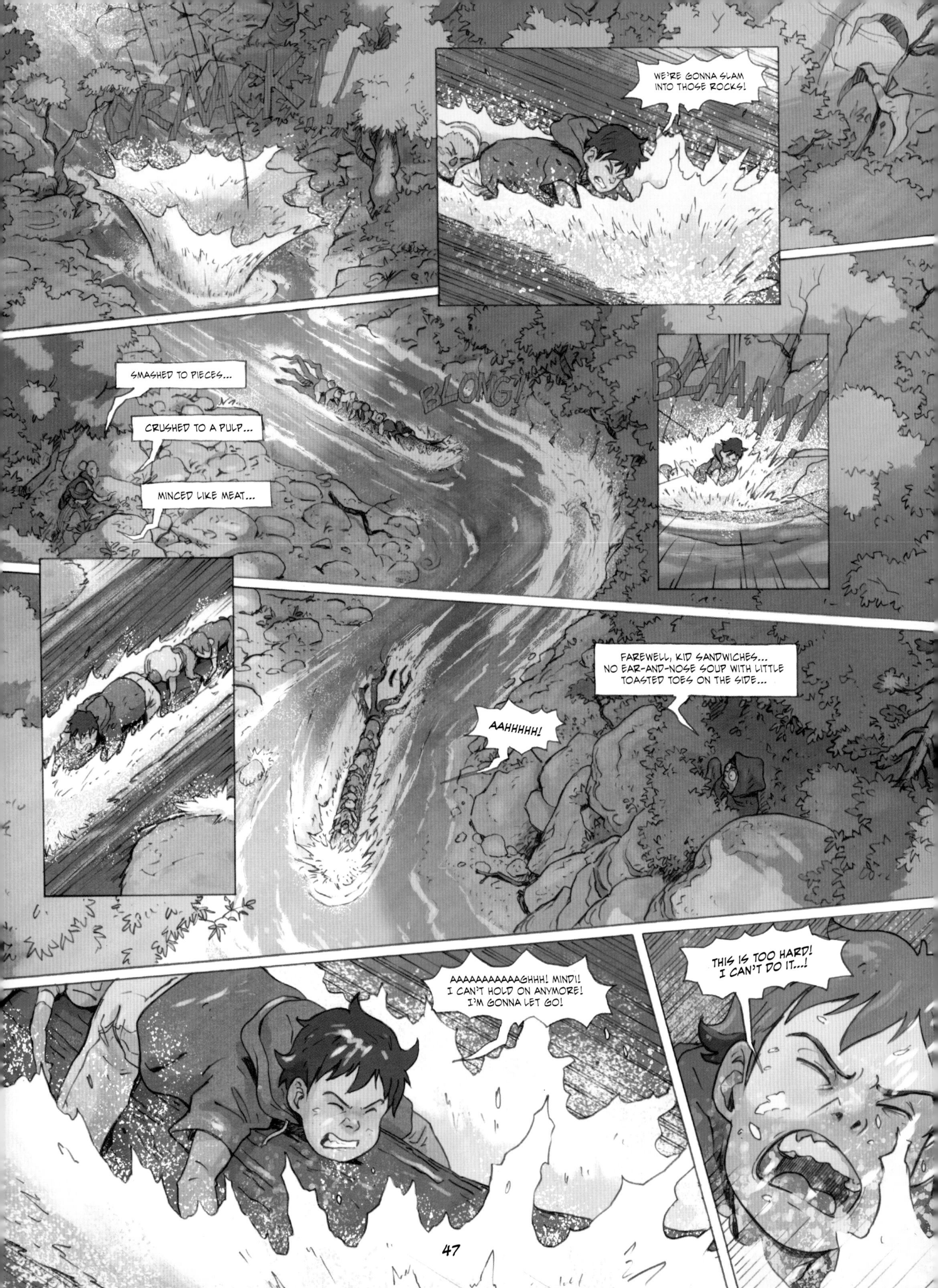
CRAAACK! !
WE'RE GONNA SLAM INTO THOSE ROCKS!
SMASHED TO PIECES...
CRUSHED TO A PULP...
MINCED LIKE MEAT...
BLONG!
BLAAAM!
FAREWELL, KID SANDWICHES... NO EAR-AND-NOSE SOUP WITH LITTLE TOASTED TOES ON THE SIDE...
AAHHHHH!
AAAAAAAAAAAGHHH! MINDI! I CAN'T HOLD ON ANYMORE! I'M GONNA LET GO!
THIS IS TOO HARD! I CAN'T DO IT...!

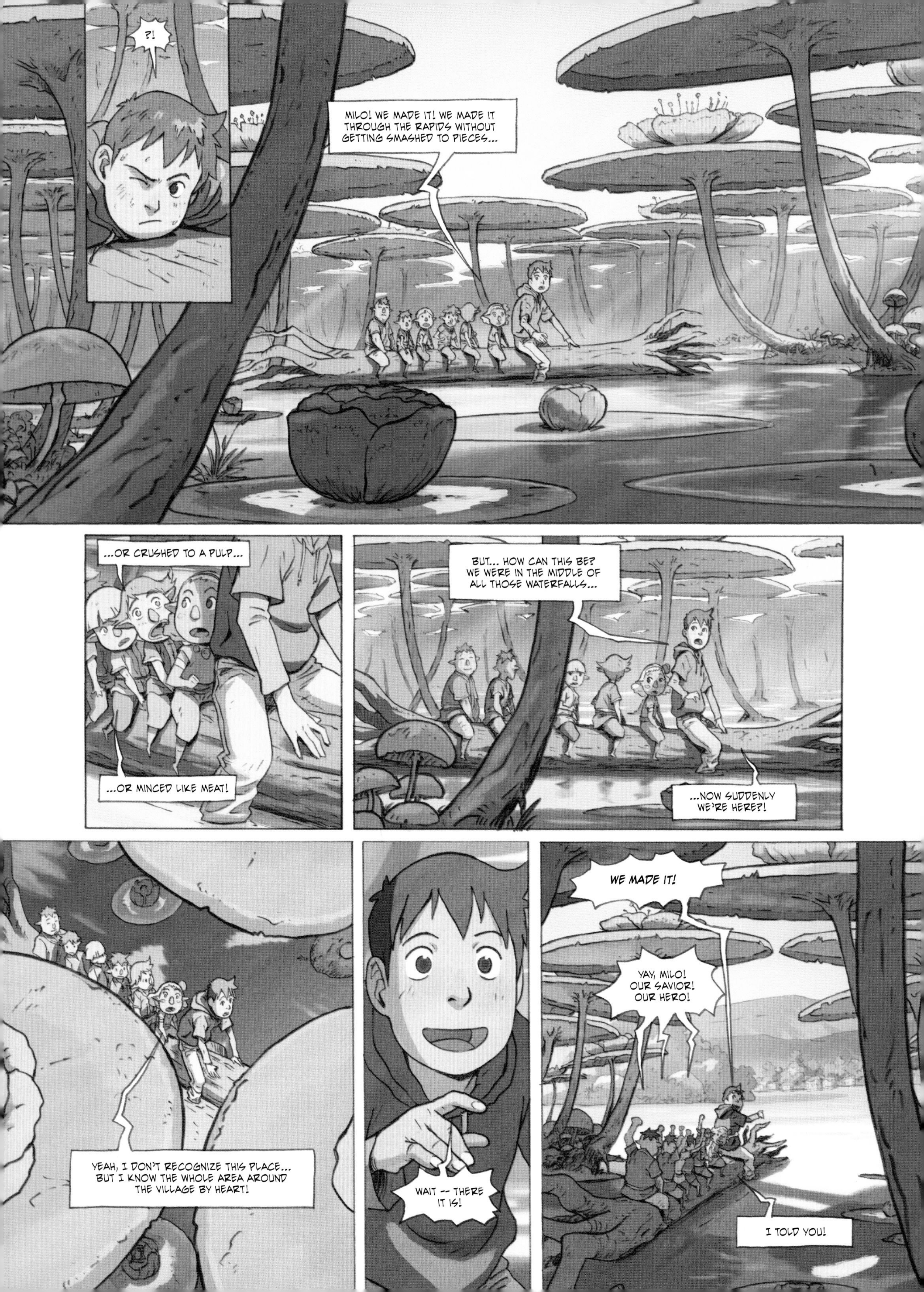
?!
MILO! WE MADE IT! WE MADE IT THROUGH THE RAPIDS WITHOUT GETTING SMASHED TO PIECES...
...OR CRUSHED TO A PULP...
...OR MINCED LIKE MEAT!
BUT... HOW CAN THIS BE? WE WERE IN THE MIDDLE OF ALL THOSE WATERFALLS...
...NOW SUDDENLY WE'RE HERE?!
YEAH, I DON'T RECOGNIZE THIS PLACE... BUT I KNOW THE WHOLE AREA AROUND THE VILLAGE BY HEART!
WAIT -- THERE IT IS!
WE MADE IT!
YAY, MILO! OUR SAVIOR! OUR HERO!
I TOLD YOU!

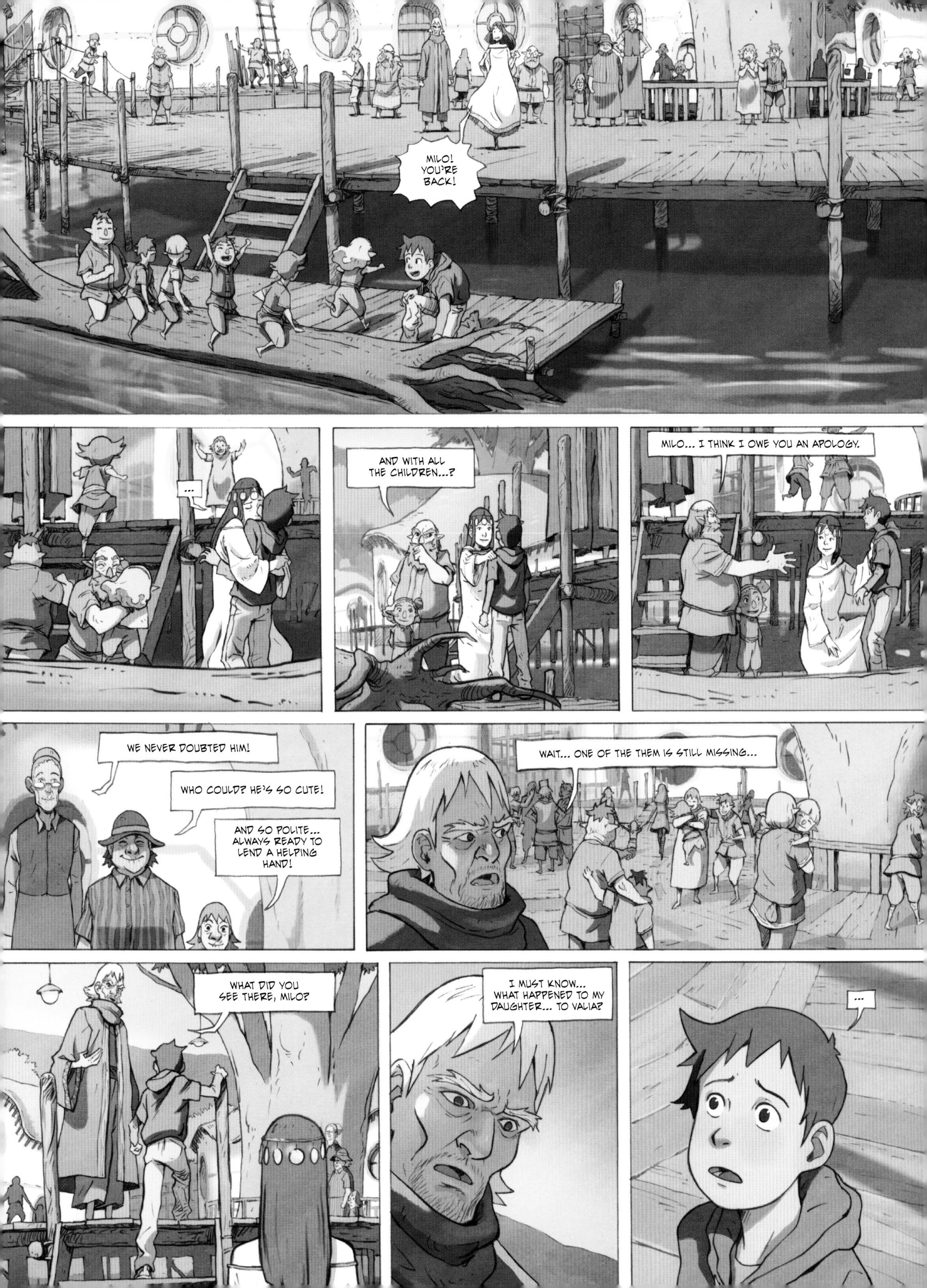
MILO! YOU'RE BACK!
...
AND WITH ALL THE CHILDREN...?
MILO... I THINK I OWE YOU AN APOLOGY.
WE NEVER DOUBTED HIM!
WHO COULD? HE'S SO CUTE!
AND SO POLITE... ALWAYS READY TO LEND A HELPING HAND!
WAIT... ONE OF THE THEM IS STILL MISSING...
WHAT DID YOU SEE THERE, MILO?
I MUST KNOW... WHAT HAPPENED TO MY DAUGHTER... TO VALIA?
...

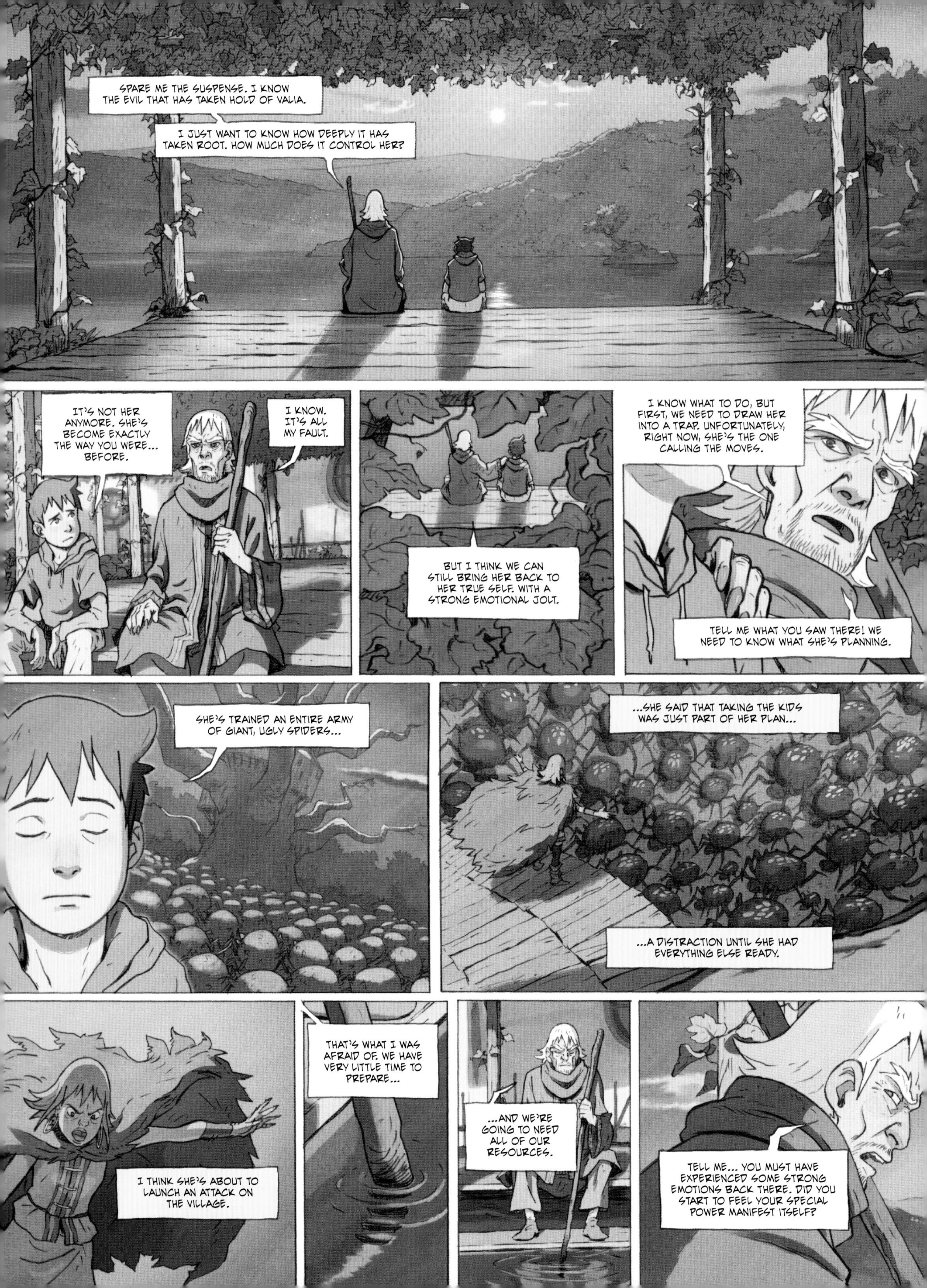
SPARE ME THE SUSPENSE. I KNOW THE EVIL THAT HAS TAKEN HOLD OF VALIA.
I JUST WANT TO KNOW HOW DEEPLY IT HAS TAKEN ROOT. HOW MUCH DOES IT CONTROL HER?
IT'S NOT HER ANYMORE. SHE'S BECOME EXACTLY THE WAY YOU WERE... BEFORE.
I KNOW. IT'S ALL MY FAULT.
BUT I THINK WE CAN STILL BRING HER BACK TO HER TRUE SELF. WITH A STRONG EMOTIONAL JOLT.
I KNOW WHAT TO DO, BUT FIRST, WE NEED TO DRAW HER INTO A TRAP. UNFORTUNATELY, RIGHT NOW, SHE'S THE ONE CALLING THE MOVES.
TELL ME WHAT YOU SAW THERE! WE NEED TO KNOW WHAT SHE'S PLANNING.
SHE'S TRAINED AN ENTIRE ARMY OF GIANT, UGLY SPIDERS...
...SHE SAID THAT TAKING THE KIDS WAS JUST PART OF HER PLAN...
...A DISTRACTION UNTIL SHE HAD EVERYTHING ELSE READY.
I THINK SHE'S ABOUT TO LAUNCH AN ATTACK ON THE VILLAGE.
THAT'S WHAT I WAS AFRAID OF. WE HAVE VERY LITTLE TIME TO PREPARE...
...AND WE'RE GOING TO NEED ALL OF OUR RESOURCES.
TELL ME... YOU MUST HAVE EXPERIENCED SOME STRONG EMOTIONS BACK THERE. DID YOU START TO FEEL YOUR SPECIAL POWER MANIFEST ITSELF?

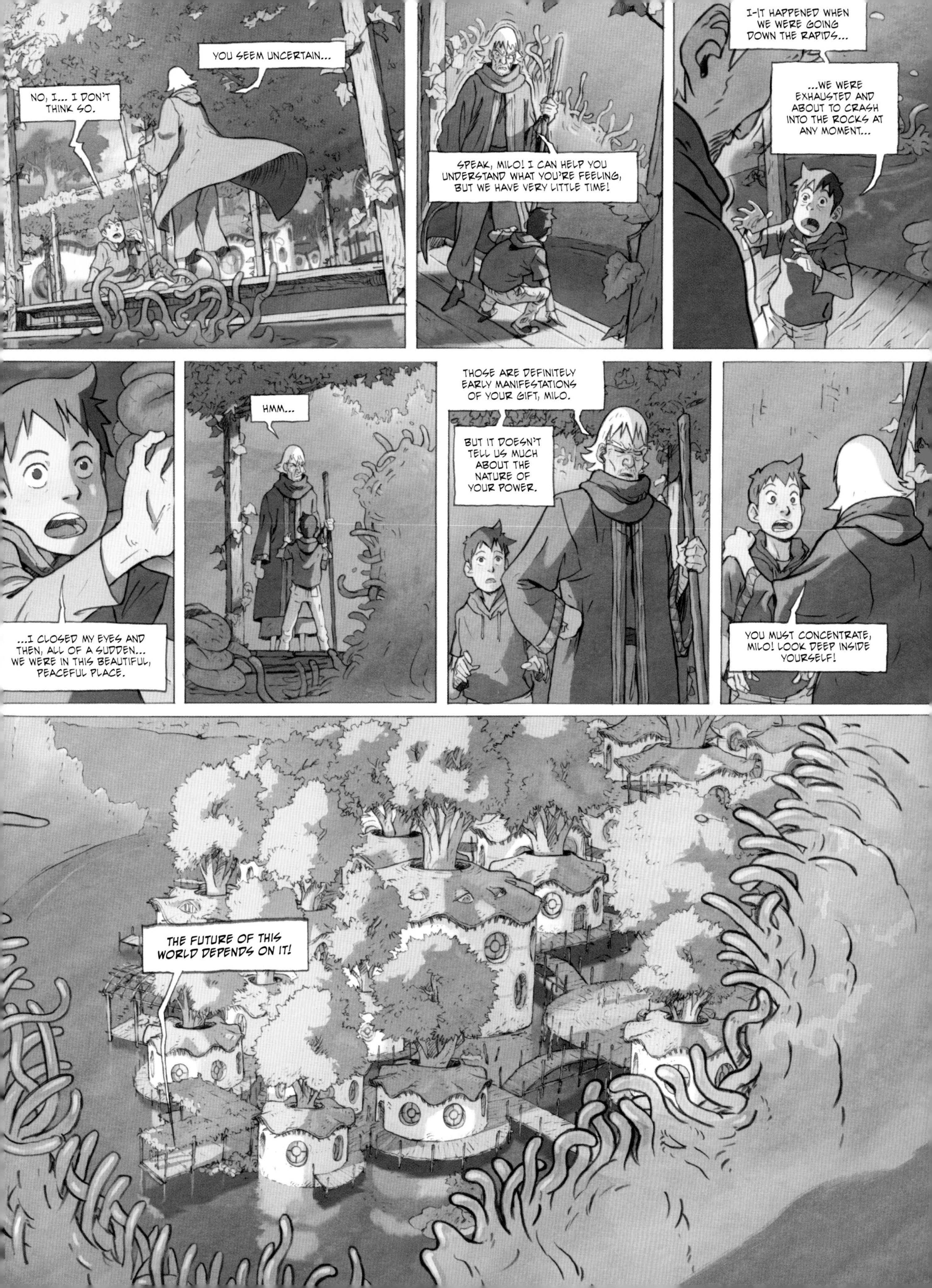
YOU SEEM UNCERTAIN...
NO, I... I DON'T THINK SO.
SPEAK, MILO! I CAN HELP YOU UNDERSTAND WHAT YOU'RE FEELING, BUT WE HAVE VERY LITTLE TIME!
I-IT HAPPENED WHEN WE WERE GOING DOWN THE RAPIDS...
...WE WERE EXHAUSTED AND ABOUT TO CRASH INTO THE ROCKS AT ANY MOMENT...
...I CLOSED MY EYES AND THEN, ALL OF A SUDDEN... WE WERE IN THIS BEAUTIFUL, PEACEFUL PLACE.
HMM...
THOSE ARE DEFINITELY EARLY MANIFESTATIONS OF YOUR GIFT, MILO.
BUT IT DOESN'T TELL US MUCH ABOUT THE NATURE OF YOUR POWER.
YOU MUST CONCENTRATE, MILO! LOOK DEEP INSIDE YOURSELF!
THE FUTURE OF THIS WORLD DEPENDS ON IT!

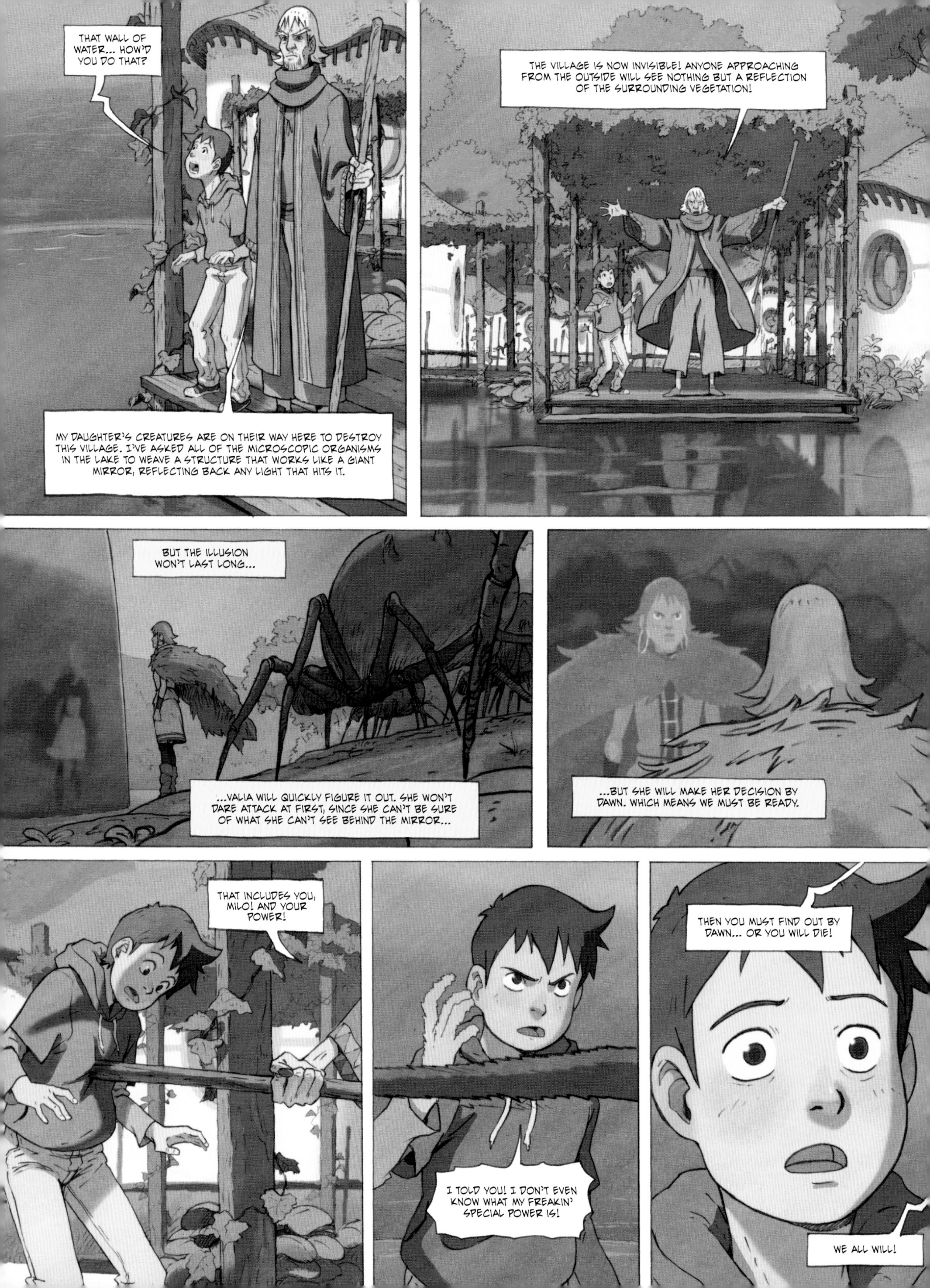
THAT WALL OF WATER... HOW'D YOU DO THAT?
MY DAUGHTER'S CREATURES ARE ON THEIR WAY HERE TO DESTROY THIS VILLAGE. I'VE ASKED ALL OF THE MICROSCOPIC ORGANISMS IN THE LAKE TO WEAVE A STRUCTURE THAT WORKS LIKE A GIANT MIRROR, REFLECTING BACK ANY LIGHT THAT HITS IT.
THE VILLAGE IS NOW INVISIBLE! ANYONE APPROACHING FROM THE OUTSIDE WILL SEE NOTHING BUT A REFLECTION OF THE SURROUNDING VEGETATION!
BUT THE ILLUSION WON'T LAST LONG...
...VALIA WILL QUICKLY FIGURE IT OUT. SHE WON'T DARE ATTACK AT FIRST, SINCE SHE CAN'T BE SURE OF WHAT SHE CAN'T SEE BEHIND THE MIRROR...
...BUT SHE WILL MAKE HER DECISION BY DAWN. WHICH MEANS WE MUST BE READY.
THAT INCLUDES YOU, MILO! AND YOUR POWER!
I TOLD YOU! I DON'T EVEN KNOW WHAT MY FREAKIN' SPECIAL POWER IS!
THEN YOU MUST FIND OUT BY DAWN... OR YOU WILL DIE!
WE ALL WILL!

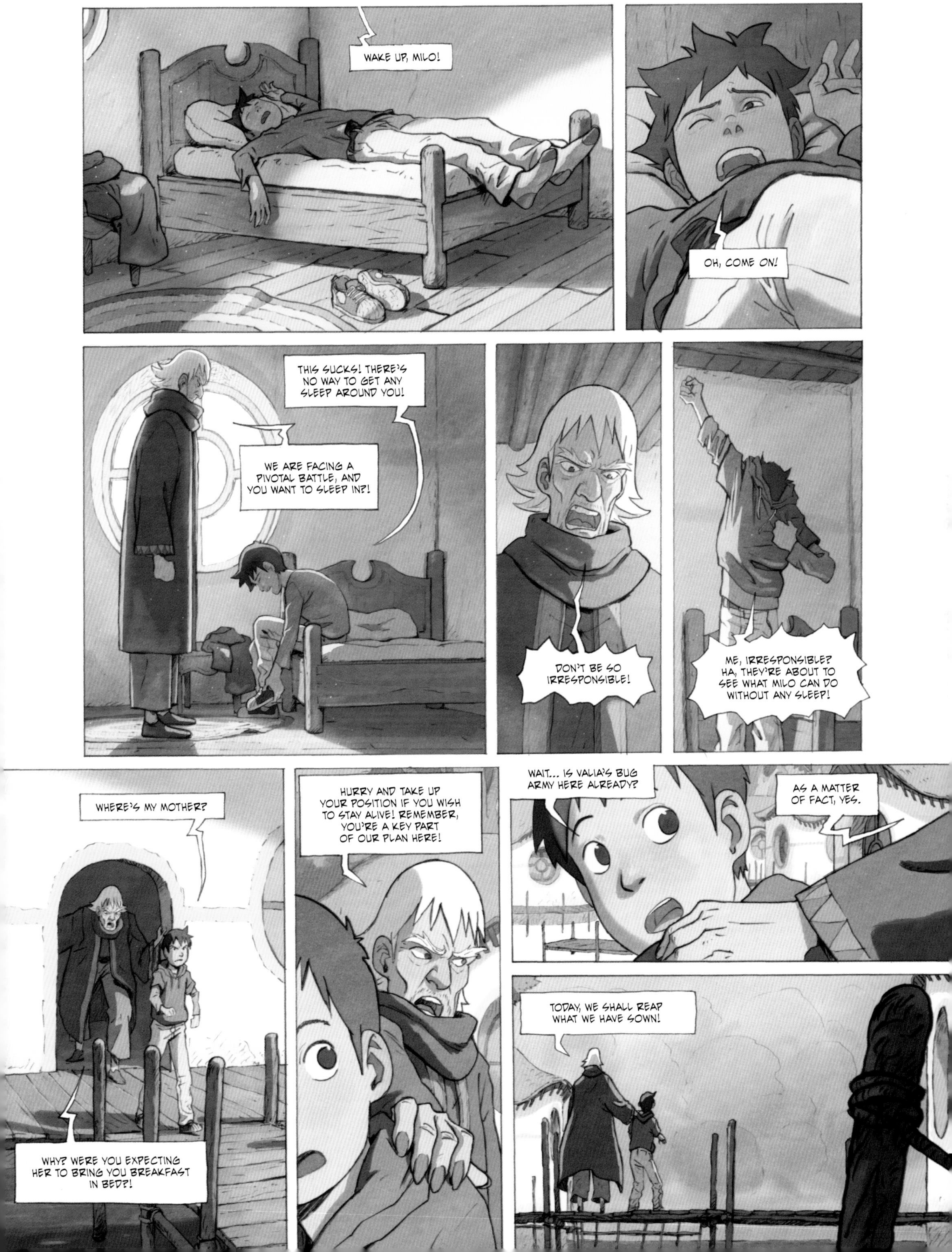
WAKE UP, MILO!
OH, COME ON!
THIS SUCKS! THERE'S NO WAY TO GET ANY SLEEP AROUND YOU!
WE ARE FACING A PIVOTAL BATTLE, AND YOU WANT TO SLEEP IN?!
DON'T BE SO IRRESPONSIBLE!
ME, IRRESPONSIBLE? HA, THEY'RE ABOUT TO SEE WHAT MILO CAN DO WITHOUT ANY SLEEP!
WHERE'S MY MOTHER?
WHY? WERE YOU EXPECTING HER TO BRING YOU BREAKFAST IN BED?!
HURRY AND TAKE UP YOUR POSITION IF YOU WISH TO STAY ALIVE! REMEMBER, YOU'RE A KEY PART OF OUR PLAN HERE!
WAIT... IS VALIA'S BUG ARMY HERE ALREADY?
AS A MATTER OF FACT, YES.
TODAY, WE SHALL REAP WHAT WE HAVE SOWN!

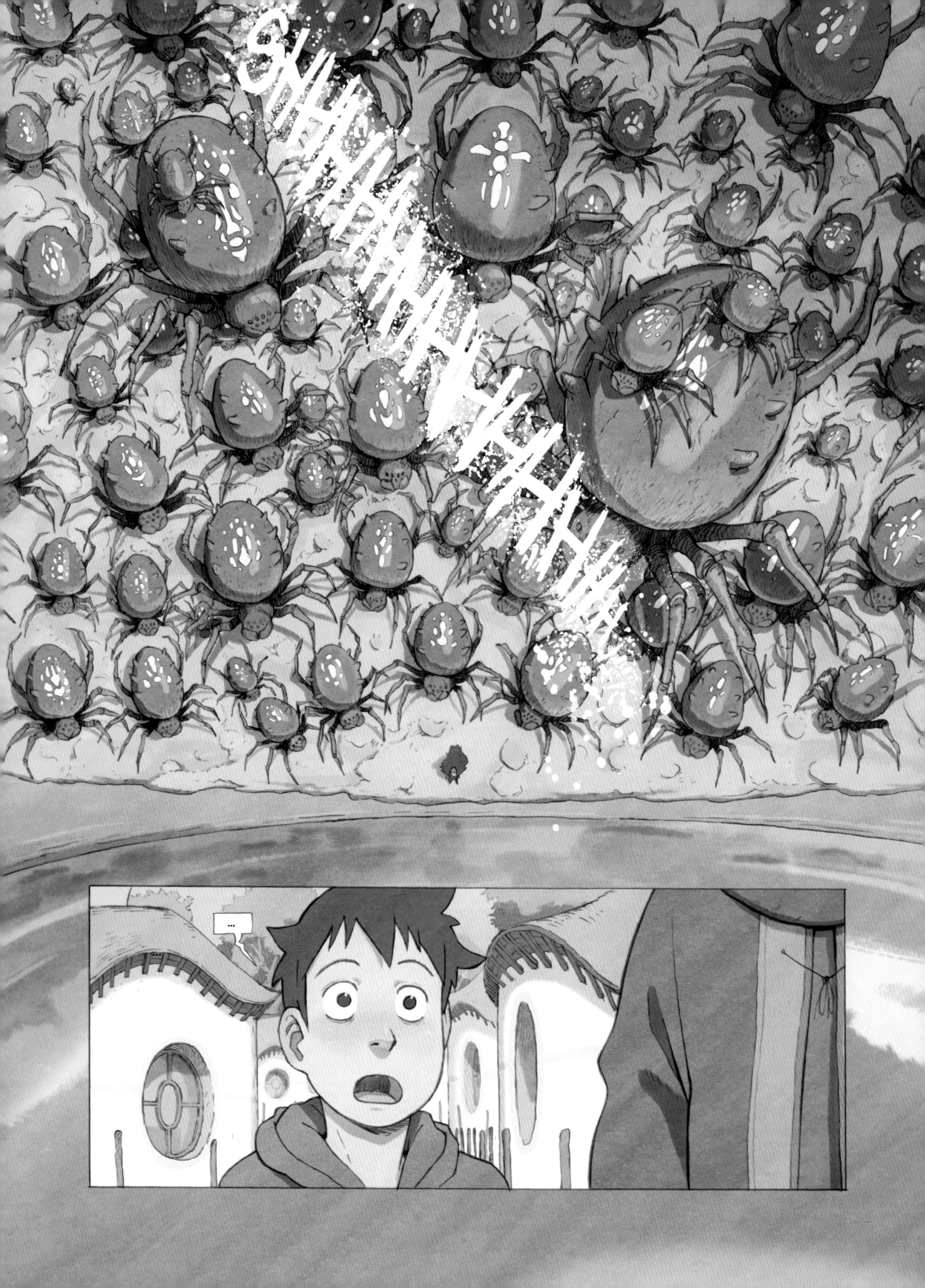
SHHHHHAAAAAAHHHH
...

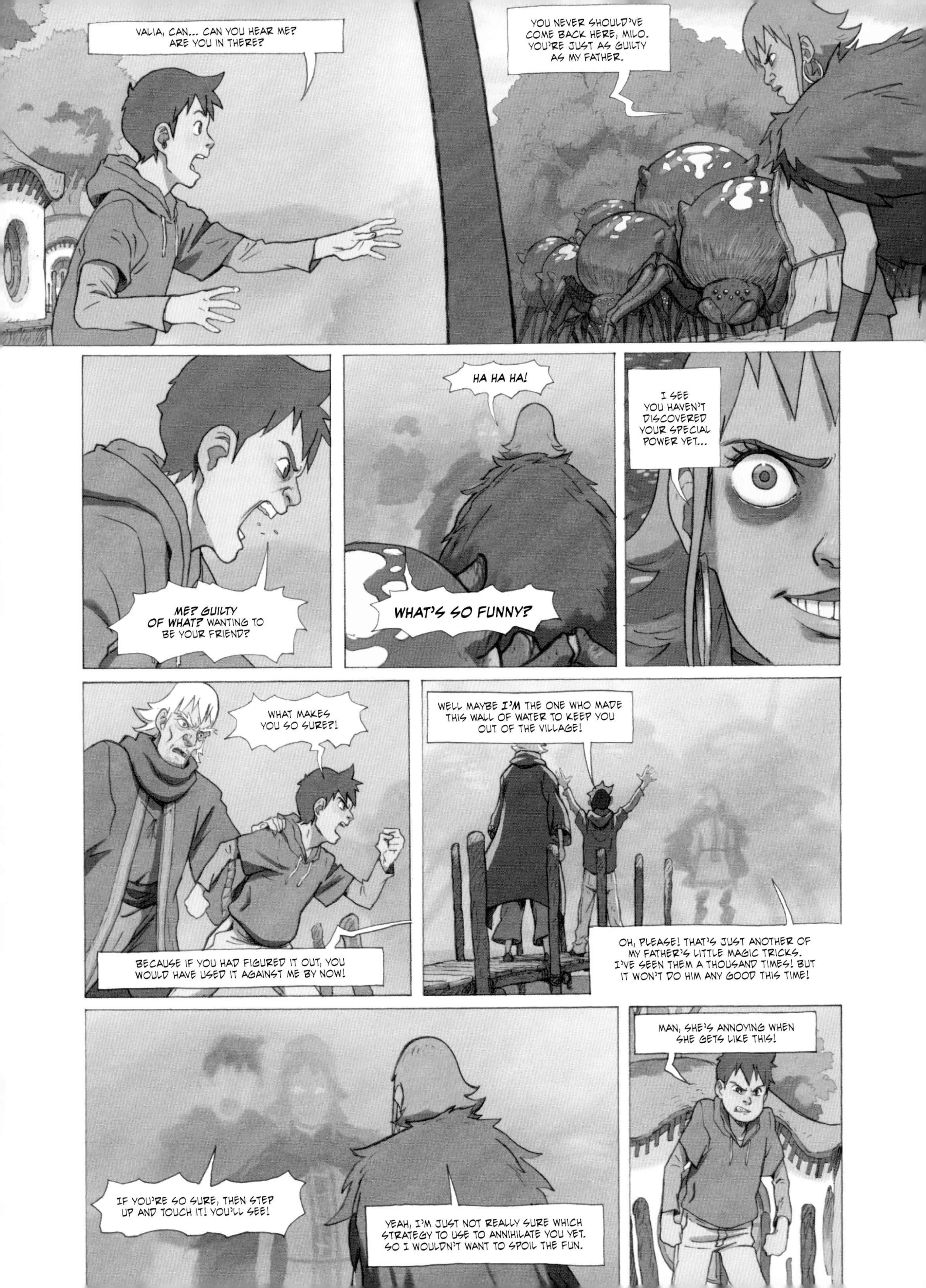
VALIA, CAN... CAN YOU HEAR ME? ARE YOU IN THERE?
YOU NEVER SHOULD'VE COME BACK HERE, MILO. YOU'RE JUST AS GUILTY AS MY FATHER.
ME? GUILTY OF WHAT? WANTING TO BE YOUR FRIEND?
HA HA HA!
WHAT'S SO FUNNY?
I SEE YOU HAVEN'T DISCOVERED YOUR SPECIAL POWER YET...
WHAT MAKES YOU SO SURE?!
BECAUSE IF YOU HAD FIGURED IT OUT, YOU WOULD HAVE USED IT AGAINST ME BY NOW!
WELL MAYBE I'M THE ONE WHO MADE THIS WALL OF WATER TO KEEP YOU OUT OF THE VILLAGE!
OH, PLEASE! THAT'S JUST ANOTHER OF MY FATHER'S LITTLE MAGIC TRICKS. I'VE SEEN THEM A THOUSAND TIMES! BUT IT WON'T DO HIM ANY GOOD THIS TIME!
IF YOU'RE SO SURE, THEN STEP UP AND TOUCH IT! YOU'LL SEE!
YEAH, I'M JUST NOT REALLY SURE WHICH STRATEGY TO USE TO ANNIHILATE YOU YET. SO I WOULDN'T WANT TO SPOIL THE FUN.
MAN, SHE'S ANNOYING WHEN SHE GETS LIKE THIS!

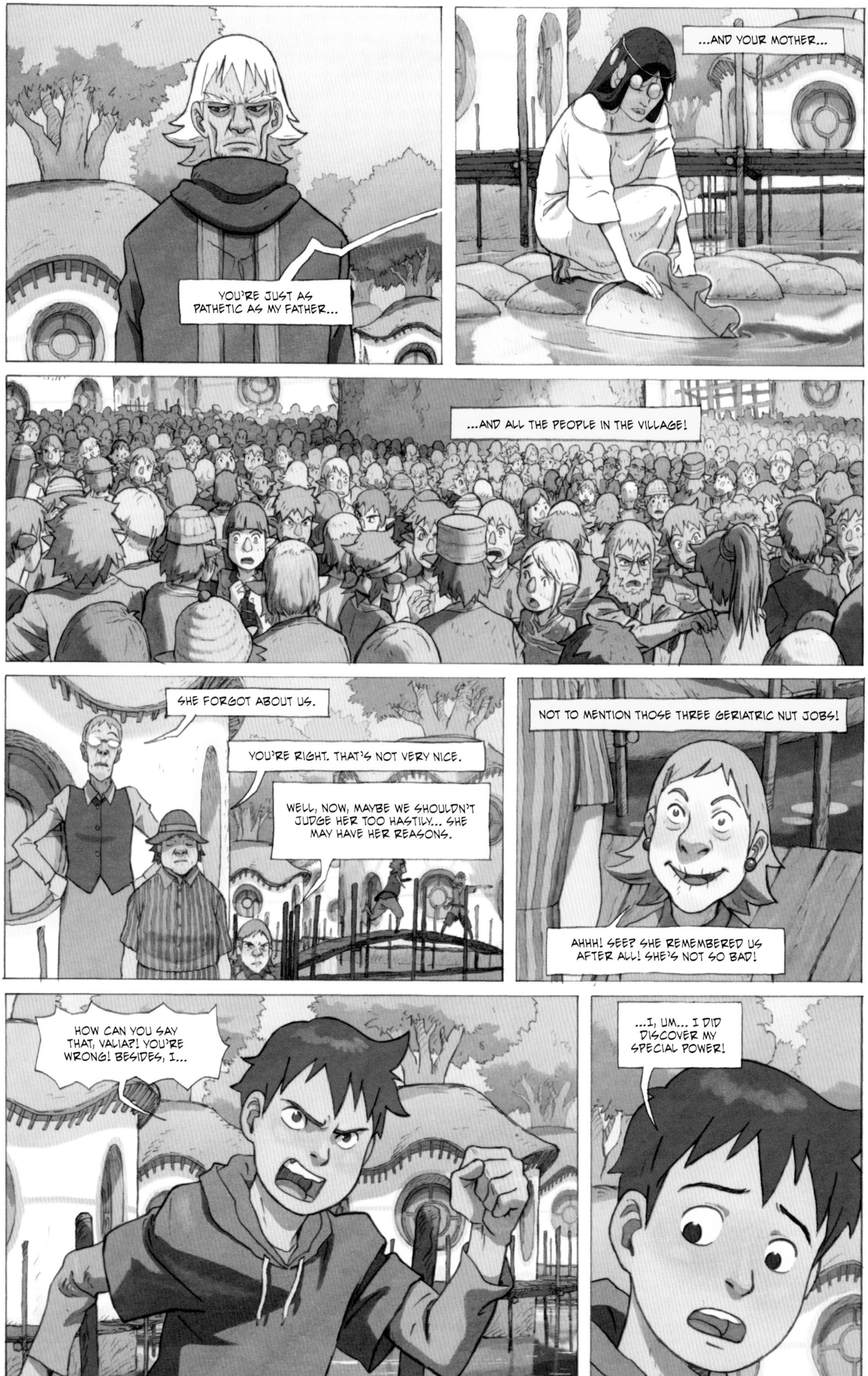
YOU'RE JUST AS PATHETIC AS MY FATHER...
...AND YOUR MOTHER...
...AND ALL THE PEOPLE IN THE VILLAGE!
SHE FORGOT ABOUT US.
YOU'RE RIGHT. THAT'S NOT VERY NICE.
WELL, NOW, MAYBE WE SHOULDN'T JUDGE HER TOO HASTILY... SHE MAY HAVE HER REASONS.
NOT TO MENTION THOSE THREE GERIATRIC NUT JOBS!
AHHH! SEE? SHE REMEMBERED US AFTER ALL! SHE'S NOT SO BAD!
HOW CAN YOU SAY THAT, VALIA? YOU'RE WRONG! BESIDES, I...
...I, UM... I DID DISCOVER MY SPECIAL POWER!

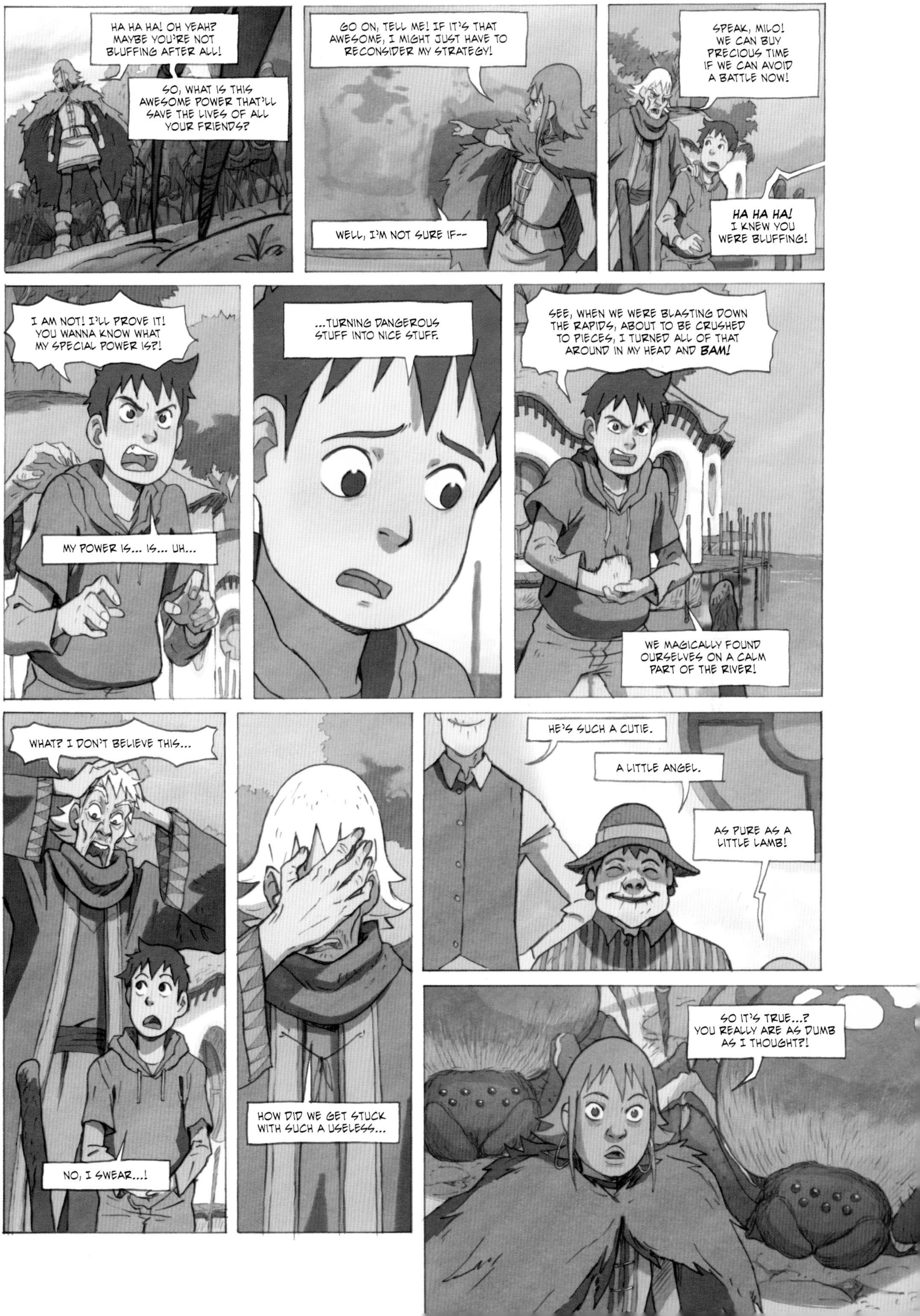
HA HA HA! OH YEAH? MAYBE YOU'RE NOT BLUFFING AFTER ALL!
SO, WHAT IS THIS AWESOME POWER THAT'LL SAVE THE LIVES OF ALL YOUR FRIENDS?
GO ON, TELL ME! IF IT'S THAT AWESOME, I MIGHT JUST HAVE TO RECONSIDER MY STRATEGY!
WELL, I'M NOT SURE IF--
SPEAK, MILO! WE CAN BUY PRECIOUS TIME IF WE CAN AVOID A BATTLE NOW!
HA HA HA! I KNEW YOU WERE BLUFFING!
I AM NOT! I'LL PROVE IT! YOU WANNA KNOW WHAT MY SPECIAL POWER IS?!
MY POWER IS... IS... UH...
...TURNING DANGEROUS STUFF INTO NICE STUFF.
SEE, WHEN WE WERE BLASTING DOWN THE RAPIDS, ABOUT TO BE CRUSHED TO PIECES, I TURNED ALL OF THAT AROUND IN MY HEAD AND BAM!
WE MAGICALLY FOUND OURSELVES ON A CALM PART OF THE RIVER!
WHAT? I DON'T BELIEVE THIS...
NO, I SWEAR...!
HOW DID WE GET STUCK WITH SUCH A USELESS...
HE'S SUCH A CUTIE.
A LITTLE ANGEL.
AS PURE AS A LITTLE LAMB!
SO IT'S TRUE...? YOU REALLY ARE AS DUMB AS I THOUGHT?!

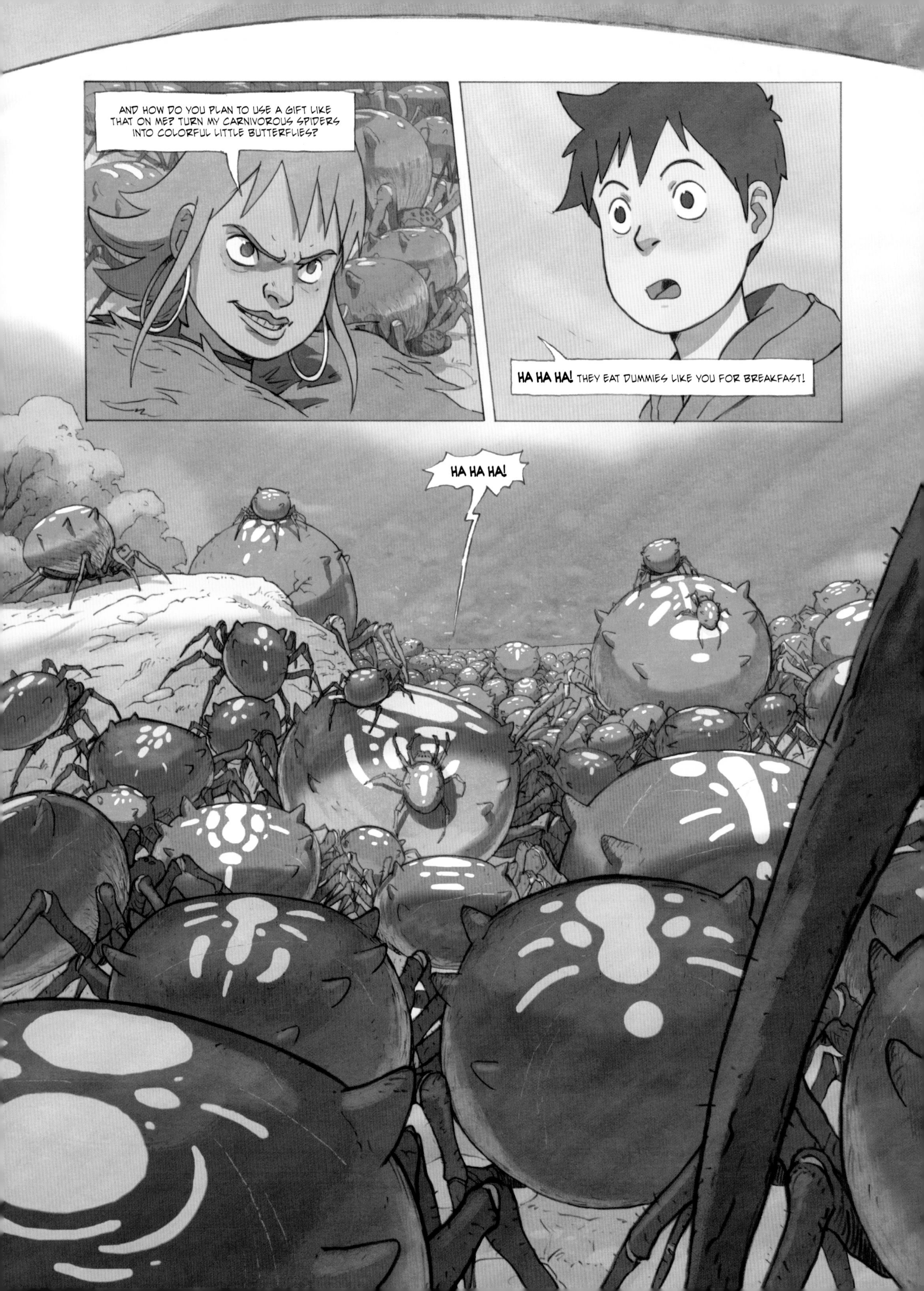
AND HOW DO YOU PLAN TO USE A GIFT LIKE THAT ON ME? TURN MY CARNIVOROUS SPIDERS INTO COLORFUL LITTLE BUTTERFLIES?
HA HA HA! THEY EAT DUMMIES LIKE YOU FOR BREAKFAST!
HA HA HA!

CHAPTER TWO

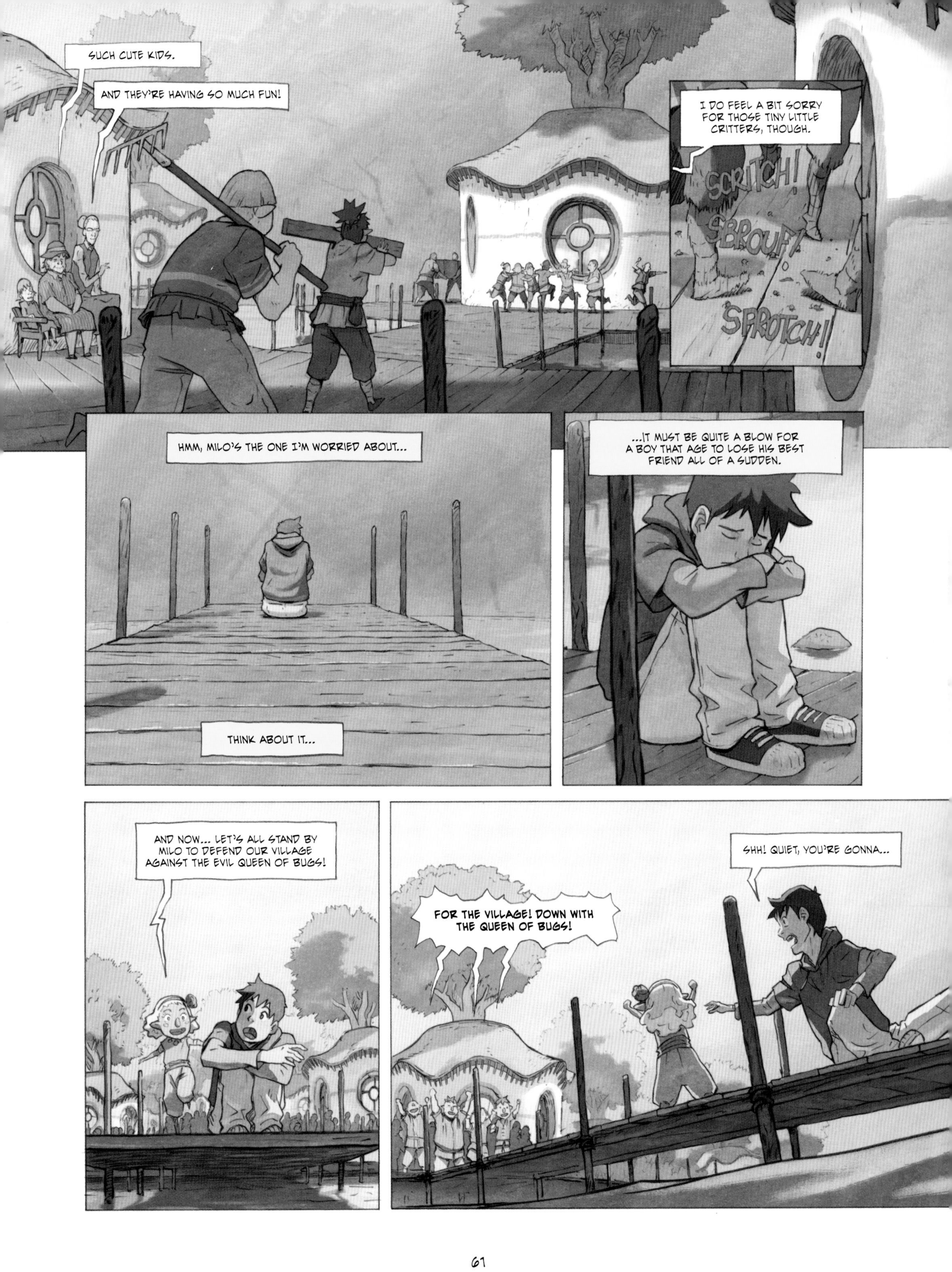

SUCH CUTE KIDS.
AND THEY'RE HAVING SO MUCH FUN!
I DO FEEL A BIT SORRY FOR THOSE TINY LITTLE CRITTERS, THOUGH.
SCRITCH!
SBROUF!
SPROTCH!
HMM, MILO'S THE ONE I'M WORRIED ABOUT...
THINK ABOUT IT...
...IT MUST BE QUITE A BLOW FOR A BOY THAT AGE TO LOSE HIS BEST FRIEND ALL OF A SUDDEN.
AND NOW... LET'S ALL STAND BY MILO TO DEFEND OUR VILLAGE AGAINST THE EVIL QUEEN OF BUGS!
FOR THE VILLAGE! DOWN WITH THE QUEEN OF BUGS!
SHH! QUIET, YOU'RE GONNA...

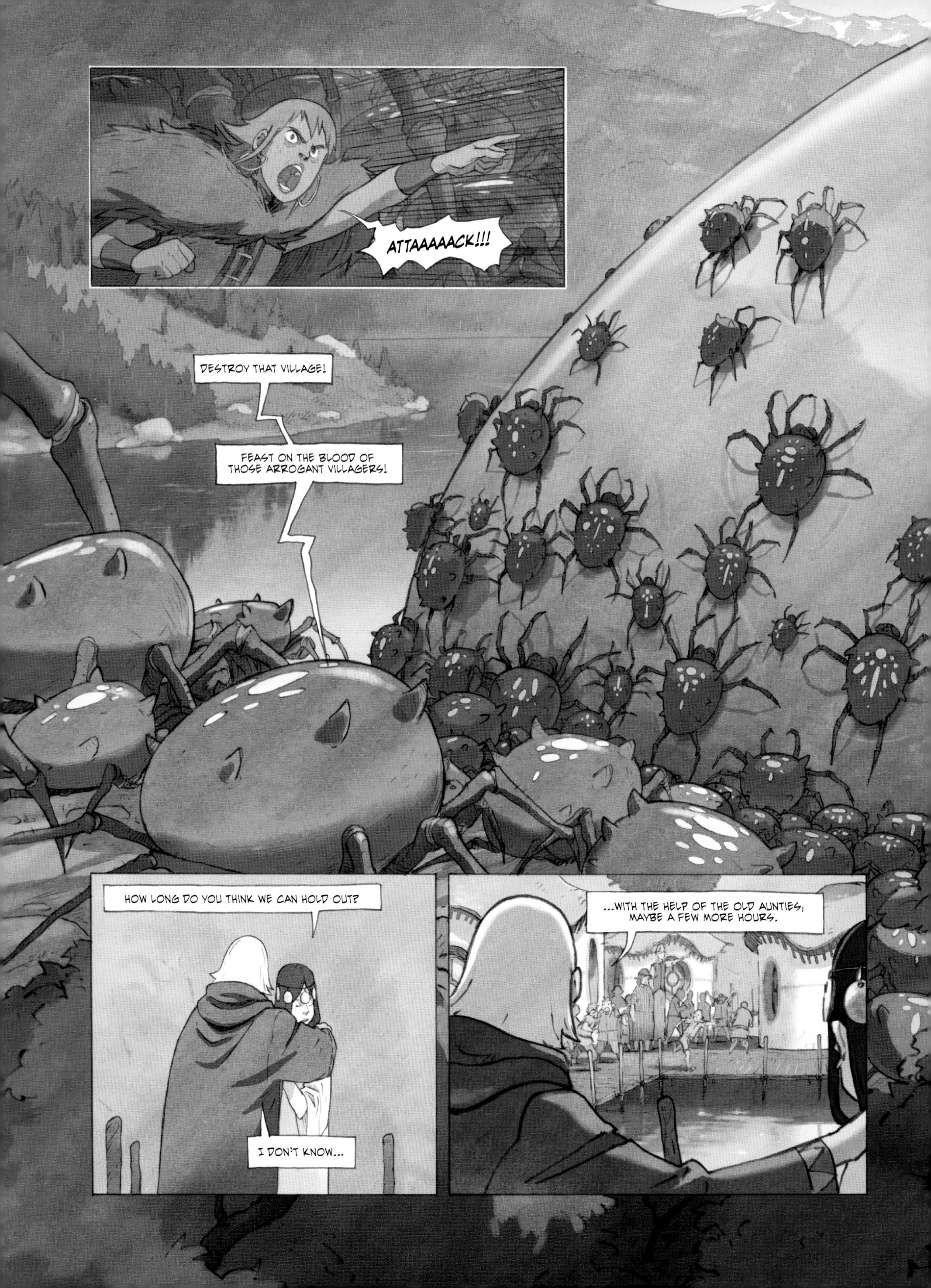
ATTAAAAACK!!!
DESTROY THAT VILLAGE!
FEAST ON THE BLOOD OF THOSE ARROGANT VILLAGERS!
HOW LONG DO YOU THINK WE CAN HOLD OUT?
I DON'T KNOW...
...WITH THE HELP OF THE OLD AUNTIES, MAYBE A FEW MORE HOURS.

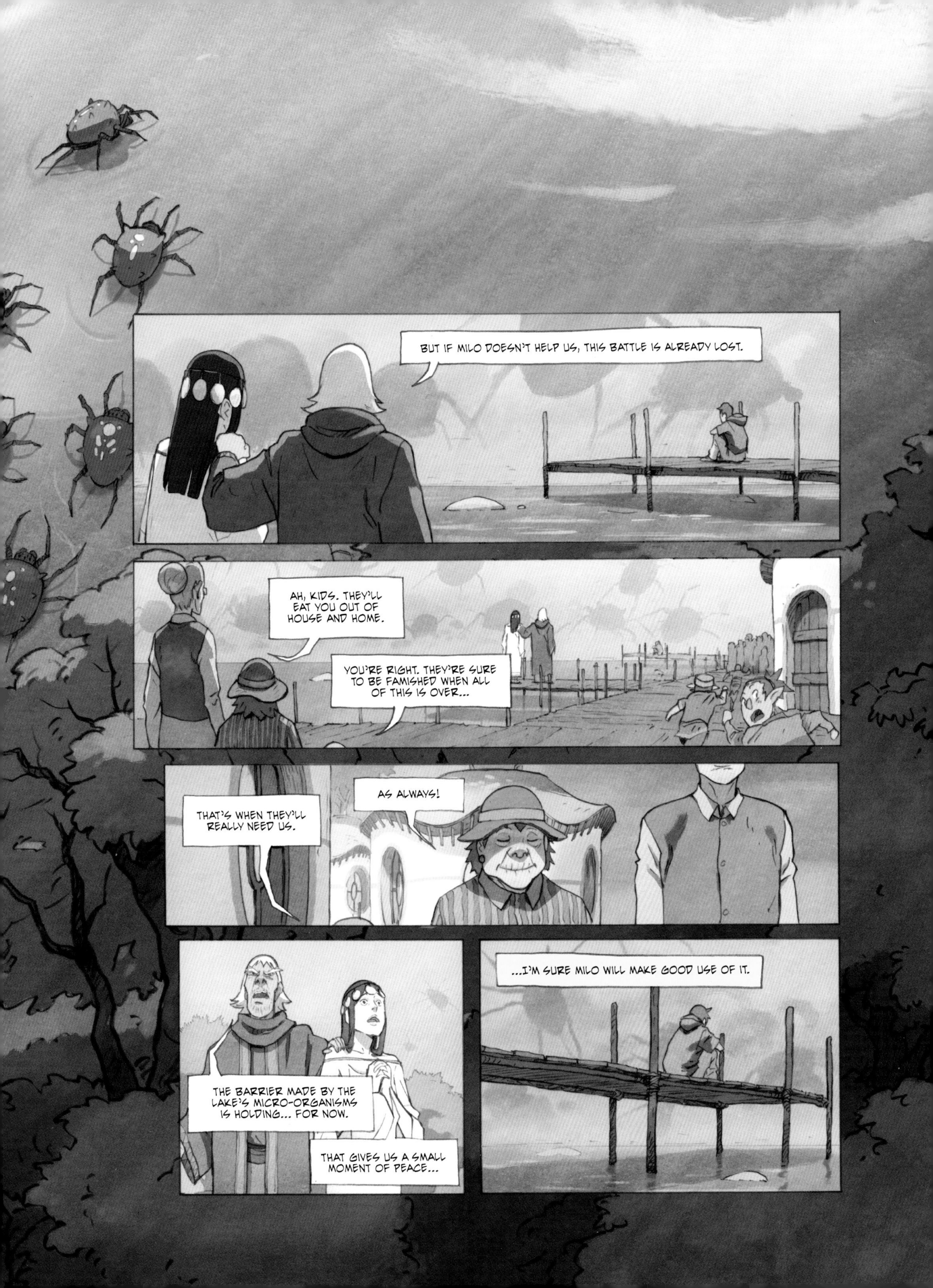
BUT IF MILO DOESN'T HELP US, THIS BATTLE IS ALREADY LOST.
AH, KIDS. THEY'LL EAT YOU OUT OF HOUSE AND HOME.
YOU'RE RIGHT. THEY'RE SURE TO BE FAMISHED WHEN ALL OF THIS IS OVER...
THAT'S WHEN THEY'LL REALLY NEED US.
AS ALWAYS!
THE BARRIER MADE BY THE LAKE'S MICRO-ORGANISMS IS HOLDING... FOR NOW.
THAT GIVES US A SMALL MOMENT OF PEACE...
...I'M SURE MILO WILL MAKE GOOD USE OF IT.

WHAT ARE YOU DOING? MEDITATING BEFORE LAUNCHING A DAZZLING COUNTER-ATTACK WITH YOUR SPECIAL POWERS?

UM, NO. I'M NOT MEDITATING. I'M JUST AS SCARED AS EVERYONE ELSE, AND I DON'T KNOW WHAT TO DO!

OH, I GET IT. YOU DON'T WANT TO TELL ME YOUR SECRET PLAN FOR GETTING US OUT OF THIS!

CLAP!
CLAP!

LISTEN UP, EVERYBODY! MILO IS CHANNELING THE FULL FORCE OF HIS MAGICAL GIFT TO FIGHT OFF THAT PAIN IN THE NECK VALIA AND THOSE BIG, UGLY BUGS OF HERS!

HUH?!

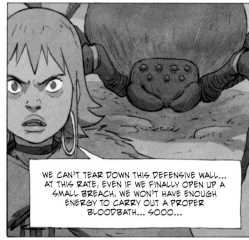

WE CAN'T TEAR DOWN THIS DEFENSIVE WALL... AT THIS RATE, EVEN IF WE FINALLY OPEN UP A SMALL BREACH, WE WON'T HAVE ENOUGH ENERGY TO CARRY OUT A PROPER BLOODBATH... SOOO...

MILO SAVED US ONCE BEFORE...

...I KNOW HE CAN DO IT AGAIN! THANKS TO HIS SPECIAL POWERS!

AAAAAAHHH!

MINDI!

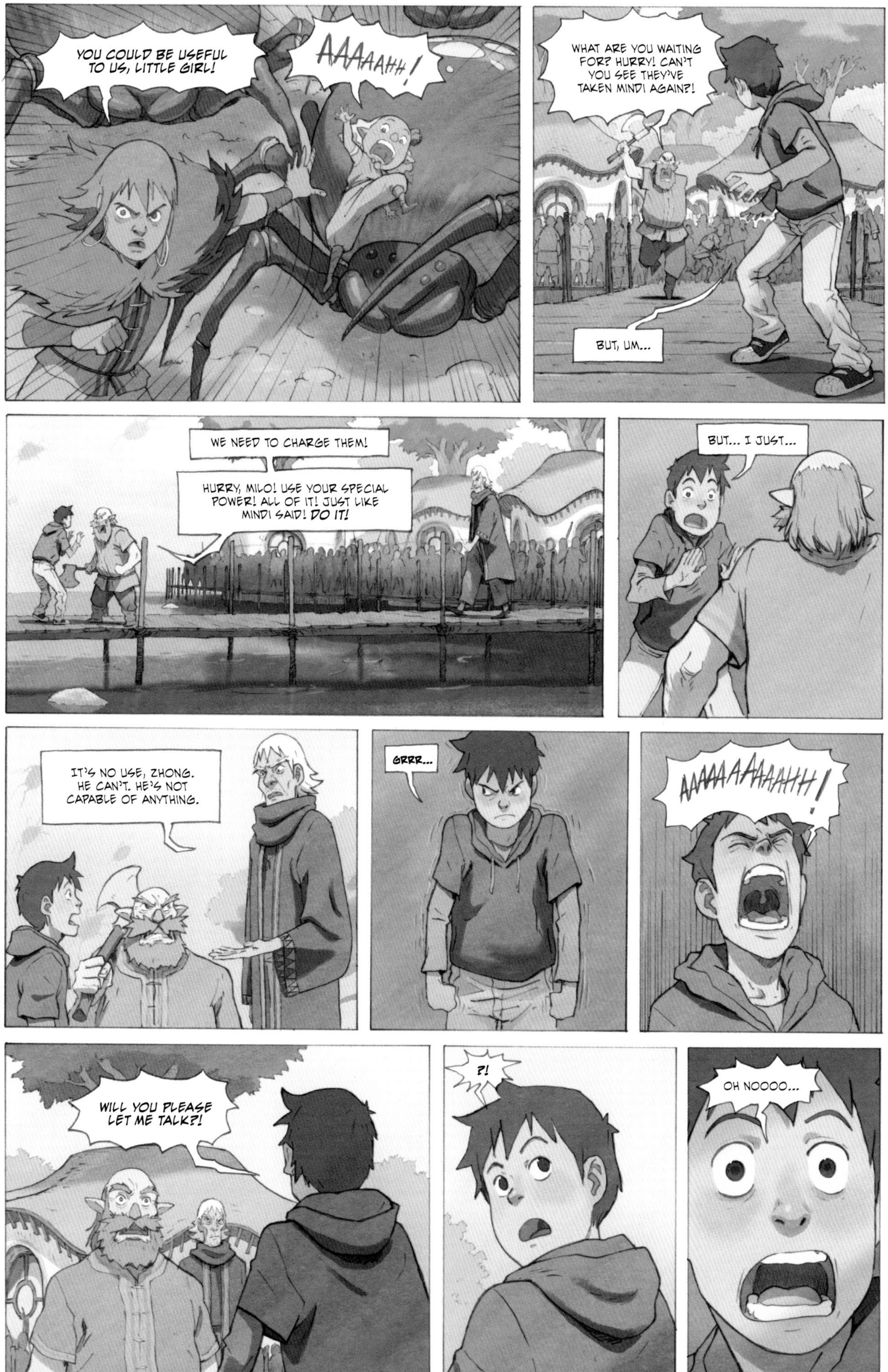

YOU COULD BE USEFUL TO US, LITTLE GIRL!
AAAAAHH!
WHAT ARE YOU WAITING FOR? HURRY! CAN'T YOU SEE THEY'VE TAKEN MINDI AGAIN?!
BUT, UM...
WE NEED TO CHARGE THEM!
HURRY, MILO! USE YOUR SPECIAL POWER! ALL OF IT! JUST LIKE MINDI SAID! DO IT!
BUT... I JUST...
IT'S NO USE, ZHONG. HE CAN'T. HE'S NOT CAPABLE OF ANYTHING.
GRRR...
AAAAAAAAAAHH!
WILL YOU PLEASE LET ME TALK?!
?!
OH NOOOO...

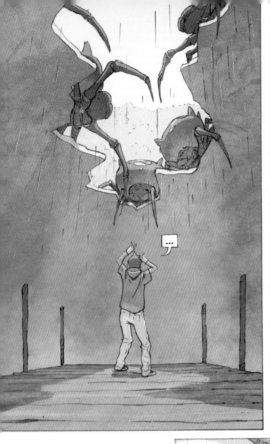

AAAAH!

THEY'RE GONNA EAT US!

WE'RE DOOMED!

THAT'S IT... OUR GOOSE IS COOKED!

WHAT DOES COOKING A GOOSE HAVE TO DO WITH ANY OF THIS?!

IT MUST BE CODE FOR SOMETHING... HE'S SENDING US A HINT TO LET US KNOW WHAT HE WANTS FOR DINNER!

WELL, WE CAN'T HAVE GOOSE. IT'S NOT EVEN GOOSE SEASON!

THIS IS THE END! THEY'RE INSIDE!

MAYBE A FROZEN ONE...?

WITH CORNBREAD STUFFING AND MASHED POTATOES. THAT'S HIS FAVORITE!

?!

!!!

I TOLD YOU NOT TO GET IN MY WAY.

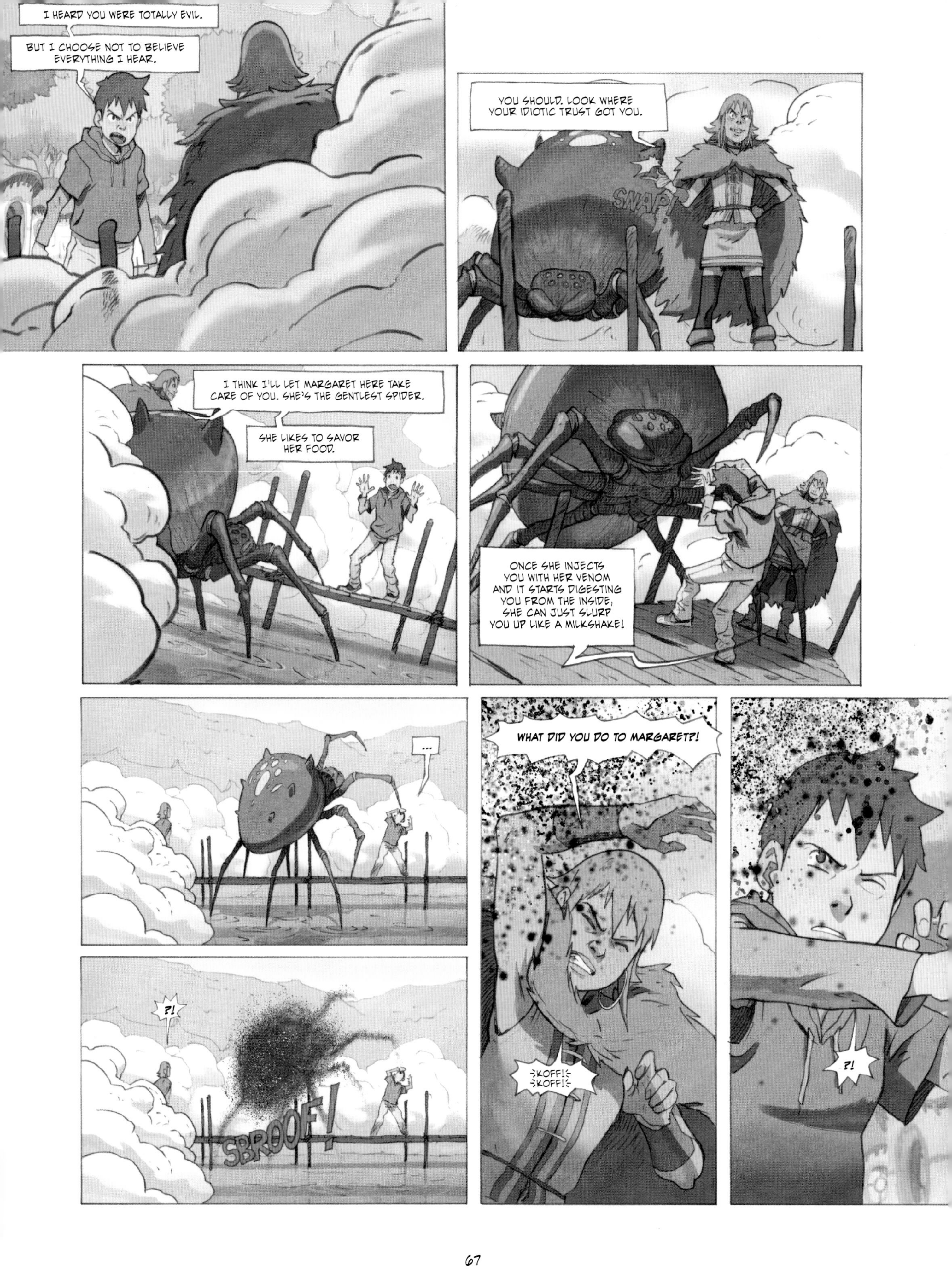
I HEARD YOU WERE TOTALLY EVIL.
BUT I CHOOSE NOT TO BELIEVE EVERYTHING I HEAR.
YOU SHOULD. LOOK WHERE YOUR IDIOTIC TRUST GOT YOU.
SNAP!
I THINK I'LL LET MARGARET HERE TAKE CARE OF YOU. SHE'S THE GENTLEST SPIDER.
SHE LIKES TO SAVOR HER FOOD.
ONCE SHE INJECTS YOU WITH HER VENOM AND IT STARTS DIGESTING YOU FROM THE INSIDE, SHE CAN JUST SLURP YOU UP LIKE A MILKSHAKE!
...
?!
SBROOF!
WHAT DID YOU DO TO MARGARET?!
KOFF! KOFF!
?!

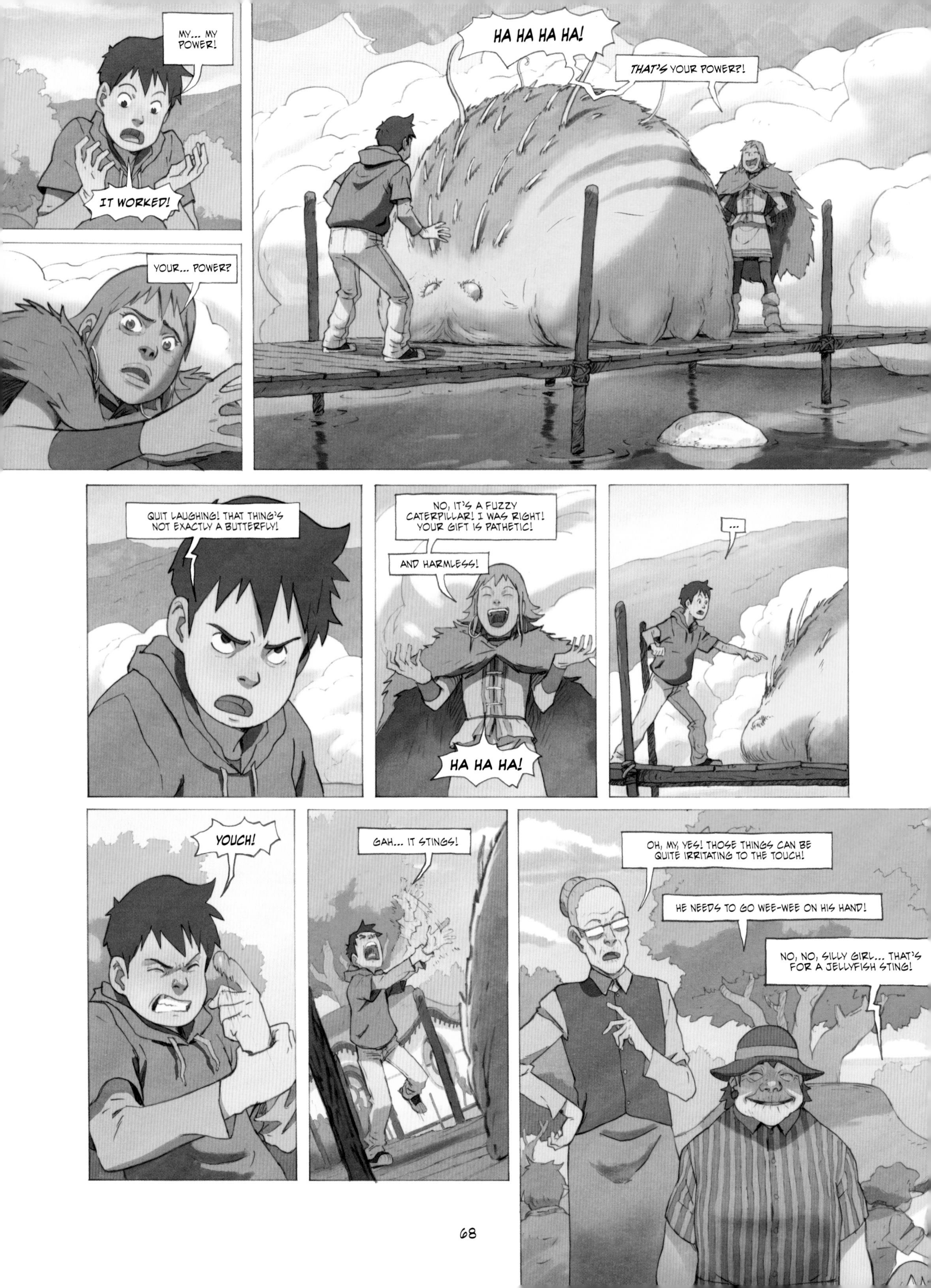
MY... MY POWER!
IT WORKED!
YOUR... POWER?
HA HA HA HA!
THAT'S YOUR POWER?!
QUIT LAUGHING! THAT THING'S NOT EXACTLY A BUTTERFLY!
NO, IT'S A FUZZY CATERPILLAR! I WAS RIGHT! YOUR GIFT IS PATHETIC!
AND HARMLESS!
HA HA HA!
...
YOUCH!
GAH... IT STINGS!
OH, MY, YES! THOSE THINGS CAN BE QUITE IRRITATING TO THE TOUCH!
HE NEEDS TO GO WEE-WEE ON HIS HAND!
NO, NO, SILLY GIRL... THAT'S FOR A JELLYFISH STING!

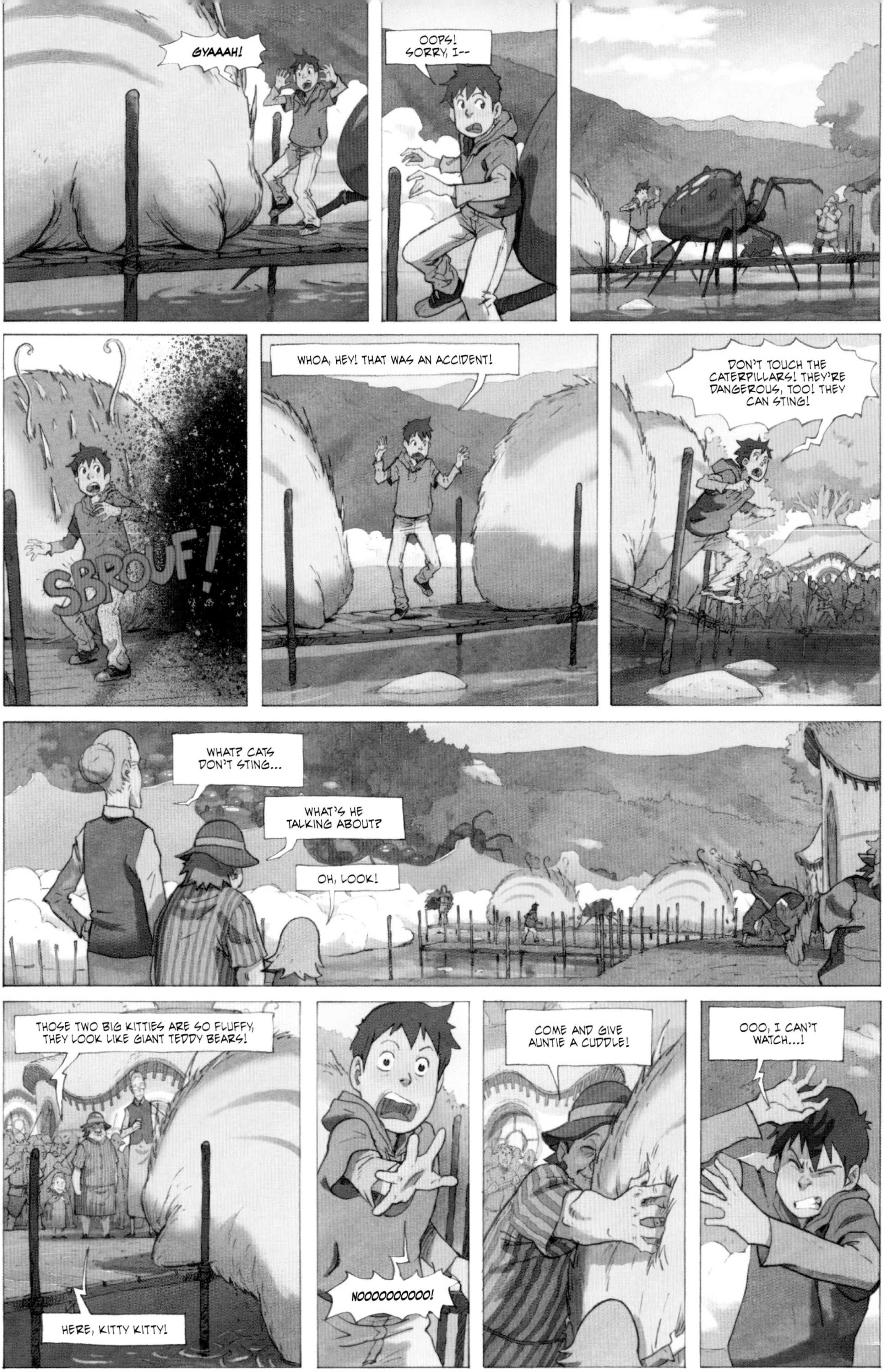
GYAAAH!
OOPS! SORRY, I--
SBROUF!
WHOA, HEY! THAT WAS AN ACCIDENT!
DON'T TOUCH THE CATERPILLARS! THEY'RE DANGEROUS, TOO! THEY CAN STING!
WHAT? CATS DON'T STING...
WHAT'S HE TALKING ABOUT?
OH, LOOK!
THOSE TWO BIG KITTIES ARE SO FLUFFY, THEY LOOK LIKE GIANT TEDDY BEARS!
HERE, KITTY KITTY!
NOOOOOOOOOO!
COME AND GIVE AUNTIE A CUDDLE!
OOO, I CAN'T WATCH...!

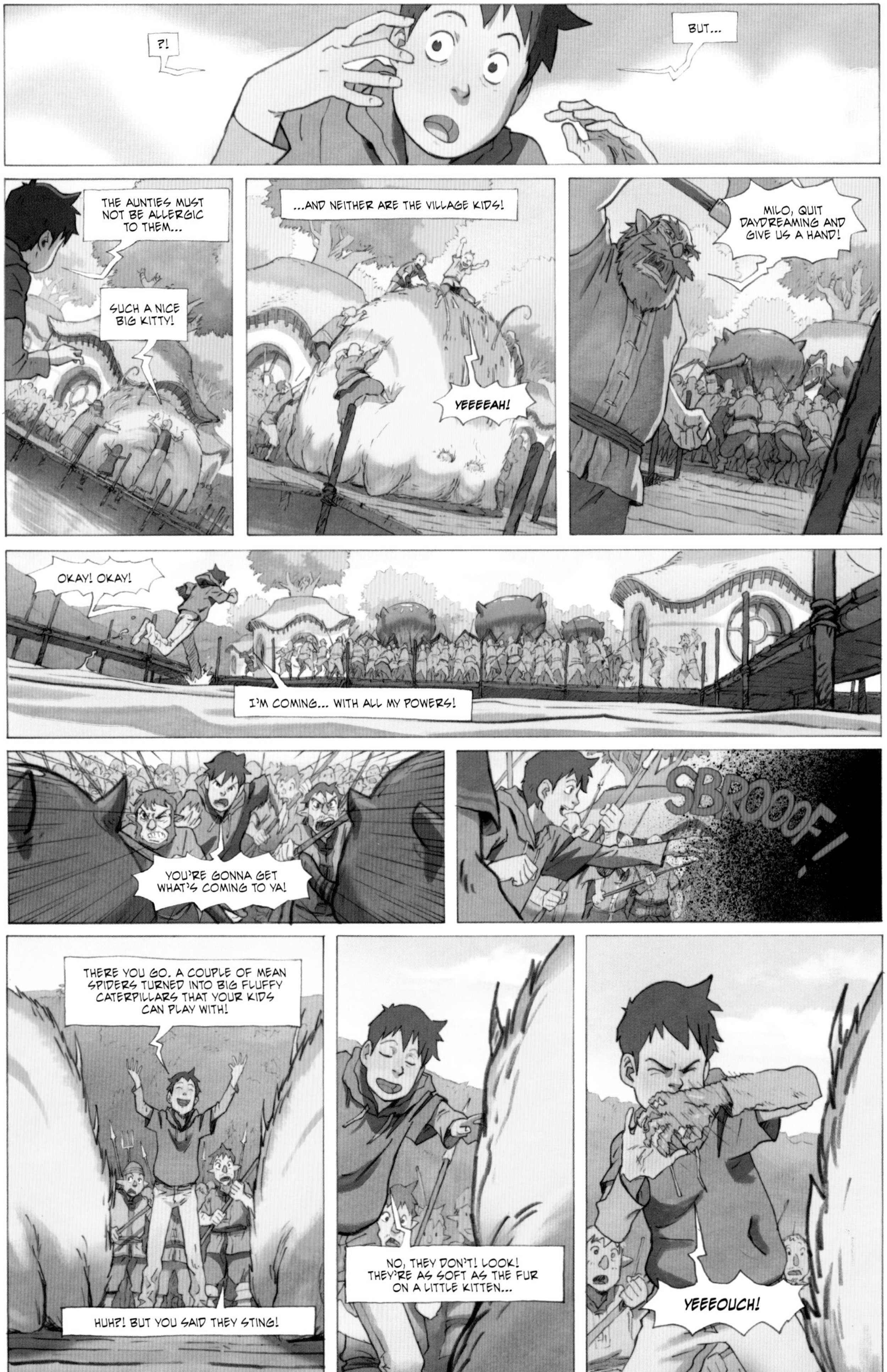
?!
BUT...
THE AUNTIES MUST NOT BE ALLERGIC TO THEM...
SUCH A NICE BIG KITTY!
...AND NEITHER ARE THE VILLAGE KIDS!
YEEEEAH!
MILO, QUIT DAYDREAMING AND GIVE US A HAND!
OKAY! OKAY!
I'M COMING... WITH ALL MY POWERS!
YOU'RE GONNA GET WHAT'S COMING TO YA!
SBROOOF!
THERE YOU GO. A COUPLE OF MEAN SPIDERS TURNED INTO BIG FLUFFY CATERPILLARS THAT YOUR KIDS CAN PLAY WITH!
HUH?! BUT YOU SAID THEY STING!
NO, THEY DON'T! LOOK! THEY'RE AS SOFT AS THE FUR ON A LITTLE KITTEN...
YEEEOUCH!

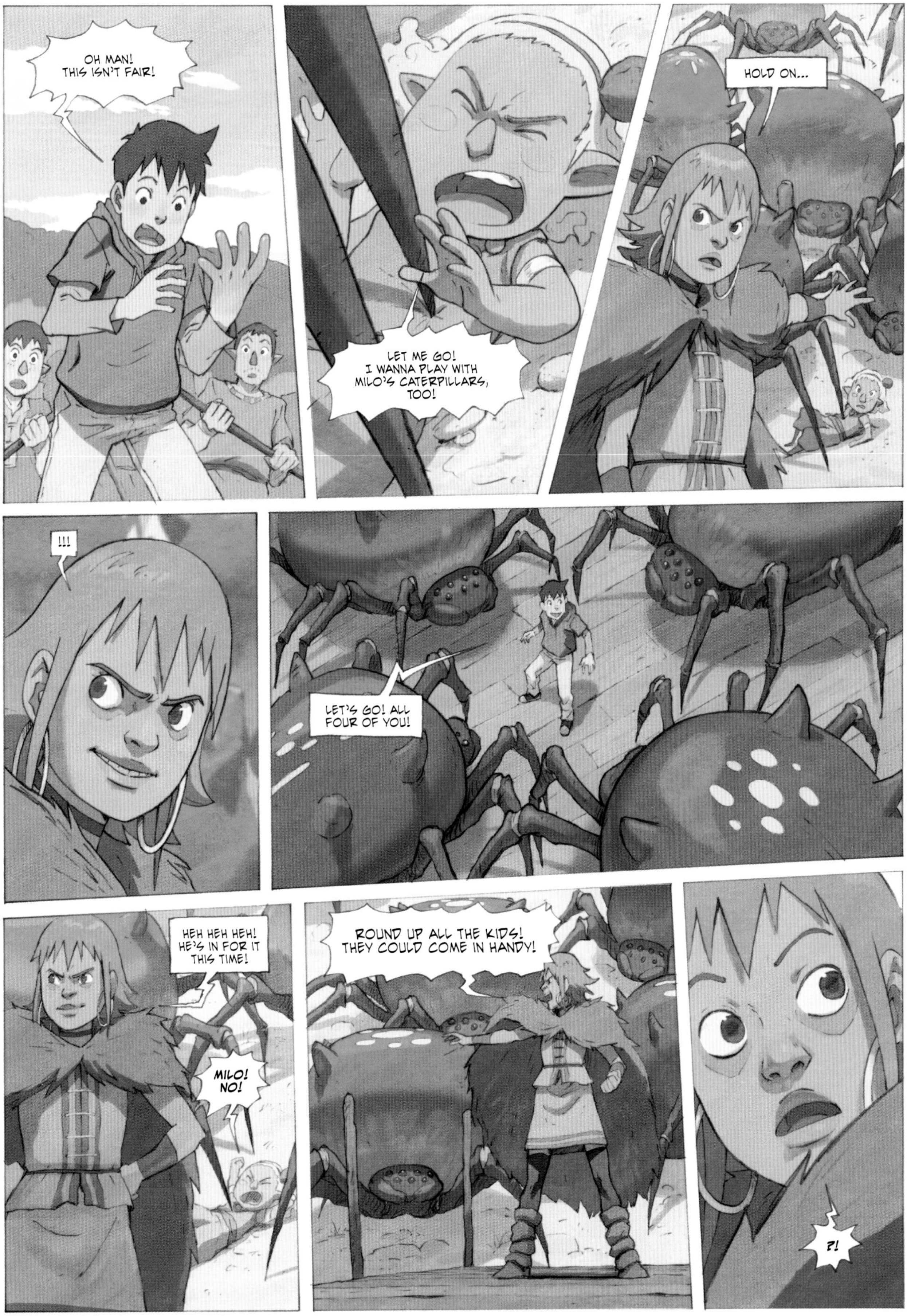
OH MAN! THIS ISN'T FAIR!
LET ME GO! I WANNA PLAY WITH MILO'S CATERPILLARS, TOO!
HOLD ON...
!!!
LET'S GO! ALL FOUR OF YOU!
HEH HEH HEH! HE'S IN FOR IT THIS TIME!
MILO! NO!
ROUND UP ALL THE KIDS! THEY COULD COME IN HANDY!
?!

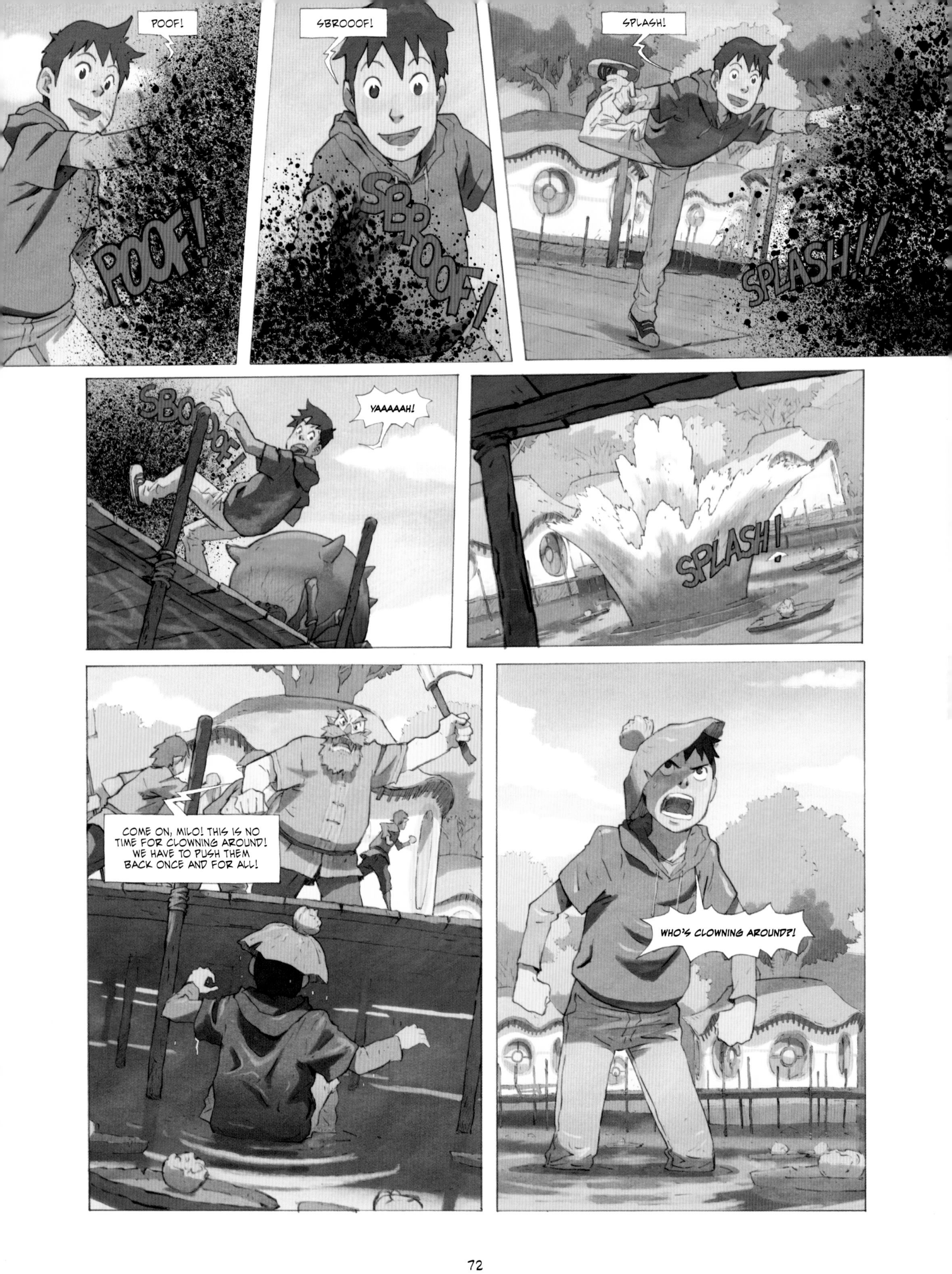
POOF!
POOF!
SBROOOF!
SBROOOF!
SPLASH!
SPLASH!!
SBOOOOF!
YAAAAAH!
SPLASH!
COME ON, MILO! THIS IS NO TIME FOR CLOWNING AROUND! WE HAVE TO PUSH THEM BACK ONCE AND FOR ALL!
WHO'S CLOWNING AROUND?!

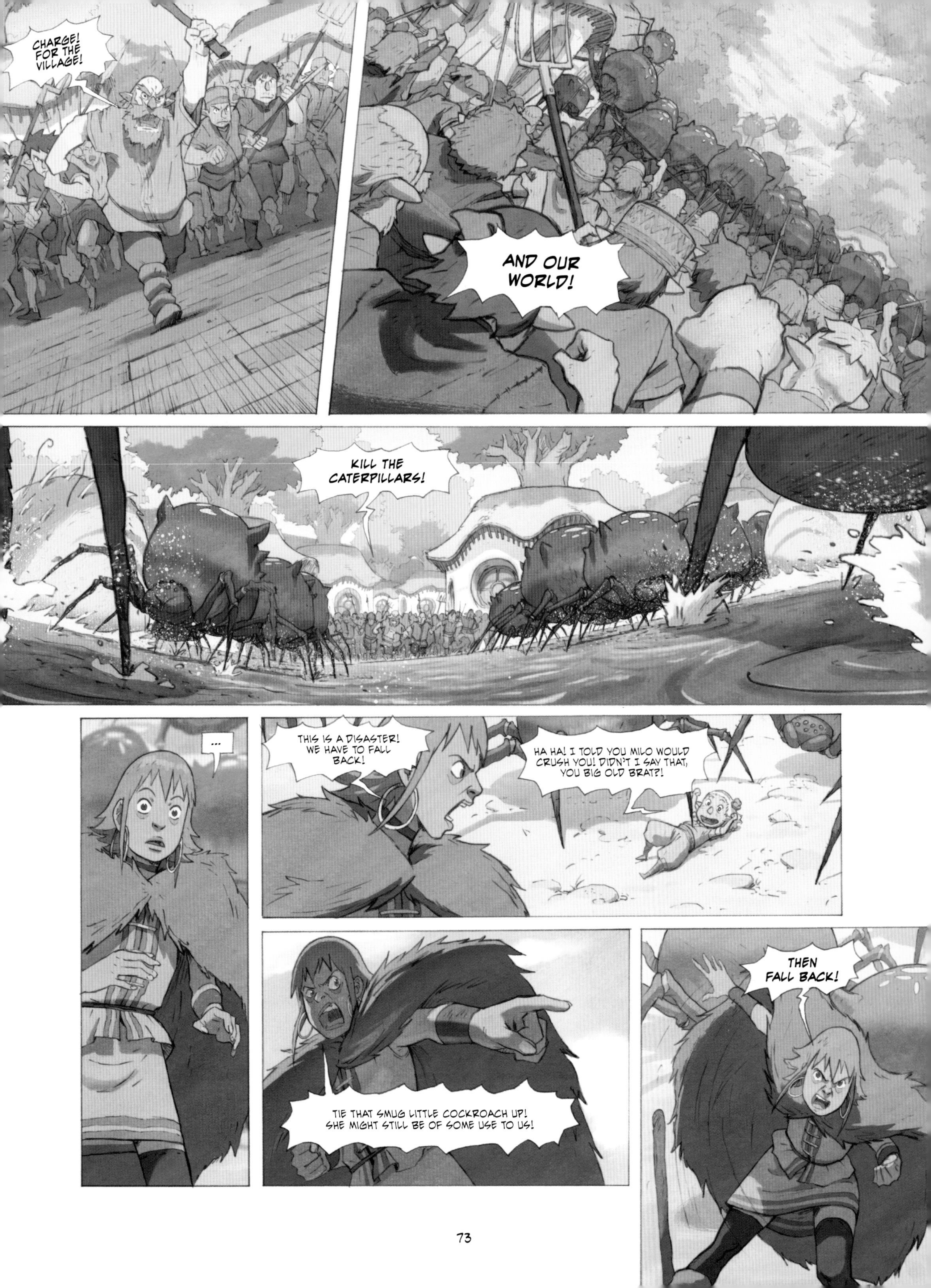
CHARGE! FOR THE VILLAGE!
AND OUR WORLD!
KILL THE CATERPILLARS!
...
THIS IS A DISASTER! WE HAVE TO FALL BACK!
HA HA! I TOLD YOU MILO WOULD CRUSH YOU! DIDN'T I SAY THAT, YOU BIG OLD BRAT?!
TIE THAT SMUG LITTLE COCKROACH UP! SHE MIGHT STILL BE OF SOME USE TO US!
THEN FALL BACK!

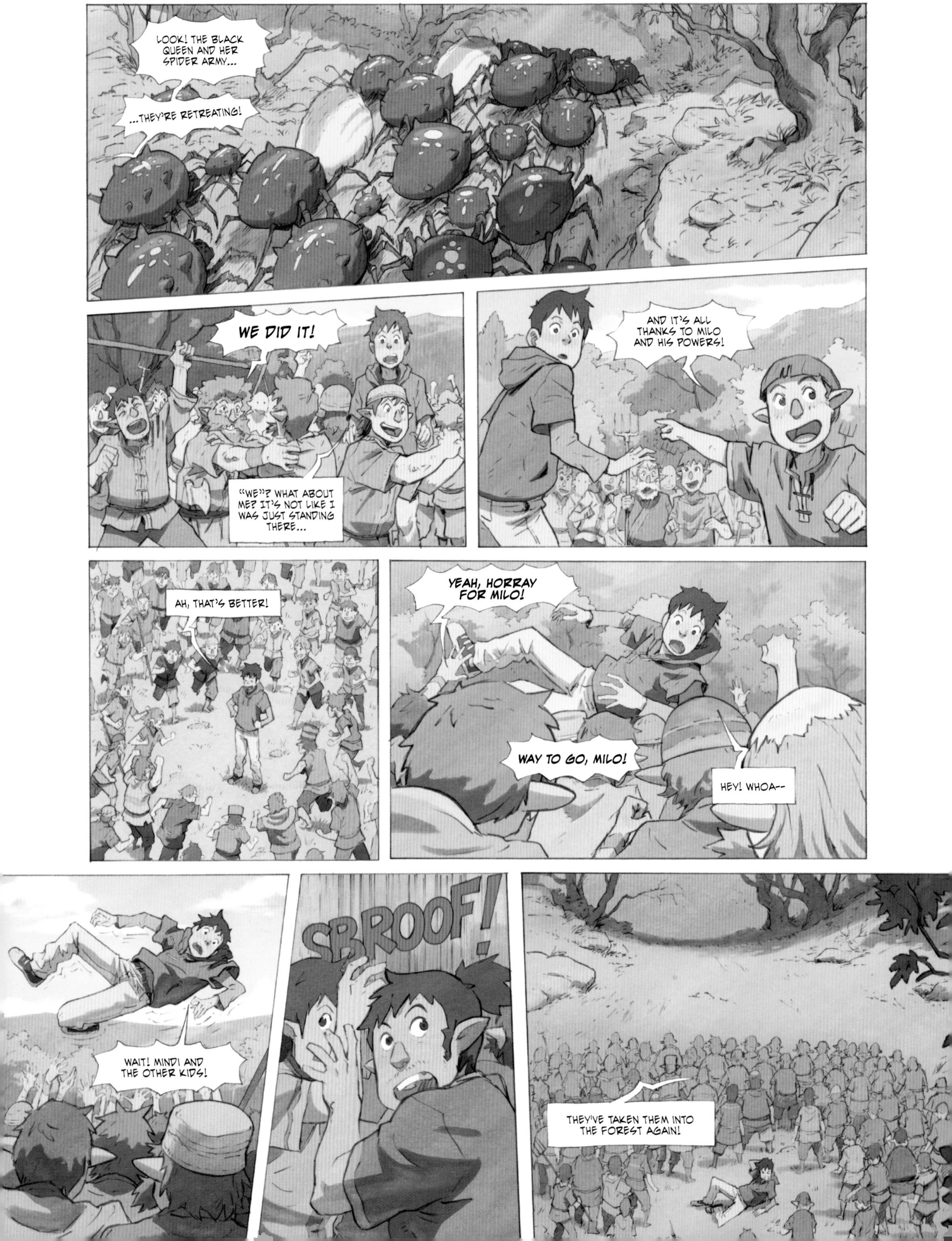
LOOK! THE BLACK QUEEN AND HER SPIDER ARMY...
...THEY'RE RETREATING!
WE DID IT!
"WE"? WHAT ABOUT ME? IT'S NOT LIKE I WAS JUST STANDING THERE...
AND IT'S ALL THANKS TO MILO AND HIS POWERS!
AH, THAT'S BETTER!
YEAH, HORRAY FOR MILO!
WAY TO GO, MILO!
HEY! WHOA--
WAIT! MINDI AND THE OTHER KIDS!
SBROOF!
THEY'VE TAKEN THEM INTO THE FOREST AGAIN!

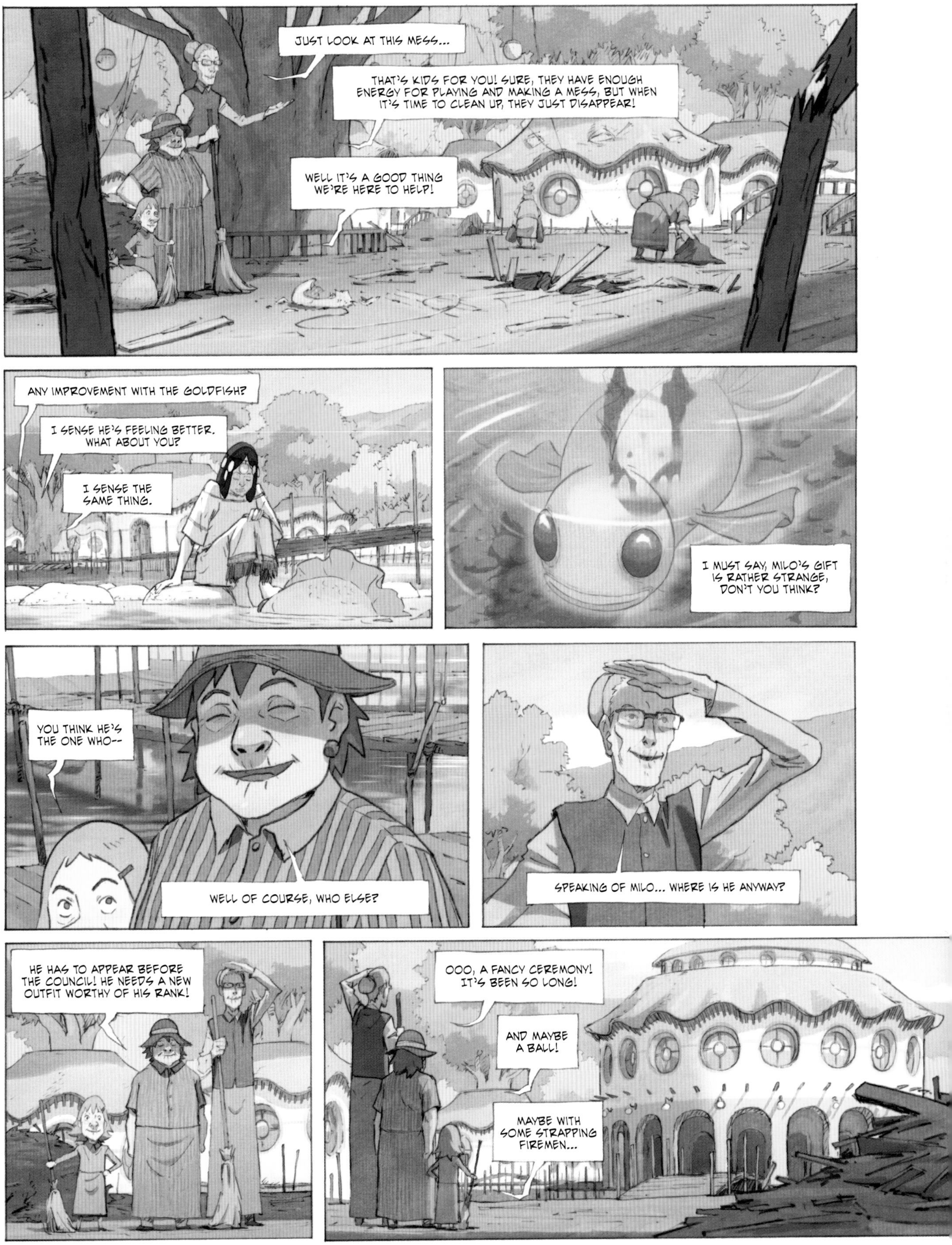
JUST LOOK AT THIS MESS...
THAT'S KIDS FOR YOU! SURE, THEY HAVE ENOUGH ENERGY FOR PLAYING AND MAKING A MESS, BUT WHEN IT'S TIME TO CLEAN UP, THEY JUST DISAPPEAR!
WELL IT'S A GOOD THING WE'RE HERE TO HELP!
ANY IMPROVEMENT WITH THE GOLDFISH?
I SENSE HE'S FEELING BETTER. WHAT ABOUT YOU?
I SENSE THE SAME THING.
I MUST SAY, MILO'S GIFT IS RATHER STRANGE, DON'T YOU THINK?
YOU THINK HE'S THE ONE WHO--
WELL OF COURSE, WHO ELSE?
SPEAKING OF MILO... WHERE IS HE ANYWAY?
HE HAS TO APPEAR BEFORE THE COUNCIL! HE NEEDS A NEW OUTFIT WORTHY OF HIS RANK!
OOO, A FANCY CEREMONY! IT'S BEEN SO LONG!
AND MAYBE A BALL!
MAYBE WITH SOME STRAPPING FIREMEN...

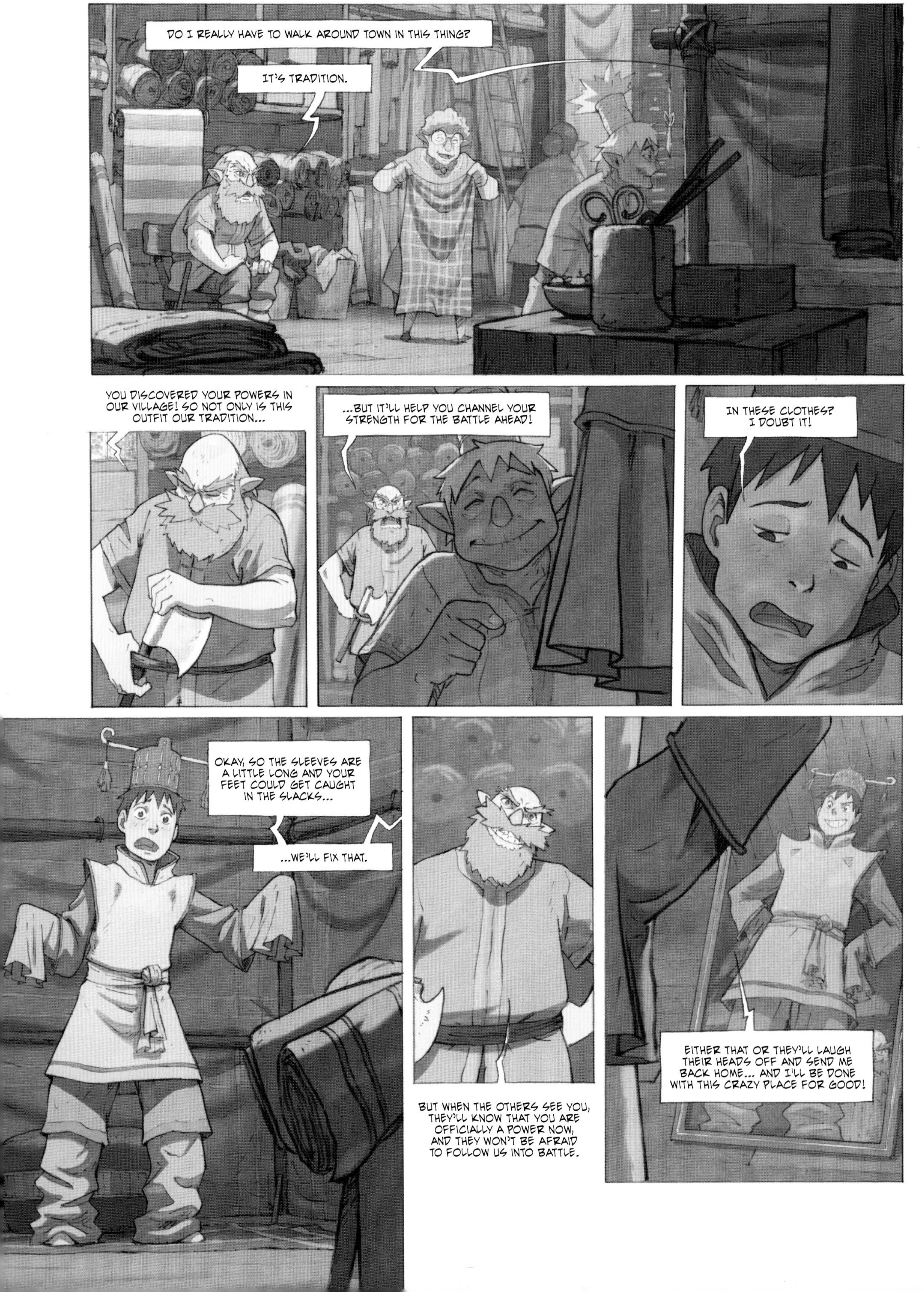
DO I REALLY HAVE TO WALK AROUND TOWN IN THIS THING?
IT'S TRADITION.
YOU DISCOVERED YOUR POWERS IN OUR VILLAGE! SO NOT ONLY IS THIS OUTFIT OUR TRADITION...
...BUT IT'LL HELP YOU CHANNEL YOUR STRENGTH FOR THE BATTLE AHEAD!
IN THESE CLOTHES? I DOUBT IT!
OKAY, SO THE SLEEVES ARE A LITTLE LONG AND YOUR FEET COULD GET CAUGHT IN THE SLACKS...
...WE'LL FIX THAT.
BUT WHEN THE OTHERS SEE YOU, THEY'LL KNOW THAT YOU ARE OFFICIALLY A POWER NOW, AND THEY WON'T BE AFRAID TO FOLLOW US INTO BATTLE.
EITHER THAT OR THEY'LL LAUGH THEIR HEADS OFF AND SEND ME BACK HOME... AND I'LL BE DONE WITH THIS CRAZY PLACE FOR GOOD!

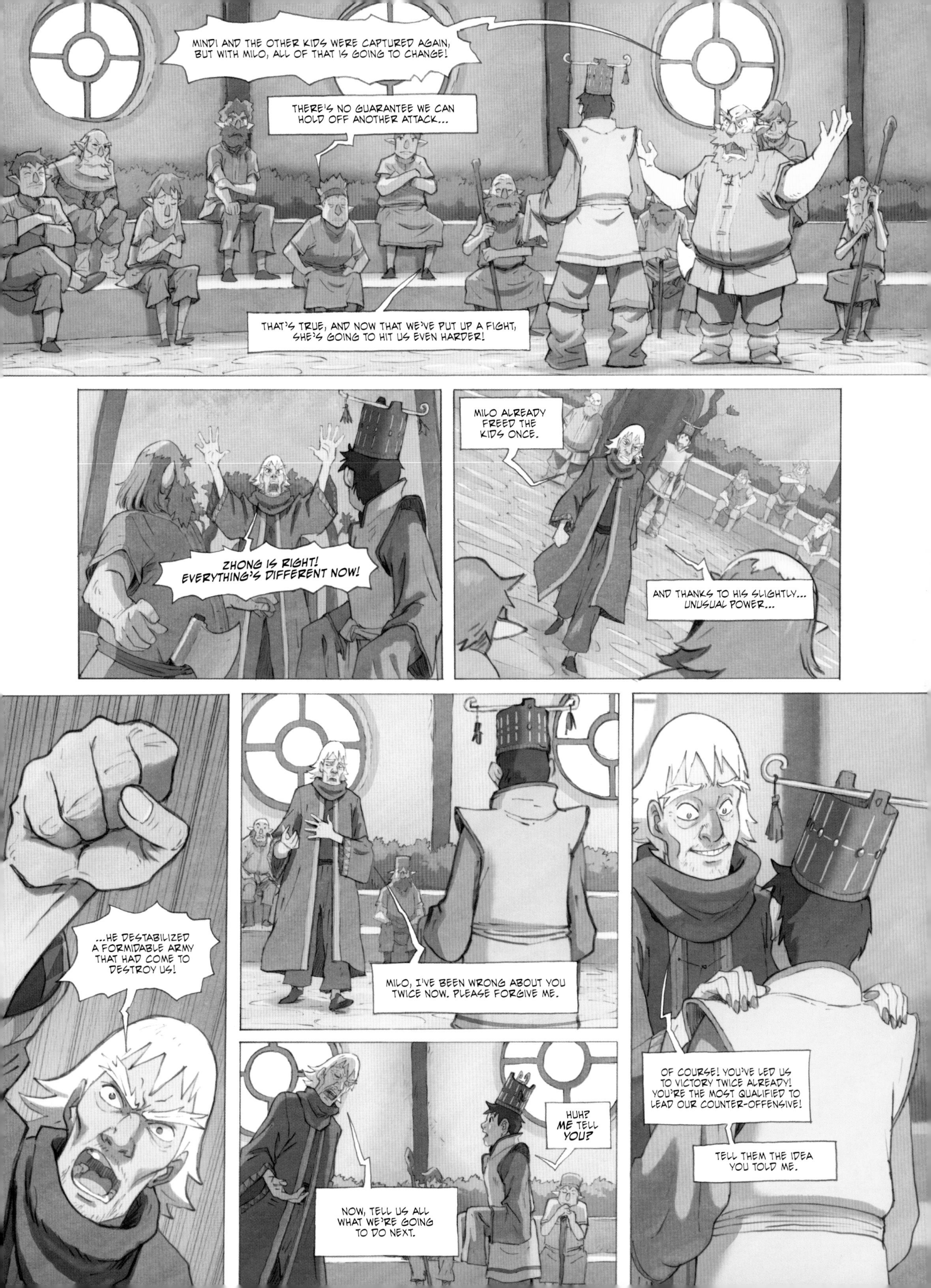
MINDI AND THE OTHER KIDS WERE CAPTURED AGAIN, BUT WITH MILO, ALL OF THAT IS GOING TO CHANGE!
THERE'S NO GUARANTEE WE CAN HOLD OFF ANOTHER ATTACK...
THAT'S TRUE, AND NOW THAT WE'VE PUT UP A FIGHT, SHE'S GOING TO HIT US EVEN HARDER!
ZHONG IS RIGHT! EVERYTHING'S DIFFERENT NOW!
MILO ALREADY FREED THE KIDS ONCE.
AND THANKS TO HIS SLIGHTLY... UNUSUAL POWER...
...HE DESTABILIZED A FORMIDABLE ARMY THAT HAD COME TO DESTROY US!
MILO, I'VE BEEN WRONG ABOUT YOU TWICE NOW. PLEASE FORGIVE ME.
OF COURSE! YOU'VE LED US TO VICTORY TWICE ALREADY! YOU'RE THE MOST QUALIFIED TO LEAD OUR COUNTER-OFFENSIVE!
TELL THEM THE IDEA YOU TOLD ME.
NOW, TELL US ALL WHAT WE'RE GOING TO DO NEXT.
HUH? ME TELL YOU?

B-BUT I...

YOU KNOW... YOUR IDEA TO BRING ALL THE VILLAGE POWERS TOGETHER.

TELL THEM.

OH, RIGHT... YEAH, WE SHOULD BRING ALL THE VILLAGE POWERS TOGETHER...!

...

TO DO WHAT, EXACTLY?

TO DO WHAT? UH...

YES, YES, YOU REMEMBER... YOUR IDEA WAS TO MOUNT AN ATTACK AGAINST THE BLACK FORTRESS IN THE MIDDLE OF THE FOREST, WHERE ALL OF THOSE EVIL CREATURES ARE GATHERED.

‡PFFF‡

ER... WELL, UM, TOGETHER, WE CAN MOUNT AN ATTACK AGAINST THE BLACK FORTRESS IN THE MIDDLE OF THE FOREST, WHERE ALL THOSE BIG, UGLY CREATURES ARE GATHERED!

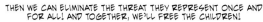

THEN WE CAN ELIMINATE THE THREAT THEY REPRESENT ONCE AND FOR ALL! AND TOGETHER, WE'LL FREE THE CHILDREN!

THANKS TO, UM... MY POWERS...

YES! ALL TOGETHER!

YEAH, I MEAN, WE ARE ACTUALLY PRETTY BRAVE...

...AND YOUR COURAGE!

I COULDN'T HAVE SAID IT BETTER MYSELF.

TOGETHER!

OUR COURAGE AND MILO'S POWERS!

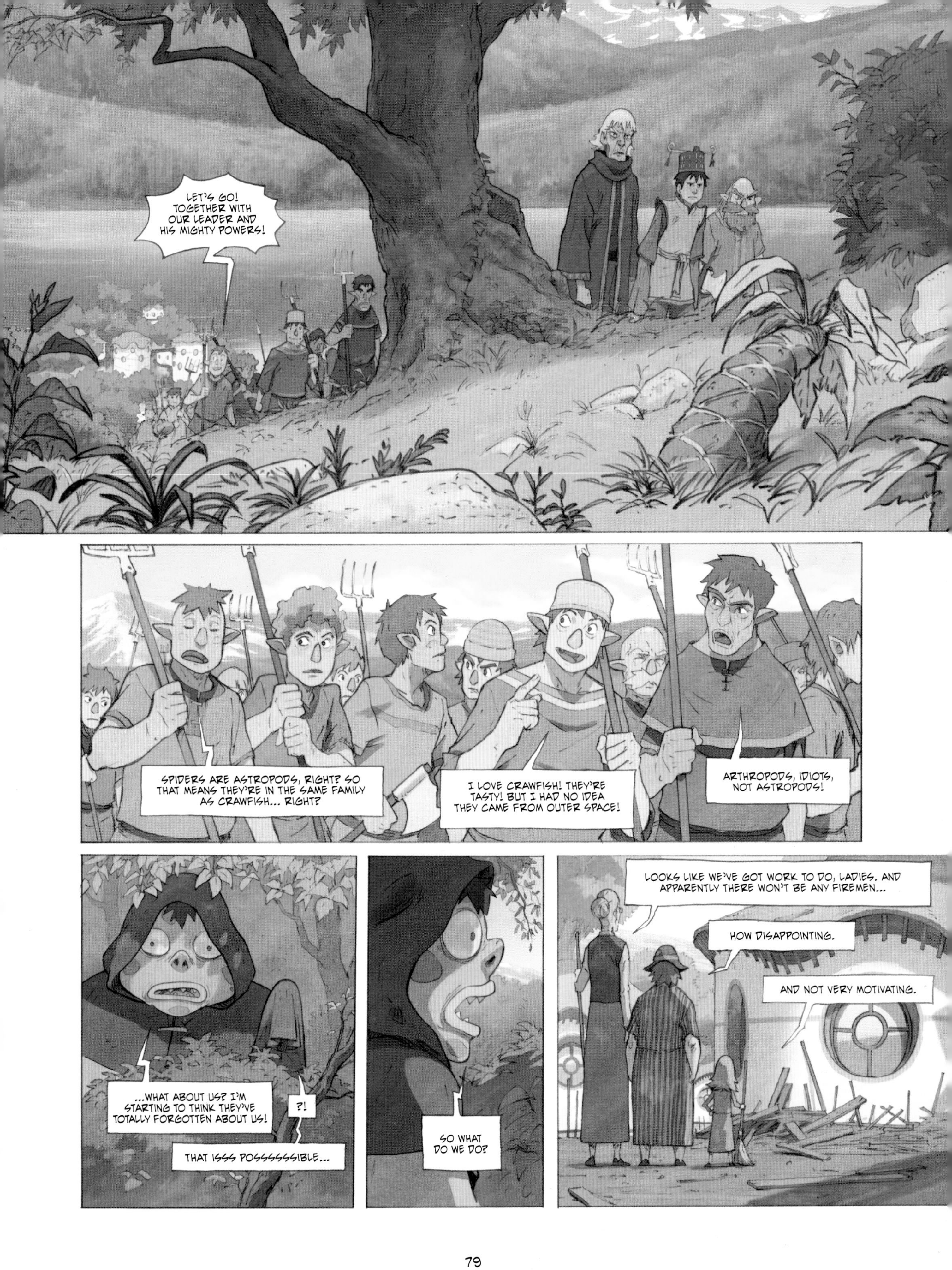
LET'S GO! TOGETHER WITH OUR LEADER AND HIS MIGHTY POWERS!
SPIDERS ARE ASTROPODS, RIGHT? SO THAT MEANS THEY'RE IN THE SAME FAMILY AS CRAWFISH... RIGHT?
I LOVE CRAWFISH! THEY'RE TASTY! BUT I HAD NO IDEA THEY CAME FROM OUTER SPACE!
ARTHROPODS, IDIOTS, NOT ASTROPODS!
...WHAT ABOUT US? I'M STARTING TO THINK THEY'VE TOTALLY FORGOTTEN ABOUT US!
?!
THAT ISSS POSSSSSSSIBLE...
SO WHAT DO WE DO?
LOOKS LIKE WE'VE GOT WORK TO DO, LADIES. AND APPARENTLY THERE WON'T BE ANY FIREMEN...
HOW DISAPPOINTING.
AND NOT VERY MOTIVATING.

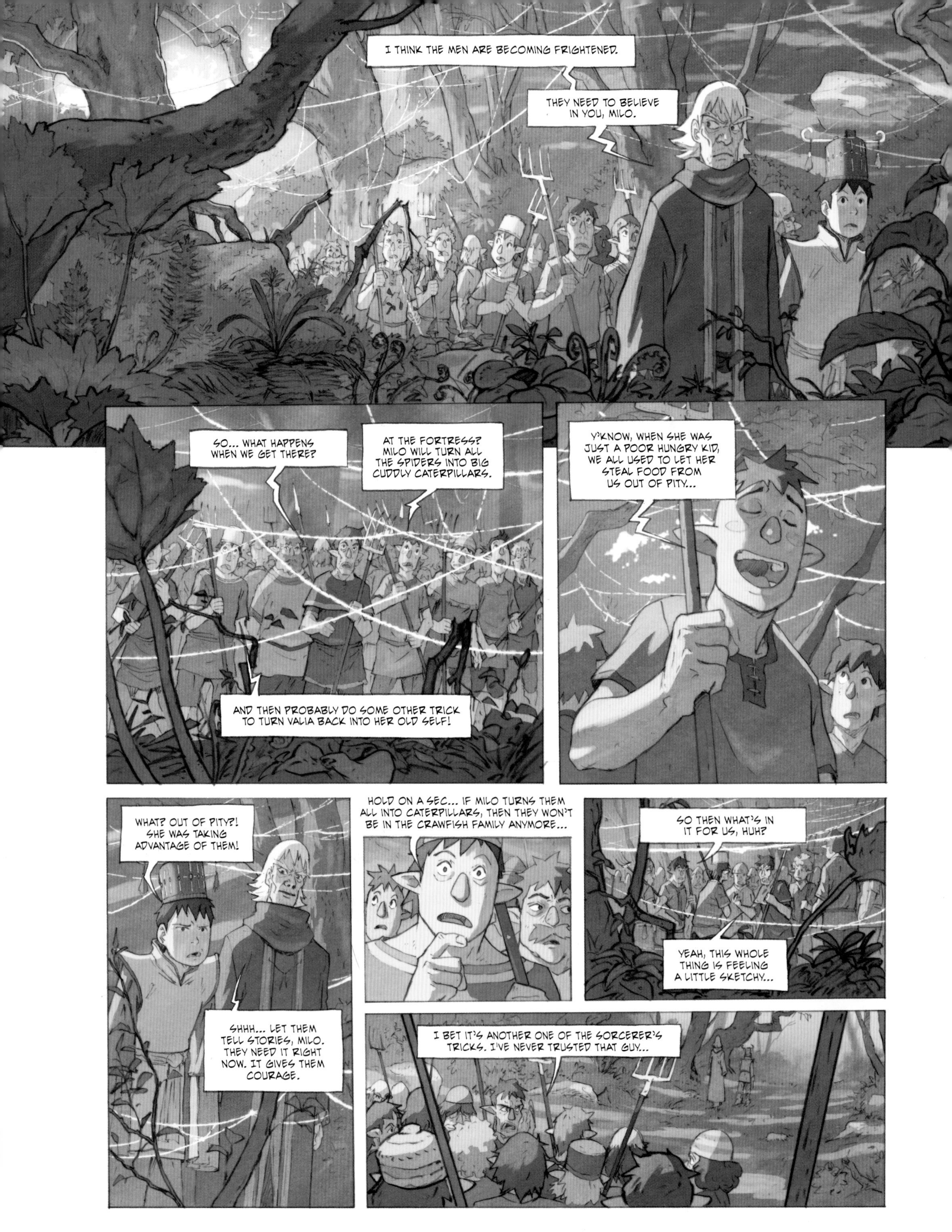
I THINK THE MEN ARE BECOMING FRIGHTENED.
THEY NEED TO BELIEVE IN YOU, MILO.
SO... WHAT HAPPENS WHEN WE GET THERE?
AT THE FORTRESS? MILO WILL TURN ALL THE SPIDERS INTO BIG CUDDLY CATERPILLARS.
AND THEN PROBABLY DO SOME OTHER TRICK TO TURN VALIA BACK INTO HER OLD SELF!
Y'KNOW, WHEN SHE WAS JUST A POOR HUNGRY KID, WE ALL USED TO LET HER STEAL FOOD FROM US OUT OF PITY...
WHAT? OUT OF PITY?! SHE WAS TAKING ADVANTAGE OF THEM!
SHHH... LET THEM TELL STORIES, MILO. THEY NEED IT RIGHT NOW. IT GIVES THEM COURAGE.
HOLD ON A SEC... IF MILO TURNS THEM ALL INTO CATERPILLARS, THEN THEY WON'T BE IN THE CRAWFISH FAMILY ANYMORE...
SO THEN WHAT'S IN IT FOR US, HUH?
YEAH, THIS WHOLE THING IS FEELING A LITTLE SKETCHY...
I BET IT'S ANOTHER ONE OF THE SORCERER'S TRICKS. I'VE NEVER TRUSTED THAT GUY...

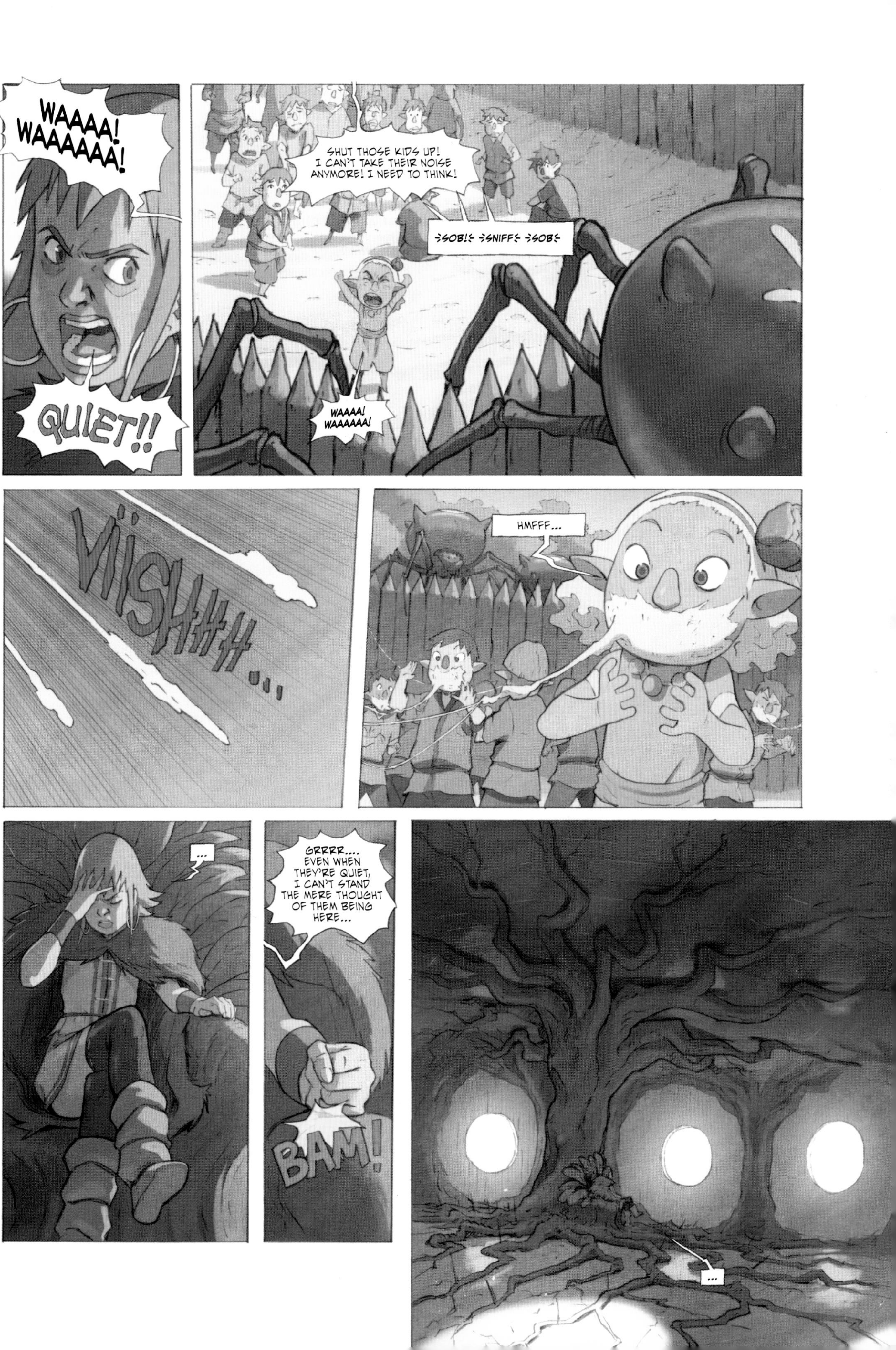
WAAAA! WAAAAAAA!
QUIET!!
SHUT THOSE KIDS UP! I CAN'T TAKE THEIR NOISE ANYMORE! I NEED TO THINK!
SOB! SNIFF SOB
WAAAA! WAAAAAA!
VÏÏSHHHH...
HMFFF...
...
GRRRR.... EVEN WHEN THEY'RE QUIET, I CAN'T STAND THE MERE THOUGHT OF THEM BEING HERE...
BAM!
...

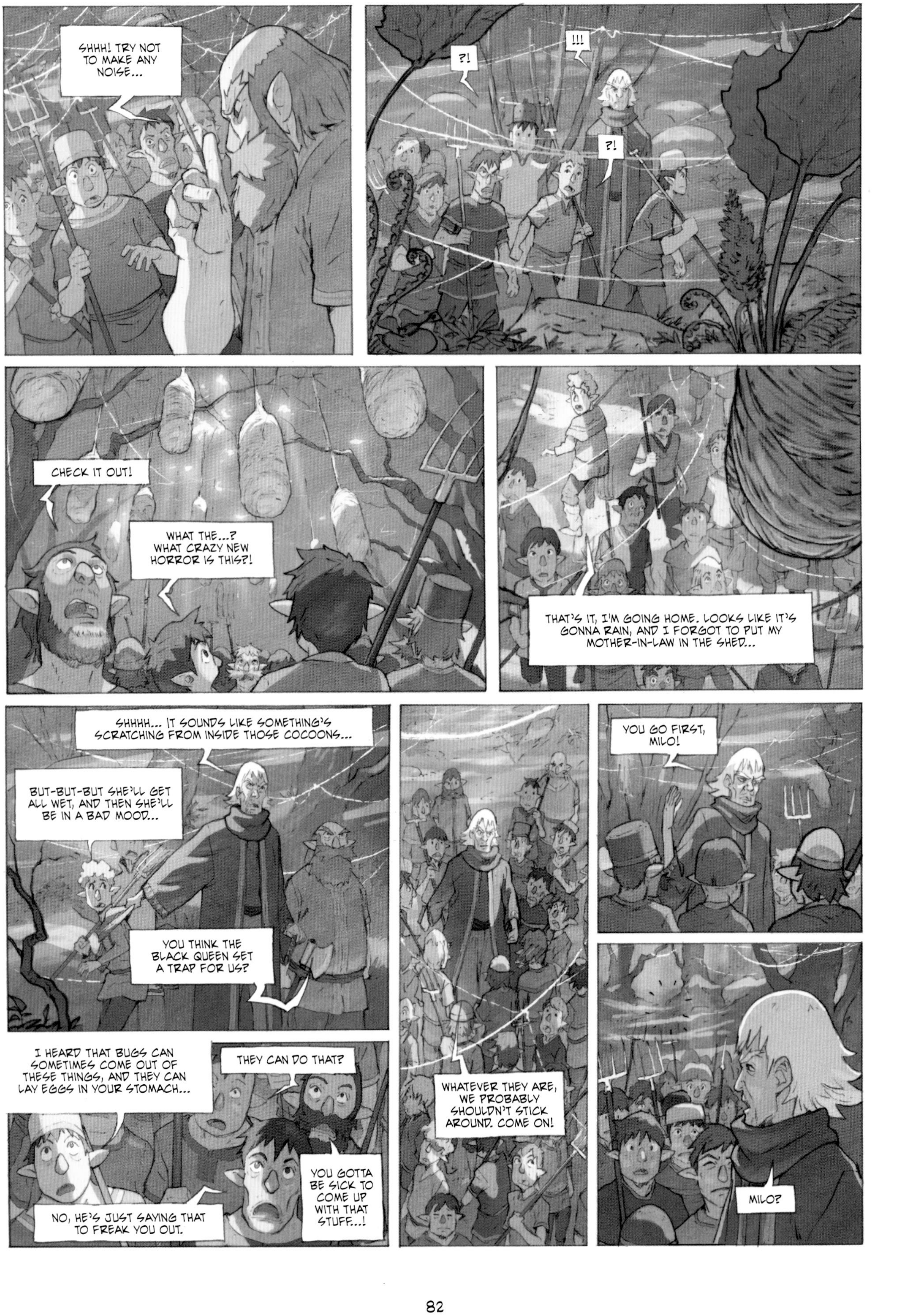

SHHH! TRY NOT TO MAKE ANY NOISE...
?!
!!!
?!
CHECK IT OUT!
WHAT THE...? WHAT CRAZY NEW HORROR IS THIS?!
THAT'S IT, I'M GOING HOME. LOOKS LIKE IT'S GONNA RAIN, AND I FORGOT TO PUT MY MOTHER-IN-LAW IN THE SHED...
SHHHH... IT SOUNDS LIKE SOMETHING'S SCRATCHING FROM INSIDE THOSE COCOONS...
BUT-BUT-BUT SHE'LL GET ALL WET, AND THEN SHE'LL BE IN A BAD MOOD...
YOU THINK THE BLACK QUEEN SET A TRAP FOR US?
I HEARD THAT BUGS CAN SOMETIMES COME OUT OF THESE THINGS, AND THEY CAN LAY EGGS IN YOUR STOMACH...
THEY CAN DO THAT?
NO, HE'S JUST SAYING THAT TO FREAK YOU OUT.
YOU GOTTA BE SICK TO COME UP WITH THAT STUFF...!
WHATEVER THEY ARE, WE PROBABLY SHOULDN'T STICK AROUND. COME ON!
YOU GO FIRST, MILO!
MILO?

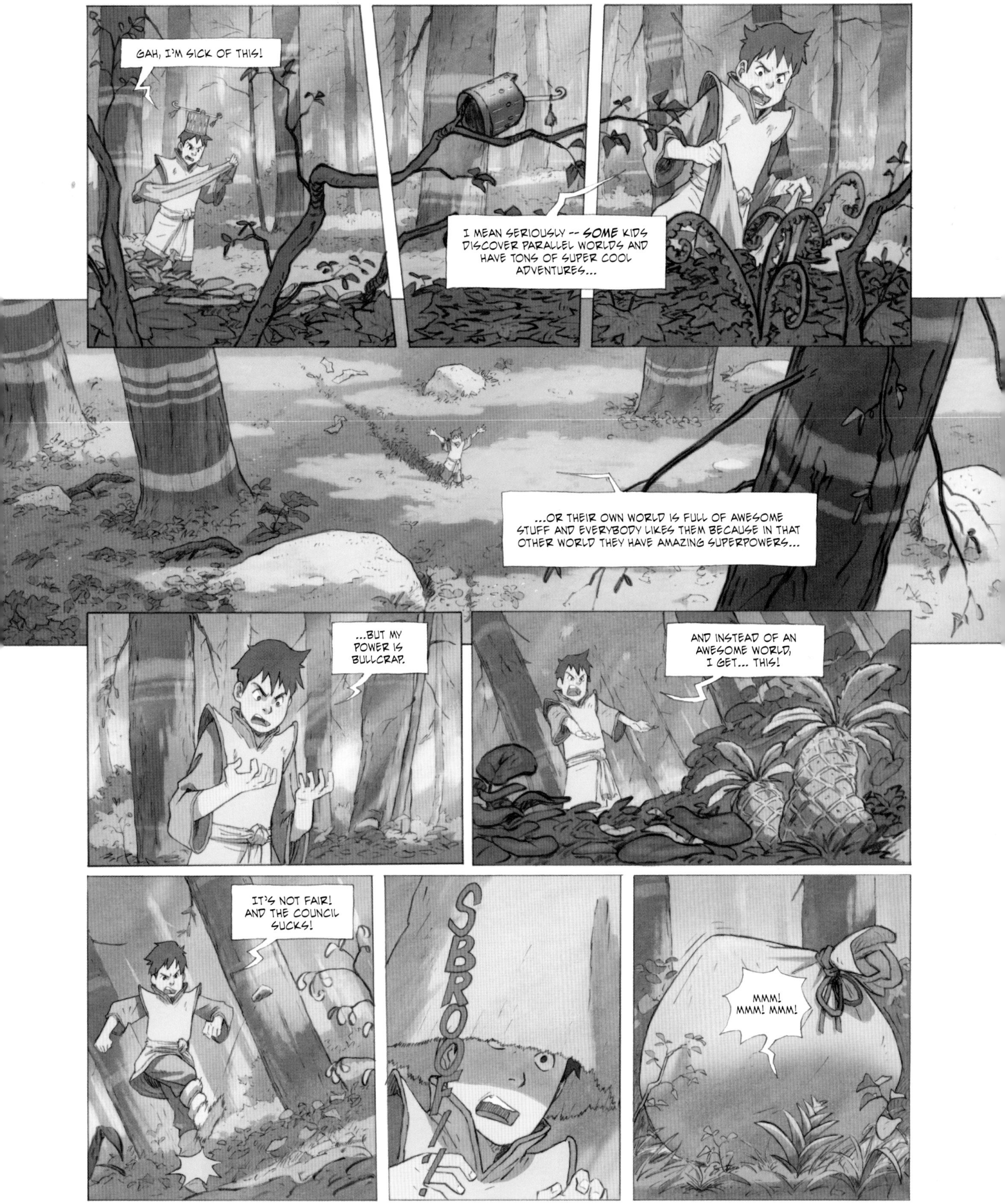
GAH, I'M SICK OF THIS!
I MEAN SERIOUSLY -- SOME KIDS DISCOVER PARALLEL WORLDS AND HAVE TONS OF SUPER COOL ADVENTURES...
...OR THEIR OWN WORLD IS FULL OF AWESOME STUFF AND EVERYBODY LIKES THEM BECAUSE IN THAT OTHER WORLD THEY HAVE AMAZING SUPERPOWERS...
...BUT MY POWER IS BULLCRAP.
AND INSTEAD OF AN AWESOME WORLD, I GET... THIS!
IT'S NOT FAIR! AND THE COUNCIL SUCKS!
SBROOF!!
MMM! MMM! MMM!

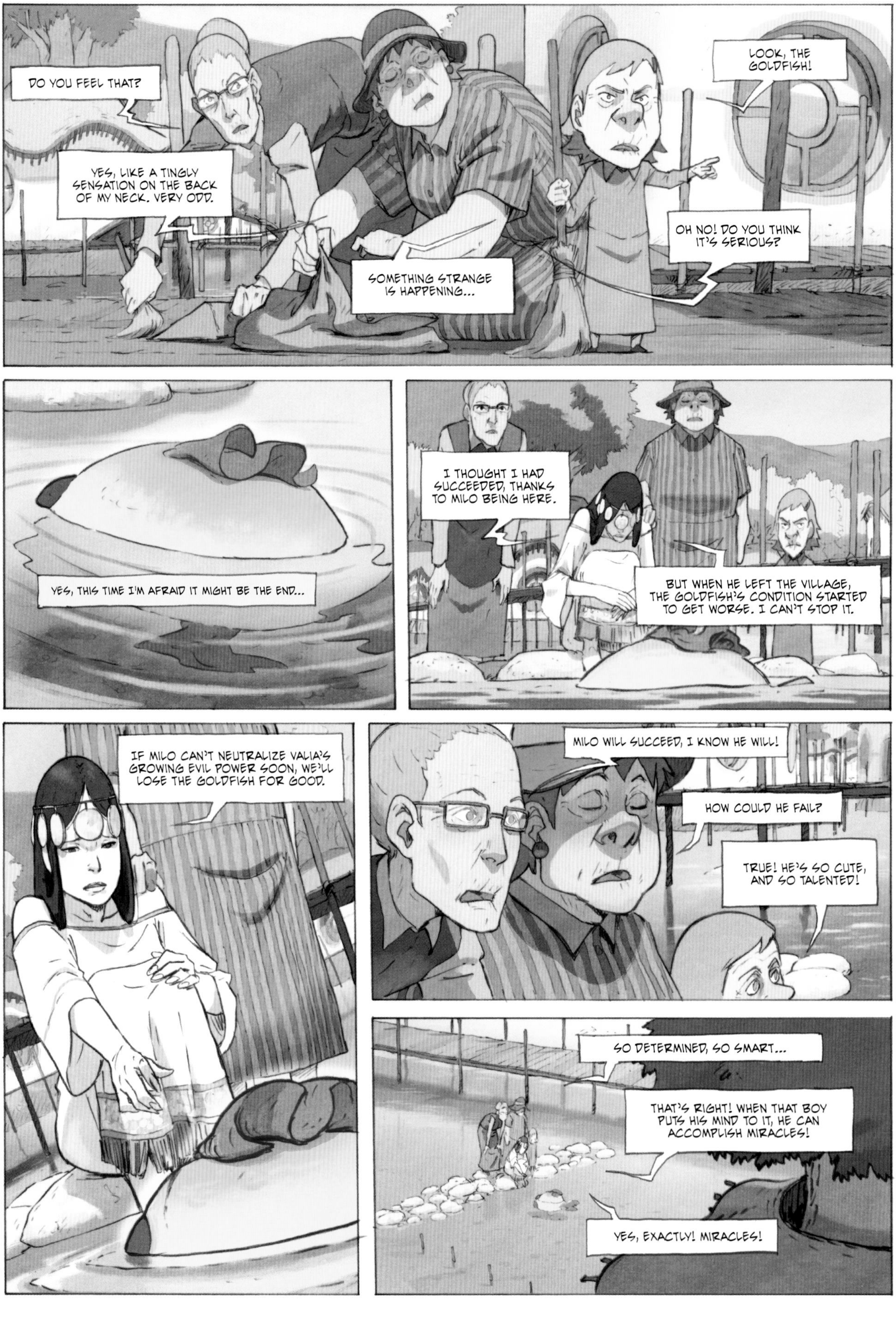

DO YOU FEEL THAT?
YES, LIKE A TINGLY SENSATION ON THE BACK OF MY NECK. VERY ODD.
SOMETHING STRANGE IS HAPPENING...
LOOK, THE GOLDFISH!
OH NO! DO YOU THINK IT'S SERIOUS?
YES, THIS TIME I'M AFRAID IT MIGHT BE THE END...
I THOUGHT I HAD SUCCEEDED, THANKS TO MILO BEING HERE.
BUT WHEN HE LEFT THE VILLAGE, THE GOLDFISH'S CONDITION STARTED TO GET WORSE. I CAN'T STOP IT.
IF MILO CAN'T NEUTRALIZE VALIA'S GROWING EVIL POWER SOON, WE'LL LOSE THE GOLDFISH FOR GOOD.
MILO WILL SUCCEED, I KNOW HE WILL!
HOW COULD HE FAIL?
TRUE! HE'S SO CUTE, AND SO TALENTED!
SO DETERMINED, SO SMART...
THAT'S RIGHT! WHEN THAT BOY PUTS HIS MIND TO IT, HE CAN ACCOMPLISH MIRACLES!
YES, EXACTLY! MIRACLES!

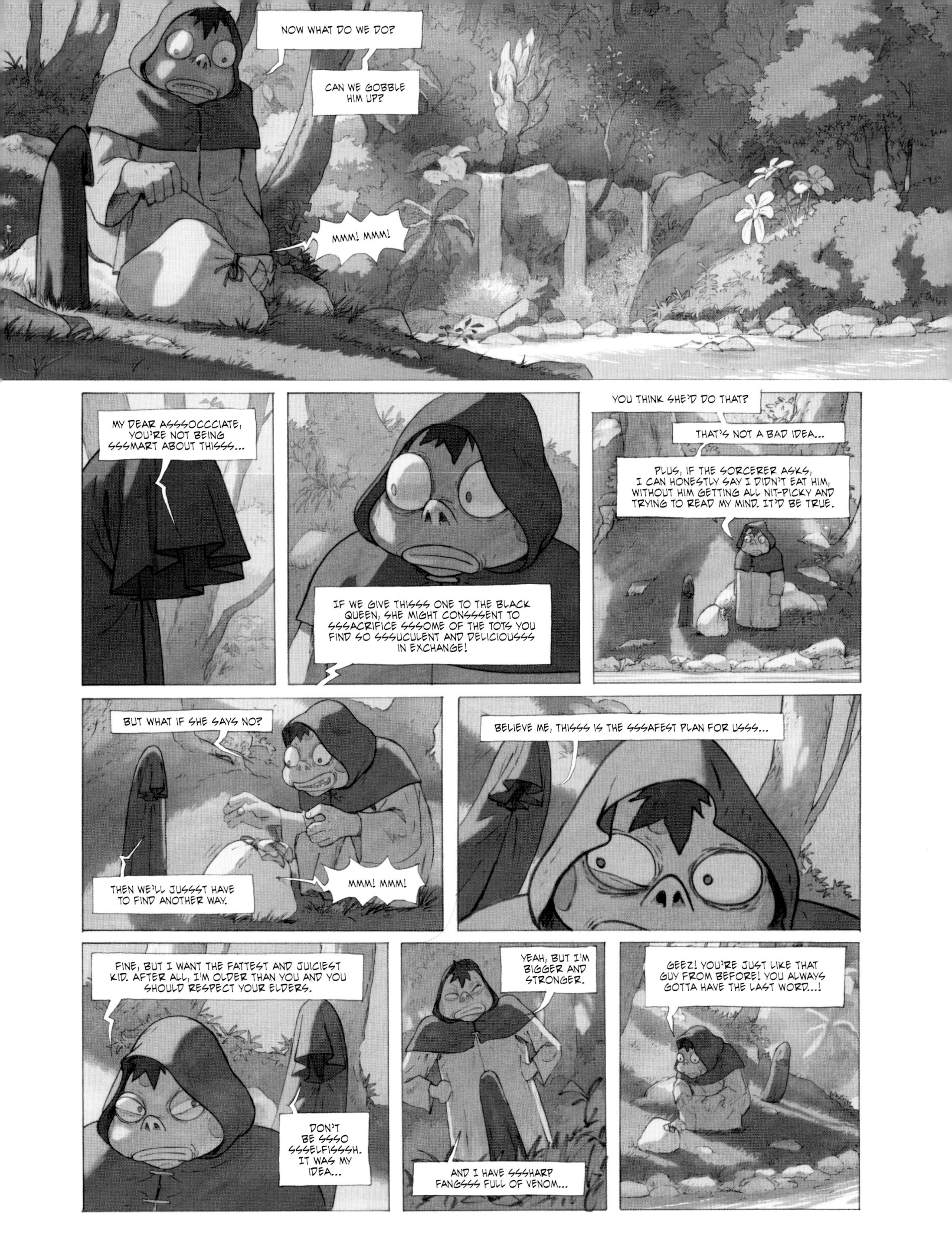
NOW WHAT DO WE DO?
CAN WE GOBBLE HIM UP?
MMM! MMM!
MY DEAR ASSSOCCCIATE, YOU'RE NOT BEING SSSMART ABOUT THISSS...
IF WE GIVE THISSS ONE TO THE BLACK QUEEN, SHE MIGHT CONSSSENT TO SSSACRIFICE SSSOME OF THE TOTS YOU FIND SO SSSUCULENT AND DELICIOUSSS IN EXCHANGE!
YOU THINK SHE'D DO THAT?
THAT'S NOT A BAD IDEA...
PLUS, IF THE SORCERER ASKS, I CAN HONESTLY SAY I DIDN'T EAT HIM, WITHOUT HIM GETTING ALL NIT-PICKY AND TRYING TO READ MY MIND. IT'D BE TRUE.
BUT WHAT IF SHE SAYS NO?
THEN WE'LL JUSSST HAVE TO FIND ANOTHER WAY.
MMM! MMM!
BELIEVE ME, THISSS IS THE SSSAFEST PLAN FOR USSS...
FINE, BUT I WANT THE FATTEST AND JUICIEST KID. AFTER ALL, I'M OLDER THAN YOU AND YOU SHOULD RESPECT YOUR ELDERS.
DON'T BE SSSO SSSELFISSSH. IT WAS MY IDEA...
YEAH, BUT I'M BIGGER AND STRONGER.
AND I HAVE SSSHARP FANGSSS FULL OF VENOM...
GEEZ! YOU'RE JUST LIKE THAT GUY FROM BEFORE! YOU ALWAYS GOTTA HAVE THE LAST WORD...!

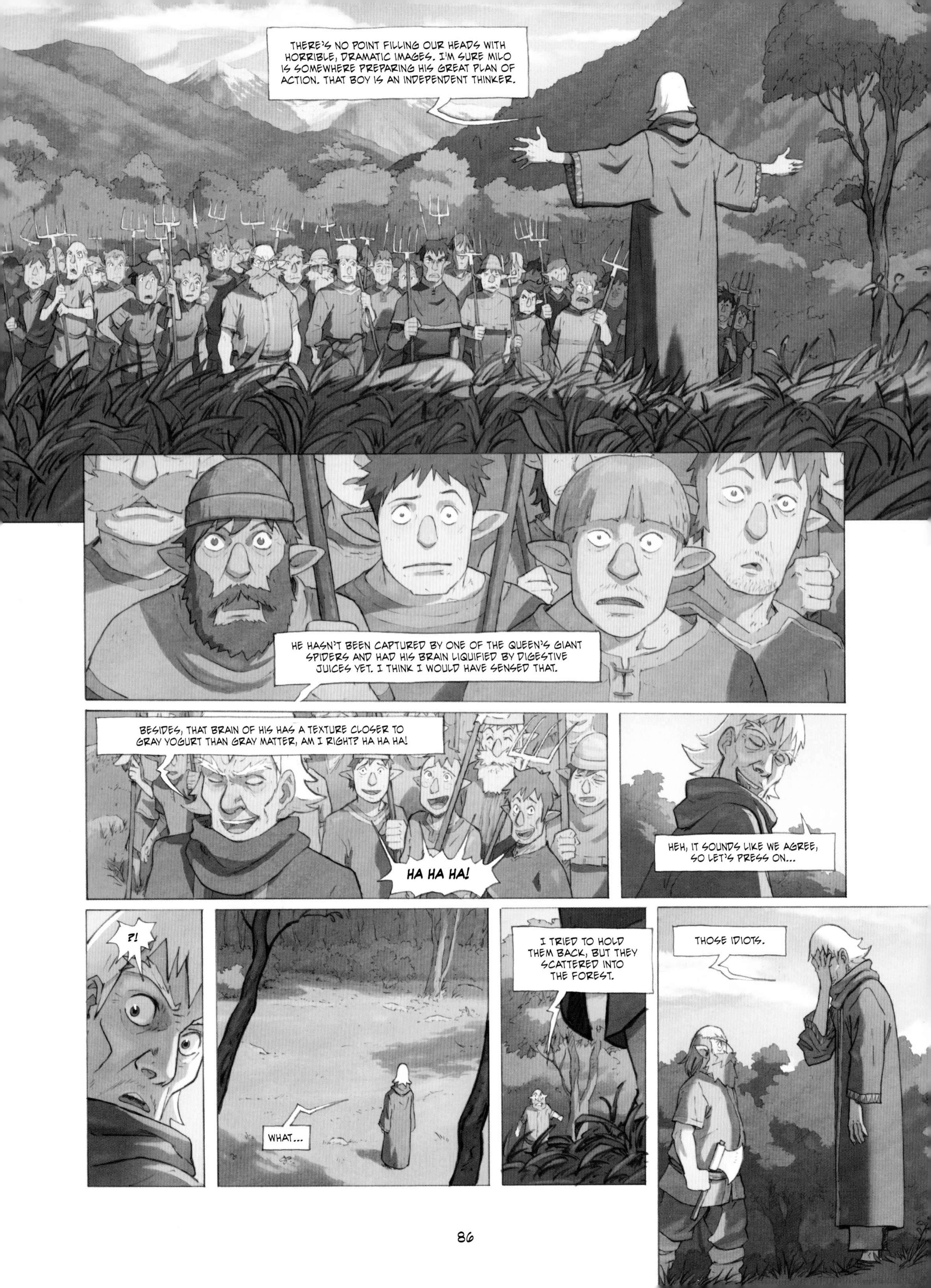
THERE'S NO POINT FILLING OUR HEADS WITH HORRIBLE, DRAMATIC IMAGES. I'M SURE MILO IS SOMEWHERE PREPARING HIS GREAT PLAN OF ACTION. THAT BOY IS AN INDEPENDENT THINKER.
HE HASN'T BEEN CAPTURED BY ONE OF THE QUEEN'S GIANT SPIDERS AND HAD HIS BRAIN LIQUIFIED BY DIGESTIVE JUICES YET. I THINK I WOULD HAVE SENSED THAT.
BESIDES, THAT BRAIN OF HIS HAS A TEXTURE CLOSER TO GRAY YOGURT THAN GRAY MATTER, AM I RIGHT? HA HA HA!
HA HA HA!
HEH, IT SOUNDS LIKE WE AGREE, SO LET'S PRESS ON...
?!
WHAT...
I TRIED TO HOLD THEM BACK, BUT THEY SCATTERED INTO THE FOREST.
THOSE IDIOTS.

YOU SURE WE CAN'T TAKE JUST ONE TINY LITTLE BITE?

I'M SICK OF CARRYING THIS PICNIC BASKET AND NOT BEING ABLE TO AT LEAST TASTE A LITTLE SAMPLE...

THE BLACK QUEEN WON'T EVEN NOTICE AND IT'LL LIGHTEN MY LOAD A BIT...

SBROOOF!

OOF!

HIS LEFT LEG, FOR INSTANCE. I BET HE DOESN'T USE THAT ONE AS MUCH AS THE OTHER ONE.

DON'T BE SSSILLY.

YOU'LL ATTRACT THE SSSORCERER'S ATTENTION.

THE SORCERER?! DON'T TALK ABOUT HIM! I DON'T WANT HIM TO TURN ME BACK INTO MY OLD FORM!

THEN DO AS I SSSAY AND FOLLOW ME!

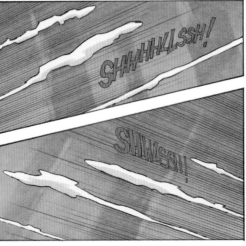

SHHHHHLSSH!

SHHSSH!

NOW WHAT DO WE DO?!

YOU KEEP GOING IF YOU WANT... I'LL JUST WAIT HERE.

HAH HAH. VERY FUNNY.

87

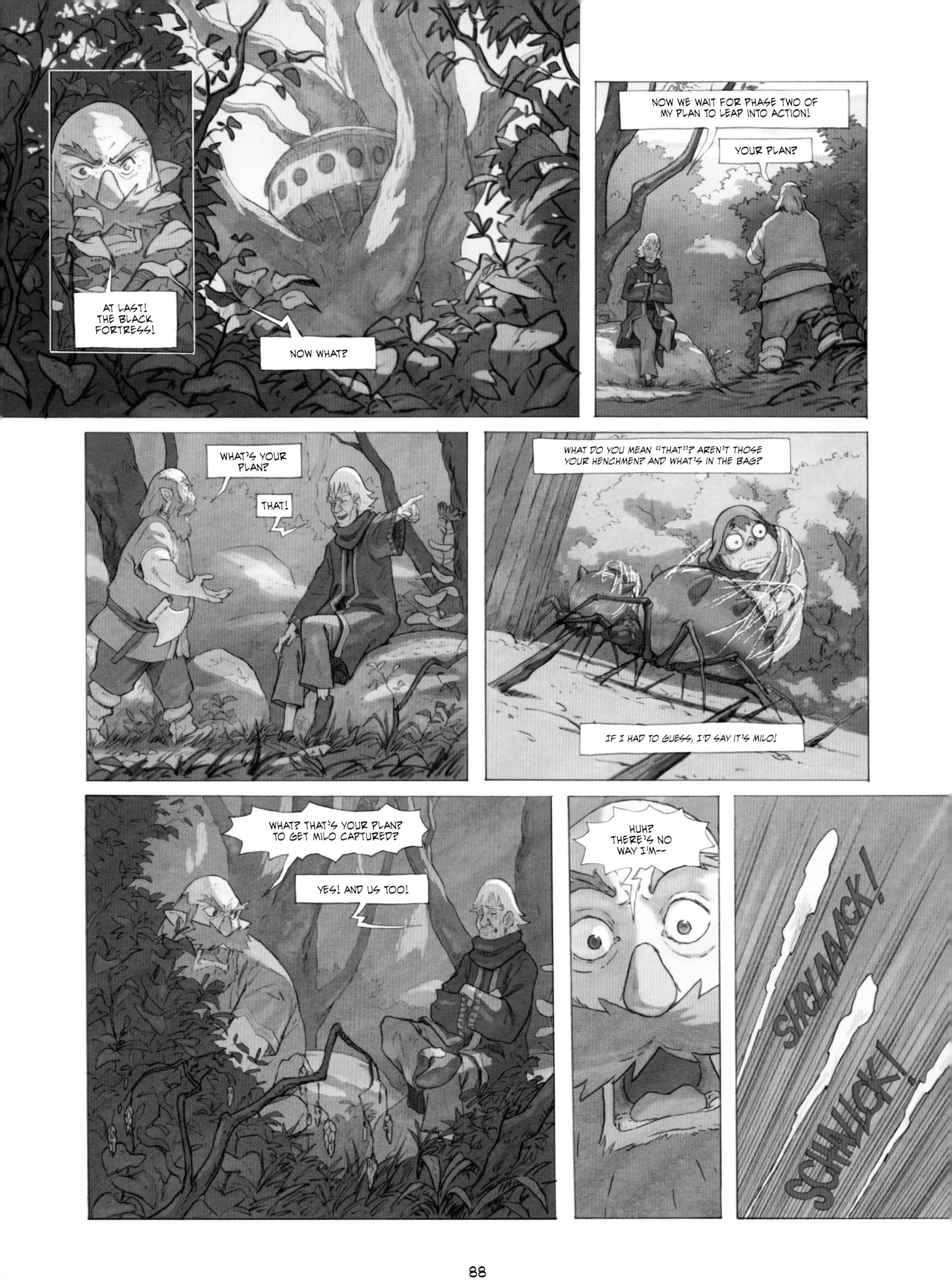

AT LAST! THE BLACK FORTRESS!
NOW WHAT?
NOW WE WAIT FOR PHASE TWO OF MY PLAN TO LEAP INTO ACTION!
YOUR PLAN?
WHAT'S YOUR PLAN?
THAT!
WHAT DO YOU MEAN "THAT"? AREN'T THOSE YOUR HENCHMEN? AND WHAT'S IN THE BAG?
IF I HAD TO GUESS, I'D SAY IT'S MILO!
WHAT? THAT'S YOUR PLAN? TO GET MILO CAPTURED?
YES! AND US TOO!
HUH? THERE'S NO WAY I'M--
SHCLAAACK!
SCHLUCK!

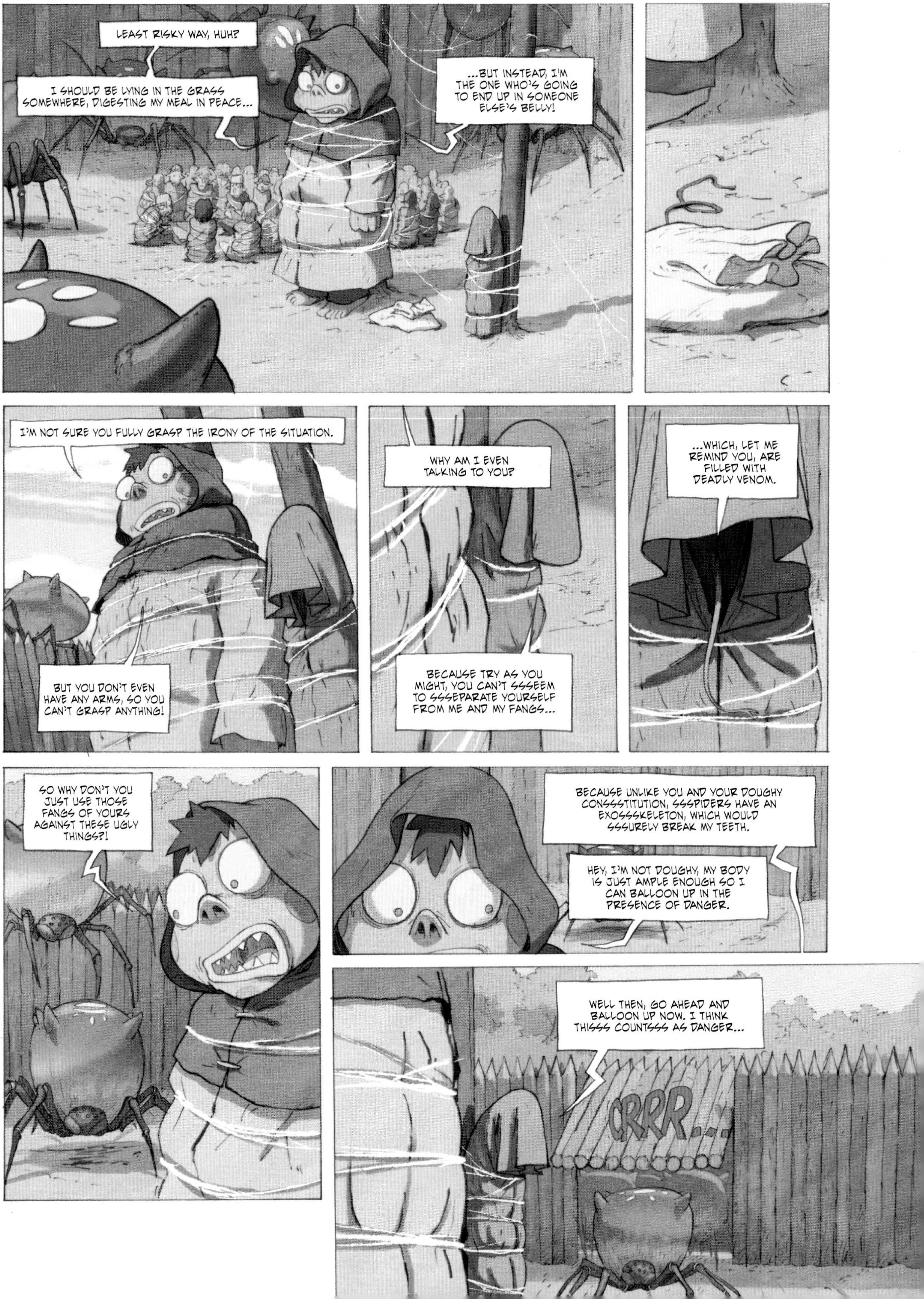
LEAST RISKY WAY, HUH?
I SHOULD BE LYING IN THE GRASS SOMEWHERE, DIGESTING MY MEAL IN PEACE...
...BUT INSTEAD, I'M THE ONE WHO'S GOING TO END UP IN SOMEONE ELSE'S BELLY!
I'M NOT SURE YOU FULLY GRASP THE IRONY OF THE SITUATION.
BUT YOU DON'T EVEN HAVE ANY ARMS, SO YOU CAN'T GRASP ANYTHING!
WHY AM I EVEN TALKING TO YOU?
BECAUSE TRY AS YOU MIGHT, YOU CAN'T SSSEEM TO SSSEPARATE YOURSELF FROM ME AND MY FANGS...
...WHICH, LET ME REMIND YOU, ARE FILLED WITH DEADLY VENOM.
SO WHY DON'T YOU JUST USE THOSE FANGS OF YOURS AGAINST THESE UGLY THINGS?!
BECAUSE UNLIKE YOU AND YOUR DOUGHY CONSSSTITUTION, SSSPIDERS HAVE AN EXOSSSKELETON, WHICH WOULD SSSURELY BREAK MY TEETH.
HEY, I'M NOT DOUGHY, MY BODY IS JUST AMPLE ENOUGH SO I CAN BALLOON UP IN THE PRESENCE OF DANGER.
WELL THEN, GO AHEAD AND BALLOON UP NOW. I THINK THISSS COUNTSSS AS DANGER...
CRRR...

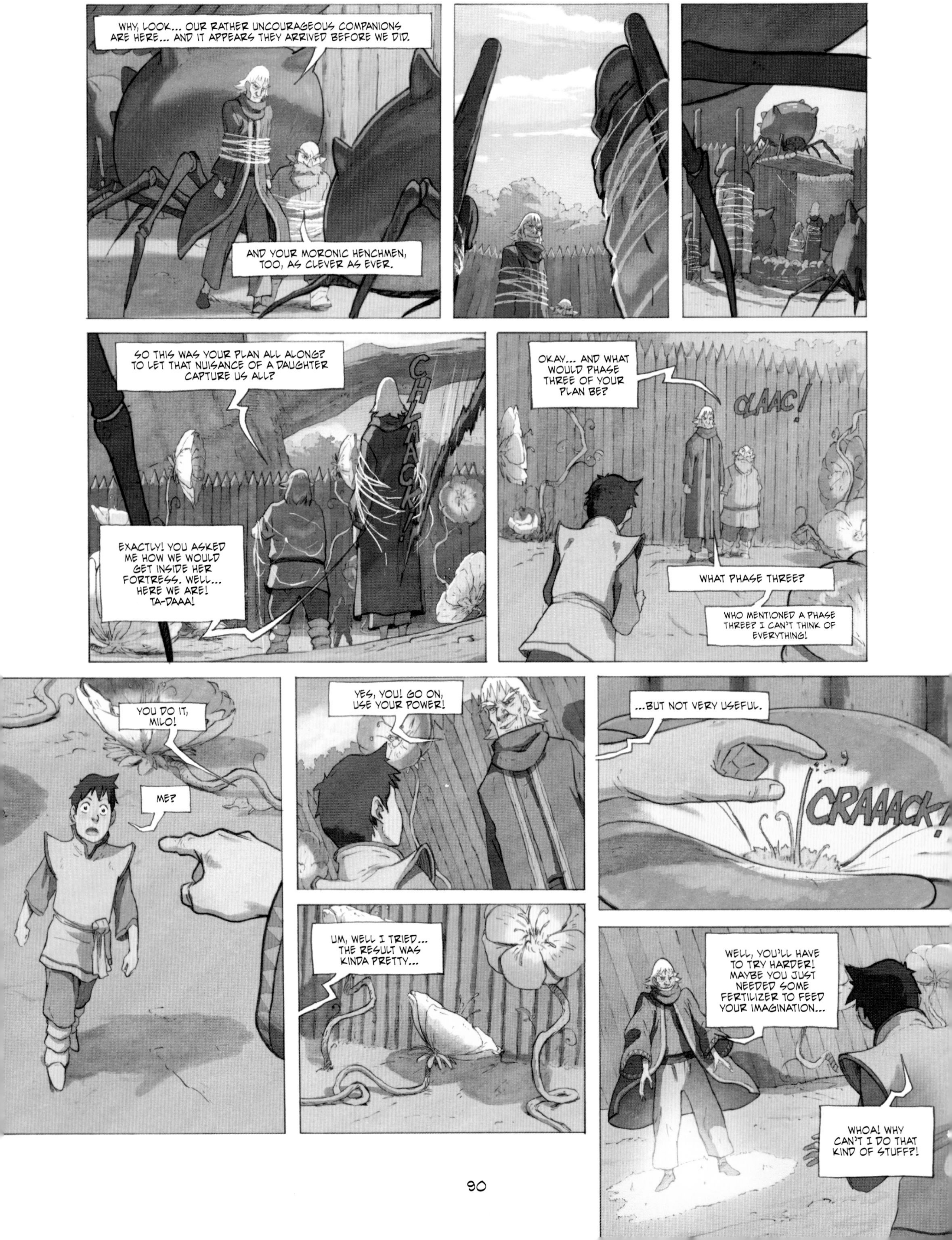
WHY, LOOK... OUR RATHER UNCOURAGEOUS COMPANIONS ARE HERE... AND IT APPEARS THEY ARRIVED BEFORE WE DID.
AND YOUR MORONIC HENCHMEN, TOO, AS CLEVER AS EVER.
SO THIS WAS YOUR PLAN ALL ALONG? TO LET THAT NUISANCE OF A DAUGHTER CAPTURE US ALL?
CHLAACK!
EXACTLY! YOU ASKED ME HOW WE WOULD GET INSIDE HER FORTRESS. WELL... HERE WE ARE! TA-DAAA!
OKAY... AND WHAT WOULD PHASE THREE OF YOUR PLAN BE?
CLAAC!
WHAT PHASE THREE?
WHO MENTIONED A PHASE THREE? I CAN'T THINK OF EVERYTHING!
YOU DO IT, MILO!
ME?
YES, YOU! GO ON, USE YOUR POWER!
UM, WELL I TRIED... THE RESULT WAS KINDA PRETTY...
...BUT NOT VERY USEFUL.
CRAAACK!
WELL, YOU'LL HAVE TO TRY HARDER! MAYBE YOU JUST NEEDED SOME FERTILIZER TO FEED YOUR IMAGINATION...
WHOA! WHY CAN'T I DO THAT KIND OF STUFF?!

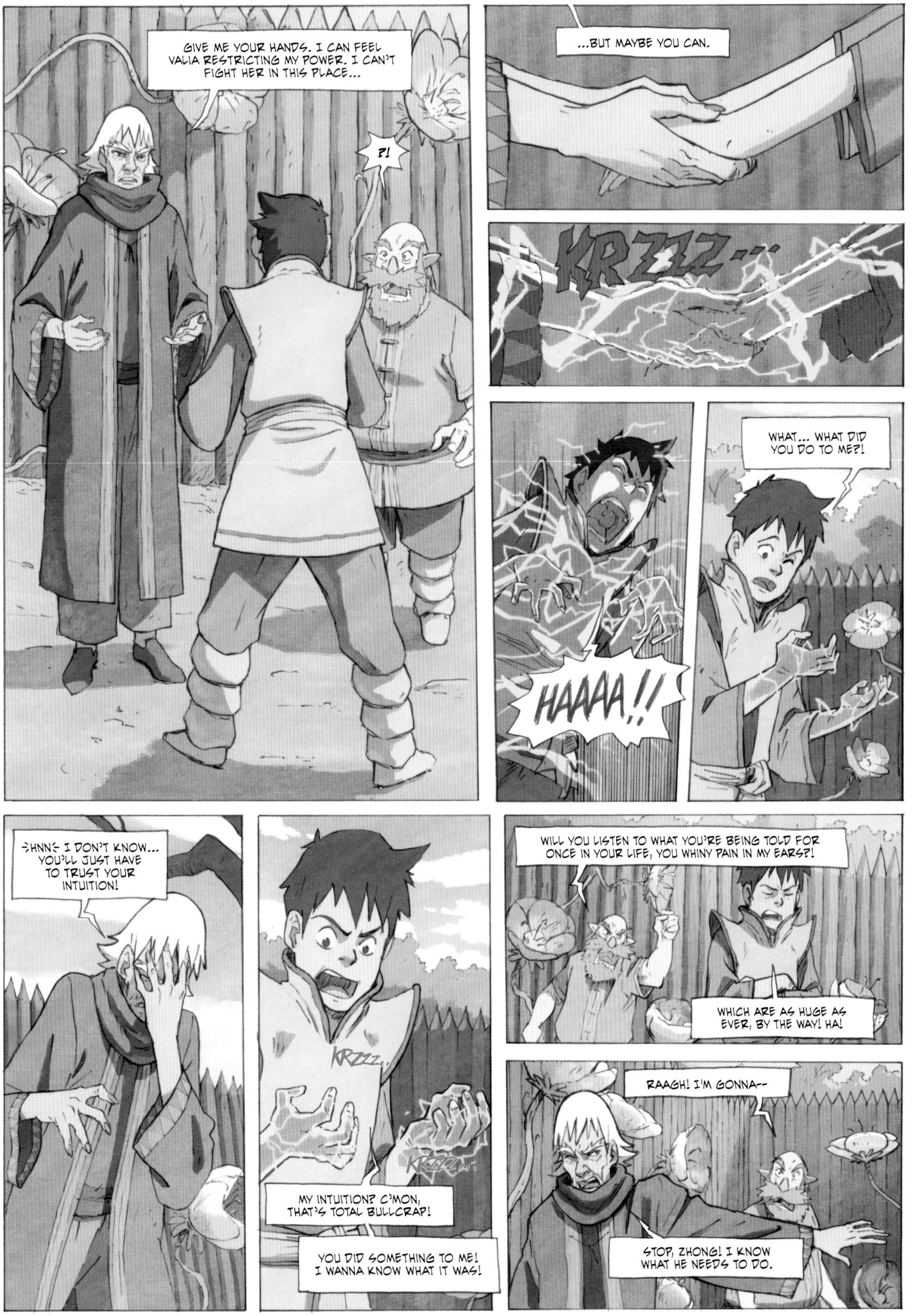
GIVE ME YOUR HANDS. I CAN FEEL VALIA RESTRICTING MY POWER. I CAN'T FIGHT HER IN THIS PLACE...
?!
...BUT MAYBE YOU CAN.
KRZZZ...
HAAAA!!
WHAT... WHAT DID YOU DO TO ME?!
~HNN~ I DON'T KNOW... YOU'LL JUST HAVE TO TRUST YOUR INTUITION!
KRZZZ...
MY INTUITION? C'MON, THAT'S TOTAL BULLCRAP!
YOU DID SOMETHING TO ME! I WANNA KNOW WHAT IT WAS!
WILL YOU LISTEN TO WHAT YOU'RE BEING TOLD FOR ONCE IN YOUR LIFE, YOU WHINY PAIN IN MY EARS?!
WHICH ARE AS HUGE AS EVER, BY THE WAY! HA!
RAAGH! I'M GONNA--
STOP, ZHONG! I KNOW WHAT HE NEEDS TO DO.

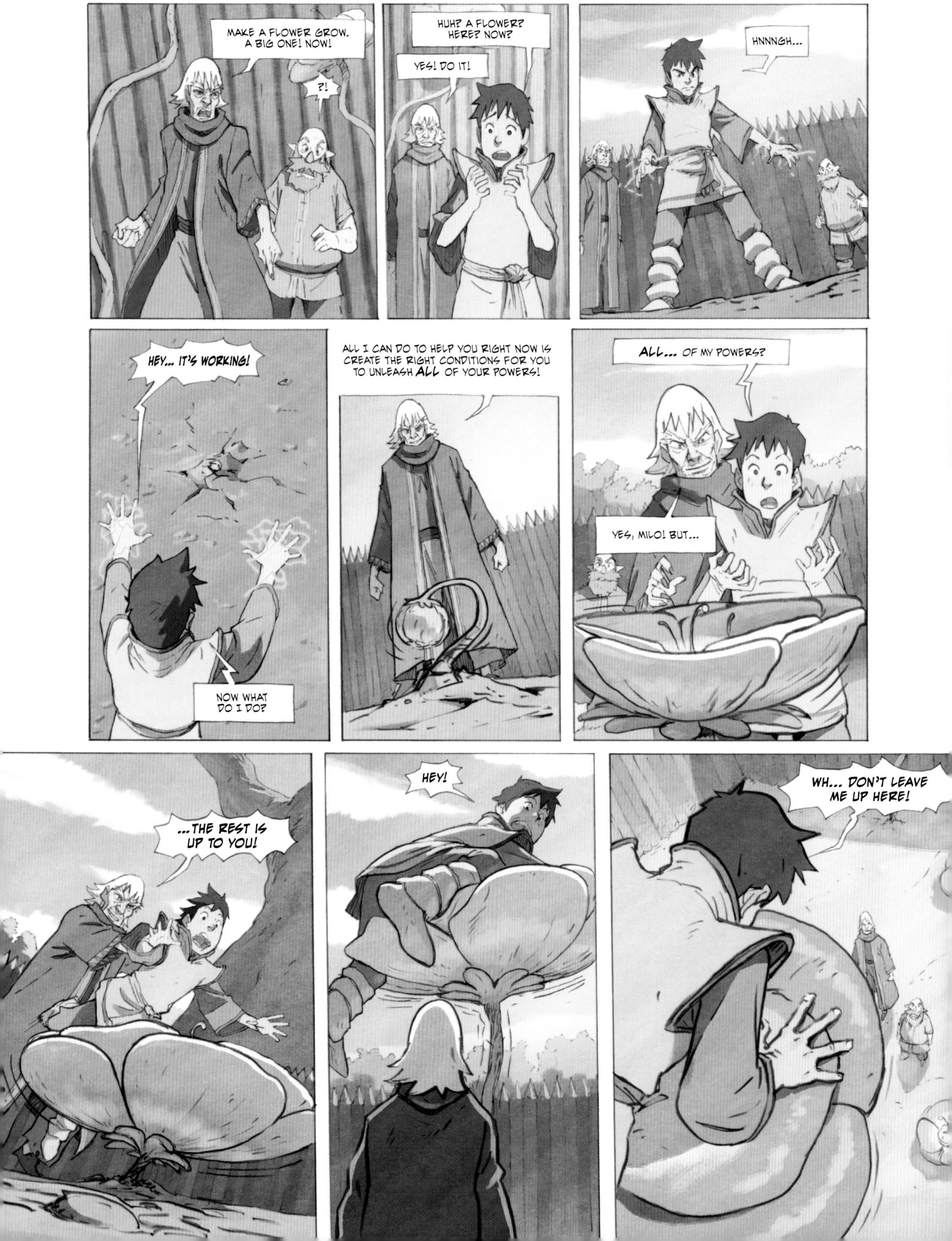

MAKE A FLOWER GROW. A BIG ONE! NOW!
?!
HUH? A FLOWER? HERE? NOW?
YES! DO IT!
HNNNGH...
HEY... IT'S WORKING!
NOW WHAT DO I DO?
ALL I CAN DO TO HELP YOU RIGHT NOW IS CREATE THE RIGHT CONDITIONS FOR YOU TO UNLEASH ALL OF YOUR POWERS!
ALL... OF MY POWERS?
YES, MILO! BUT...
...THE REST IS UP TO YOU!
HEY!
WH... DON'T LEAVE ME UP HERE!

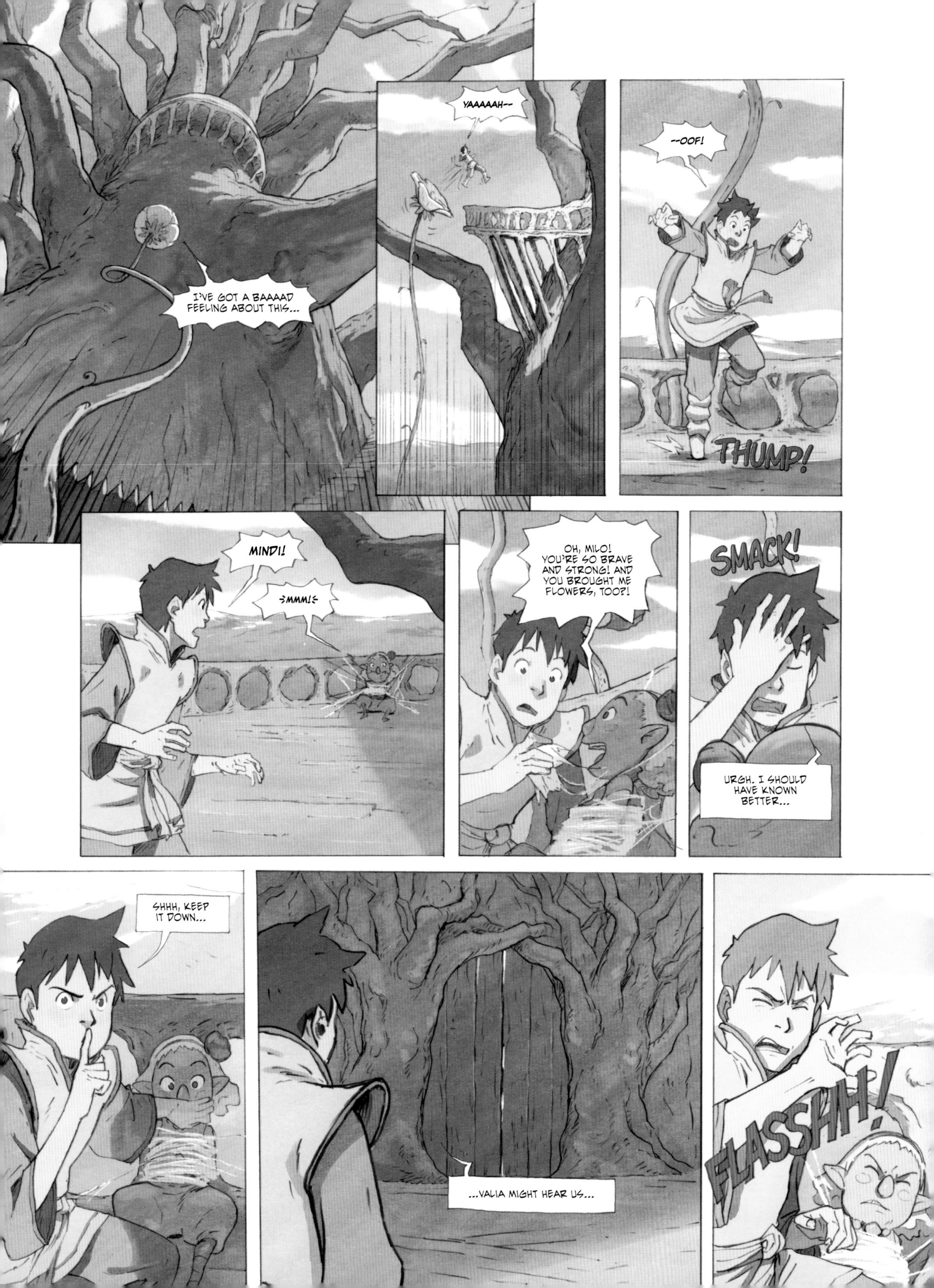
I'VE GOT A BAAAAD FEELING ABOUT THIS...
YAAAAAH--
--OOF!
THUMP!
MINDI!
MMM!
OH, MILO! YOU'RE SO BRAVE AND STRONG! AND YOU BROUGHT ME FLOWERS, TOO?!
SMACK!
URGH. I SHOULD HAVE KNOWN BETTER...
SHHH, KEEP IT DOWN...
...VALIA MIGHT HEAR US...
FLASSHH!

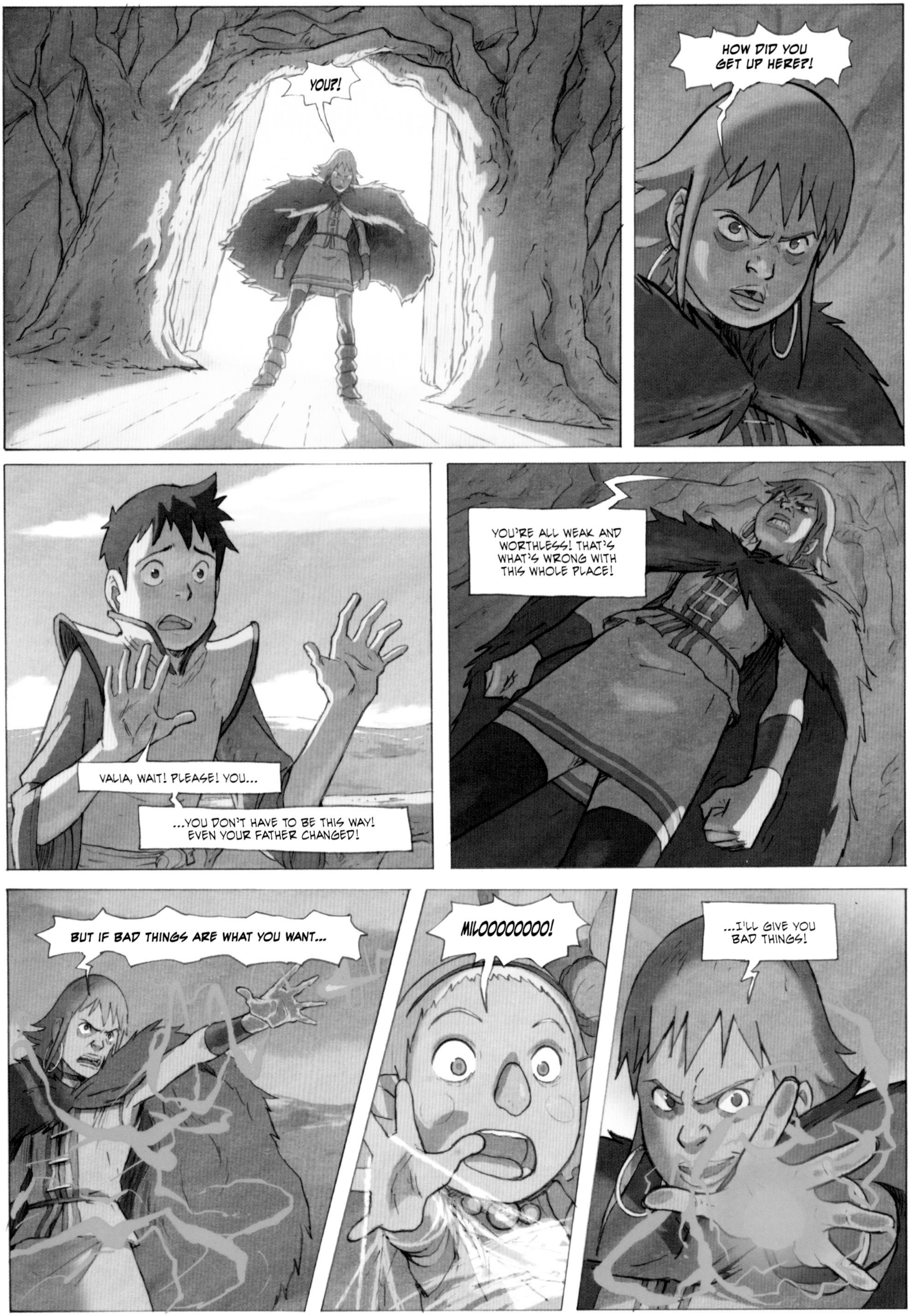
YOU?!
HOW DID YOU GET UP HERE?!
YOU'RE ALL WEAK AND WORTHLESS! THAT'S WHAT'S WRONG WITH THIS WHOLE PLACE!
VALIA, WAIT! PLEASE! YOU...
...YOU DON'T HAVE TO BE THIS WAY! EVEN YOUR FATHER CHANGED!
BUT IF BAD THINGS ARE WHAT YOU WANT...
MILOOOOOOOO!
...I'LL GIVE YOU BAD THINGS!

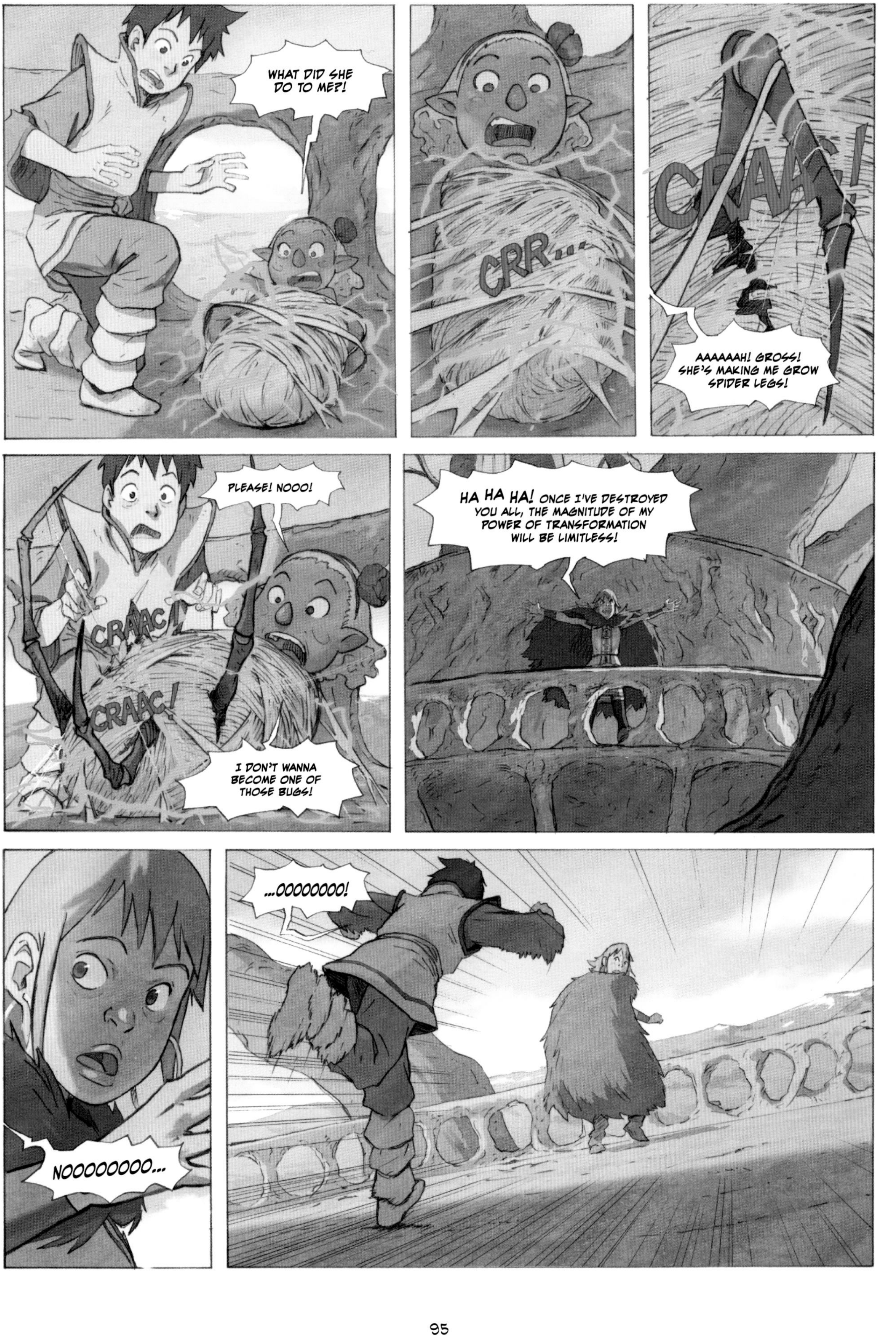
WHAT DID SHE DO TO ME?!
CRR...
CRAAC!
AAAAAAH! GROSS! SHE'S MAKING ME GROW SPIDER LEGS!
PLEASE! NOOO!
CRAAC!
CRAAC!
I DON'T WANNA BECOME ONE OF THOSE BUGS!
HA HA HA! ONCE I'VE DESTROYED YOU ALL, THE MAGNITUDE OF MY POWER OF TRANSFORMATION WILL BE LIMITLESS!
NOOOOOOOO...
...OOOOOOOO!

YOU HAVE TO DO SOMETHING!

I... I CAN'T...

LOOK WHERE THEY'RE FALLING! YOU CAN SSAY GOODBYE TO YOUR SSSNACK ONCE AND FOR ALL!

OH, NOOO...

...

...

SBROUF!

96

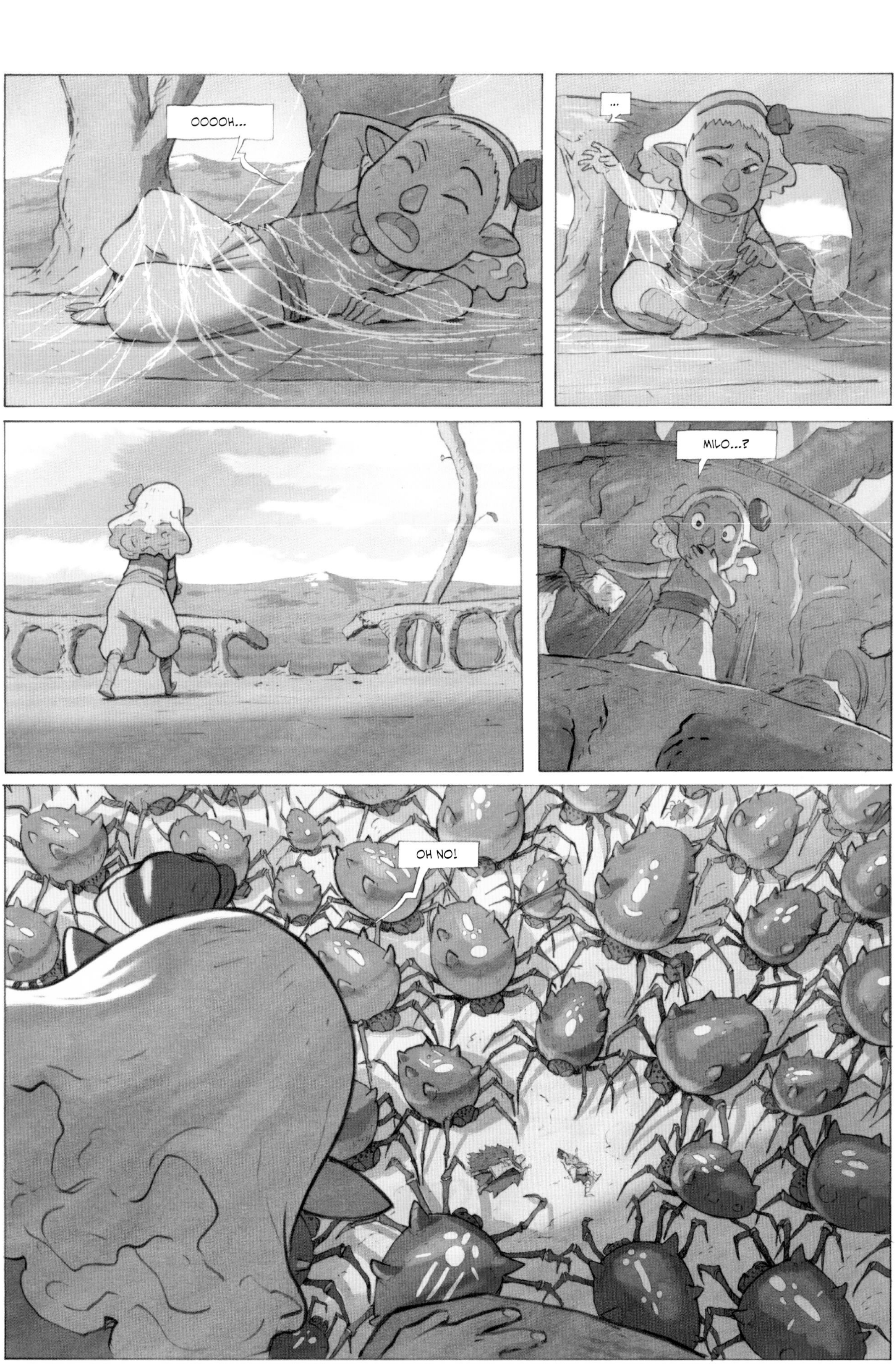
OOOOH...
...
MILO...?
OH NO!

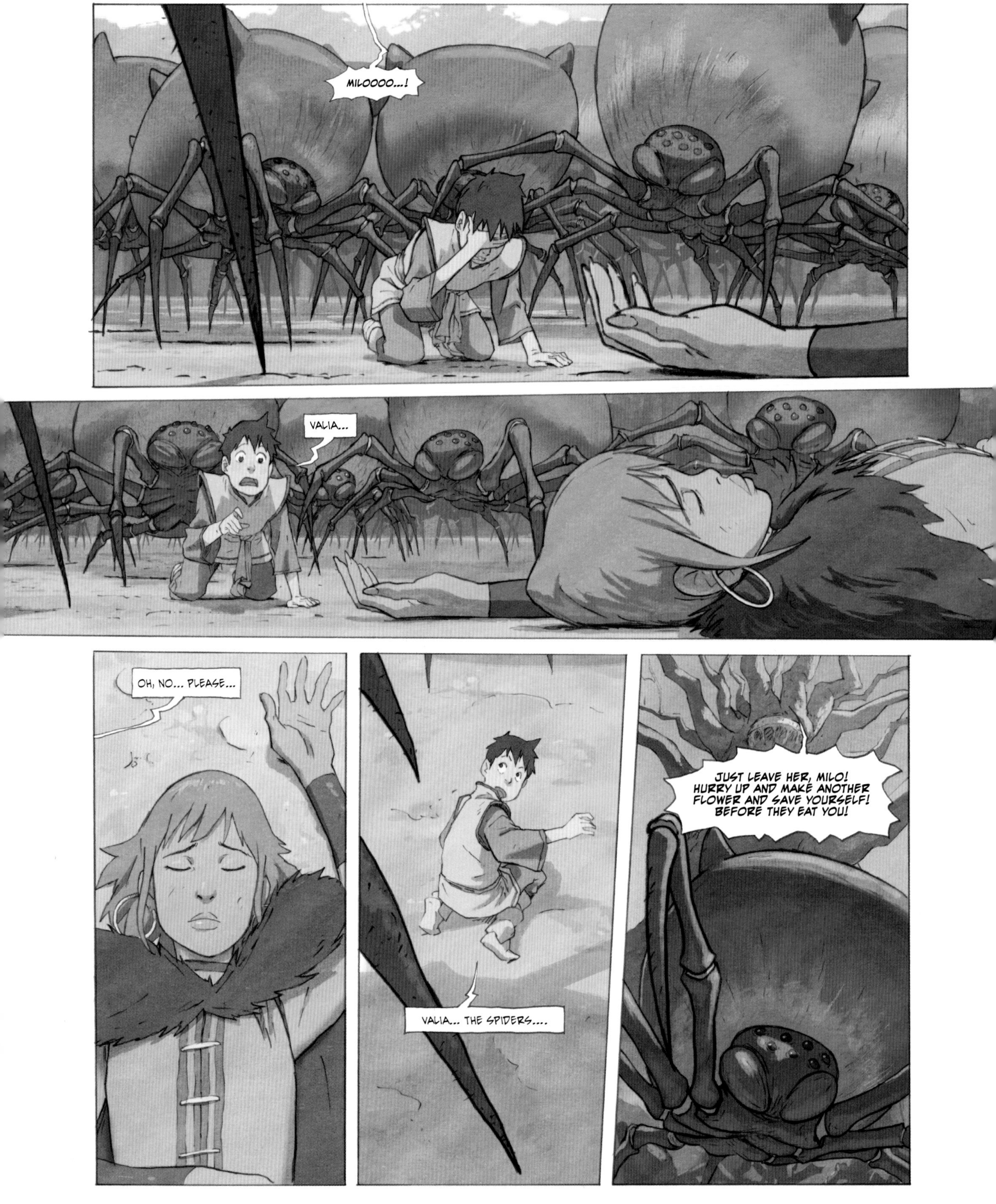
MILOOOO...!
VALIA...
OH, NO... PLEASE...
VALIA... THE SPIDERS....
JUST LEAVE HER, MILO! HURRY UP AND MAKE ANOTHER FLOWER AND SAVE YOURSELF! BEFORE THEY EAT YOU!

VALIA...

YOUR OWN BUGS ARE GONNA EAT YOU ALIVE!

MILO... IS... IS THAT YOU?

VALIA!

HOLD ON!

I WON'T LET THEM HURT YOU!

KRZZ...

KRZZ...

ENOUGH!

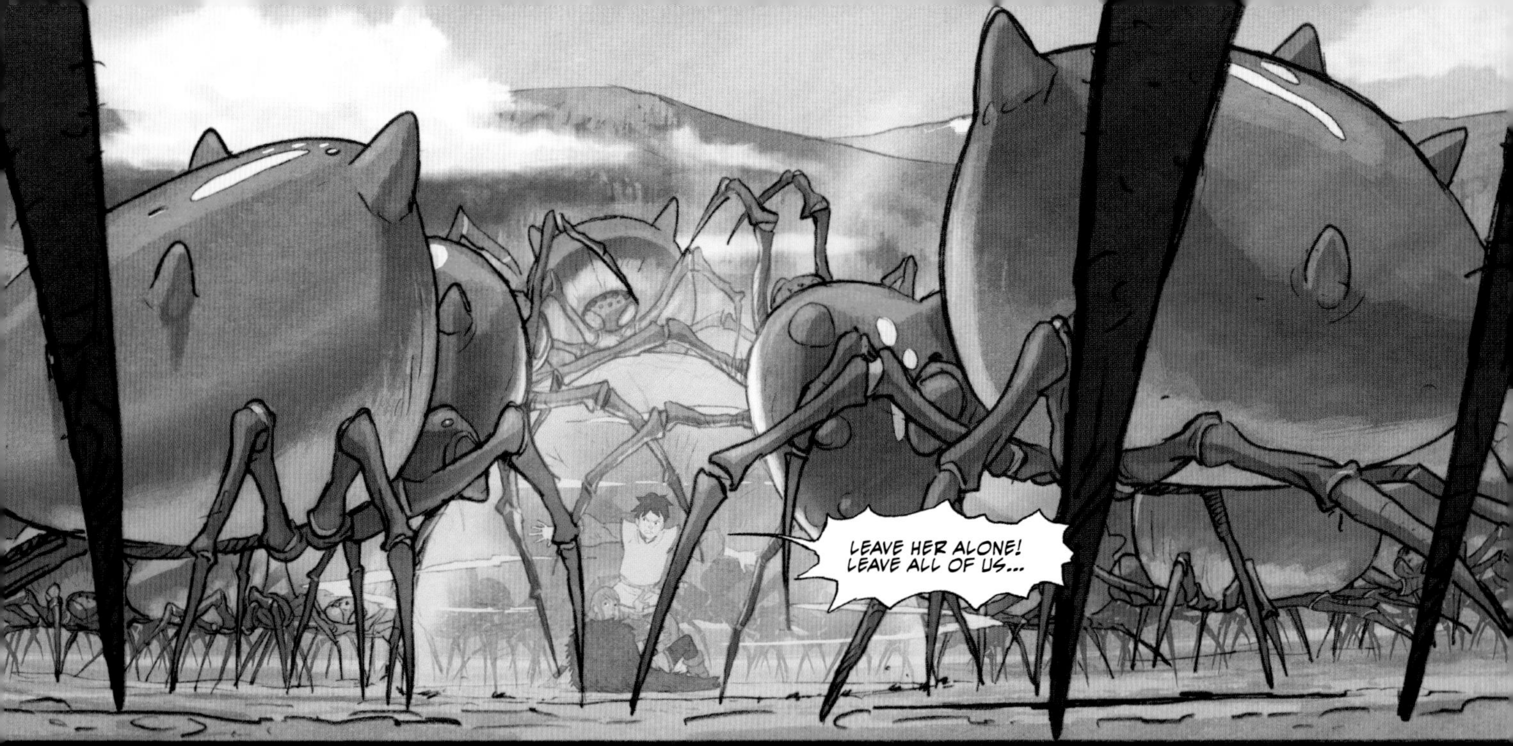
LEAVE HER ALONE! LEAVE ALL OF US...

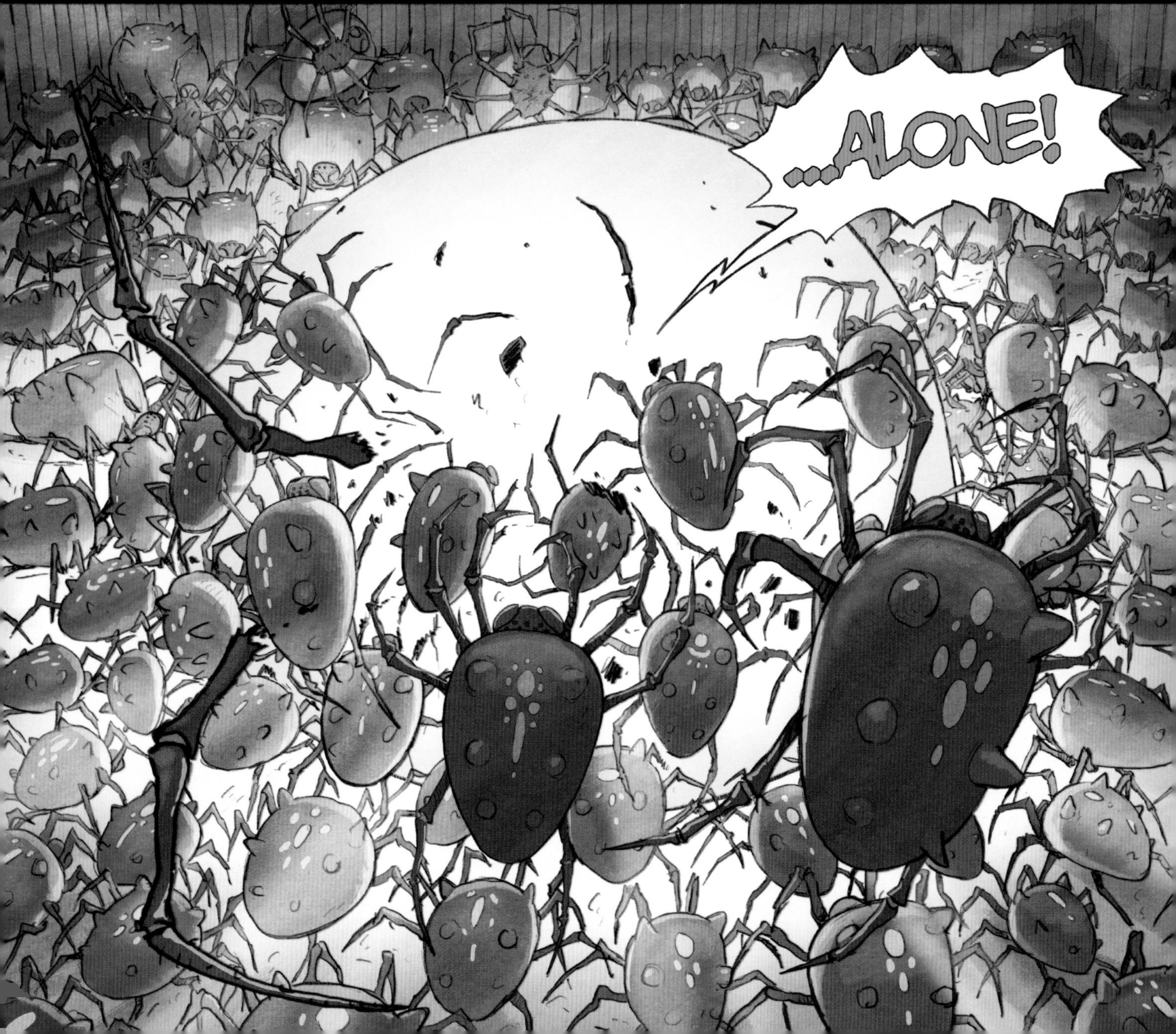
...ALONE!

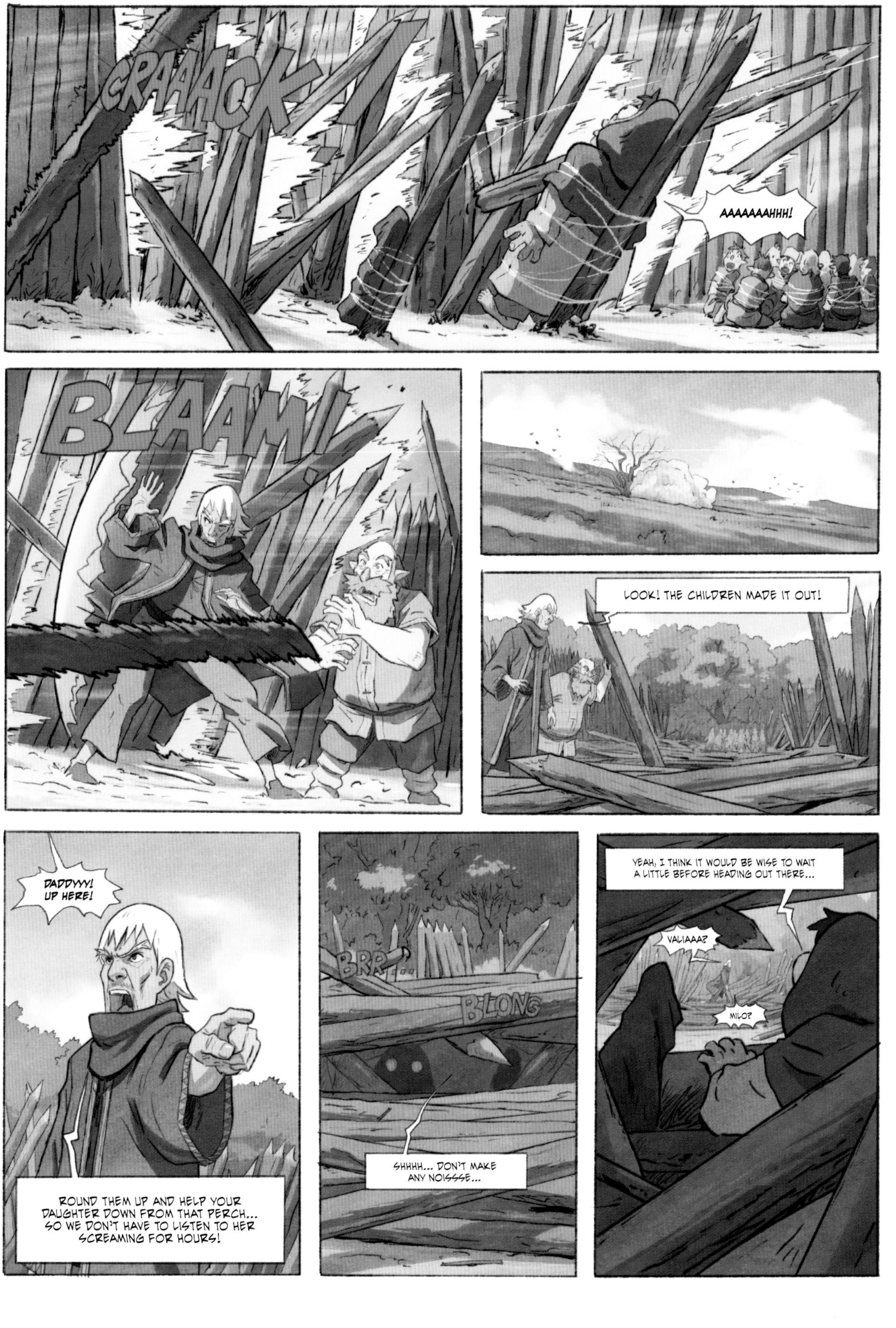
CRAAACK
AAAAAAAHHH!
BLAAM!
LOOK! THE CHILDREN MADE IT OUT!
DADDYYY! UP HERE!
ROUND THEM UP AND HELP YOUR DAUGHTER DOWN FROM THAT PERCH... SO WE DON'T HAVE TO LISTEN TO HER SCREAMING FOR HOURS!
BRR...
BLONG
SHHHH... DON'T MAKE ANY NOISSSE...
YEAH, I THINK IT WOULD BE WISE TO WAIT A LITTLE BEFORE HEADING OUT THERE...
VALIAAA?
MILO?

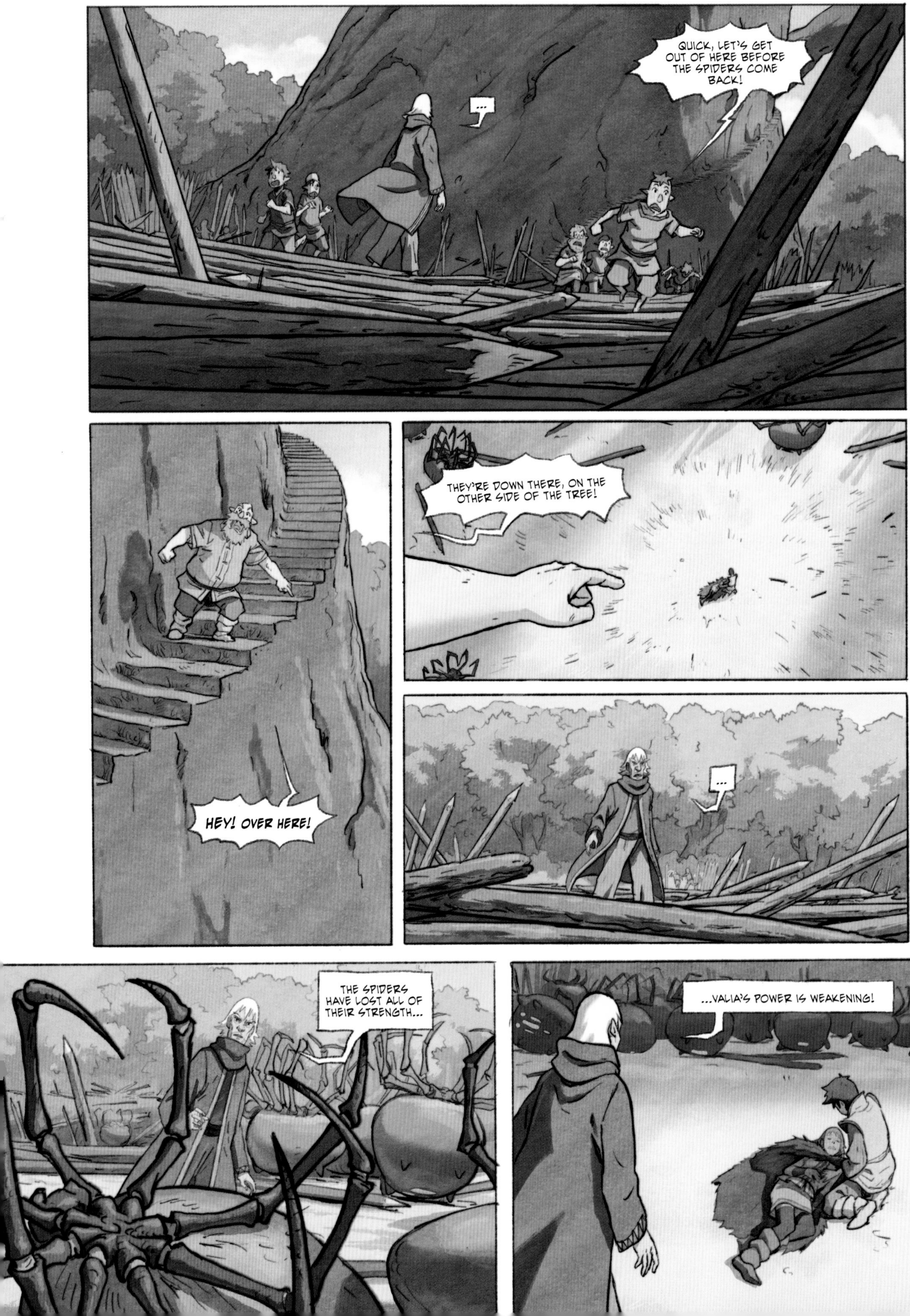
...
QUICK, LET'S GET OUT OF HERE BEFORE THE SPIDERS COME BACK!
HEY! OVER HERE!
THEY'RE DOWN THERE, ON THE OTHER SIDE OF THE TREE!
...
THE SPIDERS HAVE LOST ALL OF THEIR STRENGTH...
...VALIA'S POWER IS WEAKENING!

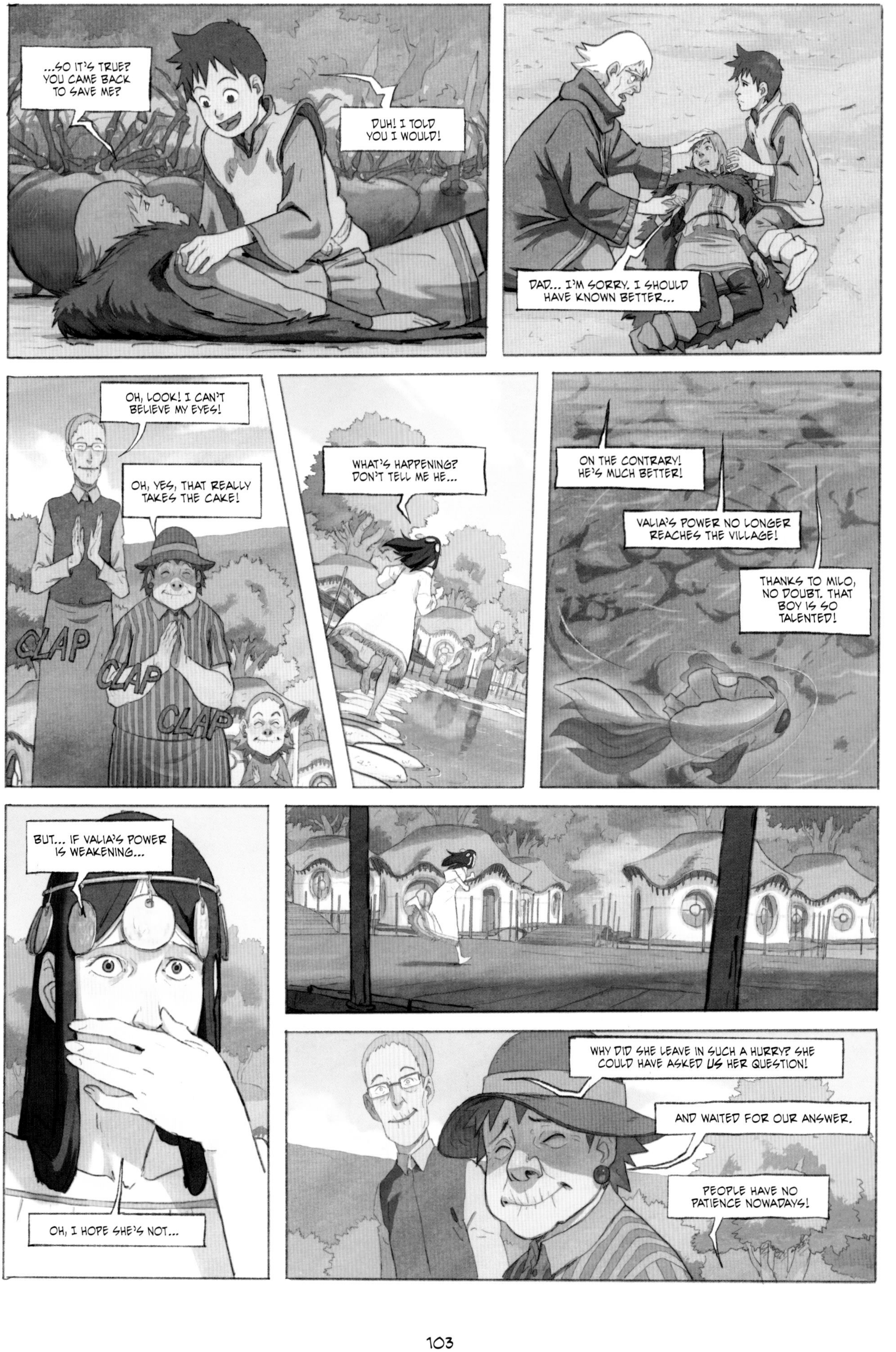
...SO IT'S TRUE? YOU CAME BACK TO SAVE ME?
DUH! I TOLD YOU I WOULD!
DAD... I'M SORRY. I SHOULD HAVE KNOWN BETTER...
OH, LOOK! I CAN'T BELIEVE MY EYES!
OH, YES, THAT REALLY TAKES THE CAKE!
CLAP
CLAP
CLAP
WHAT'S HAPPENING? DON'T TELL ME HE...
ON THE CONTRARY! HE'S MUCH BETTER!
VALIA'S POWER NO LONGER REACHES THE VILLAGE!
THANKS TO MILO, NO DOUBT. THAT BOY IS SO TALENTED!
BUT... IF VALIA'S POWER IS WEAKENING...
OH, I HOPE SHE'S NOT...
WHY DID SHE LEAVE IN SUCH A HURRY? SHE COULD HAVE ASKED US HER QUESTION!
AND WAITED FOR OUR ANSWER.
PEOPLE HAVE NO PATIENCE NOWADAYS!

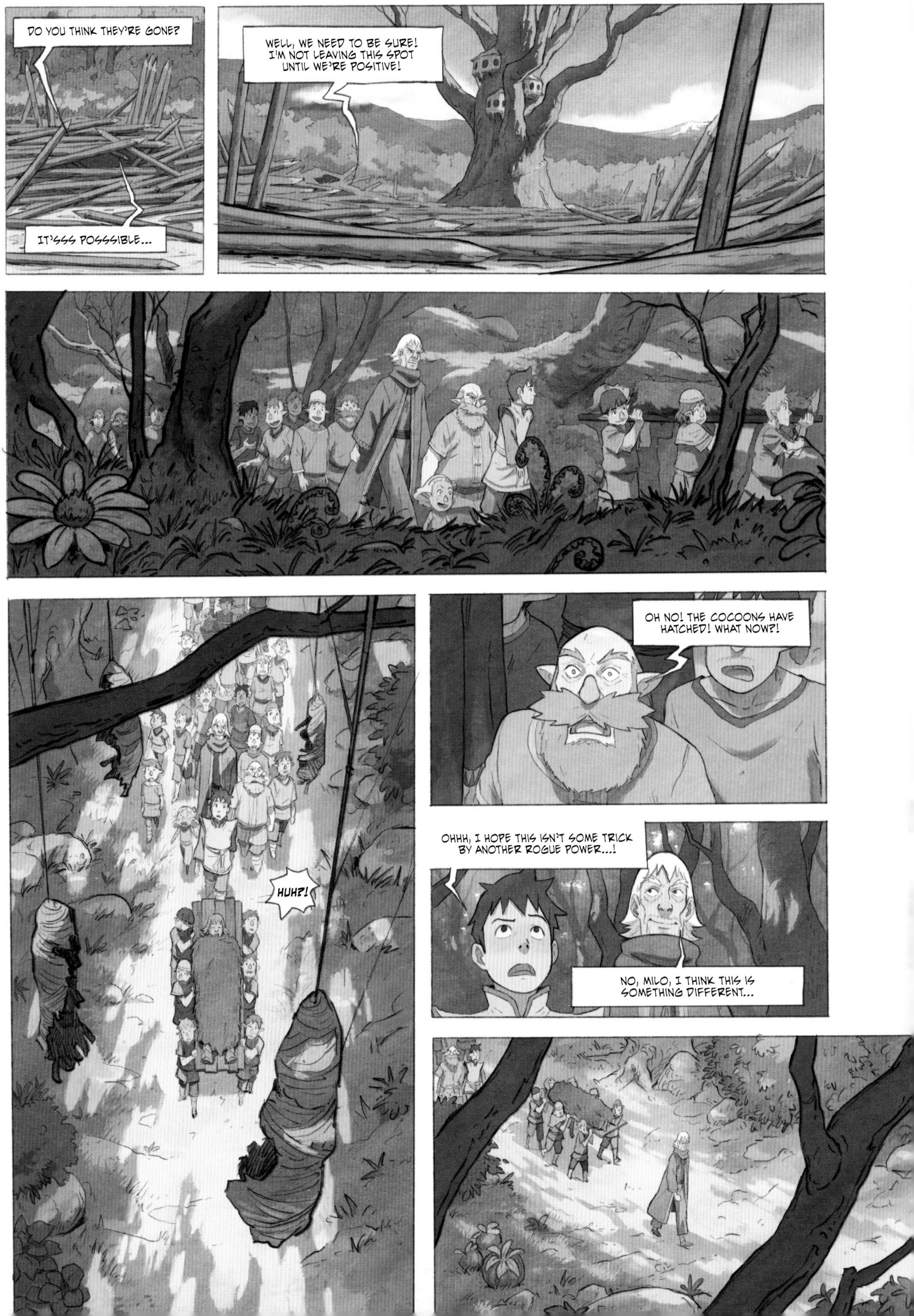
DO YOU THINK THEY'RE GONE?
IT'SSS POSSSIBLE...
WELL, WE NEED TO BE SURE! I'M NOT LEAVING THIS SPOT UNTIL WE'RE POSITIVE!
HUH?!
OH NO! THE COCOONS HAVE HATCHED! WHAT NOW?!
OHHH, I HOPE THIS ISN'T SOME TRICK BY ANOTHER ROGUE POWER...!
NO, MILO, I THINK THIS IS SOMETHING DIFFERENT...

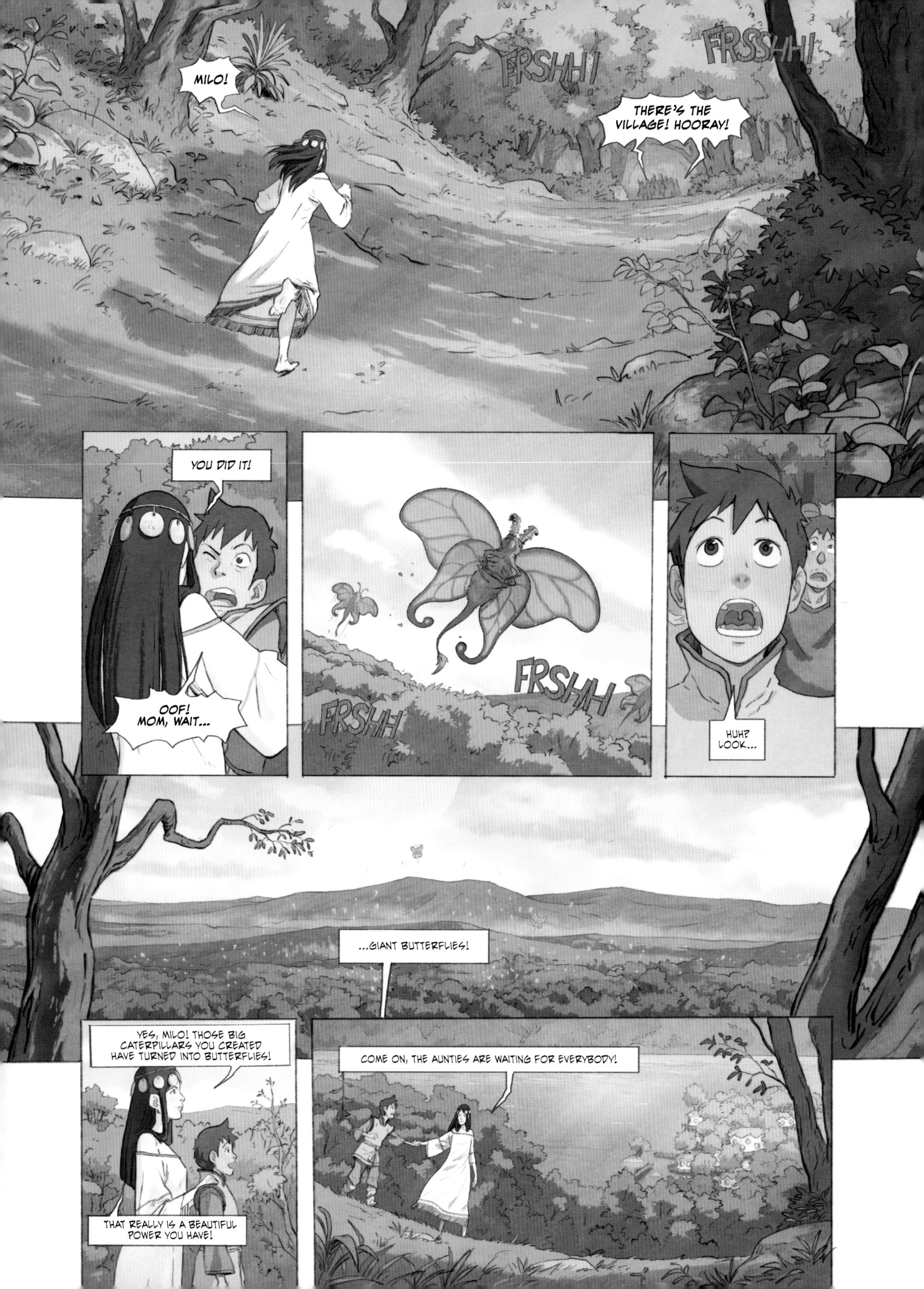
MILO!
FRSHH!
FRSSHH!
THERE'S THE VILLAGE! HOORAY!
YOU DID IT!
OOF! MOM, WAIT...
FRSHH
FRSHH
HUH? LOOK...
...GIANT BUTTERFLIES!
YES, MILO! THOSE BIG CATERPILLARS YOU CREATED HAVE TURNED INTO BUTTERFLIES!
THAT REALLY IS A BEAUTIFUL POWER YOU HAVE!
COME ON, THE AUNTIES ARE WAITING FOR EVERYBODY!

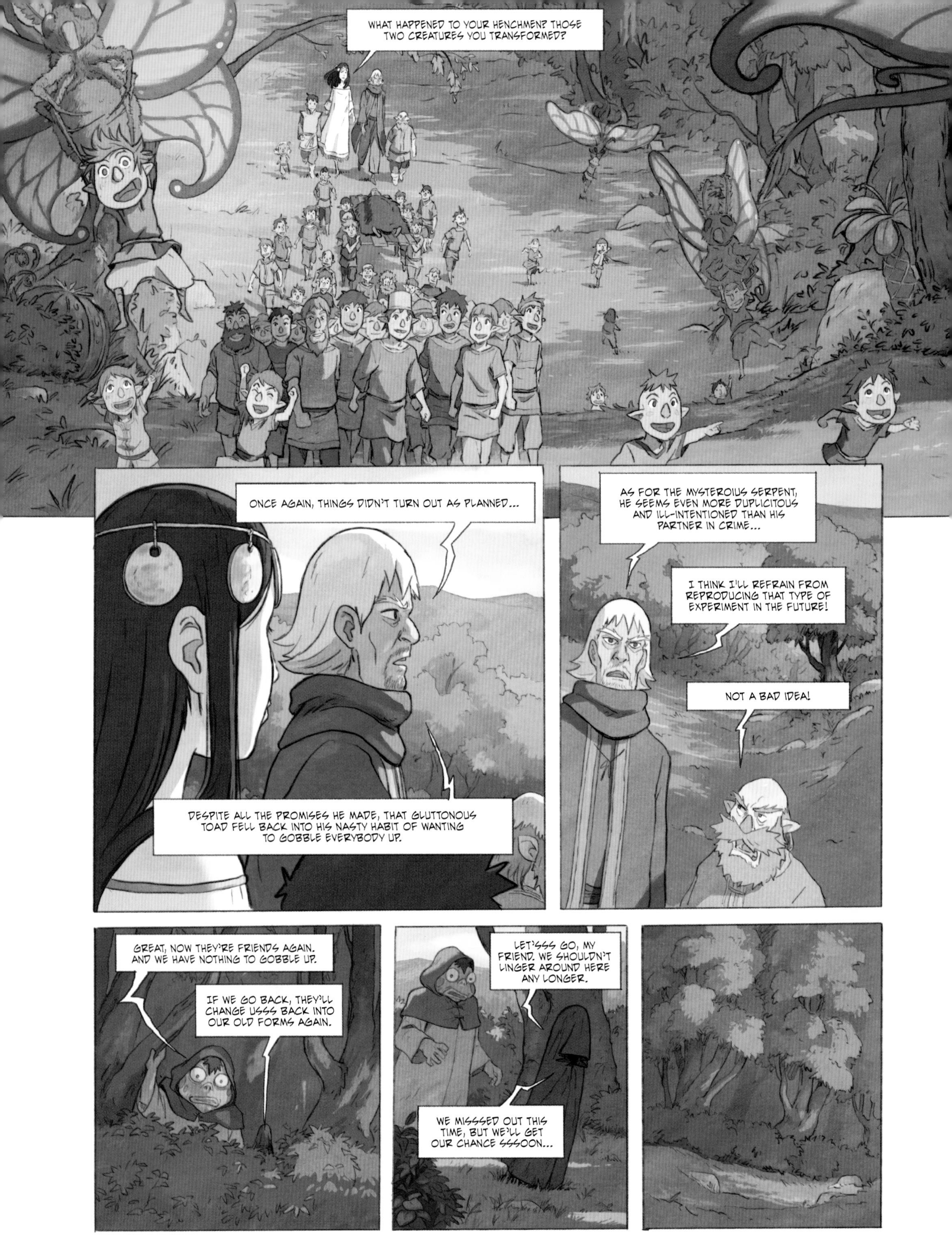
WHAT HAPPENED TO YOUR HENCHMEN? THOSE TWO CREATURES YOU TRANSFORMED?
ONCE AGAIN, THINGS DIDN'T TURN OUT AS PLANNED...
DESPITE ALL THE PROMISES HE MADE, THAT GLUTTONOUS TOAD FELL BACK INTO HIS NASTY HABIT OF WANTING TO GOBBLE EVERYBODY UP.
AS FOR THE MYSTEROIUS SERPENT, HE SEEMS EVEN MORE DUPLICITOUS AND ILL-INTENTIONED THAN HIS PARTNER IN CRIME...
I THINK I'LL REFRAIN FROM REPRODUCING THAT TYPE OF EXPERIMENT IN THE FUTURE!
NOT A BAD IDEA!
GREAT, NOW THEY'RE FRIENDS AGAIN. AND WE HAVE NOTHING TO GOBBLE UP.
IF WE GO BACK, THEY'LL CHANGE USSS BACK INTO OUR OLD FORMS AGAIN.
LET'SSS GO, MY FRIEND. WE SHOULDN'T LINGER AROUND HERE ANY LONGER.
WE MISSSED OUT THIS TIME, BUT WE'LL GET OUR CHANCE SSSOON...

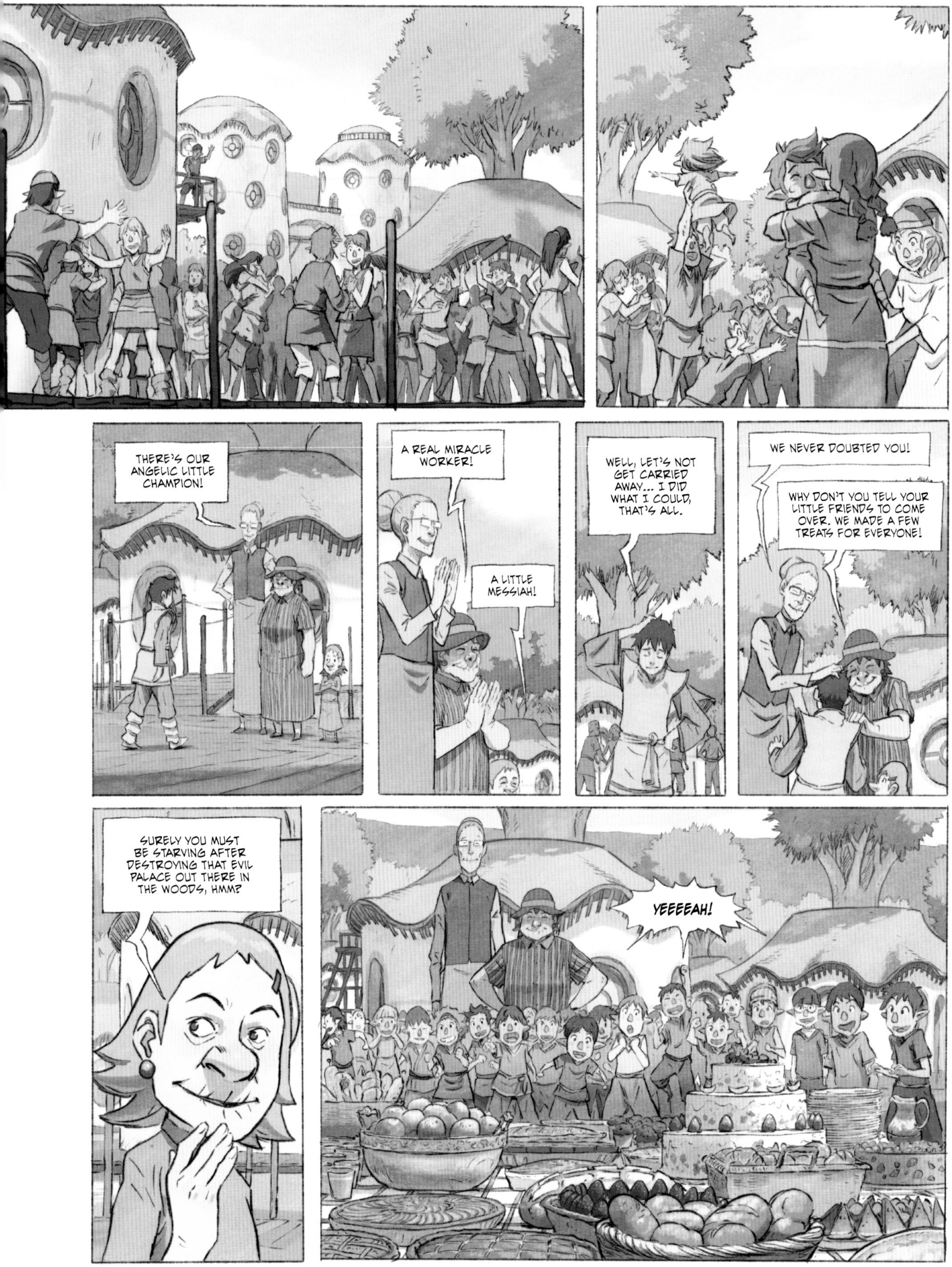
THERE'S OUR ANGELIC LITTLE CHAMPION!
A REAL MIRACLE WORKER!
A LITTLE MESSIAH!
WELL, LET'S NOT GET CARRIED AWAY... I DID WHAT I COULD, THAT'S ALL.
WE NEVER DOUBTED YOU!
WHY DON'T YOU TELL YOUR LITTLE FRIENDS TO COME OVER. WE MADE A FEW TREATS FOR EVERYONE!
SURELY YOU MUST BE STARVING AFTER DESTROYING THAT EVIL PALACE OUT THERE IN THE WOODS, HMM?
YEEEEAH!

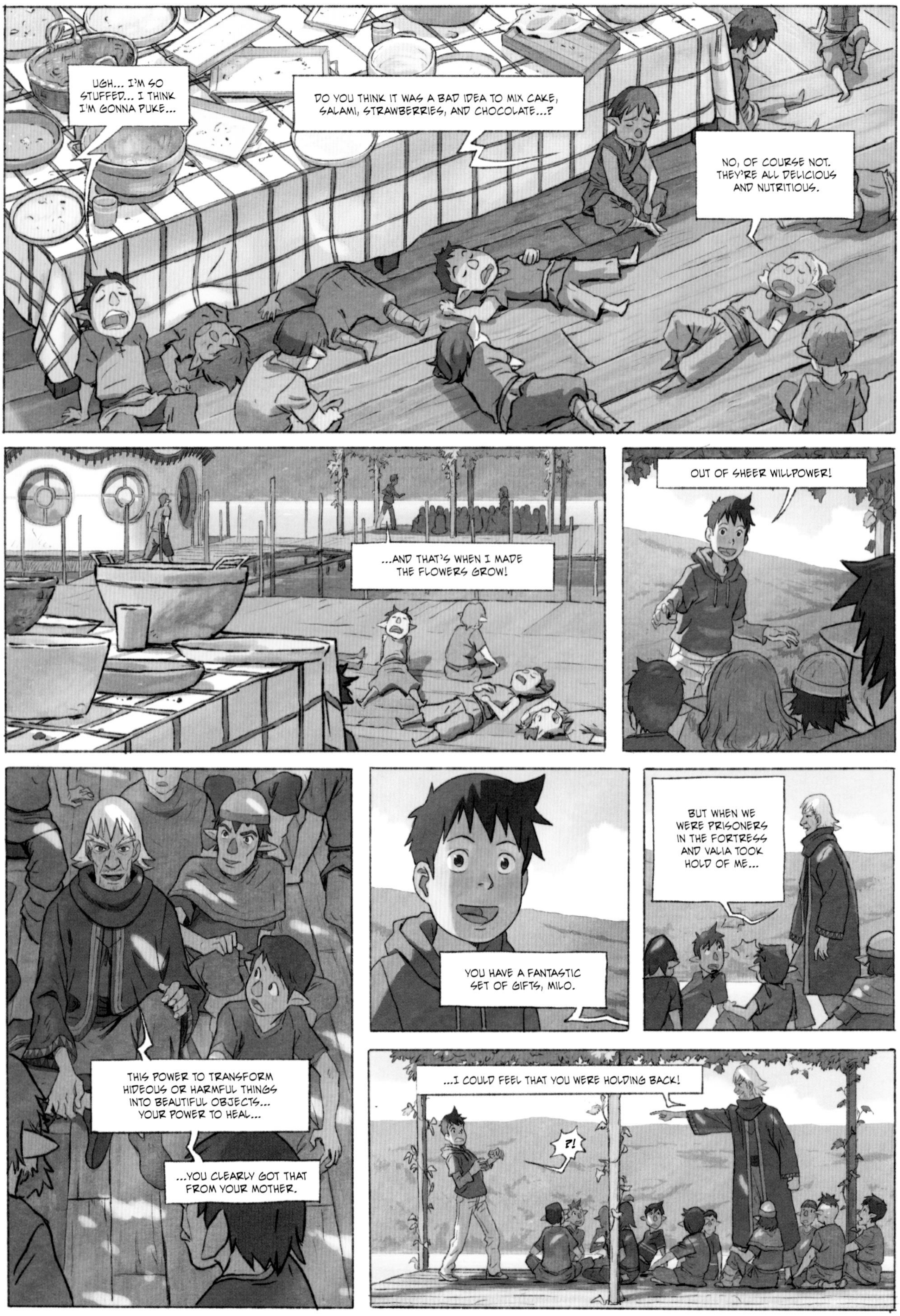

UGH... I'M SO STUFFED... I THINK I'M GONNA PUKE...
DO YOU THINK IT WAS A BAD IDEA TO MIX CAKE, SALAMI, STRAWBERRIES, AND CHOCOLATE...?
NO, OF COURSE NOT. THEY'RE ALL DELICIOUS AND NUTRITIOUS.
...AND THAT'S WHEN I MADE THE FLOWERS GROW!
OUT OF SHEER WILLPOWER!
THIS POWER TO TRANSFORM HIDEOUS OR HARMFUL THINGS INTO BEAUTIFUL OBJECTS... YOUR POWER TO HEAL...
...YOU CLEARLY GOT THAT FROM YOUR MOTHER.
YOU HAVE A FANTASTIC SET OF GIFTS, MILO.
BUT WHEN WE WERE PRISONERS IN THE FORTRESS AND VALIA TOOK HOLD OF ME...
...I COULD FEEL THAT YOU WERE HOLDING BACK!
?!

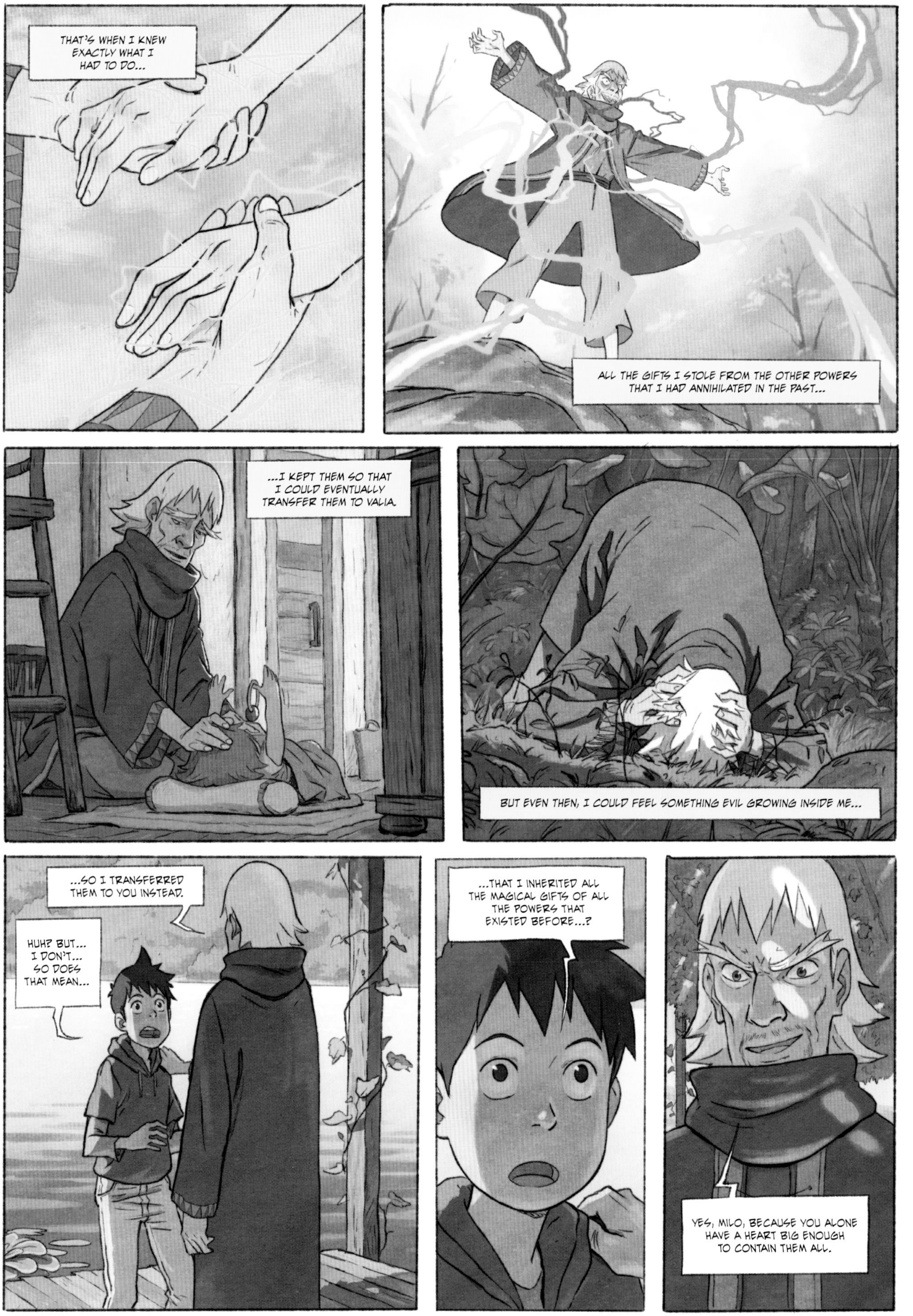
THAT'S WHEN I KNEW EXACTLY WHAT I HAD TO DO...
ALL THE GIFTS I STOLE FROM THE OTHER POWERS THAT I HAD ANNIHILATED IN THE PAST...
...I KEPT THEM SO THAT I COULD EVENTUALLY TRANSFER THEM TO VALIA.
BUT EVEN THEN, I COULD FEEL SOMETHING EVIL GROWING INSIDE ME...
...SO I TRANSFERRED THEM TO YOU INSTEAD.
HUH? BUT... I DON'T... SO DOES THAT MEAN...
...THAT I INHERITED ALL THE MAGICAL GIFTS OF ALL THE POWERS THAT EXISTED BEFORE...?
YES, MILO, BECAUSE YOU ALONE HAVE A HEART BIG ENOUGH TO CONTAIN THEM ALL.

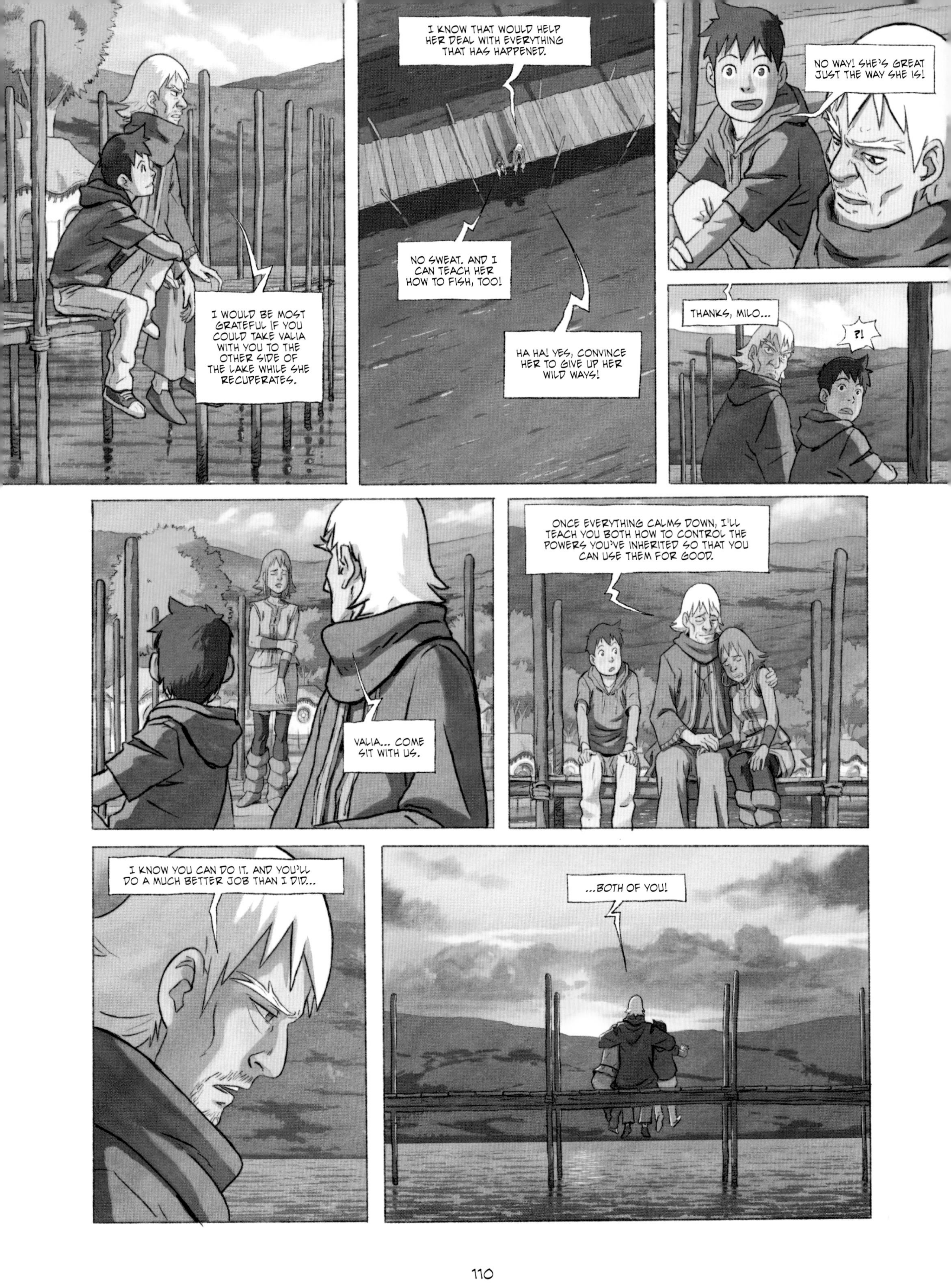
I WOULD BE MOST GRATEFUL IF YOU COULD TAKE VALIA WITH YOU TO THE OTHER SIDE OF THE LAKE WHILE SHE RECUPERATES.
I KNOW THAT WOULD HELP HER DEAL WITH EVERYTHING THAT HAS HAPPENED.
NO SWEAT. AND I CAN TEACH HER HOW TO FISH, TOO!
HA HA! YES, CONVINCE HER TO GIVE UP HER WILD WAYS!
NO WAY! SHE'S GREAT JUST THE WAY SHE IS!
THANKS, MILO...
?!
VALIA... COME SIT WITH US.
ONCE EVERYTHING CALMS DOWN, I'LL TEACH YOU BOTH HOW TO CONTROL THE POWERS YOU'VE INHERITED SO THAT YOU CAN USE THEM FOR GOOD.
I KNOW YOU CAN DO IT. AND YOU'LL DO A MUCH BETTER JOB THAN I DID...
...BOTH OF YOU!

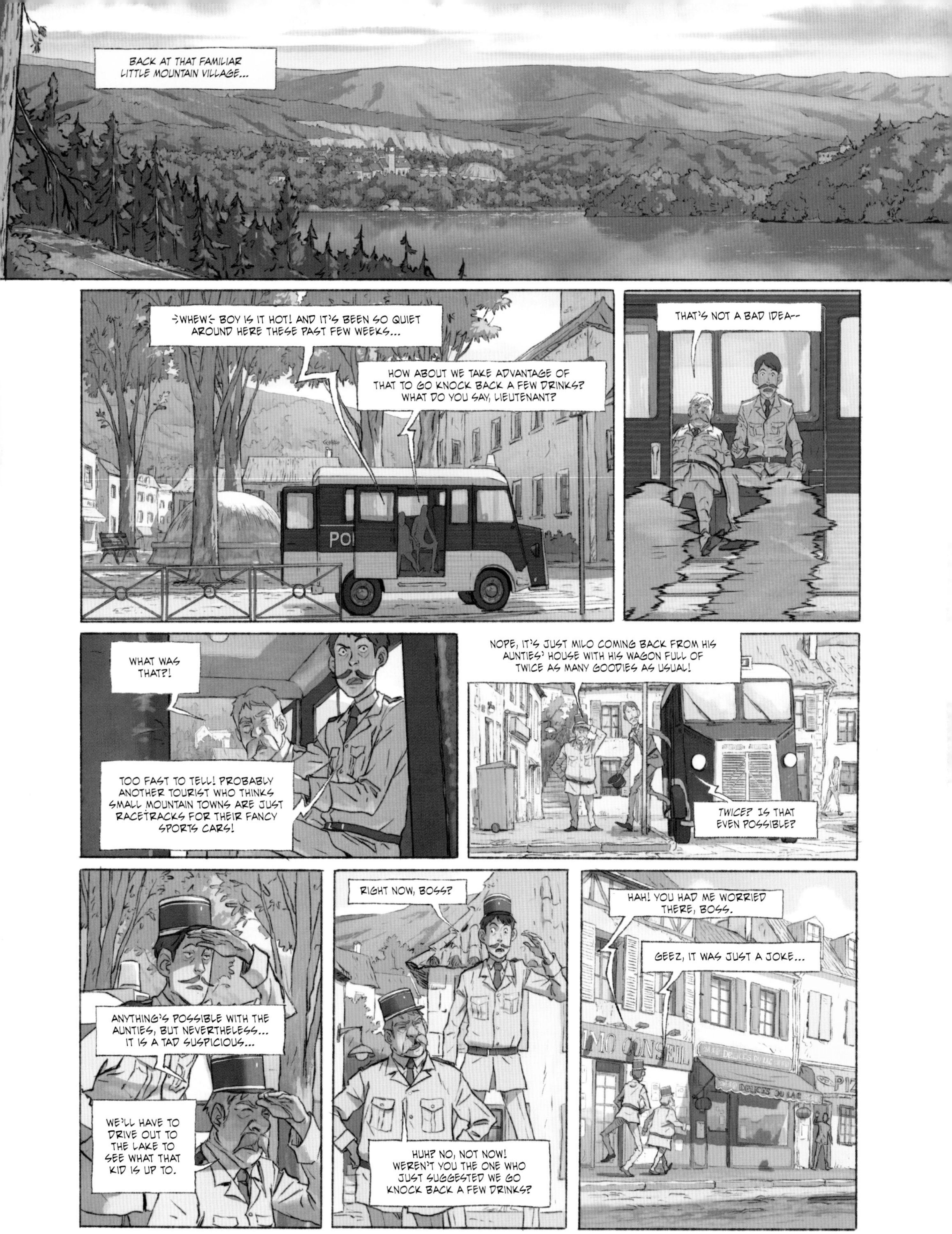
BACK AT THAT FAMILIAR LITTLE MOUNTAIN VILLAGE...
WHEW BOY IS IT HOT! AND IT'S BEEN SO QUIET AROUND HERE THESE PAST FEW WEEKS...
HOW ABOUT WE TAKE ADVANTAGE OF THAT TO GO KNOCK BACK A FEW DRINKS? WHAT DO YOU SAY, LIEUTENANT?
POL
THAT'S NOT A BAD IDEA--
WHAT WAS THAT?!
TOO FAST TO TELL! PROBABLY ANOTHER TOURIST WHO THINKS SMALL MOUNTAIN TOWNS ARE JUST RACETRACKS FOR THEIR FANCY SPORTS CARS!
NOPE, IT'S JUST MILO COMING BACK FROM HIS AUNTIES' HOUSE WITH HIS WAGON FULL OF TWICE AS MANY GOODIES AS USUAL!
TWICE? IS THAT EVEN POSSIBLE?
ANYTHING'S POSSIBLE WITH THE AUNTIES, BUT NEVERTHELESS... IT IS A TAD SUSPICIOUS...
WE'LL HAVE TO DRIVE OUT TO THE LAKE TO SEE WHAT THAT KID IS UP TO.
RIGHT NOW, BOSS?
HUH? NO, NOT NOW! WEREN'T YOU THE ONE WHO JUST SUGGESTED WE GO KNOCK BACK A FEW DRINKS?
HAH! YOU HAD ME WORRIED THERE, BOSS.
GEEZ, IT WAS JUST A JOKE...
IMO CONSEIL
DELICES DU LAC
PIZ

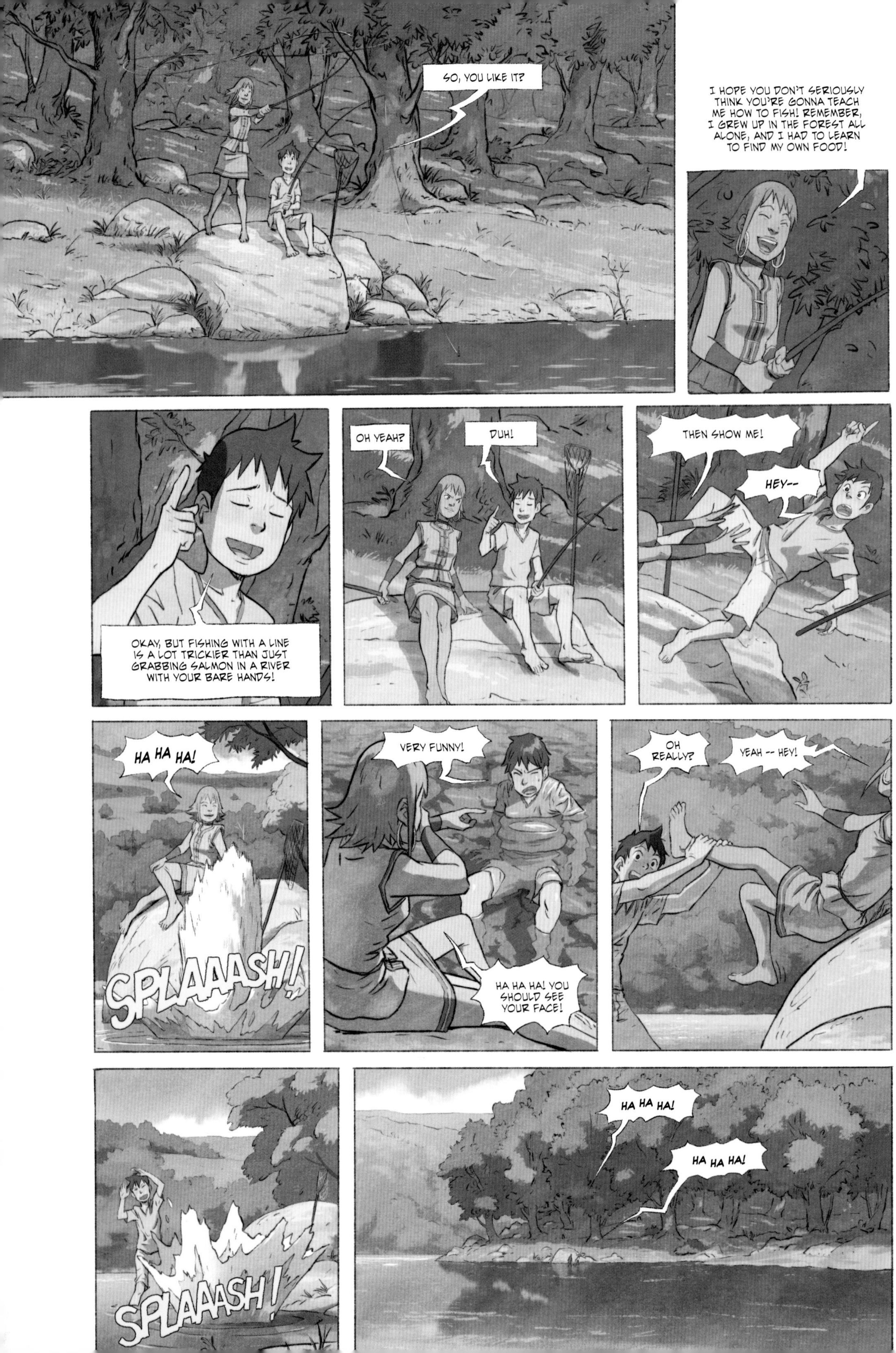
SO, YOU LIKE IT?
I HOPE YOU DON'T SERIOUSLY THINK YOU'RE GONNA TEACH ME HOW TO FISH! REMEMBER, I GREW UP IN THE FOREST ALL ALONE, AND I HAD TO LEARN TO FIND MY OWN FOOD!
OKAY, BUT FISHING WITH A LINE IS A LOT TRICKIER THAN JUST GRABBING SALMON IN A RIVER WITH YOUR BARE HANDS!
OH YEAH?
DUH!
THEN SHOW ME!
HEY--
HA HA HA!
SPLAAASH!
VERY FUNNY!
HA HA HA! YOU SHOULD SEE YOUR FACE!
OH REALLY?
YEAH -- HEY!
SPLAAASH!
HA HA HA!
HA HA HA!

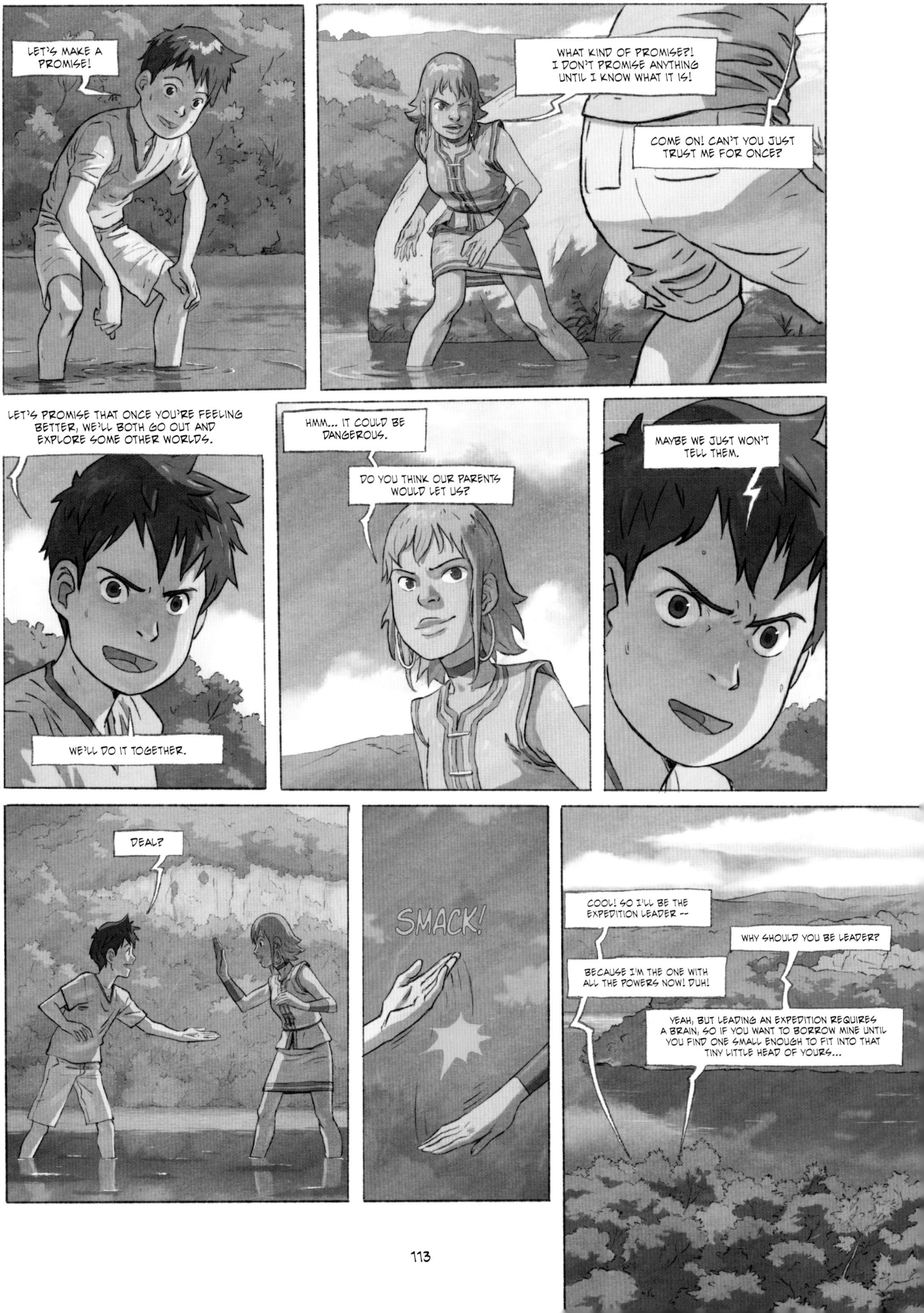
LET'S MAKE A PROMISE!
WHAT KIND OF PROMISE?! I DON'T PROMISE ANYTHING UNTIL I KNOW WHAT IT IS!
COME ON! CAN'T YOU JUST TRUST ME FOR ONCE?
LET'S PROMISE THAT ONCE YOU'RE FEELING BETTER, WE'LL BOTH GO OUT AND EXPLORE SOME OTHER WORLDS.
WE'LL DO IT TOGETHER.
HMM... IT COULD BE DANGEROUS.
DO YOU THINK OUR PARENTS WOULD LET US?
MAYBE WE JUST WON'T TELL THEM.
DEAL?
SMACK!
COOL! SO I'LL BE THE EXPEDITION LEADER --
WHY SHOULD YOU BE LEADER?
BECAUSE I'M THE ONE WITH ALL THE POWERS NOW! DUH!
YEAH, BUT LEADING AN EXPEDITION REQUIRES A BRAIN, SO IF YOU WANT TO BORROW MINE UNTIL YOU FIND ONE SMALL ENOUGH TO FIT INTO THAT TINY LITTLE HEAD OF YOURS...

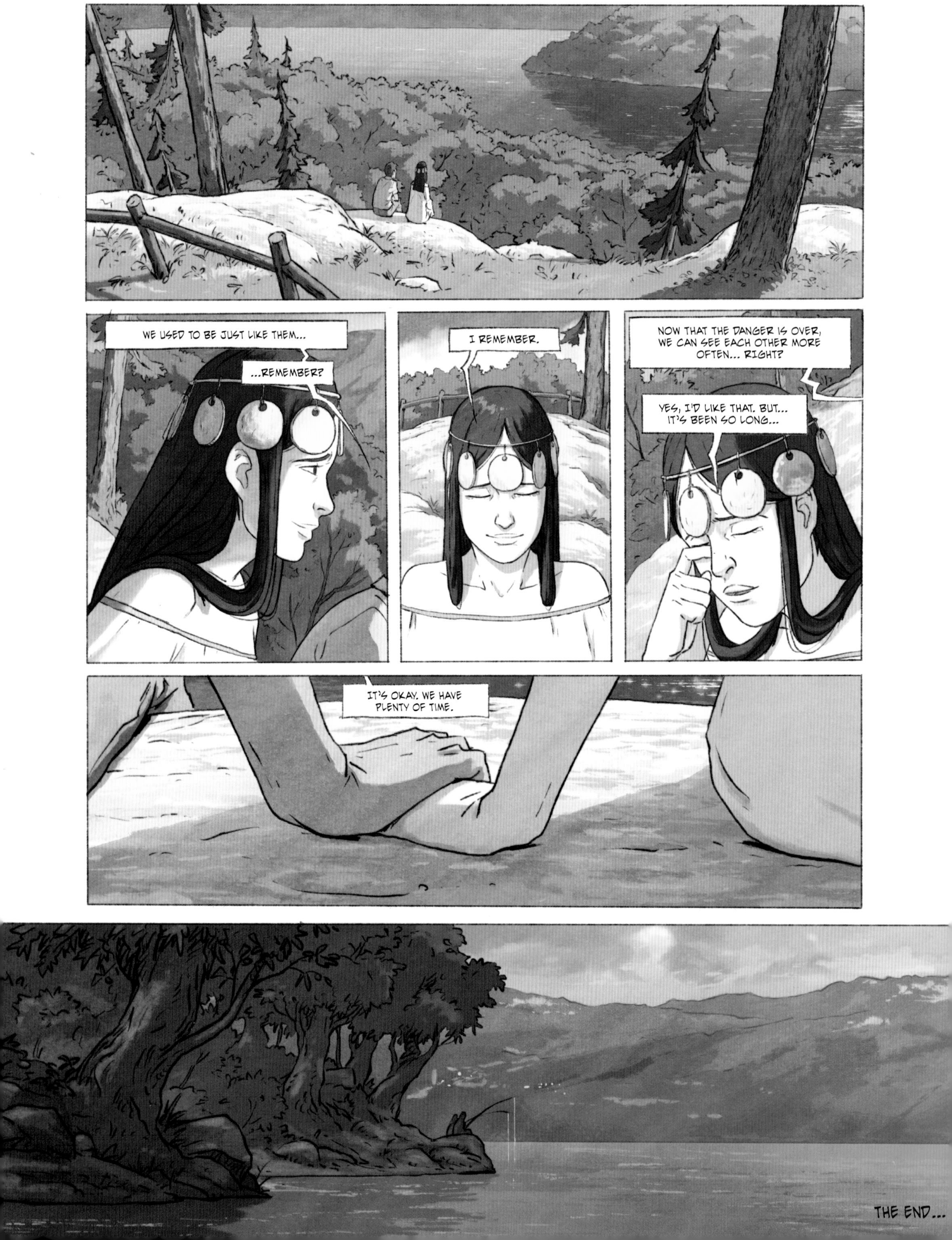
WE USED TO BE JUST LIKE THEM...
...REMEMBER?
I REMEMBER.
NOW THAT THE DANGER IS OVER, WE CAN SEE EACH OTHER MORE OFTEN... RIGHT?
YES, I'D LIKE THAT. BUT... IT'S BEEN SO LONG...
IT'S OKAY. WE HAVE PLENTY OF TIME.
THE END...

MILO'S WORLD

THE DRAWING PROCESS
BY CHRISTOPHE FERREIRA

When Richard sends his script to Christophe to illustrate, he begins by doodling the entire story in very rough thumbnail sketches (A). This allows them to see how the story will flow from panel to panel, and to decide what camera angles work best. It also allows Christophe to see how much space to leave for the word balloons. When they are both happy with the sketches, Christophe will then add more detail in pencil (B) to define important things like facial expressions. Once that stage is completed to their satisfaction, he will then render the page with even more detail and sharper lines that are clean enough to color (C). From that finished line art, the last step is adding the colors, which Christophe does mainly in the computer, using brushes and color textures that give the page the look of a watercolored painting or animated film.

(A)

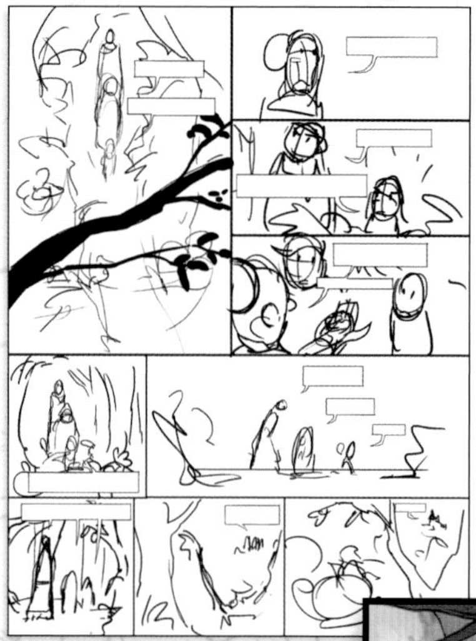

(B)

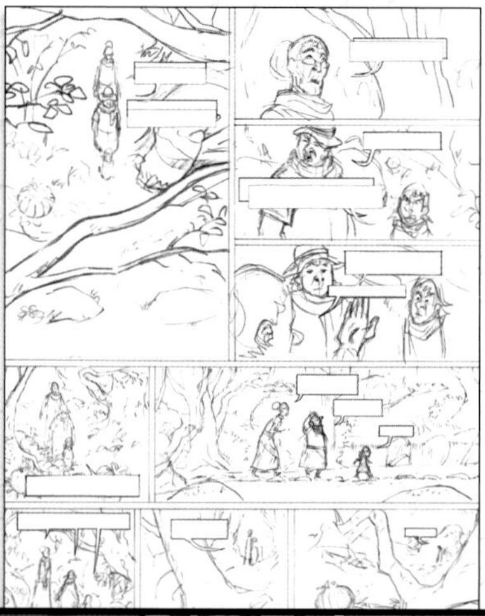

(C)

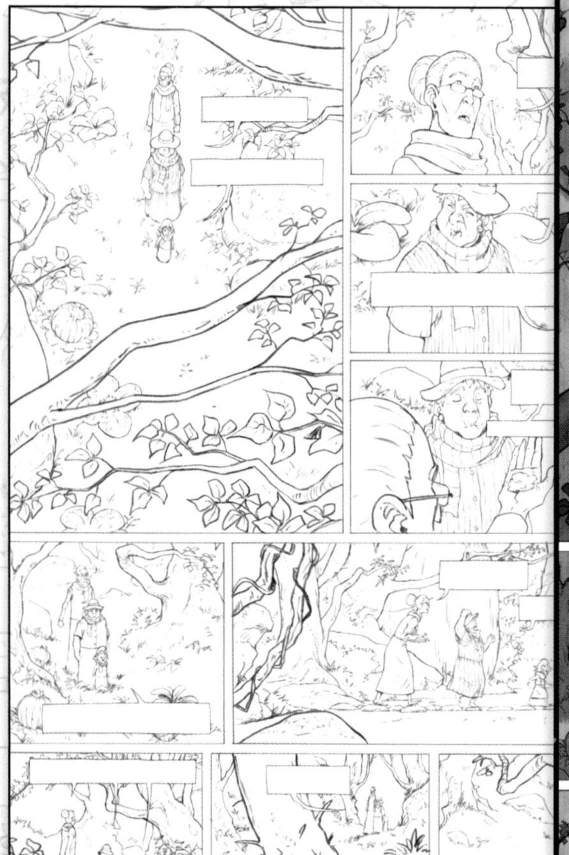

(D)

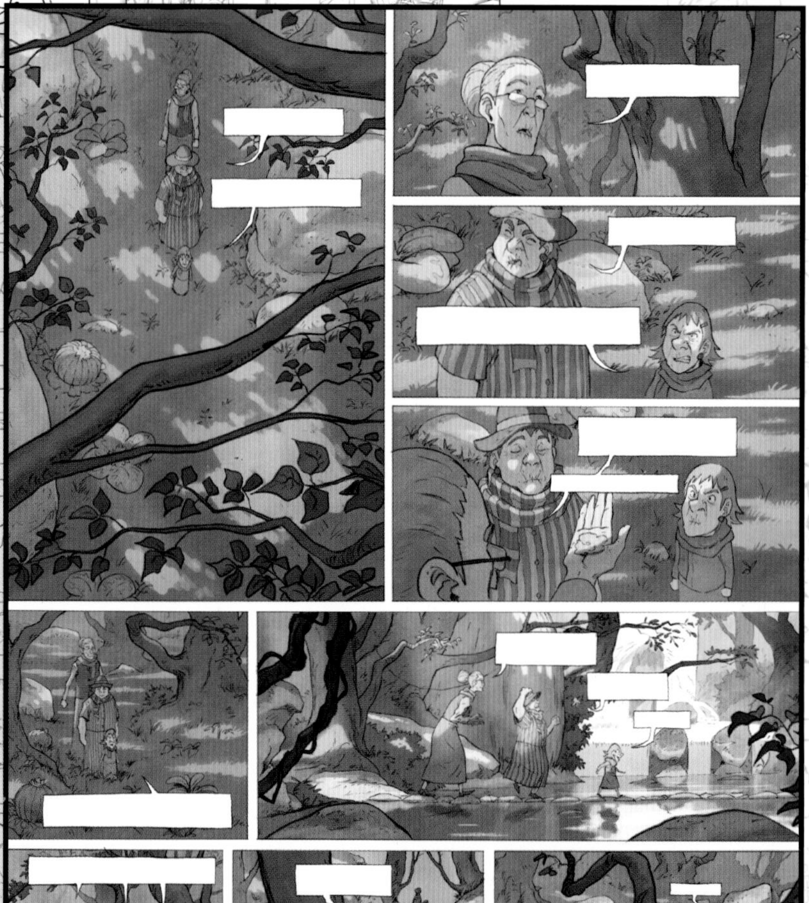

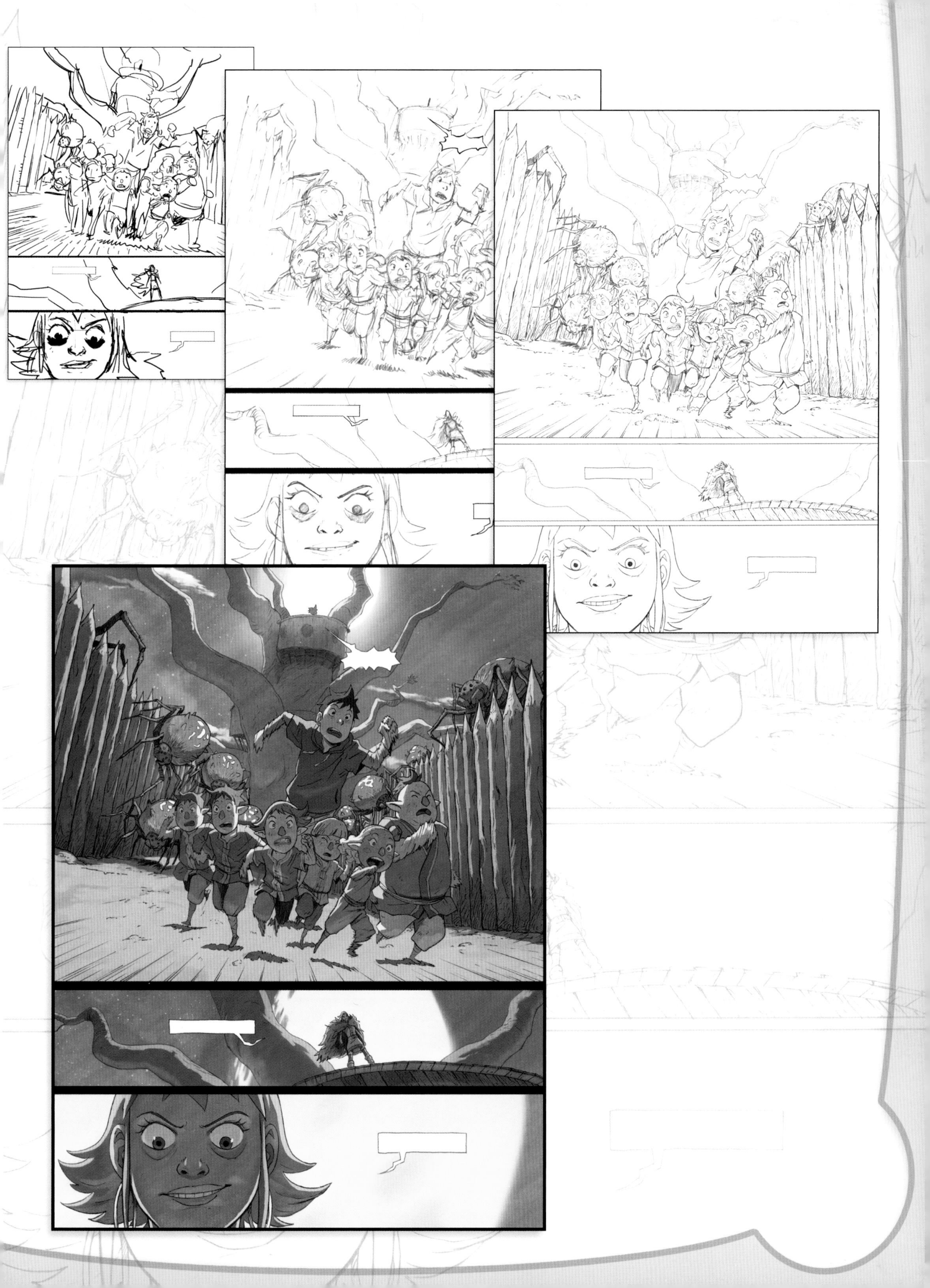

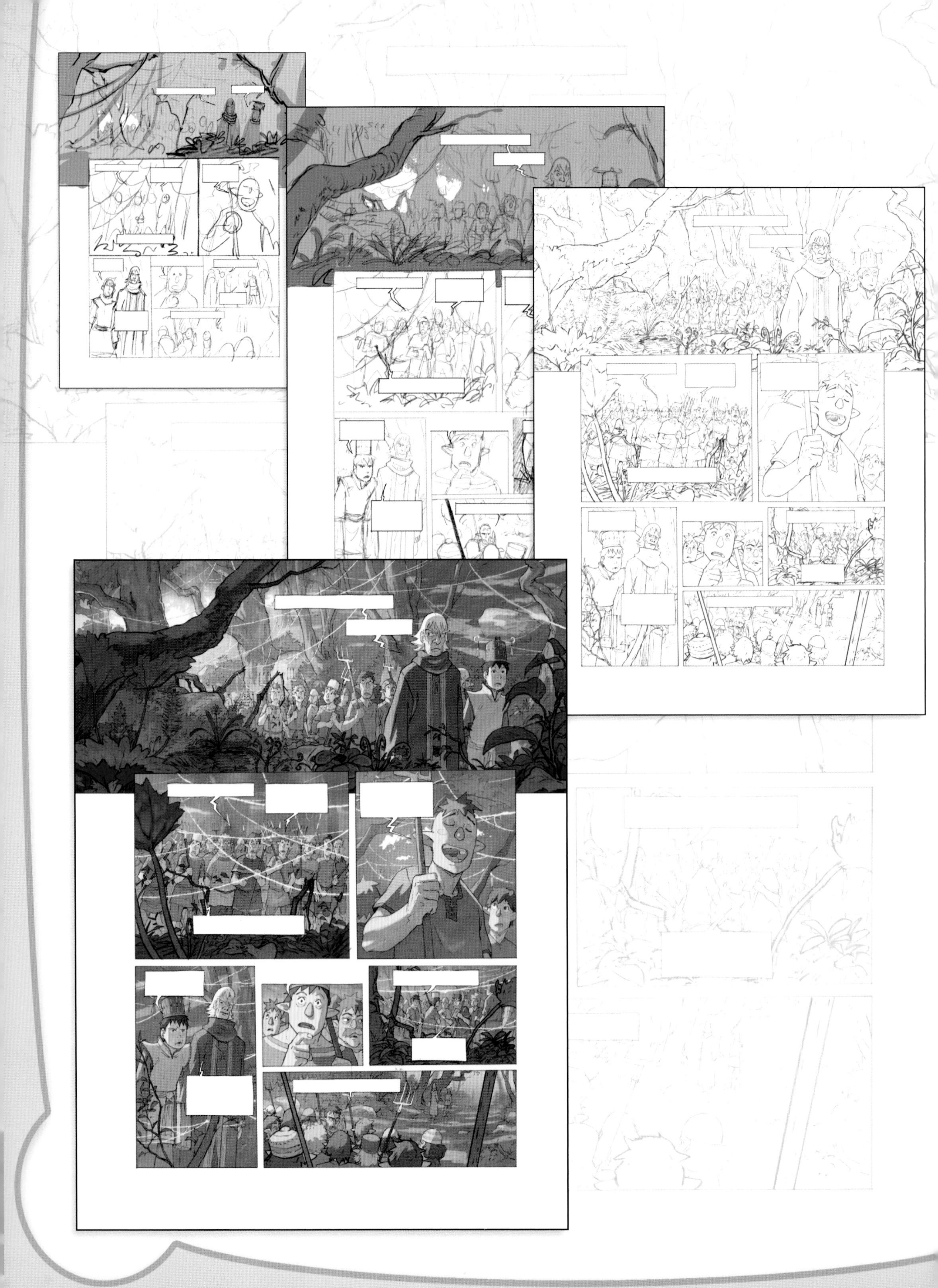

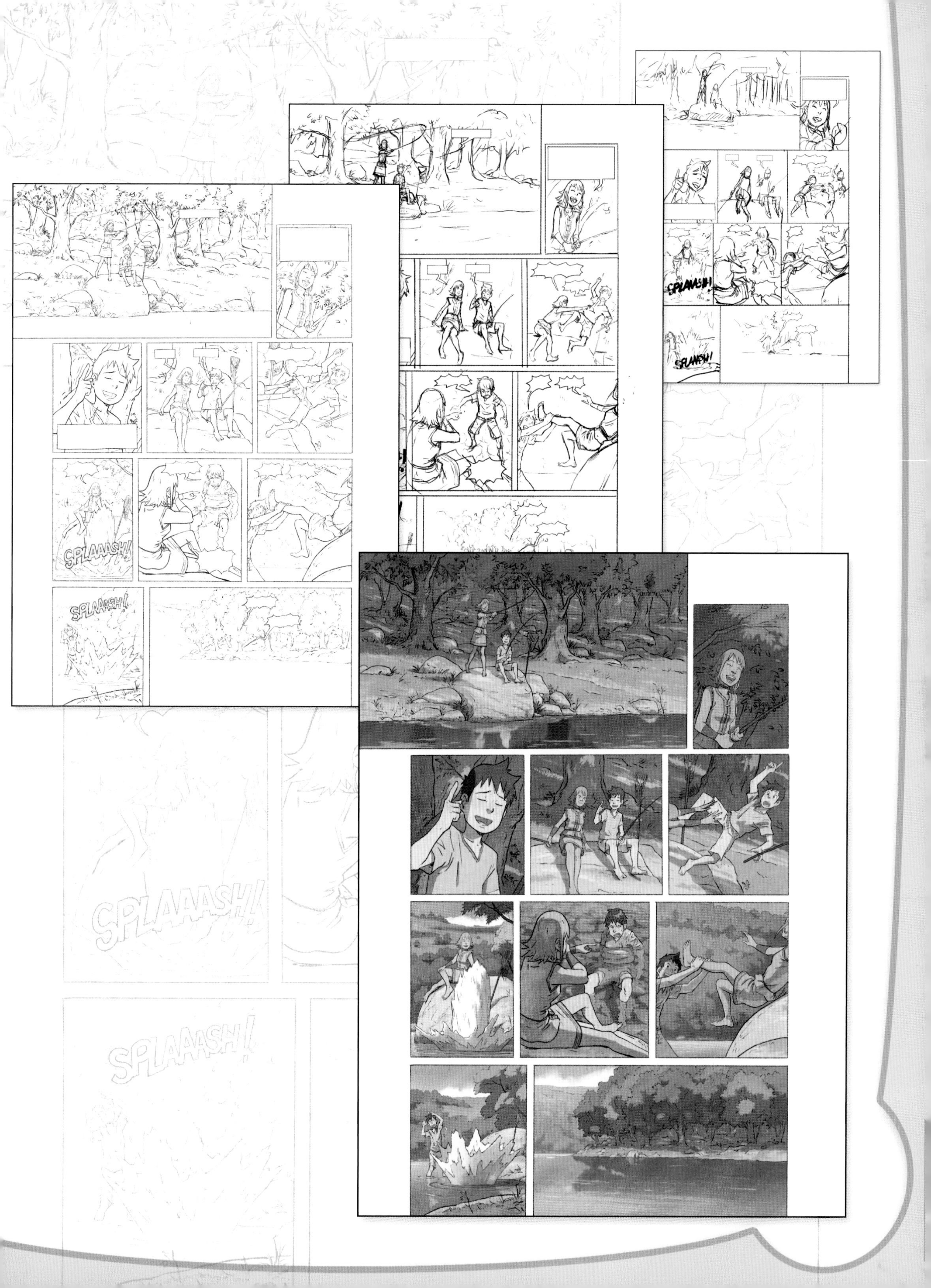
SPLAASH!
SPLAASH!
SPLAAASH!
SPLAAASH!
SPLAAASH!
SPLAAASH!

RICHARD MARAZANO is a French writer and comic book artist born in a suburb of Paris in 1971. After studying physics and astrophysics, he was pushed into comics by the legendary Jean "Moebius" Giraud who introduced him to publishers and mentored him in the creative process. Shortly thereafter, he attended the Workshop of Fine Arts Bande Dessinée in Angoulême. Since then, he has worked with artists from Europe, China, and South America in a wide variety of styles, and his works have been published worldwide in various languages. Among the eighty titles he has authored, including *Genetiks*, *The Dream of the Butterfly*, and *S.A.M.*, he has been nominated and awarded multiple times by the Angoulême International Comics Festival and Monaco Film and Literature Festival. He also received the bronze award for Best International Manga by the Ministry of Culture in Japan for his book *Otaku Blue* in 2013. *Milo's World* has been widely recognized, having won the Readers' Choice Award from *Journal de Mickey*.

He was strongly influenced by the writings of Robert Sheckley and Edgar Allan Poe as well as H.G. Wells, Nicolas Gogol, and the Strugatsky brothers, and he was deeply marked by the wit of classic movies by Billy Wilder, Ernst Lubitsch, Howard Hawks, and J.L. Mankiewicz. His stories range from science fiction to fantasy, including thrillers, adventures, dramas, and biographies, often characterized by strong compassion, a peculiar sense of irony, and a taste for foreign cultures brought back from his many travels to China, Northern Africa, and South America.

CHRISTOPHE FERREIRA began drawing comics as a child, borrowing bande dessinée from his local library in France and imitating the drawings of *Spirou*, *Asterix*, and *Leonard*. When he first saw the anime film *Akira*, his career path was decided: he would become an artist and animator. He began studying graphic design for advertising, but soon realized that there were schools that specialized in his passionate pursuit, such as the Gobelins School of Animation and Digital Design in Paris. After graduation, he attended a master class by Yasuo Otsuka, a colleague of legendary director Hayao Miyazaki, who encouraged him to continue his studies in Japan. From that fateful day in 2001, he has split his time between France and Japan before settling in Japan in 2006, creating storyboards and designs for various studios and projects, including *Hirune Hime*, *Green Lantern: First Flight*, *Fullmetal Alchemist: Brotherhood*, and *Lupin the III: Blood Seal*.

During this time, he met author and animator Alex Alice, who encouraged him to try his hand at sequential storytelling and comic book illustration. An introduction to writer Richard Marazano led to various unrealized project ideas, but after years of creative collaboration, the two finally landed on what would become *Milo's World*. First released in 2013, its success has grown internationally through six volumes. In addition to continuing Milo's adventures, they also created the three-part Greek fantasy adventure *Alcyon*.

Christophe continues to work in both France and Japan, with both animation and comics at the center of his attention.